E.T.A. Hoffmann

The Golden Pot

and other tales of the uncanny

Selected and Translated by Peter Wortsman

archipelago books

"The Sandman" originally appeared in *Tales of the German Imagination,
from the Brothers Grimm to Ingeborg Bachmann*, an anthology selected
and translated by Peter Wortsman, Penguin Classics, UK, 2012

Library of Congress Cataloging-in-Publication Data available upon request.
ISBN: 9781953861702

Archipelago Books
232 3rd Street #A111
Brooklyn, NY 11215
www.archipelagobooks.org

Distributed by Penguin Random House
www.penguinrandomhouse.com

Cover artwork by Alfred Kubin
Book design by Zoe Guttenplan

This work is made possible by the New York State Council on the Arts
with the support of the Office of the Governor and the New York State
Legislature. Funding for the publication of this book was provided by
a grant from the Carl Lesnor Family Foundation.

This publication was made possible with support from Lannan Foundation,
the National Endowment for the Arts, and the New York City
Department of Cultural Affairs.

PRINTED IN THE UNITED STATES

Contents

3   Ritter Gluck

19   Kreisleriana

31   The Golden Pot

137   The Automaton

175   The Sandman

221   Intimations from the Realm of Musical Notes

231   The Fermata

255   Counselor Krespel

285   Mademoiselle de Scudéry

371   My Cousin's Corner Window

405   Facing the Music: the Melodious Imaginings of E.T.A. Hoffmann
       An Afterword

427   Acknowledgments

There is nothing more marvelous or madder than real life.

—E.T.A. Hoffmann

The Golden Pot

Ritter Gluck

A memory from the year 1809

There are usually still a few nice days left in late fall in Berlin. The sun bursts brightly from behind a bulwark of clouds, and the moisture in the balmy air that wafts through the streets evaporates quickly. At such times you see a long row of colorful characters – dapper gents, stolid citizens with the wife and darling little ones all dressed in their Sunday best, priests, Jewesses, law clerks, prostitutes, professors, cleaning ladies, dancers, officers and the like strolling among the Linden trees toward the Tiergarten. Soon all the tables at the Café Klaus and Weber are taken; the coffee is steaming, the dapper gents light up their cigars, people talk, argue about war and peace, about Madame Bethmann's shoes, whether they were, as recently noted, gray or green, about *Der Geschlossene Handelsstaat* and counterfeit coins, and so on and so forth, until all chatter dissolves into an aria from *Fanchon*, wherein an out-of-tune harp, a few untuned violins, a consumptive wheezing flute, and a spasmodic bassoon torment their players and the listeners. Several round tables and garden chairs are pressed up close to the parapet separating the café's turf from the stately thoroughfare of the Heerstraße. There you can breathe fresh air and observe those coming and going at a far remove from the cacophonous din of that accursed orchestra; there I sit myself down to give free rein to the easy meanderings of my imagination, conversing with imagined friends and acquaintances about the sciences, art, all matters close to a man's heart. The surge of pedestrians strolling by grows ever more colorful by the moment, but nothing bothers me, nothing can scare off my fantastic conversation partners. Only the confounded trio and their perfidious waltz tear me out of my reveries. All I can hear are the screeching treble of the violin and flute and the bassoon's buzzing *basso ostinato*; the sounds swell and fade in octaves played in tandem, bombarding the eardrum, and in a spontaneous outburst, like someone gripped by an acute pain, I cry out: "What manic music! Spare us these wretched octaves!" Beside me, someone mutters: "Confounded fate! Another octave hunter!"

I looked up and only then became conscious that a man had sat down at the same table, his stony gaze directed right at me. I could not take my eyes off him.

Never had I seen a head, never a figure that made such an immediate and profound impression on me. A gently downturned nose adjoined a wide, open forehead with striking ridges that rose over bushy, light gray eyebrows, beneath which eyes blazed with an almost wild, youthful fire (though the man might well have been over fifty). The soft-edged chin stood in stark contrast with the tightly closed mouth, and a strange smile produced by the peculiar play of muscles in his sunken cheeks seemed to revolt against the deep, melancholic gravity spread across his forehead. Only a few gray locks were brushed back behind his protruding ears. A very wide, modern overcoat was draped around his big, haggard figure. As soon as my gaze fell upon the man, he looked down and went back to the business my outcry had probably interrupted. With evident delight he shook tobacco from a few little bags into a jar set before him and moistened it with red wine from a half bottle. The music had stopped; I felt impelled to speak to him.

"Thank goodness the music stopped," I said, "it was insufferable."

The old fellow gave me a fleeting glance and emptied the last bag of tobacco.

"Better no music at all," I spoke again. "Wouldn't you agree?"

"I have no opinion in the matter," he replied. "You must be a musician and professional connoisseur…"

"Not so; I'm neither. I learned to play piano and bass as a matter of good upbringing, and was told, among other things, that nothing makes a more deleterious effect than when the bass dominates with treble in octaves. At the time I took it on good authority and have since always found it borne out."

"Really?" he broke in, got up and advanced slowly and deliberately toward the musicians, often slapping the flat of his hand against his forehead with his gaze turned upward, like someone seeking to rouse a memory. I saw him talking to the musicians, whom he treated with formidable dignity. He came back, and no sooner did he sit down than they started playing the overture to *Iphigenia in Aulis*.

With half-closed eyes, his arms crossed on the table before him, he listened to the *andante*. Quietly lifting his left foot, he indicated when the voice was to start singing; now he raised his head, cast a fleeting look around, rested his left hand on the table with fingers outstretched, as if he were playing a chord on the piano, and raised his right hand in the air. He took the posture of a conductor indicating a change of tempo to the orchestra – the right hand fell, and the *allegro* began. His pale cheeks flushed a burning red; his eyebrows rose on a ruffled forehead; an inner fury enflamed his wild gaze with a fire that, little by little, displaced the smile that still hovered around his half-opened mouth. Then he leaned back, his eyebrows drawn upward, the muscles once again began to ripple on his cheeks, his eyes sparkling, a deep inner pain dissolving into desire that gripped every fiber of his being and shook him convulsively. He drew a deep breath from the pit of his chest; drops of sweat formed on his forehead; he signaled the advent of the *tutti*, when all instruments play together, and other key passages in the composition; his right hand kept time, while with the left hand he pulled out a handkerchief and wiped his face. In this way he fleshed out and added color to the bare bones approximation that those violins gave of the overture. I heard the soft, mellifluous lament of the flute once the storm of the violins and bass fizzled out and the thunder of the kettledrum dissolved; I heard the soft striking bow strokes of the cello, the plaintive murmur of the bassoon that filled my heart with a burst of indescribable melancholy; the *tutti* returned like the footsteps of a giant, the unison sounded large, and the muffled lament died down under its crushing strides.

The overture came to an end; the man let both his arms sink to his side and sat there with eyes shut tight like someone physically and emotionally drained by too great an effort. The bottle before him was empty; I filled his glass with a white Burgundy which I had ordered in the meantime. He breathed a deep sigh of relief and seemed to rouse himself from a dream. I urged him to drink; he did so without much ado, and after downing a full glass in a single gulp, he cried, "I am pleased with the performance! The orchestra did an admirable job!"

"And yet," I spoke up, "yet they only gave a faint outline of a master-piece conceived in brilliant colors."

"Am I right in supposing that you are no Berliner?"

"Quite right; I only reside here on occasion."

"The Burgundy is good, but it's getting cold out."

"Then let us go inside and polish off the bottle."

"A splendid suggestion. I don't know you, but you don't know me either. Let us not ask each other for our names; names are betimes burden-some. I'm drinking Burgundy, it isn't costing me a penny, we're having a fine time together— so be it!"

He said all this with good-natured geniality. We stepped indoors; upon sitting down, he flung open his overcoat, and I was surprised to see that beneath it he wore an embroidered cardigan, a shirt with long shirttails, black velvet leggings, and a very small silver dagger. He promptly buttoned the coat back up again.

"Why did you ask me if I was a Berliner?" I began.

"Because in that case I would have had to take my leave of you."

"A puzzling reply."

"Not in the least, it's not puzzling at all, as soon as I tell you that— well, that I'm a composer."

"I still don't follow."

"Please forgive my outburst before. I see that you haven't the faintest notion of Berlin and Berliners."

He got up and paced intently several times back and forth; then he went to the window and sang a hardly audible chorus from *Iphigenia in Tauris*, every now and then knocking on the window pane to denote a *tutti*. I noticed to my astonishment that he sang several alternate variations of the melodies all striking in their verve and novelty. I let him continue. He finished singing and sat back down. Completely taken by the man's odd behavior and the fantastic utterances of a rare musical talent, I held still. After a while he started talking again:

"Have you never composed music?"

"Yes, I have dabbled in the art; but all the music I jotted down in bursts of inspiration sounded flat and dull after the fact, so I stopped trying."

"You did wrong; for the very fact that you would scrap your own attempts is a not untrustworthy sign of your talent. You learn music as a boy because Mama and Papa want it, so you strum and fiddle away; but unbeknownst to you, little by little you become more attuned to melody. Perhaps the half-forgotten thread of a ditty with which you took unintended liberties was your first original musical idea, and this embryo, painstakingly nourished by extraneous influences, gave birth to a giant who lapped up everything around it, sucking it up and transforming it in his marrow and blood. Hah, how in heaven's name is it possible to even intimate the thousand some odd paths to musical composition! It is a broad thoroughfare, which all romp along, whooping and crying: 'We are the anointed ones! We've made our mark!' Passing through the ivory gate, you reach the realm of dreams; there are precious few who see the gate even once, and far fewer who ever pass through it! The gate might appear a bit bizarre. Madcap figures float back and forth, but they have character — some more so than others. They keep a low profile on the high road; you can only catch sight of them on the far side of the ivory gate. It is hard to ever leave that realm; monsters block the way as they do before Alzina's fortress[*]— everything whirls— everything turns— many are entrapped by their reverie in the realm of dreams, they dissolve in their dreams, they no longer cast a shadow, or else from their shadows they would become aware of that radiant beam that shines through this realm; but only a handful, awakened from their dream, rise and stride through the realm of dreams— they arrive at the truth— the supreme moment has come: contact with the eternal, an unspeakable experience! The sun looks on, it is the tonic triad, from which chords, starlike, shoot down and spin around you with flaming filaments. Enmeshed with fire, you lie there, until Psyche swings herself up to the sun."

Upon speaking these last words, he leapt up, gave me a piercing look, and threw his hands in the air. Then he sat back down again and downed the glass of wine he'd been served. A silence followed which I did not deem it seemly to break, so as not to set this extraordinary man off-track. Becalmed after a while, he continued:

"When I wiled in the realm of dreams, a thousand aches and terrors tormented me. It was late at night, and I was at my wit's end with fear of the grinning larvae of the monstrosities that besieged me, now dragging me down to the ocean bottom, now lifting me up to the heavens above.

[*] A reference to the witch in Ludovico Ariosto's (1474–1533) epic poem *Orlando Furioso* (*The Raging Roland*).

Beams of light pierced the dark night, and those beams were musical tones that enveloped me with mellifluous clarity. I woke from my aches and saw before me a big bright eye peering into an organ, and as it peered, sweet sounds arose, glimmering and getting entangled in glorious chords the likes of which I would never have conceived. Melodies streamed up and down, and I swam in this musical current – would gladly have drowned in it – when the eye looked at me and lifted me up above the roaring waves. Night fell again, and two giants in glimmering suits of armor approached me: Key Note and Fifth! They hurled me up, but the eye smiled and said: 'I know that your breast is filled with longing. The gentle, soft-voiced youth Major Third will join the giants. You will hear his sweet song, you will see me again, and my melodies will be yours.'"

He paused.

"And you saw the eye again?"

"Yes, I saw it again! For years I sighed with pleasure in the realm of dreams— here— yes, here! I sat in a lovely valley and listened to the flowers singing together. Only one sunflower kept silent and sadly turned its closed calyx to the ground. Invisible ties drew me to her— she raised her head— her calyx burst open, and from it the eye beamed at me. Notes streamed forth like beams of light from my face to the flower, which thirstily sucked them in. The leaves of the sunflower grew bigger and bigger— embers spilled from its surface— they enveloped me— the eye disappeared and I found myself in the calyx."

He jumped up at these last words and rushed out of the room with rapid youthful steps. I waited in vain for his return, resolving after a while to return to the city.

I had almost reached the Brandenburg Gate when I made out a tall figure striding toward it in the darkness and immediately recognized my curious companion from before. I spoke to him:

"Why did you rush off so suddenly?"

"I felt too hot and the sweet-voiced euphony rang out."

"I don't understand what you mean."

"All the better."

"All the worse, as I really want to completely grasp your meaning."

"Don't you hear it?"

"No."

"It's over now! Let's go! Ordinarily I am not fond of company; but— you're not a composer— you're not a Berliner."

"I cannot fathom what you have against Berliners. Here, where art is so respected and practiced at such a high level of accomplishment, I would rather imagine that a man of your artistic inclination would feel at home."

"You're mistaken. To my great distress I am damned to haunt its streets like a dead man's ghost in a desolate realm."

"A desolate realm, here, in Berlin?"

"Yes, it all feels desolate around me, since no kindred spirit ever comes my way. I stand alone."

"But what about the artists! The composers!"

"A pox on them! They carp and carp about the inconsequential — keep refining everything down to the most minute measure, keep mulling over everything just to pan out a single pitiful idea. They are forever blabbering about art, art appreciation, and what have you — they never get down to creating anything, and should they ever actually find themselves in the mood, as if impelled to bring forth a couple of artistic notions into the light of day, the terrible chill of their temperament reveals how distantly removed they are from the sun – you'd swear the stuff they churn out hailed from Lapland."

"Your judgment seems far too harsh. You must at least find the theater productions up to snuff."

"I finally forced myself to go again to the theater to see the opera of a young friend – can't remember the title. Hah, the whole world was packed into that opera! The spirits of Orcus come charging through the motley throng of well-heeled folks – every single one with his own voice and almighty tone – for heaven's sake, of course, I mean *Don Juan!* – But not the overture, which came bubbling forth *prestissimo* all in a big muddle, which I could suffer through; I prepared myself through fasting and prayer to endure it all, because I know that the euphony is overemphasized by these large-scale productions.

"Even if I must admit that Mozart's masterpieces for the most part are inexplicably neglected here, Gluck's works surely enjoy a worthy rendering."

"You think so? I once wanted to go hear *Iphigenia in Tauris*. As I entered the theater, I heard them striking up the overture. Hm— I think to myself, must be a mistake; *this* is how they do *Iphigenia*! I'm stunned when the *andante* starts up, at the beginning of *Iphigenia in Tauris*, and the storm follows hot on its heels. Twenty years lie in between! The entire effect, the whole perfectly calculated effect of the tragedy is lost. Still water— a storm— the Greeks are flung ashore, that's the opera in a nutshell!— What?

Did the composer write the overture in a mad fit, so that you can blast it off like a trumpet piece any way you want?"

"I grant you the blunder. Nevertheless, every effort is being made nowadays to valorize Gluck's works."

"Well, yes!" he responded in brief, smiling ever more bitterly. Suddenly he leapt up, and nothing could stop him. It was as if he'd disappeared in a flash, and for days I sought him out in vain in the Tiergarten.

Some months had passed, when, having tarried in a remote part of the city on one cold and rainy evening, I hastened back to my apartment on Friedrichstraße. On my way, I had to pass the theater; the jarring music of trumpets and kettledrums reminded me that Gluck's *Armide* was on the bill, and I was about to go in when near the window, where you could hear almost every note performed by the orchestra, a strange soliloquy caught my attention.

"Here comes the king— they're playing the march— oh, beat away, keep beating on the kettledrum!— it's a spirited passage! Yes, yes, they'll have to play it eleven times today— or else the procession won't be processional enough.— Hah hah— maestro— hep it up, boys!— Look there, a figurant's stuck with a shoehorn in his hands.— That's right, for the twelfth time! and always on the dominant note— oh, you powers that be, it's never ending! Now he pays his compliment. Armide thanks him respectfully.— Not again?— That's right, two soldiers are still missing! Now it's time to strike up the recitativo.— What evil spirit banned me to stay in this spot?"

"The ban has been lifted," I cried out. "Come with me!"

I seized hold of my madcap character from the Tiergarten – for the deliverer of that soliloquy was none other – grabbed him by the arm and dragged him away with me. He seemed surprised and followed quietly. We had already reached Friedrichstraße when he suddenly stopped dead in his tracks.

"I know you," he said. "You're the fellow in the Tiergarten— we talked a lot— I drank wine— got myself all worked up in a sweat— Euphony rang in my ears for two days after that— I had to endure a lot— it's over now!"

"I'm happy that chance brought us together again. Let us get better acquainted. I live not far from here; why don't we …"

"I cannot and dare not go visit anyone."

"No, you won't get away from me this time; I'll go where you're going."

"Then you'll have to accompany me for another few hundred steps. But didn't you want to attend the theater?"

"I wanted to hear *Armide*, but now—"

"Then you shall hear *Armide*, presently!"

We walked up Friedrichstraße in silence; he turned down a side street, and raced so quickly down the street that I was hardly able to keep up with him, until finally he came to a halt in front of a rather dilapidated-looking house. He knocked quite a long time before someone opened the door. Staggering around in the dark, we found our way to the staircase and climbed up to a room on the floor above, the door of which my curious companion locked behind us. I heard another door opening; soon after, he burst in with a lit candle in hand, and I was more than a bit surprised at the sight of his oddly arranged room. Old-fashioned overstuffed settees, a wall clock with gilded encasement, and a large, cumbersome mirror gave everything the somber appearance of outmoded elegance. In the middle of the room stood a small piano topped by a large porcelain inkpot, and beside it lay several sheets of lined music paper. A closer inspection of these trappings of composition convinced me, however, that nothing had been written for quite a while; the paper was all yellowed, and a thick spider's web hung over the inkpot. The man stepped in front of a cupboard in the corner of the room that I hadn't initially noticed, and as he drew back the curtain I became aware of a row of finely bound books with gilded titles: *Orfeo*, *Armida*, *Alceste*, *Iphigenia*, etc., in short, an array of Gluck's masterpieces.

"You own Gluck's complete works?" I cried out.

He made no reply, but his mouth twisted itself into a contorted smile, and the play of muscles in his sunken cheeks momentarily distorted the face into a nightmarish mask. With his stony, somber look fixed on me, he reached for one of the books – it was *Armida* – and stepped ceremoniously over to the piano. He propped up the folded music stand, which he appeared to do with pleasure, opened the book, and – how can I describe my surprise! – I saw lined sheets of paper, but with not a note inscribed on them.

He began: "Now I will play you the overture! Please be so kind as to turn the pages, and at the right time!"

I promised to do so, whereupon he played splendidly and masterfully, with full-fingered chords, the majestic *Tempo di Marcia* with which the overture begins, almost completely faithful to the original; although the *allegro* was only interlaced with Gluck's principal ideas. He introduced so many new genial twists and turns that my amazement grew by leaps and bounds. His modulated harmonies were absolutely astounding, without ever sounding grating, and he managed to adorn the essential musical ideas with so many melodic melismas that those ideas seemed to be reinvigorated again and again, ever new and rejuvenated. His face glowed; at times his eyebrows sank and a long-suppressed rage seemed about to burst forth; at other times his eyes welled up with tears of profound wistfulness. Sometimes he sang the theme in a winsome tenor voice as both his hands played artful melismas; he managed in an altogether original manner to make his voice mimic the muffled thump of the kettledrum. I kept diligently turning the page in accordance with his looks. The overture came to an end and he fell back, utterly exhausted, into the settee. He soon bestirred himself again and, while hastily flipping through many empty pages in the book, he muttered:

"All of this, my good Sir, I wrote upon emerging from the realm of dreams. But I disclosed the holy to the unholy and an ice-cold hand gripped my burning heart! My heart did not break, but I was damned to walk among the unholy like the ghost of one departed – bodyless, so that no one would recognize me until the sunflower once again lifts me up unto the eternal. Hah – let us now sing Armide's scene."

Whereupon he sang the closing scene from *Armide* with an expression on his face that gripped my heart. Here, too, his take differed in remarkable ways from the original opera; but his altered music fulfilled, as it were, the highest potential of Gluck's scene. He captured in notes all of the heightened emotion that hate, love, despair, and frenzy can express. His voice sounded like that of a youth, then deeply muffled, it welled up with an all-penetrating force. My whole being trembled— I was beside myself. When he came to an end, I threw myself into his arms and cried out with a strained voice: "What is this? Who are you?"

He stood up and measured me with a grave and penetrating look; but when I wanted to question more, he disappeared with the candle through the door and left me standing in the dark. Almost a quarter of an hour passed; I despaired of seeing him again and, orienting myself with the aid of the music stand, tried to find my way to the door, when suddenly he returned with the candle in hand, dressed in an embroidered gala frock coat, a splendid vest underneath, and a dagger dangling at his side.

I froze; he stepped toward me in a solemn manner, gently took hold of my hand, and said with a strange smile:

"I, Sir, am the Ritter Gluck."

Kreisleriana

First Series 1810

W**here did he come from? Nobody knows! Who were his parents?
Unknown!** Whose student is he? He's a good master, that much
we can give him since he plays admirably well, and since he's got common
sense and culture to boot, we can make do with him and even let him give
music lessons. And he really, truly was a kapellmeister, the diplomatically
inclined add, those, that is, in whose presence he once, when he was in a
good mood, pulled out an official document completed and signed by the
director of the ——r Court Theater which states that the Kapellmeister
Johannes Kreisler was released from his position solely because he steadfastly refused to put music to an opera written by the court poet, and also
more than once spoke in deprecating terms of the *primo uomo*, and sought
in altogether excessive, albeit incomprehensible, terms to give preference
to a young girl, one of his voice students, to sing the role of prima donna.
Yet he would nevertheless be allowed to retain the title of Royal ——r

Kapellmeister and would moreover be permitted to return to his position, were he to completely abjure certain positions and absurd prejudices – for instance, that true Italian music is gone for good, and the like – and willingly affirm his belief in the excellence of the court poet, who was generally recognized as the second Metastasio.

His friends maintained that nature tried a new recipe when cooking up his character traits, and the experiment had failed. Too little of the phlegmatic had been added to his over-excitable disposition; his imaginative faculty all too often got fired up to a dangerous degree and upset the balance of his equilibrium, a character trait absolutely essential to the artist, enabling him to get along with the world, and to compose works of the sort that the world really needs to a higher degree than they even know.

Be that as it may— enough said. Johannes was driven hither and thither by his phantasms and dreams, as if on a stormy sea, and he seemed to be seeking in vain the safe harbor that would grant him the serenity and good cheer necessary for the artist to create anything. His friends could not bring him to write down a composition and, once he had put something on paper, they were unable to keep him from tearing it up. Sometimes he only composed at night in the most agitated state of mind— he awakened his friend, who lived next door, to wildly play for him all that he had written at lightning speed— he wept tears of joy over the accomplished work— he lauded himself as the most jubilant of souls— but the very next day, the composition went up in flames.

Singing had an almost pernicious effect on him, because his imagination was practically whipped up into a frenzy and his spirit absconded to a realm into which no one could safely follow; nevertheless, he often took delight in playing strange variations in graceful contrapuntal twists and turns and imitations, elaborating on the most artful passages at the piano for hours on end. If he managed to pull this off, it put him in a chipper mood for days, and a certain roguish irony spiced up the conversation he shared with his cozy coterie of friends.

But then all at once, no one knew how or why, he disappeared. Many maintained that they detected traces of madness in him, and he had indeed at times been spotted wearing two hats, one on top of the other, with two rastrums stuck like daggers in his red waistbelt, singing merrily to himself as he hopped out the city gate – although his close friends saw nothing strange in this, since he had always been given to agitated outbursts stirred by some inner turmoil. When all inquiries as to his whereabouts came to naught, and his friends discussed what to do with his small literary estate of sheet music and other writings, Mademoiselle von B. turned up and declared that she alone would safeguard this stash of papers on behalf of her dear master and friend, whom she by no means believed to be lost. The other friends gladly consigned the whole lot to her care, and when short, mostly humorous reflections were found jotted down in pencil script on the reverse side of several pages of sheet paper, sorrowful Johannes's faithful female student made copies to pass around among his close friends, offering them as the unassuming results of the master's passing upset.

KAPELLMEISTER JOHANNES KREISLER'S MUSICAL WOES

They all went away. I could have predicted it from the whispering, foot shuffling, throat clearing, muttering in all musical keys; it was a veritable bee buzz that distracts from the repertoire and swells to a hum.

Gottlieb installed new lights and set a bottle of white Burgundy on the pianoforte. I can't play anymore, completely exhausted as I am; it's the fault of my grand old friend on the music stand, who once again swept me away, like Faust clinging to Mephistopheles' coattails, lifting my spirits so high that I lost sight of the little people scurrying around below, the prodigious din of their disquiet notwithstanding. It was a currish, uselessly wasted evening! But now I feel lighthearted and good again – did I not pull out my pencil while playing, and with my right hand jot down on page sixty-three of the score several changes of key, while the left hand kept on playing in tempo! I continue my remarks on the back side of the sheet music. Abandoning numbers and notes, like the convalescent who can't stop elaborating on his recent sufferings, I laboriously record here the hellish torments of today's tea. Not for my sake alone, but rather for the sake of all those who, guided by the Latin term *"Verte"* (I will jot it down once my plaint is completed), may from time to time turn the sheet music around, to derive delight and edification from my copy of Johann Sebastian Bach's "Variations for Piano," at the end of the thirtieth variation, published by Nägeli in Zürich. Such knowledgeable folk will immediately divine the correlation; they are well aware that the privy councillor Röderlein is a most gracious host and has two daughters whom the smart set raves about, saying that they dance like goddesses, speak French like angels, and play, sing, and draw like the Muses.

Privy Councillor Röderlein is a rich man; at his quarterly gatherings he serves the best wines, the finest dishes, and all is served in a lavish manner.

Whoever fails to have a ball at one of his teas has no style, no spirit, and above all no appreciation for the arts. Art is what it's all about; aside from tea, punch, wine, ice cream, etc., some piece of music is always presented which the smart set listens to in a very relaxed fashion. This is how it goes: after each guest has had enough time to sip any number of cups of tea, and after punch and ice cream are twice passed around, the servants set up card tables for the older, more established members of society who prefer card games to music, and who, so occupied, refrain from making undue noise, except for the jingle of small change. At this point, the younger guests crowd around Miss Röderlein; a commotion ensues, in which the following words are overheard: "Lovely young lady, please do not deny us the pleasure of your heavenly talent— oh, do sing us something, my dear."— "Impossible— I've come down with a cold— Got it at the last ball— Nothing rehearsed."— "Oh, please, please— we beg of you," etc.

In the meantime, Gottlieb has uncovered the piano keyboard and set up the music stand with the well-known book of music. The gracious Frau Mama calls over from the card table: "*Chantez donc, mes enfants!*" That is the prompt for me to play my role; I stand beside the piano, and the Röderlein girls are triumphantly led to the instrument. At this point another disagreement ensues; neither girl wants to go first.

"You know, dear Nanette, how awfully hoarse I am."

"Am I any less so, dear Marie?"

"I sing so badly."

"Oh, darling, just begin—"

And so on and so forth. It is at this point when I come up with a bright idea. (I do so every time!) Let them begin together with a duet. Said suggestion is greeted with enthusiastic applause, the book of music is leafed through, the painstakingly predesignated page is finally found, and the singing begins: *Dolce dell' anima*, etc.

The talents of the Miss Röderleins are indeed not negligible. I've been in town for five years, four and a half years of which I've been engaged as singing instructor in the Röderlein household. In this short time, Miss Nanette has managed to parrot a melody she heard ten times in the theater, and then practiced at most ten times at the piano, in a manner more or less faithful to the original. Miss Marie can manage after the eighth time, and even if she often sings a fourth note lower than the piano, the difference is readily forgiven, on account of her pretty little face and her ever so slightly rose-hued lips. The duet is followed up with the requisite acclamatory round of applause, whereupon the girls take turns singing *ariettas* and *duettinos*, and each time I hammer out the familiar accompaniment as if for the very first time.

Today, as the Röderlein girls are singing, the wife of Finance Counselor Eberstein lets it be known by her throat clearing and singing along: I've got a voice too.

To this, Miss Nanette remarks: "But Madame Finance Counselor, you, too, simply must treat us to a taste of your heavenly singing."

A new hubbub ensues. She, too, has a cold— and doesn't know any songs by heart! Gottlieb brings two arms full of books of sheet music: pages are turned and turned. First, she wants to sing "Der Hölle Rache," (Hell's Vengeance Boils in My Heart), then "Hebe! sieh," then "Ach ich liebte." (Ah, I Was in Love). Anxiously, I suggest: "Ein Veilchen auf der Wiese stand" (A Violet in the Meadow Stood). But she prefers a major genre, she wants to show off, so we stick to Constanze. Shout it out, squeal, mew, burble, gurgle, groan, grunt, quaver, warble up a storm! I play up the *fortissimo* till I'm half-deaf— Oh, Satan, Satan! Which of your hellish demons entered that throat, pinching and wedging and wrenching every note! Four strings have already snapped, a piano hammer is off. My ears are ringing, there's a roaring in my head, my nerves are shattered. Have all the impure notes of every screeching market crier's horn crowded together in this throat? It infuriates me— so I drink a glass of Burgundy! My playing is received with wild applause, and someone remarks that Madame Finance Counselor's rendition and Mozart's must have fired me up. I respond with a downcast gaze and a foolish grin.

At this point all the hidden talents in the room make themselves known and burst forth willy-nilly. The public must endure all manner of musical excesses: ensembles, finales, choruses to be performed.

"It is common knowledge that the Canon Kratzer sings a heavenly bass," the man with the short, frizzy Titus cut remarks, adding humbly that he himself is just a second tenor, though indeed the member of several song academies. All is set up in a snap to sing the first chorus from *Titus*. Which goes splendidly! Standing directly behind me, the Canon thunders out his bass as if accompanied by obligato trumpets and kettle drums in the cathedral; he hits each note perfectly, but in his haste he slows the tempo to almost twice as slow. He does remain true to himself throughout the entire performance, at least insofar as he consistently trails by a half beat. The other singers display a definite penchant for ancient Greek music, which, being devoid of harmony as everyone knows, is presented in unison; they all sing the treble with small variations by approximately a quarter tone produced by random rises and drops of pitch.

This somewhat boisterous production creates a dramatic excitement in the crowd, that is to say it causes considerable dismay at the card tables, where card players are at a loss, unable, as they had before, to add a melo-dramatic element with declamatory statements interwoven with the music, as, for instance: "Oh, I just loved to— forty-eight— I was so happy— I pass— couldn't— whist— the sweet pain of it— cards of the same color— strong suit, etc.—Things go smoothly. (So I pour myself a glass.)

That was the high point of the day's musical exposition: now it's over and done with! That's what I thought to myself, shutting the book of music and rising from the piano bench. Which is when the Baron, my antique tenor, approaches me and says: "Oh, most esteemed Kapellmeister, I have heard that you're an ace at improvisation; do improvise a piece for us! A short one! I beg you!"

To which I reply that I'm all improvised out for the day; and as we discuss the matter, a devil in the form of a dandy with two waistcoats digs up the Bach variations out from under my hat in the room next door. He thinks to himself, they're just a sweet assortment of little variations on the order of: *Nel cor mi non più sento** – *Ah vous dirai-je, maman,**** etc., and figures I can just play them off the top of my head. I hesitate; but they all chime in insistently. Very well then, I think to myself, listen up and burst with bore-dom. So then I get to it. At Variation Number 3, several ladies withdraw, followed by that little frizzy-haired fellow. The Röderleins hold on, albeit fidgeting about, till Variation Number 12, since it is, after all, their music

---

* "In My Heart I Feel No More."

** "Ah, Shall I Tell You, Mother Dear."

instructor playing. At Variation Number 15 the double-vested dandy backs off. Compelled by an exaggerated sense of politesse, the Baron sticks around till Number 30, and just keeps drinking down the punch that Gottlieb had set out for me on the piano. I would have played it out to the end, but the musical theme of this Variation Number 30 really got to me. The book of sheet music suddenly swells in my mind's eye into a giant folio, its pages covered with thousands of imitations and elaborations on the theme that I feel compelled to play. The notes come alive and flicker and leap around me— electric sparks pass through my fingertips onto the keys— the musical spirit from which it all streamed forth outflanks my rational cognition— the entire room fills with a thick cloud, and the candles burn ever more dimly— sometimes a nose peers out at me, sometimes a pair of eyes; but they promptly disappear again. So I remain seated alone with my Sebastian Bach and my Gottlieb, as if infused with a *spiritu familiari*.

I drink!— Should an honest musician ever be tormented with music as I was tormented today, and am so often tormented? I swear to God, no art is so damnably abused as is that splendid, holy *musika*, in its sheer vulnerability so easily defiled! If you have true talent, a veritable sense of art, all right then, learn music, produce something worthy of the art, and give your all to that consecrated entity. But if all you want is to warble, then do so for your own pleasure and in the privacy of your room, and don't torment Kapellmeister Kreisler and other worthy listeners with it.

Finally, I get to go home to complete my new piano sonata; but it's not yet eleven o'clock on a splendid summer night. I bet that at the cathouse next door, the girls are seated at the open window, regaling passersby on the street below with a shrill, screeching, piercing voice: "*Wenn mir dein Auge strahlet*"* – but always just the first verse. Directly across the way, somebody with lungs like Rameau's nephew is martyring a flute, and the acoustical experiments of the French horn player, next door to him, produce long, long notes. The umpteen dogs in the neighborhood are sounding off and, stirred by the sweet duet, my landlord's tomcat is serenading the neighbor's cat, whom he has had the hots for since last March, wailing sweet nothings across the chromatic scale, directly under my window (needless to say, my musical-poetic laboratory is a cheap garret room). Things quiet down after eleven o'clock; I remain seated at my perch, since I still have blank sheets of music paper and a drop of Burgundy left over, of which I promptly take a satisfying swig.

There is, I have heard, an old law that forbids noisy laborers from residing next to scholars; ought not poor, hard-pressed composers – who are, moreover, obliged to mint money out of their musical inspiration so as to continue spinning the tenuous thread of their existence – apply this law to their own circumstances and be permitted to proscribe big mouths and the blaring mob from their immediate vicinity? How would the painter engaged in depicting his ideal respond if a whole slew of grimacing ugly mugs were held up between him and his model! If he shut his eyes tight, he would at least be able to keep painting undisturbed in his imagination. Cotton balls stuffed in the ears don't help, you still hear the infernal racket – and what of the concept, the very concept of it! Now comes the chorus, now the French horns, etc.; the devil makes mincemeat of the most sublime musical ideas.

---

* "When Your Eye Beams at Me."

The sheet is covered with notes; on the white band left blank just below the title, permit me to remark why I resolved a hundred times over not to keep letting myself be tormented by the privy councillor, and why I broke that resolve a hundred times. All right, so it's Röderlein's ravishing niece who keeps me coming back to the house and who tied my artistry in a knot. Whoever has been so fortunate as to witness Miss Amalia sing the last scene of Gluck's *Armida* or the dramatic scene with Donna Anna in *Don Giovanni*, can well fathom that an hour spent with her at the piano pours heavenly balsam into the wounds inflicted upon a tormented musical instructor by all the dissonance of the day. Röderlein, who neither believes in the immortality of the soul nor in musical cadence, considers her completely useless for the maintenance of his high teas, since she refuses to sing at them, yet will sing her heart out before perfectly ordinary folk such as simple musicians, a fact that he believes does not suit her station in life. In Röderlein's view, she must surely have picked up her long-held, soaring, accordion-like notes, singing that brings rapture to my ears, from listening to a nightingale, a senseless creature that resides in the woods and from which mankind, the sensible lords of creation, have nothing to learn. Her reckless disregard of reputation sometimes goes so far that she will even allow her singing to be accompanied by Gottlieb on the violin when playing Beethoven or Mozart sonatas on the piano, a practice hardly attuned to the taste of fashionable teatime hosts or whist players.

That was the last glass of Burgundy. Gottlieb is polishing my candlesticks and seems a bit surprised by my assiduous scribbling. You would be quite right at assessing Gottlieb's age as just sixteen. His is a splendid and profound talent. But why did the father, a toll taker, have to die so young; and did the child's legal guardian have to stick him in domestic service? When Rode came to town, Gottlieb listened in from the antechamber with his ear pressed to the door of the concert hall and played what he'd heard for entire nights; all day long he went around daydreaming. The red spot on his cheek, a faithful imprint of the ring on Mlle. Röderlein's hand, might have been roused by gentle rubbing, enhancing the somnambulistic state, but really it was the mark of a heavy blow, dealt with the very opposite intention. Aside from other things, I gave him the sonatas of Corelli to practice; when he had finished, he went on a rampage rooting out the mice hiding on the floor under the old Österlein grand piano till not a one of them survived, and then with Röderlein's permission, translocated the instrument to his little room.

"Fling it off, that hateful servant's frock, my good Gottlieb, and let me at long last press you against my heart as the valiant artist you can one day become with a talent such as yours, and with your profound sense of art!" Standing behind me, Gottlieb wiped the tears from his eyes as I spoke these words to him.

Without another word, I pressed his hand in mine, we went upstairs and played the sonatas of Corelli.

The Golden Pot

A Fairy Tale for Modern Times
Bamberg 1814

The misadventure of the student Anselmus, Deputy Rector
Paulmann's Restorative Tobacco Box, and the Golden Green Snakes.

On Ascension Day, at three in the afternoon, a young man hastened through the Black Gate into the city of Dresden, running directly into a basket of apples and cakes hawked by a hideous old hag, so that every fruit and sweet cake not crushed in the collision was hurled out onto the street, and the guttersnipes gleefully shared the spoils that the scholar inadvertently flung their way. Roused by the woman's fearsome clamor, her fellow hawkers ran out from behind their carts heaped with cakes and brandy, surrounded the young man, and showered him with such vile insults that, struck dumb with upset and shame, he held out his not very amply filled purse, which the old biddy greedily snatched up and promptly pocketed. The tight ring of street vendors dissolved around him, but no sooner did the young man break free than the woman cried after him: "Run, keep running as fast as you can, Satan's child, right into the crystal ball— into the crystal ball!" The woman's shrill, croaking voice sounded so ghastly that the passersby stopped dead in their tracks, and those who had been laughing suddenly fell silent.

Even though he could make neither hide nor hair of the woman's strange words, the student Anselmus – for such was the young man's name – was so horror-stricken he quickened his steps to escape the gaze of curious onlookers.

As he elbowed his way through the well-dressed throng, he heard mutterings all around him: "The poor young man— Fie on the cursed old wench!" Strangely enough, the old woman's cryptic words had given the amusing episode a certain tragic turn, so that people who hadn't cared before now followed the student with sympathetic looks. The womenfolk readily forgave his handsome face with its expression that further intensified the ardor of his distress, as they did the lad's strong build and his garb, though it was unfashionable. His pike-gray jacket was cut as though the tailor knew the latest style by hearsay only, and the tight-fitting black satin pants gave the wearer a magister-like air, altogether out of keeping with his spritely stride and stance.

Gasping as he reached the end of the alley leading to the public bathhouse, the student slackened his pace though he dared not look up. He was still befuddled by the jumble of tumbling apples and cakes, and every kind look from this or that girl just seemed like a reflex in response to the cackling laughter mocking him at the Black Gate.

It was in this state of mind that he finally arrived at the entrance to

Lincke's Bathhouse,* where a line of festively attired visitors entered one by one. The music of wind instruments sounded from within, and the crush of merry guests grew louder and louder. Anselmus almost burst into tears. Ascension Day had always been a special holiday for him and he had likewise been inclined to participate in the festivities at this blissful establishment; he had even intended to treat himself to a half portion of coffee with rum and a bottle of Doppelbock beer, and in order to make merry had stuffed more money in his purse than was seemly or advisable. And now that fatal collision with the apple basket had drained him of all the money he had on him. Coffee, Doppelbock beer, music, and the sight of girls in pretty dresses were all out of the question now; he slunk slowly past the entrance and finally turned down the lonely path to the Elbe River, which he now had all to himself.

Finding a friendly little perch on the lawn beneath an elderberry tree growing out of a crack in the city wall, he plunked himself down and stuffed his pipe from his tobacco box, the gift from his friend, Deputy Rector Paulmann. Right there in front of his nose, the golden yellow waves of the beautiful Elbe River went purling and burbling by. Behind that, intrepid and proud, Dresden reared its bright towers into the frothy canopy of clouds covering the city and its surrounding flower-speckled meadows and green woods, while in the twilight the profile of the jagged mountains beckoned toward far-flung Bohemia.

But Anselmus, looking glumly ahead, puffed smoke clouds in the air

* Das Lincke'sche Bad (Lincke's Bathhouse) was a popular inn in a garden setting, with summer theater and concert hall, as well as one of the first open-air pools, in Dresden, in Hoffmann's day.

and gave voice to his discontent. "It's as true as the nose on my face," he said aloud, "I was born to be misery's child. That I never drew the crowning bean in my piece of cake on Three Kings' Day, that I always lost at odds or evens, that my bread and butter always fell on the buttered side – that's all water under the bridge. But isn't it godawful, when I finally decided to become a student just for the hell of it, that I should still be a loser? What kind of guy puts on a new jacket and immediately goes and messes it up with a tallow stain, or gets it caught on a cursed nail and tears a hole in it? Who else tips his hat to a privy councillor or some highborn lady, and the hat goes flying out of his hand, or else slips on the floor and falls flat on his pathetic face? Back in Halle, didn't I get it into my head, come market day, to rush headlong like a lemming and squander a full three or four pence for some banged-up pots? Did I ever even once make it on time to the registrar's office or wherever the hell you're supposed to go to register for a class? What good did it do me to leave home a half hour early and stand there in front of the door with my hand on the doorknob, about to knock, if somebody dumps a washbasin over my head, or I collide with someone else running the other way, get myself tangled up in their confounded business, and miss my appointment? Where, oh where have you gone, you blessed dreams of future good fortune, all my proud posturing of plans to become a government official! Did my unlucky star make me alienate all my would-be benefactors?

"Knowing full well that the privy councillor to whom I'd been recommended couldn't stand close-cropped hair, I had the barber painstakingly fasten a tail to my messy mop, but no sooner did I bow before the man than the unlucky tail came undone, and a feisty pug came sniffing over, snapped it up, and carried my tail as a prize to the stunned official. In a fright I lunged for it, tumbled over the table on which the councillor was having his working breakfast, and sent cup and saucer, ink bottle and blotter crashing to the floor, hot chocolate and ink spilling over the letter of recommendation. 'What the devil!' screamed the infuriated official and shoved me out the door.

"What good does it do me that Deputy Rector Paulmann got my hopes up about a clerical job? Will my unlucky star that follows me wherever I go countenance any such stroke of good fortune? Today's mishap was all I needed! I wanted to celebrate Ascension Day in style, to do it up right. I was looking forward to proudly calling out my order like every guest at the bathhouse: 'Hey waiter— a bottle of Doppelbock, please— 'n' better make it your best!' I'd've stayed up late drinking, close to pretty girls dressed to the nines. I'm quite sure I would have mustered up the courage, found a new me, so that if one or the other charming Miss asked me: 'What time might it be?' or: 'What's that you're playing?' I'd've leapt up in good form, without toppling my glass or stumbling over the bench, strode forward a step or two, gallantly bowed my head, and replied: 'At your service, Miss, it's an overture from *The Danube Maiden* by Johann Strauss,' or: 'It's about to strike six.' Could anyone have held that against me? Not on your life! And the girls would have flashed an impish smile, as expected, when I got up the nerve to prove that I too have a certain savoir faire and know how to dally with the ladies. But then the devil had to go and lead me into that damned apple basket, and now I'm reduced to sitting here alone, dipping into my tobacco box, and…"

All of a sudden Anselmus's sad soliloquy was interrupted by a strange rustle and flutter in the grass beside him; a stirring that soon rose into the branches and leaves of the elderberry tree arching over his head. First it seemed as if the evening breeze shook the leaves, and then as if cooing birds fluttered their little wings back and forth, deliberately rocking in the branches. Then a whisper and a warble rose in the air around him as if the elderberry blossoms were ringing like crystal bells. Then – he knew not how – the whisper, rustle, and ringing dissolved into a flurry of half-wafted words:

"Over, under— in between— through branches and swelling blossoms we swing, sidle, loop— little sister— little sister, swing yourself into the shimmer— swiftly, swiftly swing yourself up— down— the setting sun shoots rays, the wind of dusk hisses— rustling in the mist— blossoms sing— let's rouse our little tongues to sing along with the blossoms and branches— stars will soon sparkle— back down now— over, under, in between— swing, sidle, loop, little sister."

On and on went the bewildering babble. Anselmus thought, "It's nothing but the evening breeze bursting today into an orderly string of intelligible words." But at that very moment what sounded like a crystal bell rang three times above his head. He looked up and spotted three glimmering gold-and-green-skinned snakes wrapped around the branches, raising their heads to soak up the last rays of the setting sun. The whispering and warbling of the same words began again, and the snakes curled and slid up and down the leaves and branches. As soon as they set themselves in motion it was as if the elderberry tree scattered a thousand sparkling emeralds among its dark leaves.

"Must be the late afternoon sun stroking the elderberry," Anselmus thought, but then the little bells once again began to ring, and he saw one of the snakes stretching its little head out to him. An electric shock ran through all his limbs and sparked his innermost self – he peered upward and a pair of dark blue eyes returned his gaze with inexpressible longing, so that completely new sensation of the greatest bliss and the most profound pain threatened to explode in his chest. And as he kept gazing at the eyes with burning desire, the crystal bells sounded louder still in sweetest harmony and the sparkling emeralds fell, encircling him in a thousand little flames streaming with strands of gold.

The elderberry tree stirred, and then spoke. "You lay down in my shadow, infused with my fragrance, but you failed to fathom my secret. The fragrance is my language when inflamed by love."

The evening wind swished by and whispered, "I tickled your temples, but you didn't take the hint, the breeze is my language when inflamed by love."

The last rays of the setting sun burst through the cloud burning with words, as if to say, "I showered you with liquid gold, but you didn't grasp my meaning; the glow is my language when inflamed by love."

Ever deeper and deeper entranced by the look of those lovely eyes, his longing swelled, his desire sizzled, everything stirred and swayed as if awaking to a new and happy life. Flower petals and blossoms burst with fragrance; the scent was like the splendid song of a thousand flutes, and what they sang was echoed in the golden puff of evening clouds floating by to distant lands. But when the last rays of the setting sun faded behind the mountains, and dusk flung its cape over the surroundings, a deep raspy voice intoned from the distance:

"Hey, hey, what kind of whispered fuss is that?— Hey, hey, who seeks to

glimpse my last rays behind the mountains! Enough basking, enough singing!—
Hey, hey, o'er bush and grass, grass and stream I roam!— Hey, hey, down-down-a-
down I go— Down-down-a-down I go!"

Then the sun went silent like the stilled murmur of distant thunder, but
the crystal bells shattered in a discordant clang. All went silent and Anselmus
watched as the three shimmering and sparkling snakes went slipping along
through the grass toward the water's edge. Slithering away, they hurled
themselves into the Elbe and disappeared behind the waves; little green
flames flared up, zigzagging their way toward the city, suddenly evaporating
in a puff of mist.

SECOND VIGIL

How the Student Anselmus was taken for a drunk and a madman.
Crossing the Elbe River. The Bravour-Arie of Kapellmeister Graun,
Conradis Magen Liqueur, and the bronzed apple lady.

A proper bourgeois lady, who caught sight of Anselmus's strange doings
on her way home from a stroll with her family, stopped dead in her
tracks with her arms crossed before her and remarked: "The gentleman is
not in his right mind!"

Anselmus had embraced the trunk of the elderberry tree and kept
beseeching the branches and leaves: "Oh, just twinkle and glimmer one last
time you sweet little golden snakes, just let me hear your bell-like voices
ring again! Just wink at me one more time with your enchanting blue eyes,
one more time, I beg you, or else I'll dissolve in pain and passionate

longing!" And all the while he sighed and groaned pitifully from the bottom of his heart and, with impatient longing, kept shaking the elderberry tree, which just stood there stiff and unresponsive, fluttering its leaves, as if making light of the student's sufferings.

"The gentleman is not in his right mind!" the lady repeated, and Anselmus felt as if abruptly shaken out of a deep dream or doused with ice cold water. Only then did he see clearly where he was, and fathom that some strange spook must have muddled his mind and forced him to break out in a stream of words muttered at the top of his lungs. Profoundly embarrassed, he stared back at the lady and finally grabbed his hat that had fallen to the ground, preparing to make a quick escape.

In the meantime, the *paterfamilias* had come up close; having set down the little one he'd been carrying, he'd leaned with amazement on his walking stick and seen and heard the student's strange carryings on. Now he picked up the pipe and tobacco pouch Anselmus had let fall, held it forth, and remarked: "The gentleman had best not blubber and carry on like that in the dark, and let him not trouble decent folk if all that ails him is that he's had a drop too much to drink! Better be a good boy, go home and sleep it off."

Deeply mortified, the student let out a tearful "Ach!"

"Tut tut," the proper gent continued, "let him pay it no more mind, such things happen to the best of us, and surely on dear Ascension Day a man can be allowed to go on a bit of a bender. Such things even happen to a man of the cloth – the young gentleman is, after all, a candidate for clerical office – but if he will permit, I'll stuff my pipe from his stash of tobacco, mine having gone empty over the course of our constitutional."

As the gentleman spoke this last sentence, Anselmus was preparing to pocket his pipe and tobacco pouch, but the patriarch proceeded to slowly and carefully clean his own pipe and had already reached out to slowly stuff it from the student's stash.

Several girls from good families stopped to commiserate in a whisper with the woman and giggled among themselves while casting a contemptuous look at Anselmus. To him, it felt as if he were standing on a bed of pointed thorns and glowing hot needles. As soon as he retrieved his pipe and tobacco pouch, he immediately dashed off.

All of the wondrous things he'd seen were erased from memory, and all he recalled was that he had babbled a whole lot of nonsense at the top of his lungs under the elderberry bush, a fact he found all the more painful to recall having long harbored a visceral aversion to those who talked to themselves. Satan speaks through them, said his rector, and he had always held this to be true. To have been taken for a drunken theology student on Ascension Day – the very thought of it made him recoil.

He was just about to turn on Poplar Alley, abutting Kosel Garden, when a voice behind him called out: "Herr Anselmus! Herr Anselmus, where are you dashing off to in such haste, for a thousand heavens' sake?" The student stopped dead in his tracks, as if riveted to the ground, convinced as he was that a new misfortune was about to befall him. The voice rang out again. "Herr Anselmus, do come back, we're waiting at the water's edge!" Only then did the student realize that it was his friend Deputy Rector Paulmann calling out to him. He turned and went back to the Elbe, where he found the deputy rector with his two daughters, together with the Registrar Heerbrand, about to climb into a gondola. Deputy Rector Paulmann invited the student to join them on a ride across the Elbe, and subsequently to spend the evening at his lodgings in the suburb of Pirna. Anselmus was glad to accept, believing he would thereby escape the streak of bad luck that had befallen him today.

Once they had set out across the river, it so happened that a fireworks display was set off on the far bank in Anton's Gardens. Crackling and hissing, the rockets soared through the air and exploded, emitting a thousand sparkling streaks of fire. Anselmus sat beside the oarsman, deep in thought, when, upon seeing the reflection in the water of the flying sparks and flames, it seemed to him as if the golden snakes swam along with the current. All of the strange things he had seen under the elderberry tree leapt back into mind, and he was once again gripped by the same inexpressible longing, the burning desire that had made his breast quake with spasms of painful rapture.

"Oh, can it be you again, you little golden snakes? Sing to me, sing! Let those entrancingly lovely dark blue eyes glimmer again in your sweet song. Oh, my darlings, is it you swimming under the rippling stream!" Anselmus cried out, all the while making tempestuous gestures, as if he meant to fling himself from the gondola into the river.

"What the devil?" the oarsman cried back, grabbing him by the coat-tails. The girls who were seated beside him shrieked in terror and fled to the far side of the craft; Registrar Heerbrand whispered something into Deputy Rector Paulmann's ear, of which Anselmus only heard the words: "Fits like that— not yet noticed?"

Immediately afterward Deputy Rector Paulmann got up and sat himself down beside the student, took his hand, eyed him with a seriously grave and officious expression, and said: "What's got into you, Herr Anselmus?"

Anselmus almost lost it, overwhelmed as he was by a strange split in his mind that he could not reconcile. He clearly recognized that what he took to be the glimmer of the little golden snakes was, in fact, the reflection of the fireworks in Anton's Garden. But a feeling he'd never had before – he could not say for sure whether it was rapture or pain – convulsed in his chest, and as the boatman dipped the oar so strenuously into the surface that the river seemed to respond with furiously rushing, rippling purls of water, the young man heard in the din a furtive whisper: "Anselmus! Anselmus! Can't you see us forever drawing near? My little sister has her eye on you again. Believe! Believe! Believe in us!" And it seemed to him as if he saw in the reflection three green glowing stripes.

But when he gazed wistfully into the deep, searching to see if those precious eyes were peering back at him, he saw that the shimmer came from the reflection of the nearest lighted windows. He sat there in silence, battling with himself. The deputy rector spoke louder still: "What's with you, Herr Anselmus?"

The student replied timidly, "Oh, my dear deputy rector, if only you knew what absolutely wondrous things I just dreamt with my eyes wide open under the elderberry tree near the left garden wall, you would not hold it against me that I should seem so out of sorts."

"Heavens, Herr Anselmus," the deputy rector replied, "I always took you for such a solid young man, but to dream— to dream with your eyes wide open— and then to suddenly want to leap into the water— forgive me, but only lunatics and madmen do such things!"

Anselmus was completely nonplussed at his friend's harsh words. Paulmann's youngest daughter, Veronica, a very good-looking young girl in the flush of her sixteen years, then spoke up. "Dear father, Herr Anselmus must have experienced something inexplicable, and maybe he only thinks he was awake, unaware that he had, in fact, fallen asleep under the elderberry tree and dreamed all sorts of crazy stuff that's still running through his mind."

"And dearest Mademoiselle, honored Deputy Rector," Registrar Heerbrand added, "ought a person not also be permitted to sink into a quasi-dreaming state while still awake? The very same thing happened to me one afternoon over coffee. While lost in thought, at the precise moment of bodily and intellectual digestion, the location of a lost file suddenly leapt to mind, as if sparked by inspiration – and just yesterday a lovely, large bit of Latin text danced before my wide-open eyes."

"Oh, most honored Registrar," replied Deputy Rector Paulmann, "you always had a certain poetic leaning, which makes a person fall easily into fantastic and far-fetched notions."

But it did Anselmus's heart good, profoundly depressed as he was, to be taken for drunk or just a little batty, and despite the fact that it had grown quite dark out, for the first time he was struck by Veronica's stunning dark blue eyes without thinking of the wondrous eyes in the water. Suddenly all that odd business under the elderberry tree slipped from his mind, and he felt so lighthearted and happy; indeed, in the sway of his high spirits, he went so far as to reach out a gallant hand to help his charming defender Veronica out of the gondola, and when she proceeded to wrap her arm in his he managed so skillfully to steer her home that he only slipped once, and it being the sole muddy spot along the way, only ever so slightly soiled Veronica's white dress.

Taking note of the felicitous change in Anselmus's comportment, Deputy Rector Paulmann once again took a liking to him, and asked his forgiveness for the harsh words he'd let slip before. "Yes," he admitted, "there are indeed numerous instances in which certain phantasms that people experience and that terrify and torment them no end derive from bodily malady, for which leeches applied appropriately to the posterior can help, according to an illustrious recently deceased man of science."

Though Anselmus could not say for certain if he had been drunk, daft, or physically ill, leeches seemed in any case altogether superfluous at the present time, since the aforementioned phantasms had completely disappeared and he felt ever merrier the more he managed with little pleasantries to entertain the lovely Veronica. As usual, the frugal supper was followed by music making; Anselmus sat down to play the piano, while Veronica let her pure and lovely voice ring out.

"Precious Mademoiselle," observed Registrar Heerbrand, "your voice is clear as a crystal bell!"

"Not so!" the words slipped out of Anselmus's lips, he knew not how, and everyone eyed him with stupefied wonder. "Crystal bells ring wondrously clear in elderberry trees— ever so wondrously clear!" the student kept muttering, half to himself.

Veronica lay her hand on his shoulder and said, "What stuff and nonsense are you chattering about, my dear Herr Anselmus!"

At this, the student promptly returned to his senses and started playing again.

Deputy Rector Paulmann gave him a dark look, but Registrar Heerbrand lay a sheet of music on the stand and sang a bravura aria by Kapellmeister Graun to everyone's delight. Anselmus accompanied a few more pieces, and played an able duet with Veronica of one of Deputy Rector Paulmann's own compositions which put everyone in the merriest of moods.

It had grown rather late, and Registrar Heerbrand reached for his hat and walking stick, when Deputy Rector Paulmann took him aside and whispered in his ear, "Honored Registrar, I wonder if you could be so kind as to, um, see that our good Herr Anselmus, how shall I put it, um, in the aforementioned matter—"

"Of course, of course you can count on me," Registrar Heebrand replied, and after everyone had regrouped in a circle, he continued aloud to wit:

"There is, here in town, a most remarkable old gentleman. They say that he dabbles in all sorts of arcane studies, but since such matters are outside the scope of recognized scientific inquiry I would rather think of him as a kind of antiquarian and an experimental chemist on the side. I am, of course, referring to our noted Archivarius Lindhorst. He lives alone, as you know, in an old house far outside the city, and when he's not busy doing something else, you can find him in his library or in his chemical laboratory, the latter completely off-limits to anyone else. In addition to countless other most extraordinary books, he possesses some manuscripts in Arabic, Coptic, and a few in an indecipherable script written in some unknown tongue. He would like to have the latter copied in a faithful facsimile, and to this end is seeking someone with a steady hand able to flawlessly and precisely transcribe all these obscure signs and symbols— and to do so, moreover, in Chinese ink on fine vellum. The copyist would work under his supervision in a designated room of the house set aside for that purpose and, in addition to board and a silver dollar for the day's work, he promises a handsome present once the transcription job is done. The daily hours are from twelve to six. From three to four, you rest and eat. Since he already tried out the copying skill of a few young people and was disappointed, he finally turned to me to find him an able scribe; naturally I thought of you, my dear Herr Anselmus, since I know that you not only have a clear and neat handwriting, but that you also have a graceful and adroit hand for drawing. Should you, in these difficult times, and pending your possible steady employment, like to earn that daily silver dollar and the promised recompense once the job is done, bestir yourself to arrive tomorrow at twelve noon on the dot at the home of the archivarius, whose address you must know. But do take pains to avoid any ink flecks; if they fall on the transcription, no matter how minuscule, you'll have to start again from the beginning. And if they fall on the original, the archivarius is liable to fling you out the window, as he is a temperamental man."

Anselmus was overjoyed at Registrar Heerbrand's mention of this prospect of employment, for not only did he write with a clean and steady hand and like to draw, but it was also his true passion to transcribe with painstaking calligraphic care; so he thanked his patron in the most polite terms and promised not to miss his noontime rendezvous the next day. All night long he pictured nothing but shining silver dollars and heard their lovely clink. Who could possibly hold it against the poor fellow, just recently cheated of his dreamed-of Ascension Day on account of a freakish misadventure, a young man forced to count every penny and to forgo the pleasures that his young heart craved?

Early the next morning he gathered together his pencils, his crow quills, and his Chinese ink, convinced that the archivarius could muster no better materials than these. Among other things, he scrutinized and arranged his calligraphic masterpieces and his drawings to present to the archivarius as proof of his proficiency in the required criteria. Fortunately, everything went smoothly; he seemed to be guided by a lucky star shining over him. His neckerchief held at the first binding, no seam in his outfit burst, no stitch in his silk socks came undone, his hat didn't tumble back into the dust once he'd brushed it. In short, all went well! At precisely 11:30, the student stood in his trout-gray coat and his pitch-black garments, with a roll of manuscripts and ink drawings in his pocket, in Conradi's Apothecary on Schloßgasse, downing one— two— shot glasses of the finest stomach-calming liquor, for here, he said to himself, striking his other empty pocket, silver dollars will soon clink.

Despite the considerable distance to Archivarius Lindhorst's lonesome old house, Anselmus was standing at his door before twelve. He stood there eyeing the lovely big door knocker, but when he reached to grip it as the last loud bell rang out from the church tower and filled the air with its mighty quavering clang, the metal face twisted into a repulsive grotesque grin in the glimmering blue light of noon. Dear God! It was the face of the apple hag from the Black Gate. The sharp teeth clattered in the drooping mouth, and in the clatter a shrill voice cried: "You lunatic— lunatic— lunatic! Wait, wait! Why did you try to run! Lunatic!"

Horrified, Anselmus reeled back; he wanted to grasp the doorjamb, but his hand got entangled with the cord attached to the doorbell and tugged at it, whereupon it kept ringing louder and louder in shrill jarring notes that kept sounding through the bleak old house, the echo taunting him, "Soon you'll sink into my crystal cage!"

The student was gripped by an abject terror that made all his limbs throb with spasms of fever chills. The cord of the doorbell sank and turned into a massive transparent white snake that wrapped itself around him and squeezed him ever more tightly in its embrace so that his fragile limbs crumbled to pieces, and his blood spurted out of his veins, penetrating the transparent body of the snake and turning it red. "Kill me! Kill me!" he tried to shriek in terror, but his scream came out as a muffled wheeze. The snake raised its head and laid its long, pointy tongue against his breast, whereupon a cutting pain suddenly severed the artery running to his heart and he lost consciousness.

When he came to, he found himself stretched out on his paltry mattress, with Deputy Rector Paulmann standing over him. "For heaven's sake, my dear Herr Anselmus, what kind of devilry are you up to!?"

THIRD VIGIL
News from the family of the Archivarius Lindhorst.
Veronica's blue eyes. The Registrar Heerbrand.

The spirit peered into the deep; the water stirred and churned in foaming ripples and hurled itself with a thundering force down into the abyss that flung open its black maw to greedily drink it down. Like triumphant conquerors, the granite cliffs raised their jagged crowned heads upright, lording it over the valley below until the sun took it all into her motherly lap and embraced, nursed, and warmed her world with her rays, as with glowing arms. Then a thousand seeds slumbering beneath the bleak and barren sand suddenly awakened and stretched their little green leaves and stalks up toward the face of their mother. Like children lying content in a green cradle, the flowers rested in their buds and blossoms until they too were awakened by their mother and burst into blooms of joy, primping themselves up in delight with the light that their mother flung upon them in a thousand different hues.

But in the middle of the valley there was a black hill that rose and sank like a human breast stirred by burning longing. Mists rolled up from the abyss, balling themselves into mighty masses in an attempt to envelope the face of the mother; but she summoned up the storm that raged beneath her. When her clear rays once again stroked the black hill, a lovely fire lily sprouted from the surface in a surfeit of ecstasy, spreading its splendid petals like lips to receive sweet kisses from its mother. Then a glimmering luminescence strode into the valley; it was the youth Phosphorus. The fire lily set eyes on him and immediately implored with a burning longing, "Be mine forever, you handsome boy! I love you and would wither if you left me."

To which the youth replied, "I will be yours, you lovely flower, but then like a wayward child you will leave your mother and father, you will no longer know your playmates, you will want to be greater and mightier than all those who now frolic with you as your equals. The yearning that now warms your entire being with its soothing strength will shatter into a thousand rays, tormenting and torturing you, for one sense will engender many, and the loftiest delight the spark I thrust into you will kindle is the hopeless pain that will accompany your undoing, only to sprout again in the stalk of a strange new blossom. This spark is the seed of thought!"

"Oh," lamented the lily, "can I then not be yours in all the burning passion that consumes me? Could I possibly love you any more than I do now? And how can I still see you as I do now if your love annihilates me?"

Then Phosphorus kissed her. As if kindled by the light, she burst into flames, out of which a strange being sprung forth, hastened to flee the valley, and frolicked in infinite space, unconcerned with its old playmates and with the youth it had loved. He bemoaned the loss of his beloved, for it was only his unending love for the lovely lily that had brought him to the valley to begin with. Sharing his grief, the granite cliffs bowed their heads. But one of them spread its legs and a black winged dragon flew forth and said, "My brothers, the metals, sleep there within, but I am ever feisty and wakeful and want to help you." Flinging itself up and down, the dragon finally managed to catch the being that emerged from the lily, carried it to the hill, and wrapped its wing around it. Then she was the lily again, but the lingering thought of what she had been tore her up inside, and her love for the youth Phosphorus became a cutting pain emitting poisonous vapors which caused the other flowers that would otherwise rejoice at the sight of her to wilt and die.

The youth donned a shining suit of armor that glittered in a thousand hues. He battled the dragon, which struck the metal with its black wings with such a loud and clear knell that the little flowers blossomed back into life and fluttered around the dragon like many-colored birds, thereby vanquishing the beast. Drained of its strength, it sank down and buried itself deep in the bowels of the earth. The lily was set free; the youth Phosphorus embraced her, consumed with the burning longing of heavenly love; and the flowers and birds sang her praises in jubilant hymns. Even the high granite cliffs saluted her as queen of the valley.

"With all due respect, Herr Archivarius, honored Sir, this is oriental drivel," said Registrar Heerbrand, "but we still beg you, as is ordinarily your wont, to tell us something about your extraordinary life – perhaps an adventuresome episode from your travels, something that really happened."

"What then?" Archivarius Lindhorst fired back. "The story I just told you is the most truthful stuff I can dish out for you folks, and in a certain sense is also a part of my life. Since I come from that same valley, and the fire lily who last ruled as queen is my great-great-great-great-grandmother, which, as a matter of fact, also makes me a prince." All present broke into a burst of laughter. "Laugh to your heart's content," Archivarius Lindhorst continued. "What I just sketched out for you might seem nonsensical and loopy, but it was nevertheless not meant to be taken as twaddle or even as allegory, it's the honest truth. But had I known that the beautiful love story to which I also owe my origin would prove so unappealing, I would rather have transmitted some piece of news that my brother related on his visit yesterday."

"What's that? So you have a brother, Mr. Archivarius? Where does he live? Is he likewise in the service of the king, or perhaps an independent scholar?" The questions came from all directions.

"No!" replied the archivarius, coldly and calmly taking a pinch of snuff. "He chose the wrong direction and went with the dragons."

"Did I hear you right, worthy Archivarius," Registrar Heerbrand challenged, "he went with the dragons?"

"With the dragons?" the words echoed from every direction.

"Yes, with the dragons," Archivarius Lindhorst continued, "it was, in fact, in desperation. As you well know, gentlemen, my father died not long ago. At the most, 385 years have gone by, which is why I, too, am still in mourning; he left me a precious onyx that my brother badly wanted. We quarreled over it in an unseemly manner as my father lay dying, until he of sainted memory lost his patience, leapt up, and flung the profligate brother down the stairs. That rankled my brother, and then and there he went to live with the dragons. He now resides in a dense cypress forest on the edge of Tunis where he stands guard over a famous mystical carbuncle keenly coveted by a devil of a necromancer with a summer house in Lapland. That is why he has only a short quarter of an hour, while said necromancer is busy tending to his salamander roots in the garden, to get away and hastily fill me in on recent happenings at the source of the Nile."

For a second time, all present burst out laughing, but the student Anselmus was overcome by a strange sensation, and he could hardly look the sober, unsmiling Archivarius Lindhorst in the eye without feeling an unfathomable trembling within. Above all, the raw, albeit strangely metallic sounding voice of the Archivarius Lindhorst had a singularly invasive effect on him, sending tremors that rippled through his bones and marrow. So much for the actual objective of Registrar Heerbrand's having invited him along to the coffeehouse, not today at any rate. After the incident in front of the Archivarius Lindhorst's house, nothing could persuade Anselmus to go back and attempt a second visit, since he was absolutely convinced that only chance had spared him, if not from death, then surely from the imminent risk of having been driven stark raving mad. Deputy Rector Paulmann just happened to be passing down that same street when he saw him lying unconscious before the door with an old woman, who, having set aside her basket of cakes and apples, was bent over him; the deputy rector promptly hailed a sedan chair and so had him transported home.

"You can think of me what you will," said the student, "you can take me for a lunatic or not— so be it!— but grinning at me from the door-knocker I saw the face of the old witch from the Black Gate; what happened after that I'd rather not tell, but had I come to and espied the accursed old apple hag standing over me (for I have no doubt it was her), I'd have instantly been struck dead with fright or else gone completely berzerk." All reasoning with him was for naught, all the sound explanations of the Registrar Heerbrand and the Deputy Rector Paulmann failed to sway him, and even blue-eyed Veronica could not manage to draw him out of the glum mood he was in. He was indeed taken for mentally disturbed, and remedies were sought to distract him, whereupon the Registrar Heerbrand insisted that nothing could be more effective than productive occupation, namely the transcription of manuscripts for the Archivarius Lindhorst. It was just a matter of making the two acquainted and presenting Anselmus in the best possible light to the Archivarius Lindhorst. Since Registrar Heerbrand knew that the latter visited a certain well-known café every evening, he invited the student to have a glass of beer and smoke a pipe with him, his treat, every evening at that very café until he might manage in this way to introduce the student and have the two come to an agreement about the business of his copying manuscripts – a proposition which Anselmus gladly accepted.

"You will earn God's gratitude, esteemed Registrar, if you thereby succeed in bringing the young man back to his senses!" said Deputy Rector Paulmann.

"God's gratitude!" Veronica repeated, lifting her pious gaze to heaven, while thinking to herself that Anselmus was already a most agreeable young man even out of his right mind!

As the Archivarius Lindhorst reached for his hat and walking stick to head out the door, Registrar Heerbrand hastily grabbed the student by the hand and, blocking the old gentleman's way, said, "Most esteemed Privy Archivarius, Sir, here is the student Anselmus, of whom I spoke, the young man uncommonly skilled at transcription and drawing who would like to copy your arcane manuscripts."

"That would be most agreeable," the Archivarius Lindhorst rattled off in reply, plunking his three-cornered military hat on his head, shoving the Registrar Heerbrand and the student aside, and noisily clattering down the steps, leaving the two standing, utterly perplexed, staring at the door that he had slammed shut in their face so loudly that the hinges kept clanging.

"What a right curious old man!" remarked Registrar Heerbrand.

"C…c…curious old man!" the student stuttered after him, feeling as if an arctic current shot through his veins, so that he almost froze into an icy column.

But all the other café customers just laughed and said, "The archivarius was in another one of his quirky moods today— tomorrow he'll be meek and mild again, without uttering a word, lost in the smoke clouds of his pipe or reading newspapers. Best not to pay it any mind."

"How true," thought Anselmus, "best not to pay it any mind. Did the archivarius not say he found it most agreeable that I offered to copy his manuscripts? And why, pray tell, did the Registrar Heerbrand block his way when he was clearly on his way home? No, no, the Privy Archivarius Lindhorst is a kind man at heart and surprisingly generous – just curious in his manner of speaking. But what's that to me? Tomorrow at twelve noon on the dot I'll be at his door, let a hundred bronzed old apple hags try and stand in my way!"

FOURTH VIGIL

The Student Anselmus' melancholy. The Emerald Mirror. How the Archivarius Lindhorst flew off as a vulture and nobody was on hand to receive Anselmus.

Surely I may presume to ask you of all people, most gracious reader, a question. Have you experienced hours, indeed days and weeks on end, in your life during which all of your mundane ditherings and doings stirred up a mighty malaise that made everything you ordinarily held true and dear suddenly seem foolish and worthless? You yourself didn't know then what to do and where to turn; you were gripped by a dark inkling that in some former time there must surely have been an ardent wish fulfilled that surpassed the limited sphere of all earthly pleasure, a wish that the human spirit, like a strictly raised, timid child, dare not even express out loud. In your longing for that unknown something that wafted around you wherever you went, like a perfumed dream peopled with transparent personages that dissolve in the sharp gaze of the waking world, you fell silent, awestruck in the face of it all. You slunk about with a downcast gaze like a despairing lover, and all that you witnessed of what people were up to in the motley melee of life gave you neither pleasure nor pain, as if you no longer belonged to this world.

If, most gracious reader, you have ever felt this way, then you know from your own experience the state that the student Anselmus was in. If only I had already managed to paint a vivid picture of Anselmus so as to make you see him as I do, kind reader, for in these vigils there are still so many curious happenings to recount of his strange experiences that make it all sound like a ghost story straining the limits of the credible for ordinary folk. I fear that you will question the reality of the student and the Archivarius Lindhorst, and even harbor unjustified doubt as to the actual existence of Deputy Rector Paulmann and Registrar Heerbrand, not to speak of all the other honorable gentlemen that reside in Dresden to this day. Do try to picture yourself in the fairylike realm, prone to flashes of the greatest rapture and the most appalling horror, where the somber goddess airs her veil so that we mortals would feign catch a glimpse of her face – but a fleeting smile slips out from under her dark look, and that, dear reader, is the teasing banter that toys with us in the cloak of magic, the way a mother often tickles her favorite child. Do try, gracious reader, to put yourself in that state of mind so often at the very least revealed to us in dreams, and do take pains to recognize the reality of the aforementioned persons, as we say in common speech, flitting by. You will then, as I most sincerely hope, believe me when I maintain that this marvelous realm lies much closer to you than you previously suspected, a proximity which I have striven to intimate in my account of the strange story of the student Anselmus.

So, as I was saying, ever since that evening when he saw the Archivarius Lindhorst at the café, Anselmus sank into a dreamy brooding state that made him oblivious to any outward connection to ordinary life. He felt an unknown something stirring in his heart of hearts, provoking that wondrous pain, the physical embodiment of an ardent yearning that augurs in people a heightened state of consciousness. What he loved best was to amble alone through meadows and woods and, feeling released from all that shackled him to his tenuous existence, he was convinced, as it were, that he could only then find himself again in the foggy figments of his imagination.

Once, upon returning from a long walk, he happened to pass a curious elderberry bush beneath which, as if in the thrall of the fantastic, he had seen so many strange things that other time. He felt himself wondrously drawn to that familiar green patch of grass, but no sooner did he let himself sink down than all that he had seen before, as if gripped by heavenly rapture and impressed upon his soul by an alien will, once again wafted before his eyes in the most striking colors, as if he were witnessing it a second time. More vivid even than that other time, those blessed blue eyes peered out at him from the little head of the golden-green snake winding its way upward round the trunk of the elderberry tree, the coils of its slender body emitting the lovely crystalline tones that filled him with such ecstasy and delight. Just as he had on that Ascension Day, he embraced the tree and called to its branches and leaves, "Just one more time, whirl and wisp and wind yourself in the branches, oh lovely little snake, and let me gaze upon you! Just once more cast your lovely eyes upon me! How I love you, and will surely wither in pain and sadness if you don't come back again!" But all remained perfectly still, and as it had then, the elderberry tree once again rustled its branches and leaves in faint response. Yet for Anselmus it was as if he finally fathomed the secrets stirring deep inside, the muddle of emotions tearing up his heart with boundless longing.

"Can it be anything other," he said aloud, "than that I love you with all my heart and soul unto death, you beautiful golden little snake, that I cannot conceive of living without you, and would wither in hopeless despair if I did not see you again, if I were not able to possess you as the love of my heart— but I know that you will be mine, and then all the radiant dreams augured from on high will be granted."

So the student sought out the elderberry bush every evening when the sun had just strewn its sparkling golden rays in the tips of the trees, and called in ardent, mournful tones into the leaves and branches, clamoring after his dearly beloved, the little golden-green snake. One time when he was so engaged in his customary manner, he turned to find a tall, haggard man sheathed in a wide, light gray overcoat, glaring at him with big fiery eyes. "Hey, hey— what's all this yammering and whining? Hey, hey, why it's Herr Anselmus, who wants to copy my manuscripts."

Anselmus was more than a little taken aback at the thunderous voice, for it sounded like the same voice that on Ascension Day had called to him, "Hey, hey, what's all this jabbering and yammering, etc!" Consumed with shock and terror, he was unable to get a word out.

"What's troubling you, Herr Anselmus?" the Archivarius Lindhorst continued (for none other was the man in the light gray overcoat). "What do you want from the elderberry bush? And why haven't you come to my place to begin working?"

In truth, much as he had bucked up his resolve to pay a return visit to the home of the Archivarius Lindhorst, the student had not been able to bring it upon himself to do so. At this very moment when he was torn from the embrace of his lovely dreams, and accosted by the same hostile voice that had previously robbed him of his beloved, he was gripped by a kind of despair and impetuously fired back, "You may take me for mad or not, Herr Archivarius, it's all the same to me, but here on this tree on Ascension Day I glimpsed the golden-green snake – Ach! Eternal beloved of my soul – and she spoke to me in lovely crystalline tones. But you— you, Herr Archivarius, bellowed and hollered so horribly over the water…"

"How, pray tell, my fine fellow!" the archivarius interrupted, flashing a curious chuckle and taking a pinch of snuff.

Anselmus felt infinitely relieved just to have begun talking about that wondrous adventure, and it seemed to him perfectly in order to accuse the archivarius to his face that it was he whose voice had thundered from the distance. He pulled himself together, saying, "So let me tell all the fateful things that befell me on that Ascension Day evening, and then you can say and do and think of me what you will." He then, in fact, proceeded to relate the entire strange string of occurrences, from his unfortunate colli-sion with the apple basket to the breakaway of the three golden-green snakes in the water, and how everyone had taken him for drunk or mad. "All this," Anselmus concluded, "did I really see with my own eyes, and the clear echo of the mellifluous voices that spoke to me still resounds in my breast; it was no dream, I can assure you, and if I don't die of love and longing, I will go on believing in those golden-green snakes, regardless of the fact that I can tell from your smile, Herr Archivarius, honored Sir, that you hold these snakes to be nothing but a manifestation of my overheated and strained imagination."

"Not at all," replied the archivarius with the greatest calm and compo-sure, "the golden-green snakes you saw in the elderberry tree, Herr Anselmus, are none other than my three daughters, and it's clear that you have fallen head over heels in love with the blue eyes of the youngest, Serpentina. I was already aware of it, by the way, on Ascension Day, and since the whispering and hubbub reached my ears back at my desk at home, I called out to the mischievous little minxes that it was time to hurry home, since the sun was already setting and they had amused themselves with enough singing and sunbathing for the day."

To the student it was as if these clearly spoken words had merely con-firmed what he had long suspected, and since it suddenly seemed to him as if the elderberry bush, the wall, the grass below, and everything round about started silently spinning, he pulled himself together and prepared to reply. But the archivarius cut him off, quickly pulling off a glove from his left hand; holding the wondrously sparkling and flickering stone of a ring before the student's eyes, he said, "Look here, my dear Herr Anselmus, you may like what you see."

The student looked, and oh wonder of wonders, the stone emitted a tangle of rays from its burning fundament, and the rays spun themselves into a clearly glittering crystal mirror in which the little snakes danced and leapt, twisting and turning, now disentangling and flying apart, now winding their way back together, and when the slender, sparkling bodies rubbed up against each other they sounded in heavenly harmonies like crystal bells. Bursting with rapture and longing, the middle one extended her little head from the mirror and her dark blue eyes whispered, "Do you know me then? Do you believe in me, Anselmus? You can't love without believing! Are you able to love?"

"Oh, Serpentina, Serpentina!" Anselmus cried out in wild rhapsodies of delight, but the Archivarius Lindhorst breathed immediately thereafter on the mirror, whereupon the flickering rays of light were sucked back into focus in a crackle of sparks, and all that sparkled now was a little emerald over which the archivarius drew a glove.

"Did you see the little golden snakes, Herr Anselmus?" asked the Archivarius Lindhorst.

"Heavens, yes, and the lovely, sweet Serpentina!" replied the student.

"Hush now!" the archivarius continued. "That's enough for today. Oh, and by the way, should you decide to come to work for me, you can see my daughter often enough – or rather, to be precise, I will gladly grant you the immense pleasure of seeing her if you put your all into the work, that is, if you copy every sign cleanly and precisely. But notwithstanding the Registrar

Heerbrand's assurances of your prompt appearance, you never even presented yourself."

It was only after the archivarius mentioned the name Heerbrand that the young man once again felt as if his two feet were firmly planted on the ground and he was really the student Anselmus, and the man standing before him was the Archivarius Lindhorst. There was something frightening about the contrast between the matter-of-fact tone of the latter's manner of speaking and the wondrous apparitions he provoked from his ring like a true necromancer, a contrast further enhanced by the piercing look of his sparkling eyes beaming forth from the bony hollow sockets of his haggard, wrinkled face, as if out of an encasement. The student was gripped by the same uncanny feeling that had come over him while listening to the Archivarius relate so many fantastic things back at the café. He strained to pull himself together, and only when the archivarius asked again, "So why didn't you come to see me?" did he manage to bring himself to tell him all that had happened to him at his door.

"My dear Herr Anselmus," said the archivarius once the student had finished his story, "oh my dear Sir, I know all too well the apple hag of whom you speak; she is a wretched creature who has played all kinds of nasty tricks on me, and it is indeed reprehensible and insufferable that she would paint her face with bronze makeup to imitate a doorknocker and thereby scare away my pleasant visits. If when you come by tomorrow at noon you once again encounter her sneering and shrieking mug, kindly squirt a little of this liquor I give you into her nose and that ought to take care of it. And so adieu, dear Herr Anselmus, I tend to walk a bit quickly, and so won't propose to accompany you back to town. Adieu! Until tomorrow at twelve!"

After handing the student a little vial with a golden-yellow liquor, the archivarius rushed off at such a rapid clip that in the twilight he seemed to be swooping rather than walking down into the valley. Once he reached Kosel Garden, his overcoat billowed out behind him as the wind lifted his coattails apart so that they appeared to flutter in the breeze like a massive pair of wings, and it seemed to the student who followed the archivarius with his spellbound gaze as if a great bird were spreading its wings to take flight. As Anselmus stared into the dusk, the cawing caterwaul of a light gray vulture filled the air, and he grasped that the white fluttering which he still took to be the departing archivarius must have been the vulture from the start, even though he was baffled as to what suddenly became of the archivarius. "But it is perfectly well possible that the Archivarius Lindhorst himself flew off," the student said to himself, "since I now see and sense that all the curious characters from a wondrous world that I had heretofore glimpsed only in my most extraordinary dreams have crossed over into my conscious waking life to toy with my reason. But be that as it may! You live and burn in my breast, oh my beautiful beloved Serpentina, only you can still the boundless longing tearing at my soul. Oh, when will I peer into your blessedly lovely eyes again, my dearest, dearest Serpentina!" Anselmus cried out loud.

"That is a vile, unchristian name," muttered a deep bass voice belonging to a stroller passing beside him on his way home. Promptly roused from his reverie and realizing where he was, the student hurried on, thinking to himself, "How unfortunate it would be if in my present state I ran into Deputy Rector Paulmann or Registrar Heerbrand!" But fortunately, he encountered neither of the two.

*Madame Privy Councillor Anselmus. Cicero de officiis. Long-tailed
monkeys and other riffraff. Old Liese. The Aequinoctium.*

"There is nothing to be done with Anselmus," said Deputy Rector Paulmann. "All my good lessons, all my warnings have been fruitless, he refuses to buckle down and get serious about anything, even though he has the essential fund of knowledge, which is, after all, the foundation for all else."

But Registrar Heerbrand responded with a sly and secretive smile. "Just leave Anselmus the space and time, esteemed Deputy Rector! He's a curious case, but there's a lot of potential in him – and when I say 'a lot,' I mean he has the makings of a privy secretary, or perhaps even a court councillor."

"Court c…!?" the deputy rector exclaimed with the greatest surprise, choking on the word.

"Hush now!" the Registrar Heerbrand continued, "I know what I'm talking about. For two days now he's been bent over a work table copying manuscripts at the home of the Archivarius Lindhorst, and yesterday evening the archivarius buttonholed me at the café and said, 'That's one fine fellow you recommended, esteemed Sir! That young man's going to amount to something!' Just think of all the archivarius's connections – hush now – let's talk about it again later this year!" Having uttered these words, the registrar walked out the door with a sly smile on his lips, and left the deputy rector glued to his chair, spellbound and speechless with surprise and curiosity.

But the conversation made an altogether different impression on Veronica. "Didn't I know it from the start," she thought to herself, "that Herr Anselmus is a sharp-minded, lovable young man who's bound to make it! If only I could say for certain that he really liked me? But didn't he squeeze my hand twice that evening when we crossed the Elbe? And didn't he give me absolutely heartfelt looks when we played a duet together? Yes, yes, he's mine and I know it – and I, Veronica..." She got carried away in her imaginings, as young girls are inclined to do, already dreaming of a more formidable future. She, Madame Court Councillor, resided in a stately house on Schloßgasse or Neumarkt, or on Moritzstraße – that fashionable hat and new Turkish shawl looked great on her – as she breakfasted in an elegant dressing gown on the veranda, giving the cook her instructions for the day. "But don't you spoil that soufflé, it's the court councillor's favorite!" Below, meanwhile, she distinctly heard passing men about town remark, 'What a divine-looking lady, that Madame Court Councillor, get a load of her in that lace bonnet!" Madame Privy Councillor Ypsilon sends word via her servant inquiring, "Would Madame Court Councillor be so kind as to accompany her today to the Lincke baths?" "Thank you kindly for the invitation, but I'm terribly sorry to say that I'm already committed to take tea at the home of Madame President."

Then in her daydream, up comes Court Councillor Anselmus, done early with his work for the day, looking downright dapper in his stylish attire. "My word, ten already!" he exclaims, rewinding his golden watch and giving his young wife a kiss. "How is my dear little wife? Guess what I have for you!" he carries on flirtatiously, and pulls out of his vest pocket a lovely pair of newfangled earrings in the latest design and replacing the ordinary ones she wears.

"Oh, what lovely dainty earrings!" Veronica cries out loud, leaping up from her chair and shoving aside the task she is engaged with to feast her eyes on the earrings in the mirror.

"What in heaven's name is going on here?" exclaimed Deputy Rector Paulmann who, engrossed in his reading of Cicero's *De Officiis*, almost let the book drop out of his hands. "Everyone's having fits like Anselmus."

But at that very moment, the student Anselmus, who, contrary to his custom, had not dropped by for a number of days, burst into the room much to Veronica's fright and astonishment, for everything about him was indeed different. With a self-assurance altogether unlike him, he spoke of new possibilities in his life as he now saw it, of splendid prospects that had been proposed, some beyond the ken of ordinary folk. Bearing in mind Registrar Heerbrand's confidential remarks, Deputy Rector Paulmann was all the more concerned, hardly able to get a word in edgewise, before Anselmus let slip a hint concerning his pressing work for the Archivarius Lindhorst, elegantly and adroitly kissed Veronica's hand, and promptly up and left, dashing down the stairs and up the street.

"Acting like a court councillor already," Veronica muttered to herself, "and he kissed my hand without slipping or stepping on my foot as he usually does! And he gave me such a meaningful look. He's sweet on me and I know it!"

Once again abandoning herself to daydreaming, it seemed to Veronica as if a malevolent presence kept inserting itself among the lovely illusions; just as she emerged from felicitous reverie about her future domestic bliss as Madame Court Councillor, the hostile presence responded with sarcastic laughter and said, "All this is stuff and nonsense, and a lot of bunk to boot. Anselmus will never become a court councillor; he doesn't love you either, notwithstanding your blue eyes, slender figure, and graceful hand."

The words rushed through her like a stream of ice, a deep sense of dread dousing the cozy bliss with which she had been picturing herself in lace bonnet and elegant earrings. The tears almost rained from her eyes as she muttered aloud, "Oh, yes, of course it's true, he doesn't love me and I'll never become Madame Court Councillor!"

"Romantic drivel, romantic drivel!" cried Deputy Rector Paulmann, and then, taking up his hat and walking stick, he rushed off.

"That's just what I needed!" Veronica groaned, and became seriously vexed at her twelve-year-old sister, seated nearby, who heedlessly kept knitting away.

It was almost three o'clock already, time to clean up the room and prepare for coffee, for the Mademoiselles Osters had announced their arrival at the home of their friend. But out from behind every little cabinet that Veronica shoved aside to sweep, from behind the books of musical notes she took from the piano, behind every cup and the coffeepot she took from the cabinet, that nasty naysayer leapt forth, laughed sarcastically, fiddled with its spidery little fingers, and cried, "He'll never be your husband! He'll never be your husband!" And then when she dropped everything and fled to the middle of the room, it peeked forth with its long pointy nose from behind the oven, snarling and whining, "He will never be your husband!"

"Can't you hear, don't you see it, sister?" Veronica cried out, so petrified and trembling with terror that she didn't dare touch anything.

Quietly and with great composure, little Frances rose from her knitting frame and said, "What's wrong with you today, sister? You're tossing everything around helter-skelter with such a rattle and clatter. Let me help you."

But the merry guests had already arrived in a burst of girlish laughter, and at that moment Veronica realized that she had mistaken the oven handle for a malevolent apparition and the creak of the badly closed oven door for a stream of snarky words. Horror-stricken, she could not manage to save face fast enough to keep her friends from noticing her extraordinary tension, clearly evident in her pallor and troubled expression. After receiving her friends with a forced smile, she hastily broke off the merry chatter to tell of the confoundedly odd things that had befallen her. Veronica had to admit to having given herself over to a most peculiar string of thoughts, and to having suddenly in broad daylight fallen prey to a strange fear of spooks, which was not at all like her. She proceeded to recount in such a lively fashion how a little gray man taunted and teased her from every corner of the room. The Oster girls looked every which way around and were themselves soon gripped by fear. Whereupon little Frances appeared with the steaming coffeepot and all three came to their senses, laughing at their foolishness.

Angelica, the older of the Oster sisters, was betrothed to an officer in the army, from whom no word had been received for such a long while that she could not rule out his death or at least a serious wound to his person. This had sunk Angelica into the deepest depression, but today she was cheerful to the point of hilarity, surprising Veronica so much that she forthrightly remarked upon it.

"My dear girl," said Angelica, "I keep my Victor forever here in my heart, on my mind, and in my thoughts, and for that very reason keep my spirits high – Dear God! – always blissful to the depths of my soul! I know that my Victor is alive and well, and that I will soon see him again riding up as cavalry captain decorated for his boundless bravery. A serious but by no means life-threatening wound to his right arm inflicted by the saber slash of a hostile Hussar keeps him from writing, and the constant decampment – since of course he remains reluctant to leave his regiment – makes it all the more difficult for him to communicate with me. But this very evening he will receive the express order to stay put until he is back on his feet. Tomorrow, I'm quite certain, he'll be headed home, and no sooner having climbed into the carriage he will learn of his promotion to cavalry captain."

"But my dear Angelica," Veronica chimed in, "how, pray tell, do you now know all this to be true?"

"Don't laugh at me, dear friend," Angelica replied, "better bite your tongue, or else the little gray man will peep out of the mirror over there and flash you a punishing look! Enough of this, I cannot help but believe in certain mysterious matters, as they have often enough become visible and palpable, that is to say they have manifested themselves in my life. As a matter of fact, I don't even find it as wondrous and unbelievable as others might that there are people in this world endowed with a second sight able by certain infallible means to make their predictions come true. There is here in this city an old woman particularly adept at this. Unlike other dubious riffraff, she does not prophecy from cards, poured lead, or coffee grounds. Rather, following certain prescribed rituals in which the inquiring person participates, a wondrous muddle of all manner of shapes and figures appear in a brilliantly polished metal mirror which the old woman interprets, and from which she divines the answer to the question. I conferred with her yesterday evening and received news of my Victor, which I don't doubt for a minute."

Angelica's account sparked a ray of hope in Veronica, who promptly resolved to confer with the old woman concerning Anselmus and her hopes and prospects. She learned that the woman's name was Frau Rauerin, that she lived on a remote street near the Seetor, and that she was only available for consultation on Tuesdays, Wednesdays, and Fridays after 7 PM, but then through the night until dawn, and that she preferred her clients come alone.

It just so happened that it was Wednesday, and Veronica decided, under the pretense of accompanying the Osters home, to seek out the old woman, which she did in fact do. Once she had taken leave of her friends, who lived in the new part of town in front of the Elbe Bridge, she hastened to the Seetor and soon found herself in the remote and narrow street described by her friend, at the end of which she spotted the little red house in which Frau Rauerin was said to reside. Standing before the front door she was overcome by an unsettling feeling, a shudder of fear in her gut. Finally, she bestirred herself, her deep-seated aversion notwithstanding, to pull on the doorbell. The door opened, and she groped her way down the dark corridor to the stairway leading to the upper floor, just as Angelica had described it.

Since no one appeared, she called out in the empty hallway, "Does Frau Rauerin not live here?"

In lieu of a response came a long, clear meow, and a solemn looking big black cat with a high curved spine twirling its tail back and forth strode past her toward a door, which opened at the sound of a second meow. "Ah, the little daughter, here already? Come in, do come in!" cried the strange personage stepping out to meet her, the sight of whom gave Veronica such a fright it glued her to the ground. A tall, gaunt old hag dressed in tattered black rags! As she spoke, her protruding pointed chin wiggled, her toothless mouth squirmed out from under the shadow of her bony hooked nose, twisting into a grin, and sparkling cat's eyes flickered under thick-lensed glasses. Black bristles of hair reared out from under a kerchief wound around her head, but most repulsive of all were two big burn marks stretching from the left cheek to the nose across the loathsome face. The sight of her took Veronica's breath away, and the scream that would have brought air in and eased the pressure on her chest was squelched into a deep sigh as the witch's bony hand grabbed hold of her and drew her into the room. Inside, all was in tumult and turmoil; her ears were assaulted with a mingling of squealing and meowing and croaking and chirping.

The old crone pounded her fist on the table and cried: "Quiet, you rabble!"

At this, the whimpering monkeys climbed the top of the canopy bed, the little pigs ran under the oven, and the raven fluttered off, landing on the frame of the round mirror; only the black tomcat remained curled up cozily on the big easy chair onto which he leapt as soon as Frau Rauerin and Veronica entered the room, as if the scolding did not pertain to him.

Once the room went silent, Veronica took heart; she was no longer gripped by the sense of dread that had overcome her in the hallway – even the old woman now seemed less ghastly. Only then did she look around the room. All kinds of hideous stuffed animals hung from the ceiling, strange unidentifiable devices lay scattered about on the floor, and in the fireplace a little blue flame burned that only occasionally flared up in yellow sparks; but then came a rush from above and a flock of repulsive bats, their faces twisted in human smiles, went flapping back and forth, and every now and then the flame flared up and licked the sooty wall, at which a piercing, howling wail tore through the room, so that Veronica was once again gripped with terror and dread.

"With your leave, Mademoiselle!" the smirking old woman muttered, grabbing a big scuttle brush, dipping it in a copper kettle, and sprinkling the fireplace. The fire flared up and the room went dark in a dense blanket of smoke; but soon Frau Rauerin, who had slipped into a walk-in closet, returned with a lamp, in the flickering light of which all the animals and implements disappeared, and Veronica found herself in a simple, sparsely furnished room. The old woman approached her and said with a grating voice, "I already know what you want of me, little daughter, for what it's worth. You'd have me divine if Anselmus intends to take you as his bride once he makes privy councillor."

Veronica went stiff with surprise and fear, but the old woman contin-ued. "You already told me everything back home in your Papa's house with the coffeepot standing there before you. *I* was the coffeepot; didn't you recognize me? Little daughter, listen up! Better drop him, give up on that Anselmus, that uncouth lout; he kicked my little sons in the face, my dear little sons, the apples with their bright red cheeks which, once customers buy them, roll out of their pockets right back into my basket. He's residing with the old man – the day before yesterday he spilled that damned orpiment in my face, almost blinding me. You can still see the burn marks, little daughter! Forget about him, forget about him! He doesn't love you, he's in love with the golden-green snake, and he'll never become privy councillor since he's in cahoots with the salamanders and plans to wed the green snake. Forget about him, forget about him, I tell you!"

Veronica, who in fact was endowed with a strong and steadfast disposition and quickly overcame her girlish fear, took a step back and said with a serious and collected tone of voice, "Old woman, I heard of your gift for looking into the future, and so hoped to learn from you, perhaps a bit too eagerly and hastily, if Anselmus, whom I love and admire, will ever be mine. If, therefore, instead of fulfilling my wish you intend to taunt me with your ridiculous prattle, you're wasting your and my time, since all I wish to know is what you tell others. Since you appear to know my inner thoughts, it would perhaps have been a simple matter for you to reveal the outcome of the things that now torment and worry me, but given your shameless slander against the good Anselmus, I'll have no further truck with you. Good night!"

Veronica intended to hurry off, but the old woman fell to her knees, whining and wailing, and clasping the girl by the hem of her dress. "My little Veronica, don't you recognize old Liese, who so often carried you in her arms and pampered and coddled you?"

Veronica could hardly believe her eyes; for indeed she did recognize her old nanny, disfigured by age and by the burn marks, who disappeared many years ago from Deputy Rector Paulmann's house. The old woman now looked altogether different. Instead of the ugly stained headcloth she had a proper cap on, and instead of the black rags a flower-patterned jacket – the clothes she used to wear. She rose from the floor and, falling into Veronica's arms, continued: "Everything I told you may have sounded strange to you, but I'm sorry to say it's the truth. That Anselmus has done me much harm, even if against his will; he has fallen into the hands of the Archivarius Lindhorst and the old man wants to marry him with his daughter. The archivarius is my worst enemy, and I could tell you all kinds of things about him, things you either wouldn't understand or that would surely appall you if you did. He pretends to be the wise man, but I am the wise woman – so be it! I can tell that you're head over heels in love with Anselmus, and I will do everything in my power to ensure that you'll be happy and land in the marriage bed, as you wish."

"But tell me, for heaven's sake, Liese—" Veronica broke in.

"Hush, child, hush now!" the old woman interrupted in turn. "I know what you mean to say. I became what I became because I had to, I could not do otherwise. Now then, I know the antidote that will release Anselmus from his fatuous love of the green snake and lead him as a gracious privy councillor into your loving arms; but you have to help."

"Just tell me what I have to do, Liese, I'll do anything. I truly love Anselmus!" Veronica muttered almost inaudibly.

"I know you as a spunky child," the old woman went on. "In vain did I try to make you fall asleep with the bark of a bowwow way back when, but that's just when you opened your eyes wide to get a good look at the doggy. You used to stumble in the dark into the back room, and often scared the neighbors' children decked out in your father's housecoat. Now then, if you're serious about using my artful machinations to overpower the Archivarius Lindhorst and the green snake, if you're serious about making Anselmus a privy councillor and making him your husband, then slip out of your father's house at the next equinox at eleven o'clock and come to me; I'll accompany you then to the pathway that cuts across the field not far from here, and we'll whip up what we need, and all the wondrous things you may see will not, I hope, make you doubt our resolve. And now, little daughter, I bid you good night! Your father awaits you with hot soup."

Veronica rushed off, firmly resolving not to miss the night of the equinox, convinced as she now was that Liese spoke the truth, that Anselmus was under the thrall of an evil spell, but that she would release him from it, and soon call him hers forevermore. "Mine he will be and stay, my dearly beloved privy councillor Anselmus."

SIXTH VIGIL
The garden of the Archivarius Lindhorst along with several mocking birds. The golden pot. The English cursive script. Vile crowfeet. The prince of spirits.

"It may also well be," Anselmus said to himself, "that the extremely strong cordial, of which I partook a bit overeagerly chez Monsieur Conradi, fomented all those fearful phantasms that scared me half out of my wits at the Archivarius Lindhorst's door. Better, therefore, to stay completely sober today and watch out for any other adversity that might come my way." Just as he had outfitted himself for his first visit to the Archivarius Lindhorst, the student packed up his pen-and-ink drawings and calligraphic works, his bars of Indian ink, and his well-sharpened quill feathers, and was about to dash out the door when his eyes fell on the little flask with the yellow liquor that the Archivarius Lindhorst had given him. Suddenly, vivid memories ran through his mind of all the strange adventures he'd recently experienced, and a boundless sense of bliss and pain churned in his breast. And in spite of his firm resolve to keep a steady keel, he cried out in a tone of lamentation, "Oh, am I not going to the archivarius just to see you, my lovely beloved Serpentina?"

It seemed to him at that moment as if Serpentina's love might be the prize for a perilous task he had to undertake, and this task would entail nothing other than the copying of the Lindhorst manuscripts. He was convinced that all manner of wondrous things would befall him upon entering the house, or rather already at the door, just like before. Forgetting Conradi's cordial, he stuck the flask in his vest pocket, resolved to do just as the archivarius had told him if the bronze-faced apple peddler should accost him again with a grin. And did that pointed nose not rear up again, and those cats' eyes not flicker in the polished metal of the doorknob as soon as he reached for it at the stroke of twelve! Without hesitating, he squirted the liquor at that cursed face, and it instantly burnished and bent itself back into the glimmering round door knocker. The door opened, the bells chimed cheerfully throughout the house; *ting-a-ling— rang the thing— wing it— wing it— ting-a-ling.* Heartened, he raced up the wide, resplendent steps and reveled in the scent of rare incense that filled the air. He stopped in the hallway, uncertain on which of the stately doors to knock.

Then the Archivarius Lindhorst stepped out, dressed in a wide damask dressing gown, and greeted him. "Glad you finally kept your word, Herr Anselmus. This way, please, I'll take you straight to the laboratory." No sooner said than the old man strode up the long hallway and opened a little door that led into a corridor. Anselmus followed confidently. The corridor led into a hall, or rather a lovely greenhouse, the walls of which were lined with all sorts of rare and wondrous flowers beside tall trees with oddly shaped leaves and blossoms, the whole lot reaching all the way up to the ceiling. A marvelous dazzling light without any identifiable source spread everywhere, although there was no window to be seen. As soon as Anselmus peered at the bushes and trees, long passageways appeared, stretching into the distance – and in the dark depths of dense cypress groves he glimpsed marble basins out of which wondrous figures reared up and crystalline spurts of water surged forth, falling with a pleasant purling onto shimmering white lilies; curious whispering voices and all manner of fragrant scents swept through the forest of wondrous greenery.

The archivarius vanished, and Anselmus beheld a huge bush of glowing fire lilies before him. Intoxicated by the sweet scents of the enchanted garden, the student stood, transfixed. Then giggling and laughter filled the air and flirtatious little voices teased and taunted: "Hey, bookish boy, hey, bookish boy! Where did they dig you up? Why did you get all gussied up, Herr Anselmus? Wouldn't you like to chitchat with us awhile? We'll tell you how granny crushed an egg with her rump and how the fine young gent got a stain on his Sunday best! Do you already know the aria by heart that you learned from Big Daddy, Herr Anselmus? You look so dandy in your polished periwig and those cardboard boots!" Such were the giggled and teasing taunts hurled at him from every corner of the greenhouse, bewildering the student, who only now noticed all manner of colorful birds fluttering around him, scoffing and jeering. At that instant, the fire lily bush advanced toward him and he saw that it was the Archivarius Lindhorst, whose yellow and red glimmering flowery dressing gown had bedeviled his eyes.

"Forgive me, my dear Herr Anselmus for keeping you waiting," said the archivarius, "I had to take a passing glance at my lovely cactus that's about to burst into blossom this very night— but how do you like my house-garden?"

"Dear God, it's lovely beyond my wildest dreams, worthy Herr Archivarius," the student replied, "but I'm afraid the pied birds are giving me a bit of a ribbing!"

"What kind of jabber is this?" the archivarius called in a rage into the bush.

Whereupon a great big parrot fluttered forward, landed on the branch of a myrtle bush, and, peering at him solemnly and gravely through a pair of spectacles lodged on its twisted beak, croaked in reply, "Don't take it to heart, Herr Archivarius, my puckish parrot posse are being rambunctious again, but it's the student's own fault, since…"

"Silence! Silence!" the archivarius cut off the ancient bird, "I know those little knaves, but you'd best keep them in check, my friend! Let's go on, Herr Anselmus." The archivarius strode fleet-footed through other oddly decorated rooms; gazing, transfixed at the sight of all the curiously shaped furnishings and other obscure objects, the student could hardly keep up.

Finally, they entered a room in which the archivarius came to a halt, casting his gaze upward, which gave Anselmus time to feast his eyes on the splendid spectacle made by its simple decorations. Out of the azure blue walls grew the gilded bronze trunks of towering palm trees with colossal leaves like sparkling emeralds curling up at the ceiling. In the middle of the room, resting on three dark bronze Egyptian lions, there was a porphyry slab beset with a simple golden pot; as soon as Anselmus spotted it, he could no longer tear his eyes away. It was as if all manner of figures played in a thousand shimmering reflections in the sparkling polished gold. He saw himself with outstretched arms bursting with longing— ach!— beside the elderberry bush, Serpentina curling up and down the trunk, peering at him with her blessedly beautiful eyes. Anselmus was beside himself with mad rapture. "Serpentina! Serpentina!" he cried out loud.

Whereupon the Archivarius Lindhorst spun around and said: "What are you doing, my dear Anselmus? I believe you'd like to call to my daughter, but she's on the other side of my house in her room and is presently engaged in her piano lessons. Do come along!"

Almost out of his mind, Anselmus followed the archivarius, who dashed on ahead; the student no longer saw or heard anything until the archivarius grabbed him by the hand and said, "We've arrived at our destination!"

Anselmus awakened as if out of a dream, and noticed that he had entered a room surrounded with bookshelves in no apparent way different from any ordinary library or reading room. In the midst of the room stood a big work table with an upholstered armchair in front of it. "This, for the time being, is your workroom. It remains to be seen if in the future you will also work in the other blue library, in which you suddenly called out my daughter's name; but first I would like to convince myself of your capacity to carry out your assigned task according to my specifications."

Emboldened and confident in his conviction that his uncommon talent would greatly please the archivarius, the student pulled his drawings and transcriptions out of his satchel. No sooner had the archivarius set eyes on the first sheet, a transcription executed in the most elegant English manner, than his face lit up with a quixotic smile and he gave his head an approving shake. This he repeated with every sheet, so that the blood rushed to Anselmus's face; but when the smiles turned into scoffing sneers, the chagrinned student burst out, "The Herr Archivarius appears not altogether satisfied with my meager talents."

"My dear Herr Anselmus," the Archivarius Lindhorst replied, "you appear to have a remarkable capacity for the art of calligraphy, but if truth be told, it seems to me that I must count more on your diligence and good will than on your technical skills. But this may be more the fault of your imperfect tools than of your talents." Put on the defensive, the student lauded his much-prized skill, his mastery of Chinese ink, and his exquisite crow quills. Whereupon the archivarius handed him the sheet of English script and said, "Decide for yourself!"

Anselmus felt as if he'd been struck by lightning, compelled as he now was to assess his transcription as utterly miserable. There was no roundness in the strokes, no even-handed pressure, no balance between the big and little letters, and worse, despicable schoolboys' crowfeet often marred the otherwise rather steady lines. "And then," the Archivarius Lindhorst continued, "your ink is not durable." He dipped his finger in a glass filled with water, and upon lightly dabbing a letter it disappeared without a trace. Feeling as if a monster had him in a choke hold, the student could not utter a single word. He just stood there, wretched sheet in hand, until the Archivarius Lindhorst laughed out loud and said, "Don't let yourself be despondent, my worthy young friend; what you couldn't manage until now may well be improved upon under my tutelage. You will, in any case, find better working materials here than you had at your disposal in the past! Take heart and get to work!" The archivarius hastened to fetch a black liquid mass that emitted a singular smell, curiously colored sharpened quills, and a particularly white and smooth sheet of paper. He then withdrew an Arabic manuscript out of a locked chest of drawers, and as soon as Anselmus sat himself down to work, promptly left the room.

The student had already transcribed Arabic, so that this first assignment did not seem so difficult. "How those crowfeet crept into my lovely English script only God and the Archivarius Lindhorst may know," he said to himself, "but I swear upon my life that they didn't come from *my* hand." With every well-formed word that landed on the parchment his confidence grew, and so did his skill. The archivarius's quills did indeed lend themselves to a lovely line, and the enigmatic ink flowed pitch black and compliantly onto the blinding white parchment. As Anselmus worked away assiduously and with intense concentration, he felt ever more at ease in the solitude of the workroom; he had already completely committed himself to the task, which he hoped to complete successfully, when at the stroke of three the archivarius called him to lunch at a well-appointed table in the room next door. The archivarius was in a particularly chipper mood; he asked after the student's friends, Deputy Rector Paulmann and Registrar Heerbrand, and found many laudatory things to say about the latter. Anselmus found the good old Rhine wine quite delicious, and it made him more talkative than usual. At the stroke of four he rose from the table to get to work, and this punctuality appeared to please the archivarius.

If he had managed to effectively copy the Arabic script before the meal, the work now went all the more smoothly. Indeed, he could not fathom the speed and ease with which he now managed to mimic the ruffled characters of that foreign script. It was as if a voice emanating from his inmost soul whispered distinctly in his ear, "Oh, how could you complete this task if you did not keep *her* ever in mind and close to your heart, if you did not believe unflinchingly in *her* and her love?"

Then, in a quiet whisper came a crystal-clear reply: "I am close to you— close— close— I will help you— take heart— stick to it, dear Anselmus!— I will do my all to make you mine!"

And just as he took in every word with total rapture, the foreign characters became ever more comprehensible – he hardly even had to look at the original – it was as if a pale impression of the characters had already landed on the parchment, and all he had to do was trace them in black with a steady hand. In this manner he kept on working, infused with a sweet scent and the soothing sound of the beloved voice, until, at the stroke of six, the Archivarius Lindhorst came striding into the room and approached the work table with the same singular smile as before. Anselmus silently rose from the table, and the archivarius kept studying him with that mocking look, but no sooner did the old man glance at the transcription than every last drop of sarcasm drained from his lips and all his facial muscles tightened into an expression of utter solemnity. He no longer seemed like the same person. His eyes, which ordinarily sparkled with fire, now regarded Anselmus with an indescribably benevolent expression, his otherwise pale cheeks were infused with a soft redness, and in place of the ever-present irony that ordinarily kept his mouth clamped shut, his soft graceful lips now looked like they were about to burst into soul-searching speech. His entire figure reared up taller and statelier, his dressing gown fell like a king's mantel in wide folds around his chest and shoulders, and a narrow golden band glistened like a crown from the white curls that graced his high and open brow.

"Young man," the archivarius spoke in a muffled, solemn tone of voice, "my dear young man, even before it dawned on you, I recognized all the secret sentiments that bind you to that which is most cherished and holy to me! Serpentina loves you! A singular destiny awaits you, the fateful threads of which span a chasm of hostile forces, which will be fulfilled once she becomes yours, and if, as an essential dowry, you may lay claim to her precious possession, the golden pot. But your future happiness in higher spheres will depend on your willingness to fight for it. Hostile forces will confront you, and only the inner strength of your resistance to their rude assault can save you from disgrace and ruin. The tasks I ask of you amount to your apprenticeship; if you stick with it and persevere in what you've begun, faith and insight will allow you to achieve your immediate goal. Hold her true in your heart and *she* who loves you will help you attain the splendid treasure of the golden pot, and be happy for ever after. Be well! The Archivarius Lindhorst awaits you tomorrow at noon in his cabinet! Until then!"

With these words the archivarius gently nudged the student out the door, which he then locked behind him, and Anselmus now found himself in the room in which he had eaten, whose only door led out into the hallway.

Stunned by all the wondrous things he'd seen and heard, the student lingered in the street before the front door. A window opened above him and he looked up to see the old man, the Archivarius Lindhorst, dressed as usual in his light gray robe. "What's the matter, my dear Herr Anselmus," he called. "What are you brooding about? Can't get your mind off the Arabic? Give my best regards to Deputy Rector Paulmann if you drop by at his place, and be sure to be here tomorrow at noon on the dot. You'll find the pay for today's work in your right vest pocket."

Anselmus did indeed find the shiny coin in the designated pocket, but the sight of it hardly cheered him up. "God knows where all this will lead," he said to himself, "but even if some spook has got me in the grip of madness, I've still got my precious Serpentina under my skin, and I'd rather go under than give up on her affection – of this I'm firmly convinced, and no hostile force can uproot it. Can such a conviction be based on anything but Serpentina's love?"

*How Deputy Rector Paulmann knocked the ashes from his pipe and
went to bed. Rembrandt and the demonic Brueghel. The magic mirror
and Doctor Eckstein's remedy for an unknown illness.*

At last Deputy Rector Paulmann knocked the ashes from his pipe, and
remarked, "It's high time to get a good night's rest."

"Yes, indeed," Veronica concurred, concerned at her father's being up
later than usual, for the clock had just struck ten. No sooner did the deputy
rector retire to his bedroom and the sound of her sister Fränzchen's deep,
steady breathing make itself manifest – proof of her having fallen fast asleep
– than Veronica, who had pretended to go to sleep, quietly got up out of
bed, flung on her clothes, slipped into her coat, and escaped out into the
street.

Ever since the moment Veronica left old Liese's house, she could not get
Anselmus out of her mind. She herself could not make hide or hair of that
strange voice inside her that kept repeating again and again that his rebuffs
of her affection were fomented by a hostile presence that kept him in its
clutches, but whose grip on him she could sever with the help of magical
means. Her trust in old Liese grew day by day, and even her first impression
of her uncanny and horrific appearance faded little by little, so that everything that initially seemed bizarre and strange about her relations with the
old woman only retained a luster of quaintness and fancy which she now
found quite enticing. She therefore firmly resolved, even at the risk of
being caught sneaking off and getting herself embroiled in a thousand

troubles, to pursue this equinox adventure come what may. The fateful night on which old Liese promised to offer help and solace had finally come, and having long since quelled any concerns she might have had about wandering at night, Veronica felt elated. Quick as an arrow she shot through the lonesome streets, oblivious to the storm wind blowing and the thick raindrops it flung against her face. With a muffled drone, the bell in the steeple sounded eleven o'clock as Veronica stood before the old woman's house, soaked to the skin.

"Here already, my dear! Wait just a minute!" came a cry from above. A moment later, the old woman stood at the door carrying a basket, and accompanied by her black cat. "Come, let us go now, and carry out the actions that will favor our purpose on this fateful night," she said, reaching with a cold hand for trembling Veronica and passing her the basket, while she herself carried a cauldron, a trivet, and a spade. By the time they got to the open fields it had stopped raining, but the storm blew ever more fiercely; a thousand voices wafted in the wind, and it was as if a heart-rending scream burst from the black clouds that clustered together and soon draped everything in a dense darkness. But striding forward at a steady clip, the old woman cried out with a shrill voice: "Light, light, my lad!" Blue bolts of lightning sidled round and clashed directly in front of them, and Veronica realized that it was the cat emitting crackling sparks and lighting their way as it leapt ahead. Its fearfully horrid feline whine filled the air in brief intervals when the storm let up.

It almost knocked the wind out of her, as if ice-cold claws tore at her heart of hearts. But, taking pains to pull herself together, and clinging all the more tightly to the old woman, she said, "What must be done must be done, come what may!"

"Quite right, my little darling!" the old woman replied, "Stand firm, and I'll give you a lovely gift, and Anselmus to boot!"

At last, the old woman came to a halt and said, "We have arrived!" She dug a hole in the ground, filled it with coal, and set the tripod over it, upon which she placed the cauldron. All this she did with strange gesticulations, while the cat curled around her feet. Sparks spewed from its tail, and these lit a fire. Soon the coals began to glow and after a short while blue flames danced under the tripod. Veronica flung off her coat and veil and knelt down beside the old woman, who clasped her hands tightly and glared at her with sparkling eyes. Now the curious clumps that the old woman had plucked from the basket and dropped into the cauldron – flowers, metals, herbs, animals? Impossible to tell the difference! – began to seethe and simmer. The old woman let go of Veronica's hand and grasped an iron ladle, which she dipped into the bubbling brew and stirred while Veronica, at her behest, was made to cast her fixed gaze into the cauldron and focus all her thoughts on Anselmus. Then the old woman got busy again, casting into the cauldron sparkling scraps of metal and a lock of hair cut from Veronica's tangle of curls, as well as a ring she'd worn a long time, all the while emitting indecipherable, shrill sounding screeches and cries that tore through the night and egged on the cat that kept whining and groaning.

Would that you, esteemed reader, had been on the road to Dresden on that fateful 23rd of September. Just imagine: in vain, come nightfall, they had tried to make you stay on at the last coach stop. The genial innkeeper maintained that it was storming and raining too hard, and that in any case, it was a bad omen for anyone to venture out in the dark on such an equinox night, but you took no heed of such counsel, and rightfully thought to yourself, "I'll pay the coachman a silver dollar's tip and get to Dresden by 1 AM at the latest, where a warm meal and a cozy bed await me at the Golden Angel, or the Helm, or the stately old City of Naumberg Inn." And as the coach drives out into the darkness you suddenly see strange lights flickering in the distance.

Drawing near, you notice a ring of fire, in the midst of which a cauldron is burning, emitting billows of smoke, with red bolts of lightning and sparks shooting forth, and two figures seated beside it. The road runs straight through the ring of fire, but the horses snort and stamp their feet and rear up. The coachman curses and pleads and whips the horses, but they refuse to budge. Instinctively, you leap out of the carriage and race a few steps forward. Now you catch sight of the slender, comely girl in the thin white nightgown kneeling beside the cauldron. The storm has unraveled her braids and her long chestnut hair flutters freely in the wind. That angelically lovely face is lit up by the glaring flames shooting out from under the tripod, but terror casts an icy deathlike pallor upon it, and you can read her dread and horror in her blank look, in her upturned eyebrows, and in her mouth torn open to emit a scream of mortal terror that remains stuck in her throat, riddled by the nameless torment that clamps down on her breast. Her little hands are raised up, pressed tightly together, as if she were praying for a guardian angel to shield her from the demons of hell that, heeding the call of some potent magic spell, are about to appear. She kneels there motionless, like a marble statue. Just opposite her, a tall, haggard, copper-colored old crone with a hooked hawk's nose and sparkling cat's eyes squats on the ground, her naked, bony arms poking out from under a black cloak; she stirs a hellish brew, cackling and crying with a raspy voice above the raging, roaring wind.

I'm quite convinced, esteemed reader, that even if you had never before been stricken by fear and dread, the sight of this Rembrandtian or hellish Brueghelian tableau flashed on the canvas of life would have made the hair stand up straight on your head. But you could not tear your eyes from the poor girl entangled in these demonic machinations and, like a bolt of lightning, the electric shock that shot through your every fiber and nerve instantly fired up your brave resolve to defy the dark forces in that ring of fire. The flames consumed your dread, or rather, the resolve to come to her rescue was born of this very dread, the thought itself germinated in the throes of fear and horror, spawned by the intensity of its grip. You felt as if you were some kind of guardian angel to whom the petrified girl was pleading for help, as if you were driven then and there to draw your pistol and without any hesitation send the old crone to kingdom come!

Yet as the thought churned in your mind, you cried out, "Hey there!" or "What's going on there?" or "What the devil are you up to?" The coachman then blasted on his horn, the old crone stirred around in her bubbling brew, and everything vanished lickety-split in a thick cloud of smoke. I dare not venture to guess if you might have ever found the girl, searching for her with all your heart in the pitch-black darkness, but you would at least have broken the grip of that old crone and lifted the spell of that ring of fire into which Veronica had wandered.

But neither you nor anyone else, esteemed reader, rolled or strolled by on the 23rd of September, that stormy night so favorable to the evil work of witches, and Veronica had to crouch by that cauldron, frightened to death, until the dark deed was almost done. She was aware of the wind howling and billowing around her, of all manner of repugnant voices bellowing and blathering at the same time, but she dared not open her eyes as she sensed that the sight of the ghastly and horrific spectacle that surrounded her could well plunge her into irremediable madness.

The old woman had stopped stirring the contents of the cauldron, the cloud of smoke got thinner and thinner, and finally only a faint spirit-flame kept burning under the cauldron. Then the old woman cried, "Veronica, my child, my little darling, cast your gaze into the residue in the pot. What do you see? What do you see?" But Veronica could not bring her lips to reply, regardless of the fact that she saw all sorts of figures swirling around, one by one emerging ever more clearly. Then all at once, peering back at her tenderheartedly and reaching out his hand to her, she spotted the student Anselmus at the bottom of the cauldron. "Oh my God," she cried, "it's Anselmus, Anselmus!"

The old woman hopped to it, opening a spout at the base of the cauldron. Glowing, molten metal poured out, sizzling and sputtering, filling a small mold she set beside it. Then the old crone jumped up and, swinging herself around with wild, grotesque gesticulations, she shrieked, "Our work is done! Thanks, my lad! You kept watch— Up and at 'em! Up and at 'em!— He's coming!— Bite his head off!"

But a mighty wind squall burst about them, as if a giant eagle swooped down and batted its wings, and a terrible voice cried out: "Hey, hey!— you miserable rabble— enough is enough— you had your fun— now better run!"

Howling, the old crone collapsed; Veronica lost consciousness. She came to again in broad daylight, snug in bed, with her sister Fränzchen proffering a steaming cup of tea. "What in heaven's name is wrong with you, sister?" she said. "Here I am, standing before you for an hour or more, while you lie there unconscious, moaning and groaning, scaring the living daylights out of us! Father stayed home from school today on account of you and will be coming back any minute now with the doctor."

Veronica silently accepted the tea; as she drank, all manner of terrifying images from the night before flashed before her eyes. "Then was it all nothing but an awful nightmare that tormented me?" she asked herself. "But I really did go visit the old woman! It was the 23rd of September! Or did I already fall sick yesterday and just imagine those strange goings on? And all that made me sick was thinking incessantly of Anselmus and of that strange old woman who pretended to be Liese and just put one over on me."

Fränzchen, who had gone out, came back in again with Veronica's soaking-wet coat in hand. "Just look, dear sister," she said, "at the state of your coat. Last night's storm tore the window open and toppled the chair on the back of which it hung; the rain came pouring in and drenched your coat." These words fell as a heavy blow, since they confirmed for Veronica that it wasn't the stuff of bad dreams that tormented her, but that she really had gone to visit the old woman. The thought of it elicited a tremor of terror, and a fever chill convulsed her every limb. Gripped by spasms of cold shudders, she pulled the blanket over her head, but in doing so felt something hard pressing against her breast. She reached for it with her hand; it seemed to be some sort of medallion. When Fränzchen dashed off again with her wet coat, she pulled it out and saw that it was a small, round, brightly polished metal mirror. "Why, it's a gift from the old woman," she called out cheerfully, and it was as if fiery rays shot out of the mirror that pierced her heart of hearts and provided soothing warmth. The fever chill faded, and she felt infused by an indescribable sense of comfort and well-being. She could not stop thinking of Anselmus, and as she focused her thoughts ever more and more intensely on him, his friendly smile flashed back at her from the mirror like a live miniature portrait.

But before long, it seemed to her as if she no longer saw his image, but rather Anselmus himself in the flesh. He sat in a high-ceilinged, strangely furnished room, and kept assiduously writing. Veronica wanted to join him, tap him on the shoulder and say, "Herr Anselmus, look around for heaven's sake, it's me standing here beside you!" But that was quite impossible, for it seemed as if he were surrounded by a bright ring of fire; yet when Veronica looked more closely, it was only the shimmer of large tomes with gilded bindings. Finally, Veronica managed to capture Anselmus's attention. It was as if in order to see her, he first had to remember her existence; but eventually he smiled and said: "Ah— it's you, my dear Mademoiselle Paulmann! But why, pray tell, do you sometimes slither like a little snake?"

Veronica had to laugh out loud at these strange words, whereupon she awakened as if from a deep dream. She quickly hid the little mirror, just as the door opened and Deputy Rector Paulmann entered with Dr. Eckstein. Dr. Eckstein immediately approached the bed, reached for Veronica's wrist, took her pulse, lost in deep thought, and finally muttered, "Well! Well!" He wrote out a prescription, again took her pulse, again remarked, "Well! Well!" and left the room. But from the doctor's terse remarks Deputy Rector Paulmann still had no clear idea of just what ailed his daughter.

The library of palm trees. Fate of a disconsolate salamander.
How a black quill blandished a beet and the Registrar Heerbrand
got very intoxicated.

The student Anselmus had now been working at the home of the Archivarius Lindhorst for several days; these working hours were for him the happiest of his life, all the while serenaded as he was by the sweet sound of Serpentina's soothing words, brushed by a passing breeze, infused by a never-before-felt sense of contentment, the overall effect often lifting him to a state of ecstasy. Every need, every little worry of his miserable existence dissolved, and in this new life that rose around him like a bright sunrise, he suddenly understood all the wonders of a higher being that had heretofore stunned and frightened him. The task of transcription went very quickly as he became ever more convinced that all he was doing was tracing long familiar characters on the parchment, and he hardly had to glance at the original to copy it with the greatest precision.

The archivarius seldom made an appearance aside from at mealtimes, but it was always at the very moment when Anselmus had put the last touches on a copied manuscript. The old man then slipped him another and, after stirring the ink with a little black stick and exchanging the used quills for others with sharpened tips, promptly departed in silence.

One day at the stroke of twelve, bounding up the steps, Anselmus found the door through which he ordinarily entered locked and, dressed in his wondrous flowery dressing gown, the Archivarius Lindhorst appeared from a door on the other side and called out, "Today you enter this way, my dear

Anselmus, seeing as we are bound for the room in which Bhogovotgita's master awaits us." The archivarius led the way down the corridor and through the rooms and halls Anselmus recognized from his first visit. The student was astonished yet again by the wondrous splendor of the garden, but now he saw clearly that some curious blossoms hanging on the dark bushes were, in fact, flashy insects showing off their colors by fluttering their little wings and dancing around in a tizzy, seeming to caress each other with their proboscises. What he had previously taken to be blush- and sky-blue-colored birds were fragrant flowers, and the scent they dis- seminated rose from their calyxes in sweet pulsations that mingled with the burble of distant fountains and the rustling of careening perennials and tall trees to produce mysterious chords of melancholy longing.

But the mocking birds, which had teased and taunted him that first time, once again fluttered round his head and cried incessantly with their fine-tuned beaks, "Herr Studiosus, Herr Studiosus, what's the rush?— Don't keep your head in the clouds or else you'll fall and break your nose.— Ha ha, Herr Studiosus!— Put your scholar's smock on!— Godfa- ther Screech Owl will dress your wig!" Such was the serenade of stuff and nonsense that bombarded his ears until he left the garden.

Finally, the Archivarius Lindhorst strode into the azure-blue chamber; the porphyry with the golden pot had disappeared, and in its place in the middle of the room stood a table draped in violet-colored velvet, on top of which lay the familiar writing tools, with an armchair pulled up in front. "My dear Herr Anselmus," said the Archivarius Lindhorst, "you have already faithfully copied a number of manuscripts at lightning speed and to my great satisfaction; you have earned my trust; the most important task is still to be accomplished. That is the copying, or rather painted reproduction, of certain works written in unusual characters that I keep stored in this room and that can only be copied on the spot. From now on you will therefore work here, but I must urge upon you the greatest care and concentration; one false stroke, or heaven forbid, a single inkstain dripped on the original will spell your doom."

Anselmus noticed little emerald-green leaves growing from the golden stems of the palm trees; the archivarius plucked out one of these leaves and Anselmus realized that what he took for a leaf was, in fact, a rolled-up sheet of parchment, which the old man unraveled and spread out before him on the table. The student was quite surprised by the strangely convoluted characters, and at the sight of the many dots, strokes, faint lines, and curlicues that sometimes seemed to imitate plants, sometimes moss, sometimes animals, he almost lost faith in his capacity to precisely copy it all. The sight of it made him sink into deep thought.

"Courage, young man!" the archivarius chimed in. "If you have tried-and-tested faith and true love in your heart, Serpentina will help you!" His voice sounded like ringing metal, and as the petrified student looked up, he saw the Archivarius Lindhorst standing there before him in all his regal splendor, just as the old man had appeared in the library on his first visit. Anselmus felt impelled to fall down on his knees in veneration, but the archivarius promptly climbed the stem of a palm tree and disappeared among the emerald leaves. The student realized that the prince of spirits had spoken to him and thereupon arisen to his ethereal study, from whence, perhaps sending the beneficent rays of planets as celestial envoys, the prince might hold court and enlighten the student as to how to proceed with him and the lovely Serpentina. It may well also be, Anselmus thought, that news awaited the archivarius from the wellspring of the Nile or that a magus from Lapland sought an audience – in any case, he had best concentrate on the task at hand.

So resolving, he proceeded to study the strange characters on the parchment roll. The wondrous music came wafting in from the garden and he inhaled its sweet scents; the mocking birds kept snickering, but he no longer grasped their meaning, which suited him just fine. At times it also seemed as if the emerald leaves of the palm trees rustled quietly, and as if the lovely crystal bells he had first heard under the elderberry bush on that fateful Ascension Day resounded in the room. Marvelously fortified by the ringing and the glimmer, Anselmus applied himself ever more intently to the transcription of the parchment, and before long he knew, as if in his heart of hearts, that the characters conjoined to express nothing other than these words: "Announcing the wedding of the salamander with the green snake." Then little crystal bells chimed a triad of notes, and the words "Anselmus, dear Anselmus!" were whispered from among the leaves, and – wonder of wonders! – the green snake slithered down the stem of the palm tree.

"Serpentina, lovely Serpentina!" Anselmus cried out, enraptured to the point of madness. For as he looked closer he saw that it was a charming, lovely girl gliding toward him, peering at him with inexpressible longing in her dark blue eyes, the like of which he could heretofore only dream of. The leaves appeared to droop and give way, thorns sprouting from the stem, but Serpentina twisted and twirled herself adroitly, drawing after her a fluttering robe shimmering in a brilliant blaze of color which, clinging to her slender body, slipped along unfettered, without catching on the spikes and thorns of the palm tree. She sat herself down beside Anselmus on the same chair, slung her arm around his shoulder and pressed him to her so that he felt the hot breath blowing from her lips and the electric warmth of her body.

"Dear Anselmus," she whispered, "soon you will be all mine; having won me over with your faith and your love, I will grant you possession of the golden pot that will bring us both eternal bliss."

"Oh, my sweet and lovely Serpentina," Anselmus said, "if I can have you, nothing else matters; if only you'll be mine I will gladly be swallowed up by all the wondrous and strange things that have befallen me ever since the moment I first saw you."

"I know that the arcane and whimsical web my father often likes to weave in jest stirs terror and trembling in your heart, but I hope it won't happen again now that I have come, my dear Anselmus, to set you straight from the bottom of my heart about everything down to the smallest detail, everything you need to know to get my father's game and grasp what makes him and me tick."

To Anselmus it seemed as if he were so completely entwined and entangled with her presence that he could only move in tandem with her, and as if it were her pulse coursing through his every fiber and nerve. He listened intently to her every word that resounded in his innermost self and, like a brilliant ray of light, sparked heavenly delight in him. He had his arm wrapped around her slenderer than slender waist, but the iridescent, glimmering material of her robe was so smooth, so slippery, that it seemed to him as if she could slip away, and he shuddered at the thought that she might at any moment slip free of his grip. "Don't leave me, oh my lovely Serpentina," he involuntarily cried out, "it's you and you alone I live for!"

"I shan't leave ere I've told you all that your love for me will let you comprehend," added Serpentina. "Know then, my beloved, that my father hails from the wondrous species of the salamanders, and that I owe my existence to his love for the green snake. In ancient times, the mighty spirit-prince Phosphorus ruled over the enchanted land of Atlantis, and the elemental spirits were his subservient vassals. One day the salamander that Phosphorus loved best – it was my father – happened to go walking around in the splendid garden that Phosphorus's mother had adorned with the most luxuriant flowers and flora, when he heard a tall lily sing softly, 'Press your little eyelids shut till my lover, the morning wind, rouses you from sweet slumber.' He stepped toward it, aroused by its scent, whereupon the lily spread its leaves and he espied her daughter, the little green snake, curled up asleep in its calyx. The salamander was gripped by burning love for the beautiful serpent and took her away, pursued in vain by the essence of the flower's wordless lament, which called out to every corner of the garden in search of her beloved daughter. For the salamander had carried her off to Phosphorus's castle and begged his father, 'Marry me to my beloved, for she shall be mine forever.'

"'Fool, what are you asking!' cried the spirit-prince. 'Know that the lily was once my lover and ruled at my side, but the spark I ignited in her threatened to consume her, and only the defeat of the dark dragon whom the earth spirits now keep shackled in chains saved the lily, allowing her leaves to grow strong enough to enclose and preserve the spark. But if you embrace the green snake, your hot blood will burn away her body, and a new being will arise from the ashes and fly off.'

"But the salamander did not heed the spirit-prince's warning. With burning longing, he embraced the snake, who promptly moldered into a pile of ashes out of which a winged being was born and flew off. Overcome by despair, the salamander ran through the garden in a fit of fury, spewing fire and flames, laying waste to everything in his path, burning the most beautiful flowers and blossoms whose wailing filled the air. Infuriated, the spirit-prince grabbed the salamander and said: 'Your fire is consumed— the flames are extinguished, the glare died out— you are banished to the realm of the terrestrial spirits. Let them tease and taunt you and keep you captive until the fire is rekindled and erupts from the belly of the earth, spewing forth your essence in the body of a new being.' And the poor salamander sank down, its spark extinguished.

"But the surly old earth spirit, Phosphorus's gardener, stepped up and said, 'My Lord, who more than I should rage at the salamander's excesses! Did I not polish all the lovely flower petals he burned down with traces of my rarest metals? Did I not painstakingly tend to and nurture their sprouts and squander some of my finest pigments? And still I stand by the poor salamander, for it was love alone that drove him to despoil the garden – the same force that so often consumed you too, my Lord, and drove you to despair. Spare him from this painful punishment!'

"'His fire is extinguished,' said the spirit-prince. 'But in that unfortunate future, when the language of nature is no longer comprehensible to the human species, when the elemental spirits are banished to their remote realms and only still mutter in muffled echoes to the ears of man, when the last inkling of the harmonic sphere is reduced to an endless longing for that wondrous realm when faith and love still fueled the human spirit – in that unhappy time the salamander's spark will be reignited, but only man will greet its glimmer, and the salamander will be compelled to endure the hardship of a tenuous existence. But he will retain more than just the memory of his original state, he will once again live in holy harmony with all of nature, he will fathom its wonders, and the power of his brother spirits will stand at his disposal. He will find the green snake again curled up in a bush of lilies, and the fruit of their union will be three daughters who will appear to man in the bodily shape of their mother. In springtime they will nestle in the branches of the dark elderberry bush and let their sweet crystalline voices ring. If in that spiritually wanting, destitute, hard-hearted time, a young man should happen to overhear their song, if one of the little snakes should gaze upon him with her sweet and lovely eyes, the sight of her will awaken in him an inkling of that faraway, wondrous land, to which he can bravely strive to raise himself up and gain entry once he has cast off the burden of the ordinary. If his love for the snake rouses in him a faith in the wonders of nature, and his own existence can fully and passionately partake, then the snake will be his. But the salamander may not cast off his heavy burden and return to live with his brothers until three young men have been found to be wed to the three daughters.'

"'Permit me, my Lord,' said the earth spirit, 'to give the three daughters a gift that will embellish their lives with the three found mates. Each will receive from me a pot made of the finest metal I possess, and I will polish it with rays emanating from a diamond; our wondrous realm as it presently exists in harmony with all of nature will be mirrored in its glimmer in a blinding burst of loveliness; but from inside the pot, the moment they wed, a fire lily will burst forth whose eternal blossoms will shower the youth deemed worthy with its sweet scent. In no time at all he will understand their language and fathom the wonders of their realm, and go with his beloved to live in Atlantis.'

"It must now be clear to you, dear Anselmus, that my father is that salamander of whom I spoke. Disregarding his higher nature, he has been obliged to submit to the petty constraints of ordinary life, hence the frequent moody fits that make him take it out on others. He often told me that we now have an expression for the state of mind that the prince of spirits Phosphorus set as a precondition for anyone seeking to wed my sisters and me; however, it is an expression which is all too often inappropriately misused nowadays: that such an individual need be of a childlike poetic disposition. This disposition is often found in youths who are scorned by the crowd on account of the great simplicity of their manner and because they are totally lacking in worldly sophistication. Oh, my dear Anselmus! You grasped the meaning of my song and my glance under the elderberry bush – you love the little green snake, you believe in me and want to be mine forever! The lovely lily will blossom from the golden pot and we will be united and live together in bountiful bliss in Atlantis! But I make no secret of the fact that in the terrible fight with the salamanders and the earth spirits the black dragon broke free and took flight. Phosphorus has once again taken the vile creature captive, but from the black feathers that fell to the

earth in combat, evil spirits sprouted in opposition to the benevolent salamanders and their allied spirits. That old crone who is so hostile to you,
dear Anselmus, and who, as my father well knows, seeks possession of the
golden pot, owes her existence to the mating of a dragon feather fallen in
combat and a wild beet. She is well aware of her origin and her power, for
in the restless mutterings and convulsions of the captured dragon, many a
mysterious secret constellation was revealed to her. She employs every
means at her disposal to control from the outside in, which my father
opposes with the bolts of light that shoot out of his salamander soul. She
gathers all the hostile essences to be found in poison plants and venomous
animals and, mixing them in a potion that maximizes their potency, arouses
evil spirits that burden human minds with dread and horror and subject
them to the wiles of the demons let loose in the dragon's struggle. Beware
of that old hag, dear Anselmus; she hates you because your childlike, pious
disposition already circumvented some of her evil spells. Stay true – true to
me – and soon you'll get what you want."

"Oh, my Serpentina," cried Anselmus, "how could I ever stop cherish-
ing you, how can I not love you forever!" The burning tingle of a kiss lingering on his lips, he awakened as if from a profound dream to find that
Serpentina had disappeared. The clock struck six, and the student realized
with a heavy heart that he hadn't copied so much as a single word; concerned at what the archivarius would say, he peered at the page and – oh,
wonder of wonders – the copy of the enigmatic manuscript lay finished
before him. Upon closer scrutiny, he became convinced that he had copied

Serpentina's account of her father, the favorite of the spirit-prince Phosphorus in the magical land of Atlantis.

At that moment, the archivarius walked in dressed in his light gray overcoat, with his hat on his head and his walking stick in hand. Peering at the parchment Anselmus had covered in that strange script, the old man took a pinch of snuff and smiled. "Just as I thought! Here's the silver thaler I promised, Herr Anselmus! Now, let's go mark the moment at Lincke's Bathhouse— follow me!"

The archivarius strode swiftly through the garden, in which the air was filled with such a pandemonium of singing, whistling, and chatter that Anselmus was deafened, and he thanked heaven to finally find himself out on the street. They had hardly advanced a few steps when they ran into the Registrar Heerbrand, who gladly tagged along. At the door to the tavern, they stuffed their pipes with tobacco, and the registrar bemoaned not having brought along a tinderbox. "You want a light?" the archivarius exclaimed scornfully. "Take all the fire you need!" Whereupon he snapped his fingers, emitting a stream of sparks, giving light to all.

"Will you get a load of that little chemical trick!" Registrar Heerbrand remarked to the student. But Anselmus was awestruck, and could not help but muse with a shudder of emotion on the history of the salamander.

At Lincke's Bathhouse, the Registrar Heerbrand, ordinarily an even-tempered, quiet man, drank so much strong Doppelbock beer he started singing student songs in a squeaky tenor, and nudged everyone, "So are you my friend or not!" Until, finally, after the archivarius was already long gone, Anselmus had to take the registrar home.

Ninth Vigil

How the student Anselmus came somewhat to his senses. The punch party. How the student Anselmus mistook the deputy rector for an owl, thereby making the latter very angry. The ink spot and its consequences.

All of the strange and wondrous things that befell Anselmus daily took him altogether out of the loop of his ordinary life; he had long since stopped frequenting old friends, and every morning he impatiently awaited the stroke of twelve to return to his paradise. Even though he was devoted heart and soul to the lovely Serpentina and to the miracles of the fairy realm he encountered at the home of the Archivarius Lindhorst, he could not help but think every now and then of Veronica; indeed, it sometimes seemed to him as if she came, blushing, to confess her ardent love, hoping to tear him from the grip of the phantoms that teased and taunted him. It was sometimes as if a strange irresistible force suddenly took hold of him and drew him back to the forgotten Veronica, compelling him to follow her wherever she wished, as though he were chained to her. The very same night that Serpentina had first made herself manifest in the form of a bewitchingly beautiful girl, when the wondrous secret of the marriage of the salamander and the green snake was revealed to him, Veronica appeared in his mind's eye more vividly than ever. Indeed, when he awakened from deep sleep, it became crystal clear to him that he had only been dreaming; he was now convinced that Veronica, with a pained expression that touched him deeply, was actually standing by and lamenting the fact that he seemed intent on forfeiting her ardent love for the lure of those fantastic illusions that would only lead to his dissolution and eventually bring about his rack and ruin. Veronica looked more enticing than he had ever before noticed; he could hardly get her out of his mind, and this caused him great anguish that he hoped to quell with a morning stroll.

A magical force beyond his control drew him in the direction of the Pirna Gate; he was just about to turn down a side street when Deputy Rector Paulmann came walking up and called out to him from behind. "Hey, hey! My good Herr Anselmus, mercy, mercy, where in heaven's name have you been keeping yourself? We haven't seen hide nor hair of you in God knows how long. Do you know that Veronica longs to sing another number with you? Come along then, it looks like you were already headed in my direction."

Having no choice but to accept, Anselmus went along with the deputy rector. As they stepped inside the house, Veronica came rushing toward them decked out in her most enchanting dress, so that her flabbergasted father asked, "Why dressed to the nines, dear daughter, are we expecting company? But here I've brought along Herr Anselmus!"

As Anselmus chivalrously kissed Veronica's hand, he felt a soft squeeze that ran like a feverish rush through every fiber and nerve of his body. Veronica was merriment and comeliness incarnate, and when Paulmann finally retired to his office she managed through all manner of teasing and sly quips to so excite the student that he lost all restraint and chased the cheeky girl around the room. But the demon of awkwardness once again took hold; he knocked into the table and Veronica's lovely sewing box fell to the floor. Anselmus picked it up; the lid had flown open and a little round hand mirror peaked out, into which he cast an eager glance. Veronica drew quietly behind him, laid a hand on his arm and, nestling up against him, peered over his shoulder into the mirror. It was as if an inner turmoil welled up in Anselmus— a psychic whirlpool of thoughts and images flashed and faded— the Archivarius Lindhorst— Serpentina— the green snake— until finally things calmed down and all the disparate pieces came together in his conscious mind. It suddenly became clear to him that he had always been thinking of Veronica, that the figure who appeared before him yesterday in the blue room was none other than Veronica, and that the fantastic legend of the marriage of the salamander with the green snake had not been told to him, but had rather been born of his own imagination. He himself wondered at his flights of fancy and simply ascribed it to the exalted states brought on by his love for Veronica, as well as his work for the Archivarius Lindhorst, in whose rooms, moreover, he was overwhelmed by a stupefying scent. He had to laugh out loud at his madcap illusion of being in love with a little snake and at having taken a portly privy archivarius for a salamander. "Yes, indeed, it's Veronica!" he cried out, turning his head and peering right into the girl's blue eyes, imbued with love and longing.

A muffled "Ach!" escaped from her lips, which at that moment burned with longing to press against his.

"Oh, how lucky I am," sighed the ecstatic student, "all the stuff of yesterday's dreams became real today and is truly to be mine."

"And do you really want to marry me when you become a privy councillor?" Veronica asked.

"Absolutely!" Anselmus replied.

At that moment, the door creaked open and Deputy Rector Paulmann burst in. "Well then, my dear Herr Anselmus, I won't let you slip away today, so long as you can make do with a meager bowl of soup, after which

Veronica will whip up a splendid coffee to be enjoyed in the company of Registrar Heerbrand, who promised to drop by."

"Oh, most esteemed Deputy Rector, don't you know that I am committed to go to the Archivarius Lindhorst to continue my transcription?"

"Look here, my young friend," said Deputy Rector Paulmann, proffering his pocket watch, indicating the time of half past twelve. Anselmus realized that it was much too late to go to the Archivarius Lindhorst's house, and acceded all the more gladly to the deputy rector's wishes, as he would have the opportunity to gaze at Veronica all day long, and to exchange furtive looks, a gentle squeeze of the hand, and even hope for a secret kiss. Anselmus's hopes and dreams were now so confirmed in his mind that he grew ever more giddy, convinced as he now was that he would soon be freed of the batty fancies that had threatened to turn him into a complete lunatic.

The Registrar Heerbrand did indeed drop by as promised after dinner, and once the coffee had been sipped with great delight and darkness had fallen, he let it be known with a chuckle, rubbing his hands together, that he had brought something along with which – once Veronica had applied the magic touch with a whisk of her gracious hands and mixed it properly, thereby titling and paginating its intoxicating properties, as it were – they would all make merry together on that cool October evening.

"Well then, out with that secret something you've got hidden away, most esteemed Registrar!" cried the deputy rector.

Herr Heerbrand reached three times into his satchel and retrieved, one by one, a bottle of arak, lemons, and sugar. Less than a half hour later, the intoxicating vapors of an ambrosial punch rose from Paulmann's dining room table. Veronica proffered the drink, which soon sparked all manner of merry chatter among the friends. But as soon as the potent spirit of the liquor rose to Anselmus's head, all the images of the fabulous phenomena he'd recently experienced leapt back to mind. He saw the Archivarius Lindhorst decked out in his damask dressing gown that sparkled like phosphorus. And he once again felt compelled to believe in Serpentina. Seething inside him, it all welled up again. Veronica offered him a glass of punch, and as soon as he took hold of it, he gently stroked her hand with a poignant sigh, "Serpentina Veronica!" And he drifted back into deep dreams.

But then Registrar Heerbrand exclaimed in a loud voice, "A marvelous old geezer, though he may leave us none the wiser, long life to the Archivarius Lindhorst all the same! Let's drink to that, Herr Anselmus!"

Roused out of his dreams, Anselmus clinked glasses and announced, "It all comes from the fact that the archivarius is really a salamander who, in a fit of fury, lay waste to the garden of Phosphorus, the prince of spirits, after he lost the little green snake."

"Come again?" asked Deputy Rector Paulmann.

"Yes, indeed, honored Registrar," the student rattled on, "that's why he is compelled to serve as the royal archivarius and set up house here in Dresden with his three daughters, who are, in fact, three little green snakes that lounge around in the elderberry bush, singing enticing songs like sirens and seducing unsuspecting young men."

"Herr Anselmus! Herr Anselmus!" cried Deputy Rector Paulmann. "Do you have a screw loose? In heaven's name, what kind of utter gobbledygook are you babbling?"

"He's right," the Registrar Heerbrand chimed in, "that fellow, the archivarius, is a damned salamander who with his shifty fingers plays fiery tricks, spewing smoldering slime that burns holes in your overcoat. Yes, indeed, you're quite right, little brother Anselmus, and whoever doesn't take my word for it is my sworn enemy." Whereupon the Registrar Heerbrand struck so hard with his fist on the table that the glasses rattled.

"Registrar! Are you mad?" cried the vexed deputy rector. "*Herr Studiosus, Herr Studiosus*," he said, turning to Anselmus, "what kind of madness are you up to again?"

"Ach!" said the student, "you're nothing but an odd bird— a wig-combing old eagle owl, Herr Deputy Rector!"

"What did you say? I, a bird— an eagle owl— a hairdresser?" shrieked the deputy rector in a simmering rage. "Sir, you are mad— stark, raving mad!"

"And the old lady's put one over on you," Anselmus added, "even if she's low class, and her father was nothing but a scruffy feather duster and her mother a measly wild beet, she got her grounding from all kinds of lowdown creatures – the poison-tongued riffraff she grew up with."

"That is a scurrilous slander!" Veronica cried out with burning fury in her eyes. "Old Liese is a wise old woman and the black cat is no hostile creature, but a cultivated young man of high breeding and her first cousin."

"Can the salamander eat without scorching its whiskers and wincing in pain?" said the Registrar Heerbrand.

"No, no!" Anselmus cried out. "Not now or nevermore will he manage; and the green snake loves me, since I'm a childlike spirit and looked Serpentina in the eyes."

"The tomcat will scratch them out!" Veronica shouted back.

"Salamander— salamander beats them all— all," howled Deputy Rector Paulmann at the top of his lungs. "But am I in a madhouse? Am I myself mad? What kind of crazy mumbo jumbo am I muttering? Me too, I'm bonkers— bonkers!" Whereupon he leapt up, tore the wig off his head, and hurled it hard against the ceiling, so that the crushed curls creaked and totally unraveled, spreading puffs of powder around the room.

Then the student and the registrar grabbed the punchbowl and the glasses and hurled them against the ceiling, so that the shards scattered in a cacophonous clang. "Long live the salamander— death to the old hag— shatter the metal mirror— scratch the tomcat's eyes out! Birdy— Birdy flying high— eagle owl— salamander!" This is what the three screamed and howled higgledy-piggledy, like men possessed. Bursting out in tears, Fränzchen leapt up and left the room, but Veronica lay on the sofa whimpering in pain and misery. Suddenly, the door flew open and everyone fell silent as a little man in a gray coat strode in. His face had something strangely grave about it, and an unduly large pair of spectacles graced the bridge of his inordinately twisted nose. His head was bedecked by a curious wig that resembled a cap of feathers.

"A great good evening to you all," the droll little man snorted, "might I find a certain young scholar Herr Anselmus here? Permit me to convey respectful greetings from Herr Archivarius Lindhorst, who waited in vain today for Herr Anselmus, but bids him respectfully not to miss the usual time tomorrow." With that, he headed back out the door, and everyone saw that the grave little man was actually a gray parrot.

Deputy Rector Paulmann and Registrar Heerbrand exploded in a burst of laughter that thundered through the room as Veronica wept and moaned, ridden with unimaginable grief. A lightning bolt of horror flashed through the student's fit of madness and he dashed out the door and ran through the streets, oblivious to all. Instinct directed him back to his apartment, to the refuge of his little room.

Shortly thereafter, Veronica strolled peacefully and affably over to his place, asked him why in his inebriated state he had caused her such a fright, and warned him to mind he not fill his head with new delusions when next he works for the Archivarius Lindhorst. "Good night, good night, my dear friend," she whispered and blew him a kiss. He wanted to take her in his arms, but the phantom figure faded, for she was but the stuff of dreams, and he woke up cheerful and refreshed.

He himself had to laugh out loud at the effects of the punch, but as soon as he thought of Veronica he was infused with a beneficent feeling. "I owe it to her alone," he said to himself, "that I survived that ridiculous ordeal. Truth to tell, I was pretty much in the same fix as someone who believes he's made of glass, or someone who fears going out lest he be eaten by chickens because he believes he's a barleycorn. But as soon as I become privy councillor, I'll marry Mademoiselle Paulmann and be happy ever after." And when at noon he strode through the Archivarius Lindhorst's garden he wondered no end how all this could have once seemed so strange and magical to him. He saw nothing but a perfectly ordinary broken flower pot filled with all kinds of geraniums, stalks of myrtle, and the like. Instead of those resplendent many-colored birds that teased him there were nothing but a few sparrows fluttering about that gave off a disagreeable crowing as soon as they became aware of him. The blue room also looked altogether different than when he first saw it, and he could not fathom how for a single second he could have been taken by that garish blue and the unnatural golden stems of the palm trees with their misshapen flashing leaves.

The archivarius regarded him with an altogether quizzical ironic smile and asked, "Well, how did you like that punch yesterday, my dear Anselmus?"

"Oh, but surely the parrot…" Anselmus replied, deeply embarrassed, before falling silent as he realized that the parrot was just part of the phantasmagoria of his drunken state.

"But I myself was there in that raucous company," the Archivarius Lindhorst let slip, "didn't you see me? With all the mad goings-on I was almost badly injured, since I was seated in the terrine at the precise moment the Registrar Heerbrand reached for it to hurl it against the ceiling, and had to hastily retreat into the bowl of Deputy Rector Paulmann's pipe. Adieu then, Herr Anselmus – work well. I'll pay you your silver coin for yesterday's missed day of work, seeing as you've done such a splendid job till now."

"How could the archivarius babble such mad drivel?" Anselmus muttered to himself as he sat down at the work table to copy the manuscript the old man had, as usual, spread out before him. But he saw that the parchment was covered with an apparent hodgepodge of so many strangely twisted characters and curlicues that muddled his vision without offering his eyes a single respite that it seemed well-nigh impossible to copy it faithfully. Indeed, taking in the whole of it at first glance, the parchment resembled a motley veined slab of marble or a moss-covered stone. His bewilderment notwithstanding, he wanted to do what he could, and taking heart, dunked the quill, but the ink refused to flow. He flicked the quill tip impatiently and – dear God! – a big dab dropped on the original manuscript spread out before him. Hissing and hurtling, a blue bolt of lightning shot forth from the fleck and with a terrible crash sidled round the room and struck the ceiling. A dense vapor emanated from the walls, the leaves began to rustle as if stirred by a storm, and blinking basilisks burst forth in a flickering crackle of flames, igniting the vapor, so that rolling sheets of fire hailed down on Anselmus. The golden trunks of the palm trees turned into giant snakes whose horrible heads clashed with cutting metallic clangs and entwined their scaled bodies around the student.

"Madman! Now you must suffer the punishment for your brazen outrage!" cried the terrible voice of the crowned salamander that appeared like a blinding ray of light in the flames above the snakes and now spewed vengeful cataracts of fire upon poor Anselmus; it was as if the pelting flood of fire thickened around his body and congealed into a solid ice-cold mass. But as Anselmus's limbs pulled tighter and tighter together and grew rigid, he lost consciousness. When he came to again, he could not move, as if he were hemmed in by a glimmering flash of light against which he collided if he even tried to lift a hand or make some other movement. Hell's bells! There he sat in a corked crystal flask on a shelf in the library of the Archivarius Lindhorst.

TENTH VIGIL

The sufferings of the student Anselmus in the glass bottle.
Happy life of the Kreuzchüler and the Faithful. The Battle in
the Archivarius Lindhorst's Library. Victory of the Salamander
and Liberation of the student Anselmus.

I presume that I am right to doubt, dear reader, that you have ever been held captive in a glass bottle – unless of course, bewitched by some vivid elfin dream, you found yourself constrained in such a sorry condition. If that was ever the case, then you will painfully empathize with the student Anselmus in his miserable state, but if you have never chanced to dream this sort of circumstance, for my sake and that of the poor student, just let your lively imagination lock you for a moment or two in a crystal decanter. You're ringed by a blinding glimmer, all the objects surrounding you appear to be encircled and illuminated by a brilliant rainbow – everything in the room trembles and teeters and drones in the grip of that shimmer. You float inertly and motionlessly in a frozen block of ether that holds you in its vise grip, so that your mind attempts in vain to command your dead body. The prodigious weight presses down heavier and heavier on your chest – with every breath you sap the last little reserves of air that still wafts up and down in that tight space – your arteries swell up and, riddled with abysmal terror, every nerve ending twitches in a bleeding struggle for life.

Take pity, esteemed reader, on the student Anselmus, gripped by this undefinable ordeal in his glassed-in enclosure. Even so, he felt that death could not release him; had he not just now awakened from that profound faint, still swimming in his torment as the morning sun shone bright and bounteous in his room, gripped anew by his ordeal? He could not budge, but his thoughts struck against the glass, jarred by the deafening clang, and instead of the words that his mind would ordinarily have drawn from his throat, all that he perceived was the muffled roar of madness. Whereupon he cried out in despair: "Oh, Serpentina— Serpentina, save me from this hellish agony!" It was as if a flurry of quiet sighs came fluttering around him and landed on the bottle like green, transparent elder leaves. The clamor let up, the blinding, bewildering burst of light faded, and he breathed a bit more freely. "Am I myself not to blame for my own misery?

Ach! Did I not commit an outrage against you, oh my lovely, beloved Serpentina?! Did I not harbor vile doubt of your very existence? Did I not lose faith and with it everything else that might make me happy? Now will you nevermore be mine, the golden pot is lost to me, I will nevermore discover its wonders. Let me but catch a glimpse of you one last time, and hear your soft sweet voice, my darling Serpentina!"

Thus clamored Anselmus, torn by sharp, cutting pain, when a voice beside him replied, "I don't for the life of me know what you're wailing about, Herr Studiosus!"

For the first time, Anselmus noticed that five other bottles stood beside him on the shelf, and in these he spotted three students from the Kreutz-schule and two law clerks. "Oh, gentlemen, my comrades in misery," he cried out, "how in heaven's name do you manage to look so calm, indeed so buoyant as the cheerful looks on your faces suggest? You sit just like me imprisoned in glass bottles, can't bestir yourself or move a muscle, and can't even think a reasonable thought without stirring a jarring racket of clang-ing and banging, without whipping up a whirlwind in your head. But they certainly don't believe in the salamander and the green snake."

"What are you jabbering about, Herr Studiosus," a student countered, "we've never been better off than now, since the precious coins the mad Archivarius pays us for all kinds of crazy copying do us a lot of good. We no longer have to learn by heart any tedious Italian choral works, we can drop by every day at Joseph's or some other beer hall, drink our fill of Doppelbock beers, look a pretty girl in the eye, sing "Gaudeamus igitur" like a real student, and live it up."

"The gentleman is quite right," a clerk remarked, "I too am rolling in precious coins, just like my esteemed colleague next to me, and go strolling to my heart's delight on the Weinberg, instead of being cooped up between four walls all day long copying legal briefs."

"But most esteemed Sirs," Anselmus countered, "don't you realize that the whole lot of you are enclosed in glass bottles, unable to stir, let alone go strolling about?"

Whereupon the Kreutzschule student burst out in a hearty laugh and cried out, "The Herr Studiosus is off his rocker, he thinks he's enclosed in a glass bottle and is, in fact, standing on the Elbe Bridge peering down into the water. Let's get going!"

"Ah," Anselmus sighed, "they never set eyes on the lovely Serpentina, they haven't the faintest idea of freedom and faith and life in love; that is why, in their ignorance and coarse sensibility, they don't feel the oppressiveness of their imprisonment by the dread salamander. But I, poor lackless soul, must wither away in ignominy and misery if she whom I love beyond reason does not come to my rescue."

Whereupon Serpentina's voice wafted and whispered in the room around him, "Anselmus, you must believe, love, hope!" And every sweet syllable streamed into the student's prison, and the crystal of his clear enclosure gave way so that the prisoner's chest could stir and heave! The torment of his condition diminished little by little and he realized that Serpentina still loved him, and that it was only her intercession that made his stay in the bottle somewhat bearable. He paid no more mind to his feeble-minded fellow sufferers, but focused his mind and all his thoughts on lovely Serpentina.

All of a sudden, a repugnant muffled muttering emanated from the far side of the bottle. It soon became apparent that this muttering came from an old coffeepot with a half-broken lid standing just opposite him on the shelf. The more closely he looked, the more the hideous features of a shriveled old hag's face came into focus, and soon he shuddered at the sight of the apple peddler from the Black Gate standing there before the shelf. She grinned and laughed and called out in a shrill voice, "Poo-poo, my pretty boy! So now you've got to sit it out! Bottled up in a crystal decanter! Didn't I predict it long ago?"

"Just keep sneering and jeering, you cursed ghoul," said the student, "it's all your doing, but the salamander will get you, you vile wild beet!"

"Ho ho!" the old hag retorted. "Not so proud! You kicked my little son in the face, you burned my nose, and still I'm well disposed toward you, you rogue, because you're otherwise a well-heeled sort, and my little girl likes you. But you'll never get out of the crystal decanter if I don't lend a hand; I can't clamber up to reach you, but my godmother, the rat who lives on the floor above your head, will gnaw the board you're balanced on in two. Then you'll come tumbling down and I'll catch you in my apron so that you don't break your nose, but keep your smooth pretty face intact, and I'll carry you to Mademoiselle Veronica, whom you must marry if you're to become a privy councillor."

"Get off my back, you devil's spawn," cried the student Anselmus in a fit of rage, "it's only your hellish intrigue that spurred me on to the sins that I must now expiate. But I will patiently endure it all, and can only sit out my time here enveloped by the love and solace of my darling Serpentina! Hear me now, you old witch, and despair of ever winning me over! I defy your force, I am forever bound in love to Serpentina – I don't ever want to become a privy councillor – I never want to see Veronica again, she who, swayed by your wiles, lured me to evil ends! If the green snake can't be mine, I'll waste away in longing and pain. Off with you, off with you, you despicable shape-shifting hag!"

The old woman laughed so hard the walls rattled, and she screamed, "Then sit it out and rot in the bottle, but now it's time to get to work, since my business here is of a different sort." She flung off her black coat and stood there in her repulsive nakedness, then she whirled around in circles, and great folios came tumbling down from the shelf. Out of these she ripped leaves of parchment, artfully binding them together, and wrapped her body in that hodgepodge of material so that she was soon dressed as if in a multicolored suit of armor. Spewing fire, the black tomcat leapt out of the inkwell on the desk and yowled at the old crone, who shouted out with joy, and together they disappeared through the door. Anselmus noticed that they headed for the blue room, and soon he heard in the distance a hubbub of hissing and howling. The birds screeched in the garden, the parrot cawed, "Stop! Stop! Thief! Thief!"

At that very moment the old crone came trotting back into the room with the golden pot clutched under her arm, shrieking wildly with grotesque gesticulations, "Good luck! Good luck! My little son! Kill the green snake! Up and at 'em, my little son!"

It seemed to Anselmus as if he heard a flurry of deep sighs, the voice of Serpentina. Gripped with horror and despair, he gathered all his strength, striking against his crystal enclosure with a force so great his nerves and arteries threatened to burst. A cutting clang ran through the room, and the archivarius appeared in the doorway in his glimmering damask dressing gown, crying out, "Hey, hey, you ragtag riffraff, you frightful spooks— you spawns of witch's spell— This way— Watch out!"

The old crone's black hair stood like bristles on her head, her fiery red eyes sparked and sputtered with hellish fire and, biting down hard on the pointy teeth studding her jaw, she cried, "Here, kitty, kitty! Sic 'em, sic 'em, lickety-split!" Cackling and sneering, she pressed the golden pot hard against her and, reaching in, flung fistfuls of glimmering earth at the archivarius. But as soon as each clump of earth touched his dressing gown it was transformed into a blossom and fell to the ground. Then the lilies on his gown flickered and flared up, and the archivarius hurled the flaming lilies at the witch, who howled in pain. But as soon as she leapt up and shook the parchment coat of armor, the flames were extinguished and the lilies crumbled into ash. "Up and at 'em, my boy!" the old crone shrieked, whereupon the tomcat leapt into the air and hurtled at the archivarius in the doorway.

But the gray parrot came swooping down and dug his twisted beak into the nape of the cat's neck, so that fiery red blood spurted out, and Anselmus heard Serpentina's voice thundering, "Touché! Touché!"

Then in a fit of fury and despair, the old hag leapt at the archivarius; she chucked the pot behind her and splayed the lanky fingers of her withered fist to claw at the archivarius, but he promptly tore off his dressing gown and flung it at her. Blue crackling flames sputtered, sparked, and blustered from the sheets of parchment, and the old crone tossed about, wailing in pain, digging her fingers into the pot to shovel out ever more earth, and tearing page after page of parchment out of the books to try and tamp the blazing flames. Once she had managed to pat herself down with enough earth and parchment, the fire went out. But then, as if issuing from the archivarius's inner reserve, flickering, crackling rays darted at her. "Hey, hey, up and at 'em – victory to the salamander!" the archivarius's voice droned through the room and a hundred bolts of lightning curled in fiery rings around the old hag.

Swirling and whirling about, the tomcat and the parrot were locked in furious combat, until finally, with a mighty flutter of its wing, the parrot knocked the cat to the ground, grasping and piercing it with its claws so that the cat howled and moaned in terrible death throes. With a sharp thrust of the beak, the parrot hacked its eyes out, so that a burning ooze spurted out. A dense cloud of smoke rose from under the dressing gown, where the old crone had fallen to the ground; her howling, her infernal, piercing wailing faded in the distance. The billowing smoke cloud accompanied by a terrible stench dissolved; the archivarius lifted the dressing gown and beneath it lay a ghastly white beet.

"Herr Archivarius, honored Sir, I bring you my defeated foe," said the parrot, proffering a black hair in its beak.

"Very good, my dear friend," the archivarius replied, "here, too, lies my vanquished enemy. Be so good as to dispose of the remains; this very day as a modest reward you will get six coconuts and a new pair of spectacles, since, as I see, the tomcat made a shambles of your old pair."

"Ever your faithful servant, my praiseworthy friend and patron!" the parrot replied, well pleased. Clasping the beet in its beak, it flew out the window that the archivarius had opened.

The old man retrieved the golden pot and cried out, "Serpentina, Serpentina!"

But as the student peered at the archivarius in joy and relief at the demise of the vile old hag who had precipitated his ruin, the old man was once again transformed into the majestic figure of the prince of spirits, who now peered up at him with a look of indescribable grace and dignity. "Anselmus," said the prince of spirits, "not you, but a hostile principal that wreaked havoc in your heart and sought to divide and conquer your spirit was to blame for your faltering belief. You have kept faith, be free and rejoice!"

A flash of light pulsed in the depth of Anselmus's heart, and the lovely triad of the crystal bells rang louder and mightier than ever before in his ears – his nerves and fibers quivered – and as the resounding music swelled ever more in the room, the glass shattered, and the student tumbled into the arms of his beautiful beloved, Serpentina.

ELEVENTH VIGIL

Deputy Rector Paulmann's indignation at the madness that erupted in his family. How the Registrar Heerbrand became privy councillor and how on the frostiest day of the year strolled about in silk socks and shoes. Veronica's confession. Betrothal beside the steaming soup bowl.

"But tell me, most worthy Registrar, how that confounded punch could have so gotten into our heads and made us carry on like a pack of monkeys?" Thus spoke Deputy Rector Paulmann the following morning upon entering the room and finding it still strewn with broken shards and the remains of his hapless wig, dissolved by punch into its constituent parts. After the student Anselmus had raced out the door, Deputy Rector Paulmann and Registrar Heerbrand kept crisscrossing the room, shaking all over, screaming like lunatics, and knocking their heads together, until Fränzchen finally managed with great effort to lead her befuddled father to bed. Then the registrar sank, all tuckered out, onto the sofa, Veronica having fled the scene and taken refuge in her bedroom.

Looking pale and downhearted, with a blue handkerchief wrapped around his head, the Registrar Heerbrand sighed, "Oh my dear Deputy Rector, the punch that Mademoiselle Veronica lovingly prepared is not to blame for wreaking havoc, no! It was finally all the fault of that damned student! Haven't you noticed that he's been off his rocker for the longest time? Don't you know that insanity is infectious? One fool makes many, as the preacher says. Begging your pardon, but it's an old saying; this is particularly true when you've downed a drop, as you are thus prone to mad doings and can easily be unwittingly influenced to imitate an addled wingman. Can you believe it, Deputy Rector, that I still feel dizzy when I think of the gray parrot?"

"Stuff and nonsense!" the deputy rector interrupted. "Rubbish! It was the archivarius's little old secretary with a gray coat wrapped around himself looking for Anselmus."

"That may well be," the Registrar Heerbrand admitted, "but I must admit I'm in a sorry state; all night long I heard a strange piping and tooting."

"That was me," the deputy rector replied, "I snored up a storm."

"That may well be as you say," the registrar continued, "but— oh, my dear Deputy Rector! It was with good reason I sought to bring us a bit of good cheer yesterday, but that student spoiled everything. You don't know the half of it, oh, Deputy Rector, kind Sir!" Registrar Heerbrand jumped up, tore the kerchief from his head, embraced the deputy rector, and gave him a hearty handshake. Yet again, he cried: "Oh, Deputy Rector, Deputy Rector!" and, reaching for his hat and walking stick, promptly stormed out the door.

"That Anselmus will never again cross my threshold," Deputy Rector Paulmann muttered to himself, "for I can see all too clearly now that with his confounded lunacy he drives the best people bonkers and robs them of their ounce of reason. Now the registrar has lost his marbles – I'm okay for the moment, but the devil who came pounding at my door yesterday in a drunken tizzy might finally manage to break in and play his game. So get thee hence, Satan! Away with that Anselmus!"

Veronica became quite pensive. She did not say a word, but simply smiled strangely from time to time, and preferred to be alone. "Anselmus has gotten under her skin too," the deputy rector fumed spitefully, "but it's a good thing he doesn't turn up, I know that he's afraid of me – which is why he won't dare drop by." Paulmann spewed these last words at the top of his lungs.

Whereupon Veronica, who happened to be present, burst out crying. "How could Anselmus possibly come here, corked up as he's long been in a glass bottle!" she sobbed.

"Come again? What's that you say?" Deputy Rector Paulmann cried out. "Dear God, oh, dear God, now she, too, is babbling nonsense – soon she'll be off her rocker. Oh, that accursed, wretched student Anselmus!"

He immediately ran off to fetch Dr. Eckstein, who smiled and kept repeating, "I see! I see!" Still, he didn't prescribe any remedy, but rather added in passing, "Case of nerves! It'll cure itself. Take her outside. Go for a walk. A little distraction. Theater. 'Sunday's Child.' 'The Sisters from Prague.' It'll be all right!"

"The doctor's never been so loquacious," Deputy Rector Paulmann thought to himself. "Why, he's downright chatty."

Many days, weeks, and months passed. Anselmus had disappeared, but even Registrar Heerbrand never came a-knocking. It was not until February 4th that the registrar, dressed in a new suit of the finest material, in shoes and silk stockings, the chill outside notwithstanding, came traipsing in at noon on the dot with a big bouquet of fresh flowers in his hands, stunning the deputy rector with his fancy getup. Registrar Heerbrand approached the deputy rector in a right festive manner, embraced him with due decorum, and said, "Today, on the name day of your gracious daughter, Mademoiselle Veronica, let me say everything I've long held in my heart! On that unfortunate evening when, stuffed in the pocket of my waistcoat, I brought by all the ingredients of that noxious punch, I had intended to convey some good news and celebrate the happy day in merriment, already knowing that I was to be named privy councillor at court. The official patent *cum nominee et sigloi principis* I now bring you in the selfsame pocket."

"Well, I'll be, Herr Registrar— I mean to say, Herr Privy Councillor Heerbrand!" the deputy rector stammered.

"But, wait, my esteemed friend," the newly dubbed Privy Councillor Heerbrand continued, "you alone can make my happiness complete. For the longest time I have secretly loved Mademoiselle Veronica, cognizant of certain friendly looks she cast in my direction that clearly indicated that she may not be averse to my affection. In short, esteemed Deputy Rector,

I, Privy Councillor Heerbrand, respectfully request the hand of your gracious daughter Mademoiselle Veronica, who, should you not object, I would soon like to make my wife."

Deputy Rector Paulmann clapped his hands together in complete surprise, and replied, "Well, well, well, Herr Registrar – Herr Privy Councillor, I mean to say – who would have thought it! Well, if Veronica does indeed love you, I for my part have nothing against it; perhaps her present gloom is only a function of her concealed love for you, honored Privy Councillor! You know how moody women can be."

At that very moment, Veronica entered the room, pale and troubled, as she generally was these days. Privy Councillor Heerbrand immediately approached her, found well-chosen words to greet her on her name day, and handed her the fragrant bouquet along with a little packet. And as she opened it, a pair of glimmering earrings sparkled up at her. Her cheeks flushed with a fleeting redness, her eyes twinkled, and she cried out, "Oh, my God! Can these be the very same earrings I tried on several weeks ago, and which I found so enthralling?"

"How can that be possible," Privy Councillor Heerbrand replied, somewhat taken aback and a bit chagrinned, "seeing as I just bought them for a pretty penny an hour ago on Schloßgasse?"

But Veronica wasn't listening, already stationed in front of the mirror, assessing the effect of the jewels that now dangled from her dainty little ears. Deputy Rector Paulmann proceeded to reveal to her with a grave expression and solemn tone of voice his friend Heerbrand's elevation in rank and his request for her hand in marriage.

Veronica gave the privy councillor a piercing look and said: "I've known for the longest time that you wanted to marry me— So be it then! I promise you my heart and hand, but I must immediately reveal to you both, my father and my betrothed, things that weigh heavy on my heart— right now, even if the soup that my sister Fränzchen has just set on the table should grow cold."

Without waiting for the deputy rector's or the privy councillor's reply, ignoring the words of protest visibly about to spill from their lips, Veronica continued, "You can take my word, dear Father, that I loved Anselmus with all my heart, and as the Registrar Heerbrand himself, henceforth promoted to privy councillor, assured us, Anselmus had it in him to achieve like honors. I decided to marry him and no one else. But then it seemed as if strange inimical forces were tearing us apart, and I sought the help of old Liese, who had been my nanny and is now a wisewoman, a great magician. She promised to help me to make Anselmus all mine. We went at midnight on the winter equinox to the crossroads, she conjured up the spirits of hell, and with the help of the black tomcat we managed to fabricate a metal mirror in which, by focusing my thoughts on Anselmus, I had only to peer to make him mine in heart and soul. But now I sorely regret having done all that, I renounce all of Satan's arts. The salamander vanquished the old crone; I heard her cries, but I could not help her. No sooner was she reduced to a beet and devoured by the parrot than my metal mirror shattered with a piercing clang."

Veronica fetched the two pieces of the broken mirror and a lock of hair from her sewing box and, handing them to Privy Councillor Heerbrand, continued: "Here, take this, my dear Privy Councillor, take these broken pieces of the mirror and fling them at midnight tonight from the bridge over the Elbe, from the spot crowned with a cross; the current of the raging river is not frozen below. However, keep the lock of hair and wear it against your faithful heart. I renounce Satan's arts, and gladly grant Anselmus his happiness, for he is henceforth bound to the green snake, who is far lovelier and richer than I. I will love and honor you, dear Privy Councillor, as your legally wedded wife!"

"Oh God! Oh God!" Deputy Rector Paulmann cried out in pain, "my daughter has gone mad, she's gone mad— she can nevermore become Madame Privy Councillor— she's gone mad!"

"Certainly not!" Privy Councillor Heerbrand chimed in, "I am well aware of the fact that Mademoiselle Veronica had a certain fondness for that confounded Anselmus, and it may be that in a fit of passion she turned to the old wisewoman who, as I can tell, can be no other than the card- and coffee-grain reader at the Seetor – in short, the raving old crone. And it cannot be denied that there are indeed secret arts that exert their inimical influence on people's destinies, we've read about it in old books, but what Mademoiselle Veronica said about the victory of the salamander and the liaison between Anselmus and the green snake is just the stuff of poetic allegory – a poem, as it were, wherein she celebrates in song her parting with the student."

"Take it for what you will, my dear privy Councillor!" Veronica interrupted. "Perhaps for the stuff of a foolish dream."

"By no means do I do so," replied Privy Councillor Heerbrand, "since I am also well apprised of the fact that Anselmus was propelled by arcane forces that egged him on to all manner of mad doings."

Unable to keep silent any longer, Deputy Rector Paulmann exploded. "Hold still, for heaven's sake, hold still! Have we once again been overcome by the insidious effects of that damned punch, or is Anselmus's madness infecting us? Herr Privy Councillor, what nonsense you speak again! I am willing to believe that love has made you both a bit addled in the brain, but marriage will soon enough iron things out. Else I'd be concerned that you, too, esteemed Privy Councillor, had gone off your rocker, and would then worry that your progeny might inherit the derangement of the parents. Now then, I give my fatherly blessing to your happy union and permit you to kiss as future husband and wife." This happened forthwith, and so it was that before the soup went cold, the betrothal was arranged.

A few weeks later, as she had foreseen, Madame Privy Councillor Heerbrand sat at the bay window of a lovely house near the New Market, and cast her smiling gaze at the fancy folk rushing by. And they in turn, peering up over their lorgnettes, remarked, "Why, it's that lovely Madame Privy Councillor Heerbrand, isn't she looking well!"

TWELFTH VIGIL

News of the realm to which Anselmus retreated as the Archivarius Lindhorst's son-in-law, and how he lived there with Serpentina. Conclusion.

How deeply I felt in my heart of hearts the profound bliss of the student Anselmus who, bound in body and soul to the lovely Serpentina, retreated with her to the mysterious and wondrous realm for which, imbued with strange intuitions, he had always longed, and that he now recognized as his true home. Overwhelmed by this feeling, I was reluctantly compelled to acknowledge the insufficiency of my every expression, dear reader, in a faltering attempt to put the splendid surroundings of our friend Anselmus into words given the spiritual impoverishment and paltry limitations of my petty little life, which put me in a foul mood. I skulked about as if in a dream – in short, I fell into the sorry state Anselmus had suffered, which I described for you in the fourth vigil. How dispirited I felt, after running through the eleven vigils I had successfully written up, convinced as I now was that the insight necessary to add on the twelfth as a satisfactory conclusion would forever elude me; every time I sat down, come nightfall, to complete the work, it seemed as if spiteful spirits (it might well have been relatives – perhaps first cousins – of the murdered witch) held before me a polished plate of metal in which I saw my sorry self, pale, bleary-eyed and melancholy, like the Registrar Heerbrand in the throes of his post-punch hangover, as I struggled to find the phrases to paint a picture of that never-glimpsed realm. I finally flung my pen down and hastened to bed, so that I might at least dream of our blissful Anselmus and his lovely Serpentina. This had already been going on for many days and nights when, altogether unexpectedly, I received the following note from the Archivarius Lindhorst:

Your Excellency has, as I have learned, set down in eleven vigils the singular adventures of my worthy son-in-law, the former student, now poet, Anselmus, and are presently wracking your brain as to how in a twelfth and final vigil to describe his happy life in Atlantis, whereto he retreated with my daughter to live on the handsome estate I possess there. Much as I regret that in the process you revealed my true nature to your reading public (as this might well cause me a thousand inconveniences in my service as privy archivarius; indeed it might even spur some in the college to question how a salamander can legally and with binding consequences swear an oath to serve the state, and how, if at all, he can be entrusted to conduct important business, since according to Gabalis and Swedenborg, elemental spirits are not to be trusted), and notwithstanding the fact that my best friends may now be inclined to eschew my embrace, fearing that I might in a sudden excess of cockiness transmit a spark and singe their hairpiece and Sunday best, it is nevertheless my intention to be of assistance to Your Excellency in the completion of this work, since the text contains much that is praiseworthy concerning my dear married daughter and myself (would that I could already have married off the other two).

Consequently, should you wish to write the twelfth vigil, I advise you to descend the damned five flights of steps of your abode, leave your miserable little chamber, and hasten to my door. In the palm tree room, with which you are already familiar, you will find all the necessary writing materials, and will then in a few select words be able to reveal to your readers what you have seen. That would be better than attempting a rambling description of a life only known to you from hearsay.

Your Excellency, I remain respectfully your most humble servant,
The Salamander Lindhorst
Pleno Titulo Privy Court Archivarius

This admittedly somewhat harsh, yet on the whole still friendly, note from the Archivarius Lindhorst was most welcome. Whereas it seemed quite certain that the strange old man was well aware of the curious manner in which I learned of what befell his son-in-law (which I must, alas, keep secret from you, esteemed reader), he did not take it as badly as I had feared; he did, after all, offer of his own accord to help me complete my work, from which I am inclined to conclude that he basically gave his accord that his wondrous existence in the spirit world should become known in print. It may be, I thought, that he thereby hoped to have a better chance of finding the mate for each of his remaining daughters, for perhaps a spark may fall into the heart of this or that young reader, igniting in him a longing for the green snakes and propelling him to seek them out and find them curled around the elderberry bush on Ascension Day. From the misfortune that befell Anselmus when he was bottled up in the glass flask, such a worthy suitor will have learned his lesson, to guard against all doubt and disbelief. At eleven o'clock on the dot I extinguished my study lamp and slipped off to the house of the Archivarius Lindhorst, who was already waiting for me in the vestibule.

"You made it to my door, my most esteemed friend! So glad you didn't misconstrue my good intentions. Do come in!" With these words he led me through the dazzling glimmer of his garden to the azure-blue room in which I spotted the violet desk at which Anselmus had worked. The archivarius disappeared, but reappeared again a moment later with a lovely golden goblet in hand, from which a blue flame danced upward. "Here," he said, "I bring you the beloved beverage of your friend, the Kapellmeister

Johannes Kreisler.* It is arak flambé, sweetened with sugar. Have at least a little nip, while I toss off my dressing gown and make myself comfortable, and while you sit and look and write, enjoying your precious company, bobbing up and down in the goblet."

"As you please, honored Herr Archivarius," I replied, "but if I am to enjoy the drink, you surely will not…"

"Don't you worry, my fine friend," the archivarius cried. Then he flung off his dressing gown and, to my considerable amazement, stepped into the goblet and vanished in the flames.

Fearlessly I blew aside the flames and partook of the drink— it was ambrosial!

⁓

Can't you hear the emerald green leaves of the palm trees softly rustling and sighing as if caressed by the cool breath of the morning wind? Roused from sleep, they bestir themselves as if stoked by heavenly harp strings, whispering secrets of faraway wonders! The azure hue is released from the walls and floats up and down like a fluffy fog, but blinding beams of light shoot through the mist that whirls like a child's exultant joy and rises to immeasurable heights, vaulting over the crests of the trees. But ever more blinding beams cut through the haze until, in a burst of sunlight, the boundless expanse of the grove opens to reveal Anselmus standing before me.

Glowing hyacinths and tulips and roses raise their fair heads and, like sweet notes, their blended scents salute the blessed youth: "Stroll, oh stroll

---

* One of Hoffmann's literary alter egos and pen names.

among us, beloved boy, you who understand our essence – our scent is the longing for love – we love you and are forever yours!"

The golden beams of light burn in glowing tones: "We are fire ignited by amorous fervor – their scent is the longing, but fire is desire, and do we not reside in your breast? We are yours!"

The dark bushes rustle – the tall trees beckon: "Come to us! You, oh blessed one, dearly beloved! Fire is desire, but hope is our cool shadow! We rustle round your head, whispering sweet nothings, for love lives in your heart, and so you understand." The fountains and brooks burble and bubble: "Oh, dearly beloved, don't rush by so quickly, pause a moment to peer into our crystal surface – your image lives in our midst, that look that we lovingly preserve, for you have understood!"

A flock of brightly colored birds burst into a triumphal chorus of twittering and tweeting: "Give ear, give ear to our song, we are joy incarnate, we are bliss, the rapture of love!"

But Anselmus looks with longing at the resplendent temple rising in the distance. The artful columns look like trees, and the capitals and cornices like acanthus leaves twirled and twisted into splendid wreaths dangling as wondrous adornments. Anselmus approaches the temple, gazing in ecstasy at the brightly colored marble and the magnificent moss-covered steps. "Oh no," he cries out, as if in an excess of rapture, "she cannot be far!"

Then Serpentina, in all her grace and splendor, emerges from the temple carrying the golden pot out of which a lovely lily has sprouted. The inexpressable bliss of her endless longing glowing in her lovely eyes, she looks at Anselmus and says, "Oh, my beloved, the lily has burst from its calyx, the greatest good has been fulfilled, can there be any happiness like ours?"

Anselmus wraps his arm around her with the fervor of his burning desire, whereupon the lily bursts into flames above his head. The trees and bushes rustle louder, and the fountains frolic all the more merrily, the birds and all sorts of brightly colored insects dance in the swirling bursts of air— a joyful, frolicking, jubilant tumult in the air— in the waters— on dry ground— celebrating the revelry of love! Now streaks of light flash through the bushes. Diamonds glimmer from the ground like sparkling eyes! Glittering geysers shoot out of the fountains. Wondrous scents waft about with the beating of wings. They are the elemental spirits rendering homage to the lily and proclaiming the fulfilment of Anselmus's bliss. Then Anselmus raises his head as if engulfed by the glimmer of an apotheosis! Is it glances? Is it words? Is it song? I can hear it distinctly, "Serpentina! My belief in you, my love, has let me tap nature's innermost essence! You brought me the lily that sprouted out of the golden core, tapping earth's primal force before Phosphorus ignited the idea – it is the recognition of the harmony of all being, and in this recognition let me live in the bounty of its bliss forevermore. Jubilant, I have known the highest truth, that I must love you forever, oh Serpentina! Never will the golden rays of the lily fade, for like faith and love, knowledge springs eternal."

I am indeed beholden to the magical arts of the salamander for affording me this vivid vision of Anselmus frolicking on his estate in Atlantis, which I found cleanly inscribed in my own handwriting on paper lying on the yellow table there before me after it all disappeared in a flash as if swallowed by a fog. However, I felt myself pierced and torn by a sudden burst of pain.

"Oh, you, lucky Anselmus, who cast off the burden of the mundane responsibilities of daily life! Who, borne aloft on the wildly waving wings of your love of the beauteous Serpentina, now live in bliss and delight on your estate in Atlantis! Whereas I, poor soul! Soon, all too soon, in a matter of minutes, I find myself removed from that lovely hall, hardly an estate in Atlantis, returned to my miserable garret room, my spirit burdened by the beggarly needs of sustaining life, my vision encumbered by a thousand hardships as if cloaked in a thick fog, at the thought that I myself may never set eyes on the lily!"

Then the Archivarius Lindhorst tapped softly on my shoulder and whispered, "Be still, be still, my fine friend! Don't be so upset! Were you not yourself just transported to Atlantis, and do you not yourself at least possess a goodly domain as the poetic estate of your spirit? Is Anselmus's blessed state anything other than a life enshrined in poesy, revealed in the sacred harmony of all being as the most profound secret of nature?"

The Automaton

1814

The Talking Turk made quite a splash, indeed he became the talk of the town. Young and old, high society and the hoi polloi, all came in droves, from morning to night, to hear the oracular pronouncements whispered to the curious by the stiff lips of that wondrous living-dead figure. In fact, the entire configuration of the automaton was such – there being general consensus that its artistry was far superior to that of similar trick gimmicks often shown at trade and county fairs – that everyone was drawn to it. In the middle of a room of moderate size containing only the necessary equipment sat the life-sized, well-proportioned figure, dressed in fine and tasteful Turkish garb, on a low, three-legged settee. The artist would shove this back on request to dispel any suspicion of contact with the floor.

The Turk's left hand lay relaxed on a knee, the right hand resting on a little freestanding table. The entire figure was, as previously mentioned, well-proportioned, but what stood out as particularly remarkable was the head; a truly oriental, intelligent-looking physiognomy made the whole thing look far more alive than even those wax figures made to resemble the animated faces of noted individuals. The figure was surrounded by a light parapet that prevented visitors from coming too close, for only those who sought to satisfy their curiosity as to the overall structure – insofar as its creator allowed this to be seen without revealing its secret – and those posing questions were accorded the privilege. If, as was customarily the case, you whispered a question into the Turk's right ear, he first turned his eyes, then his entire head, in the direction of the one asking, and believing in the actuality of the breath that emanated from his mouth, you were likewise inclined to believe that the answer really did come from inside the figure.

Once several questions had been posed, the creator inserted a key into the figure's left side, and cranked up the clockwork with considerable creaking. At this point, upon the spectator's request, he also lifted a hatch, within which you beheld a gear box with cogs that did not seem to have any effect on fomenting the automaton's speech, and yet by all appearances occupied so much space that it would have been impossible to hide a person, even if he were smaller than the famous dwarf August who crawled out of a pie crust. Aside from the movement of the head that occurred each time just prior to the answer, the Turk sometimes also raised his right arm and either waved a finger in warning or with a wave of his entire hand dismissed the question. If this happened, then only the repeated urging of the asker might elicit a rather ambiguous or petulant response. All this clockwork might presumably be connected to the movement of the head and arm, even if, here too, the intercession of a thinking person seemed all the more likely. The spectator ran himself ragged with conjectures as to the source of the wondrous message, closely examining walls, an adjoining room, the apparatus, all to no avail. The more they were examined by the Argus-eyes of the most skillful mechanics, the more the figure and its creator felt under observation, and the more uninhibited its comportment became. The creator spoke and joked with spectators in the most distant corners of the room, and let his mechanical creation make its movements and answer questions, as if it were a freestanding, independent being that required no contact with him. Indeed, he could not refrain from breaking into a markedly ironic chuckle when, after circling the tripod and banging on the table, going so far as to lift the figure closer to the light and peering into its core with spectacles and a magnifying glass, expert mechanics swore that the devil alone could make sense of the wondrously intricate clockwork. All attempts at an explanation were for naught, and the hypothesis that the breath emanating from the figure's mouth could be produced by hidden valves, and that the creator himself as a wily ventriloquist gave the answers, was instantly refuted, when at the selfsame instant the Turk offered an answer to a question posed by a spectator, the creator conversed loudly and distinctly with the very same spectator.

Despite the figure's tasteful outfit and the inscrutable mystery of its entire makeup, the public's interest in it would have soon waned if its creator had not managed to attract attention in another way. This added interest lay in the nature of the answers given by the Turk, that each time tended with deep insight into the individuality of the questioner, sometimes full of a dry wit, sometimes rather vulgar and droll, and then again spirited and incisive, and painfully on the mark. The questioner was often startled by a quizzical peek into the future explicable only from the standpoint of the questioner's own soul-searching self-examination. The mystery was, moreover, all the more enigmatic in that, while the questions were posed in German, the Turk often replied in a foreign tongue known to the questioner, and all agreed that it would hardly have been possible to formulate such a succinct and apt response in such few words in any other language. In short, every day brought word of new quick-witted, trenchant responses by the wise Talking Turk, and every evening a heated discussion as to which was more amazing, the enigmatic similarity between the figure and a living human persona, or rather the insight into the individuality of the questioner, and the uncommon brilliance of the answers.

Two academic friends, Ludwig and Ferdinand found themselves a part of just such a discussion. Both friends were compelled to admit, to their great shame, that they had not yet visited the Turk, despite the fact that fashion, so to speak, compelled a visit so as to be in the know about the miraculous answers to the many captious questions.

"I have a profound aversion," said Ludwig, "to all these figures that not only emulate the human mien, but also mimic human comportment, these veritable statues of a living death or a still life. From early childhood I fled in tears when I was taken to a wax museum, and to this day I cannot enter such a display without being gripped by an uncanny feeling of dread. I'm inclined to cry out, in Macbeth's words, 'Thou hast no speculation in those eyes / Which thou dost glare with!' when I perceive all the vacant, dead, glassy looks of wax sovereigns, famous heroes and infamous murderers, and villains directed at me. I am convinced that the vast majority of people feel much the same way, if not to the same degree of repulsion, since most people tend to whisper in wax museums; you seldom hear a loudly uttered word. Such decorum is not the consequence of reverence for the lofty personages depicted, but rather the effect of the uncanny, the grisly, that compels a stunned pianissimo from the spectator. The movements of lifeless figures that mimic the human have an altogether sinister effect on me, and I am absolutely convinced that the lingering memory of your wondrous, quick-witted Turk with his rolling eyes, turning head, and lifted arms, like some necromantic monster, would hound me in sleepless nights. Which is why I prefer not to pay him a visit, but would rather hear secondhand all the witty and astute things he says to this or that questioner."

"As you must know," Ferdinand affirmed, "everything you just said concerning the exceptional mimicking of the human, of the living-dead quality of wax figures, echoes my own sentiments to a T. In the case of mechanical automatons, however, it's really a matter of the manner in which the creator seizes the thing. One of the most accomplished automatons I ever saw is Enslen's The Voltigeur;* as truly impressive as I found its vigorous movements, the effect of its suddenly remaining seated on a tightrope and the friendly nod of its head struck me as particularly bizarre: no doubt no one else was gripped by that sense of dread that such figures easily engender in extremely excitable individuals. In the case of our Talking Turk, I believe there is another explanation. Based on the description of those who have seen him, the appearance of this well-put-together, dignified figure plays a

---

* Johann Carl Enslen (1759–1848), a German traveling painter, exhibitor and creator of panorama structures, and early pioneer in photography. His Voltigeur was featured as part of an elaborate show displayed in Berlin, which incorporated a mechanical automaton with trick mirrors, laterna magica, and camera obscura, and greatly inspired Hoffmann.

strictly secondary role, and his eye rolling and head turning surely serve only to effectively deflect our attention, to take our eyes off the actual key to his secret functioning. It is perfectly possible – perhaps, based on empirical evidence, even certain – that a breath should waft from the Turk's mouth; we cannot, however, necessarily conclude from this that said breath is stirred by the spoken words. There is no doubt whatsoever that a human being is capable, via some hidden and unknown acoustic and optical mechanical contrivance, to establish a connection with the questioner such that it sees him, hears him, and can whisper answers. The fact that no one, not even one of our most skilled mechanics, has yet hit on the slightest clue as to how this connection is facilitated proves that the creator's device must have been very cleverly conceived, and so, from this standpoint, his creation merits the closest attention. What seems all the more remarkable and really fascinates me is the intellectual insight of the human being behind it all, seemingly enabling the Talking Turk to delve into the psychic depths of the questioner – there is often such profound insight and at the same time such an eerie interplay of lightness and darkness in the answers as to approach an 'oracular' pronouncement, in the strictest sense of the word. Many friends who have witnessed it themselves have told me such astounding accounts in this regard that I admit to being intrigued, and I can no longer withstand the urge to put the wondrous seer of the unknown to the test myself. I have decided to go there tomorrow morning, and am herewith most cordially inviting you, dear Ludwig, to set aside all your dread of living dolls and accompany me."

As much as Ludwig bristled, after several other friends beseeched him not to exclude himself from the amusing expedition, and to accompany them tomorrow morning to get to the bottom of the secret of the miraculous Turk, he was ultimately obliged to give in so as not to be taken for a crank.

Ludwig and Ferdinand did indeed go with a group of merry youths, who got together for that express purpose. Although the Turk was undeniably decked out in Oriental splendor and, as already mentioned, had a most becoming head, upon entering the exhibition space Ludwig was struck by a sense that the whole thing was rather droll, and when finally the device's creator stuck a key into his side and the wheels began to whir, it all seemed to him so insipid and outdated that he could not help but cry out, "I do say, my dear fellows, we may have roast meat in our belly, but His Excellency the Turk has the entire gizmo, roasting spit and all!"

Everyone laughed, and the creator, who did not seem to appreciate the joke, immediately closed off the cogwheels to further viewing. Whether the jovial mood of the merry gents displeased the wise Turk, or the morning did not find him in a good mood, his answers – even to some downright witty, spirited questions – all remained uninteresting and flat; Ludwig, in particular, had the misfortune that his questions were never understood and elicited altogether skewed replies. The dissatisfied friends were about to skip out on the automaton and his creator, when Ferdinand spoke up. "I dare say, gentlemen, none of you are overly impressed by the Talking Turk, but perhaps it was our fault; perhaps our questions were not up to snuff. The fact that he should now turn his head and raise his hand," (which the figure did indeed do) "appears to confirm my supposition! I can't say why, but I am inclined to pose another question which, if on the mark, should restore the automaton's honor." Ferdinand stepped up to the figure and whispered a few words into its ear; the Turk raised an arm, indicating that he refused to reply, but when Ferdinand would not let up, the Turk turned his head to him.

Ludwig noticed how Ferdinand suddenly turned pale, but after several seconds of silence asked another question, and immediately received an answer. With a forced smile, Ferdinand addressed his friends. "Gentlemen, I can assure you that, at least for me, the Turk has upheld his honor; so that the oracle can remain mysteriously oracular, however, please spare me from revealing what I asked and what he answered."

As much as Ferdinand took pains to hide his upset, his troubled state of mind was all too apparent in his strained effort to appear cheerful and nonchalant, and had the Turk given them the most wondrous, apt answers, his friends would not have been gripped by the peculiar, almost chilling feeling evoked by Ferdinand's evident tension. His prior mask of mirth had vanished, and in lieu of his ordinarily loquacious conversational manner he now spoke only a word or two here and there, and parted from the others in a moody silence.

"Dear friend," Ferdinand began as soon as he found himself alone again with Ludwig, "I cannot hide the fact from you that the Turk touched me in my heart of hearts, indeed that he cut me to the quick with his words, so much so that I won't be able to get over the pain until death brings the fulfillment of the terrible oracular pronouncement."

Ludwig regarded his friend with a look of total surprise and dismay, but Ferdinand continued: "I now see that the invisible being that mysteriously communicates with us through the Turk has potent powers at his disposal, that penetrate our innermost thoughts with a magical force; it may well be that by some strange sway he can clearly and distinctly predict the future fomented by the mystical connection between our inner selves and the world around us, and thus knows all that will befall us in days to come, just as there are people endowed with the unfortunate visionary ability to fore-tell death at a given time."

"You must have posed a most peculiar question," Ludwig replied, "but perhaps you yourself put too much store in the oracle's ambiguous answer, reading too much into what the capricious play of chance may have coin-cidentally appeared to reveal as penetrating and pertinent, and thus ascribe a mystical perspicacity to the altogether ingenious person who expresses himself through the Turk."

"In your reference to so-called chance," Ferdinand objected, "you have just now contradicted a contention on which we always agreed in the past. But in order to lay it all on the line so that you may grasp my profound upset and distress at what I heard today, I must tell you something about my earlier life that I have kept from you until now. Many years have passed since I returned to B—— from my late father's East Prussian estates. In K—— I met with several young Courlanders who likewise sought to make their way to B——; we journeyed together in three horse-drawn postal coaches. As you can well imagine, since we were all of an age burst-ing with a frenzy of expectations, and riding out into the world fitted with purses to meet our needs, our lust for life brimmed over with an unchecked exuberance. The wildest whims were jubilantly realized, and I can still remember that we plundered Madame Postmaster's store of provisions in

M——, where we stopped at noon. Her protestations notwithstanding, we paraded with our booty up and down before the storehouse, smoking up a storm, in full view of the crowd until, summoned by a merry blast of the postal horn, we drove off again.

"In the giddiest of moods, we pulled in to D—— where we resolved to spend a few days to take a turn in the lovely surroundings. Every morning we went on a merry expedition; once we climbed the slopes of the Karlsberg and roamed around in the vicinity until late that evening, and when we got back to the inn we were welcomed by a lovely punch we'd ordered that morning, and which, drained by galivanting around in the salt sea air, we dispatched with pleasure. Without being really drunk, the pulse in my veins pumped and thumped, and my blood ran like a burst of flames, sparking all my synapses. And when at last I made it back to my room, I flung myself on my bed; but despite my fatigue, my sleep was not much more than a dreamy half slumber in which I remained aware of everything going on around me. It seemed to me as if I heard a muffled whisper in the room next door, and I finally deciphered a manly voice that said: 'Sleep then if you must, but be ready at the appointed hour.' A door was opened and shut, whereupon a deep silence set in, soon interrupted by a few quiet chords played on a pianoforte.

"You know, my dear Ludwig, what magic there is in musical notes resounding in the still of the night. That's just the way it was, as if some spirit voice were speaking to me in those chords. I completely surrendered myself to that pleasant impression, convinced that it would lead to a pleasant follow-up, a fantasia or some charming piece of music, but imagine my state of mind when the divine voice of a woman sang the following words in a heart-stirring melody:

Mio ben ricordati
s'avvien ch'io mora,
quanto quest' anima
fedel t'amo.
Lo se pur amano
le fredde ceneri
nel urna ancora
t'adorerò!*

"How can I begin to describe the mix of emotions of that never-before-experienced, never anticipated feeling stirred up in me by those long, drawn-out, now surging, now fading notes! When that altogether strange melody, like nothing I'd ever heard before – oh, it was the deep, blissful melancholy of fervent love itself – when she cooed her lovely canto in simple melismata, now soaring high so that each note tinkled like a crystal bell, now sinking low so that it seemed to die out in the muffled sobs of desperate lamentation, it felt as if a nameless rapture quivered through my innermost self, rendering me breathless, as the pain of that endless longing contracted spasmodically in my chest, and I myself dissolved in nameless,

---

* An aria from *Allessandro nell' Indie*, an opera libretto about the Indian campaign of Alexander the Great, by Pietro Metastasio (1698–1782), set to music more than ninety times, first by Italian composer Leonardo Vinci (1690–1730), whose version premiered in Rome on January 2, 1730.

heavenly bliss. I did not dare budge; all of me, my soul, my entire disposition spilled into my hearing. The string of notes had long since gone silent when a burst of tears finally gave vent to the surge of emotion that threatened to do me in.

"Sleep must finally have overtaken me, since when I shot up out of bed, awakened by the shrill blast of the postal horn, the bright sunlight of morning flooded my room, and I realized that it was only in my dream that I had been privy to the greatest happiness, the most profound bliss to be found in this life on earth. A lovely, budding young girl entered my room – it was the singer – and she spoke to me in a sweet voice: 'You must have recognized me again, my dear, dear Ferdinand! I know that all I had to do was sing to completely come alive in you again; for every note I sang was already present in you and only had to resound in the echo chamber of my heart.' What unnamable rapture swept through me as I saw that it was the beloved of my soul whom I bore in my heart since early childhood, from whom a cruel turn of fate had made me part, but whom I was ecstatic to have found again. But my fervent love resounded again in that melody so full of ardent yearning and, in our words, our looks were transmuted into musical notes that coalesced like a burst of fire.

"But now that I was fully awakened, I had to admit to myself that no recollection from early in life accorded with that most radiant dream vision – it was the first time that I ever set eyes on that lovely girl. I overheard loud and hefty chatter emanating from the street in front of the inn – mechanically I picked myself up and hurried to the window; an older, well-dressed gentleman quarreled with the porters who had broken something on the postal carriage. Finally all was resolved, and the man called up to my room:

'Everything is now in order, we're ready to depart.' I became aware of a woman peering out the window of the room directly next to mine, but she promptly pulled her head back so quickly, that since she had on a rather wide-brimmed travel hat, I caught no sight of her face. When she strode out the door, she turned and looked back up at me and— Ludwig! It was the singer, my dream vision— the glance of those heavenly eyes fell upon me, as if the pitch of a ringing crystal pierced my breast like the thrust of a dagger, and I felt a physical shot of pain, so that every nerve and fiber in my body set to tingling, and I froze in a fit of nameless rapture. One, two, three, she had climbed into the carriage— the postilion blasted a lively ditty as if to taunt me. A moment later, the carriage had turned a corner and disappeared.

"Like a man lost in dreams, I remained stationed at the window. The Courlanders burst into my room to fetch me for a previously arranged expedition— I didn't utter a word— they took me for ill— how in heaven's name could I have expressed in words the slightest inkling of what I'd experienced! I refrained from asking after the stranger who'd occupied the room next to mine, for it seemed to me as if any word regarding the identity of that lovely vision spilled from profane lips would defile the precious secret of my heart. I vowed then to carry my secret faithfully and be forever true to her who had now become the eternally beloved of my heart and soul, even if I never set eyes on her again. You, my dearest friend, must surely recognize the state of mind in which I felt I'd put myself; you will, therefore, not think badly of me for forsaking all my other responsibilities in an effort to track down the slightest clue as to the identity and whereabouts of my unknown beloved. Given my disposition, the company of the boisterous Courlanders became repulsive to me; heading off an inevitable confrontation, one night I up and left, and hurried off to B—— to pursue my pressing concern of the moment.

"As you know, from an early age I had a knack for drawing; in B—— I came under the influence of skilled masters in the art of the miniature, and within a short amount of time I managed to fulfill my sole object, namely to paint a faithful likeness of the unknown beauty. Secretly, behind closed doors, I painted her portrait. No other human eye has ever seen it, for I painted another picture of the same dimensions, had it measured for a medallion, and took great pains to replace it with the picture of my beloved. I have worn it ever since then dangling against my breast.

"This is the first time I have ever spoken of the most important moment in my life, and you, Ludwig, are the only living soul to whom I revealed my secret. But today a strange, inimical force broke into the sanctuary of my innermost self! Upon approaching the Turk, thinking of my heart's beloved, I asked: 'Will I ever again experience a moment like the one during which I was completely happy?' As you no doubt noticed, the Turk did not want to reply; but finally, when I would not let up, he said, 'My eyes peer into your breast, but the mirrorlike polish of the golden medallion you wear blocks my view – turn the picture toward me!' I am at a loss for words to describe the feeling that made me tremble all over. You will surely not have failed to notice the stir that swept through me. The picture really did lie against my breast, as the Turk declared; I turned it around without attracting notice and repeated my question, whereupon the automaton said, in a solemn tone, 'Oh, you poor unfortunate soul. At the precise moment you see her again you will have lost her forever!'"

Ludwig was about to attempt to cheer up Ferdinand, who had fallen into a dark brooding state, with a few consoling words, when they were interrupted by the approach of several acquaintances.

Rumors of the wise Turk's latest mysterious response spread through the city, and people tore their hair out trying to guess what infelicitous prophecy could have so upset an open-minded fellow like Ferdinand. The friends were bombarded with questions – so much so that, to help Ferdinand out of a tight fix, Ludwig felt obliged to dish up a doozy of a yarn that gained more credence the further it wandered from the truth. The same group of friends that had egged on Ferdinand to visit the wondrous Turk gathered once a week, and at their very next get-together the Turk was once again on everybody's tongue, since, much as Ferdinand tried to hide his sorry state, the whole gang kept peppering him with questions about what the automaton could possibly have said to make him so downhearted. Ludwig felt all too poignantly how deeply his friend must have been shaken up upon having the buried secret of his fantastical love uncovered by a strange, horrid force. Like Ferdinand, he too was firmly convinced that the piercing look of that mysterious entity able to uncover deepest secrets might well also have the ability to forge a link between the future and the present. Ludwig felt compelled to believe the oracle's pronouncement, but the hostile, shameless revelation of the cruel fate foretold to his friend set him against the being hidden behind the Turk. Consequently, he took a steadfast stand in opposition to the artwork's countless admirers. While they pronounced that there was something altogether remarkable in the natural movements of the automaton that enhanced the effect of the oracular pronouncements, he maintained that it was precisely those eye and head movements that lent an indescribably absurd element to the honorable Turk, and it was due to this that he had let slip a bon mot, vexing the unseen creator behind the device, which ill humor the latter had exhibited with a slew of insipid and meaningless replies.

"I must admit," Ludwig continued, "that at first sight the figure immediately reminded me of an altogether delicate and finely crafted nutcracker that a cousin of mine once gave me for Christmas when I was a little boy. The device in the shape of a little man had a deadpan comic expression, and by means of an ingenious hidden mechanism, his big eyes would come twisting and popping out of his head whenever he cracked a nut, which gave the entire figure such an absurdly animated manner that I played with it for hours on end, and transformed the wooden dwarf in my hands into a mystical mandragora root. All of the perfectly fashioned marionettes I later encountered seemed stiff and lifeless compared with my splendid nutcracker. So much had been said of the wondrous automata at the Danzig Arsenal that I could not possibly resist paying it a visit when I finally found myself in Danzig some years ago.

"Soon after I entered the hall, an old German soldier came striding toward me and fired his rifle, the reverberation of which rang out with an ear-splitting intensity against the vaulted ceiling. More shenanigans of that sort, which I have since forgotten, from time to time took me by surprise, until finally I was led into the hall occupied by the God of War, terrible Mars himself, and his entire court entourage. He sat decked out in rather grotesque attire on a throne adorned with weapons of all sorts, ringed by tribunes and warriors. As soon as we set foot in front of the throne, a few tympanists started beating their drums, and pipers sounded out something awful, so that the spectator felt inclined to hold his hands over his ears to block out the cacophonous clang. I remarked that the God of War had a wretched military band, altogether unworthy of his majesty, and everyone agreed.

"Finally, the banging and the piping stopped; the tribunes started turning their heads and stamping with their halberds, until the God of War himself rolled his eyes a couple of times, leapt up out of his seat, and appeared to want to stride toward us. But soon after that, he plunked himself back down on his throne, and there was more drumming and piping, until all returned to its former wooden silence.

"After having surveyed all these automata, I said to myself in parting: 'I prefer my nutcracker!' And now, my good Sirs, after having witnessed the wise Turk, I say it again: 'I prefer my nutcracker!'"

Everyone had themselves a good laugh, but agreed that Ludwig's take on the matter was more amusing than earnest, since aside from the extraordinary mindfulness evidenced time and again by the automaton's answers, the undetectable link between the hidden being and the Turk, that not only spoke through the device but also produced the figure's movements in response to the questions, proved altogether remarkable, and was, in any case, a testament to mechanical and acoustical wizardry.

Even Ludwig himself had to admit that this was true, and everyone was full of praise for the automaton's unknown creator. Whereupon, an elderly gentleman who generally said little, and this time, too, had not taken part in the conversation, rose from his chair, as was his wont when he wished to add a few words (which were always absolutely pertinent to the subject at hand), and in his polite manner began, "If you will be so good as to permit me a word— I bid you most respectfully, kind Sirs! You rightfully extoll this most unusual work of art, that has for such a long time now riveted our attention; you are, however, ill-advised to refer to the ordinary man standing by it as an artist, since he has played no part whatsoever in those aspects of the work that we justifiably find to be so sublime; said credit belongs, rather, to a man well versed in all the related arts, who has for many years resided within the walls of our city, and whom we all know and hold in high regard."

Stunned by his pronouncement, everyone peppered the old man with questions, and he continued, "I mean no one other than Professor X———. The Turk had already been here for two days without anyone taking any particular notice of it; Professor X———, on the other hand, made haste to go see it, since everything related to automata intrigues him. No sooner had he heard of a few of the Turk's answers than he pulled aside the artist standing by and whispered some words in his ear. The latter turned white in the face, and after the departure of the few curiosity-seekers who had found their way there, he promptly locked the door. The posters advertising the Turk disappeared from the street corners where they had been plastered on walls, and nothing more was heard of the wise Turk until two weeks later a new announcement appeared, and the Turk was now found to be adorned by his splendid headgear and enveloped by the inscrutable riddle, as we see him today. Ever since that time, his answers have also become so quick-witted and profound. But there can be no doubt that all this is the doing of Professor X———, since all the while the artist withheld his automaton from public view he paid the professor daily visits, and also, as we well know, the professor spent many consecutive days in the hotel room in which the figure stood and in which he still stands today. You all surely know, my good Sirs, that the professor has a collection of the most splendid, exquisite automata, albeit all outfitted with a musical element. He has long been in correspondence and competition with Court Counselor B—— concerning his collection as well as the magical arts, and you will, I'm quite sure, concur that it can only be him and him alone likely to arouse general amazement. Yet even though he is glad to show off his rare artworks to anyone who so wishes and who takes real pleasure in seeing them, he continues to work and create in complete secret."

Although it was common knowledge that the professor, whose principle scientific research interests were in physics and chemistry, also liked to dabble on the side with mechanical artworks, no one among the group of friends suspected he had a hand in the savvy Talking Turk, and it was only from hearsay that anyone knew of the cabinet of wonders of which the old gentleman spoke. Ferdinand and Ludwig felt a strange excitement at the old man's account of the professor and his influence on the curious automaton.

"I cannot deny," said Ferdinand, "that the prospect of approaching Professor X—— for an explanation now gives me a flicker of hope at unraveling the secret that weighs so awfully on my heart. It is indeed possible that I might find some solace in pursuing my suspicion of a mysterious connection between the Turk – or rather the hidden person utilizing him as a vehicle for oracular pronouncements – and myself, and that in so doing I may perhaps diffuse the effect of those terrible words. I have consequently decided to make the mysterious man's acquaintance, under the pretext of wanting to see his collection of automata, and since, as we've heard, his devices have a musical element, you might find it of interest to accompany me."

"As if it were not enough," replied Ludwig, "for me to stand by you in word and deed in this unsettling matter! I cannot deny that when the old man spoke of Professor X——'s influence on the talking machine, all sorts of strange thoughts ran through my mind, although it may well be that I am seeking far-fetched explanations for something lying right under our nose. Is it not conceivable, to posit an explanation close at hand, that the unseen person was cognizant of the fact that you wore a picture in a pendant hanging against your breast, and could not an informed guess have led to the seemingly portentous pronouncement? Perhaps with his grim augur the unseen person simply sought to get back at us for our mockery of the wisdom of the Turk."

"As I already told you before," Ferdinand replied, "no one ever saw the picture, and I never told another living soul of the effect of that incident on my life. The Turk could not possibly by any ordinary means have been apprised of it all! Perhaps the far-fetched explanation you seek comes closer to the truth!"

"What I mean to say," Ludwig remarked, "even though I seemed just now to suggest the contrary, is that our automaton really is one of the most remarkable devices I've ever seen, and everything appears to suggest that whoever may be directing its functioning is privy to a more profound understanding than ever suspected by those who flippantly gawk and puzzle over the puzzling. The figure is nothing more than the form of a communication, but there can be no doubt that this form is skillfully fashioned, since its overall appearance as well as the automaton's movements are geared to deflecting the spectator's attention, so as to guard the secret, and in a sense to optimally prime the questioner in anticipation of the responding entity. No human being could possibly be hidden inside this figure, of this there can be no doubt; the fact that we believe the answers emanate from the Turk's mouth is surely based on some acoustical illusion; just how this is accomplished, how the person answering is set in such a position to observe those asking the questions, to examine them and respond in an intelligible manner, is and remains a riddle to me. It presupposes a keen acoustical and mechanical know-how, an exceptional perspicacity, or perhaps rather a consequent slyness on the part of the creator, who employed every means to pull the wool over our eyes.

"I must admit to being less interested in the disclosure of this secret, overshadowed as it is by the most extraordinary fact that the Turk can often peer deep into the innermost recesses of the heart and soul of the questioner, as you yourself observed even before it was proven to you. It is as if the responsive being were somehow, by a means unknown to us, able to exert a psychic influence, indeed to establish such a spiritual rapport with us that it appears to grasp our state of mind, to fathom our entire internal makeup. Even if it does not clearly reveal the secret we harbor, it calls forth, in an ecstatic state fostered by the strange spiritual principle's rapport with us, intimations of all things buried in our breast, which are illuminated by our mind's eye. It is the psychic force that plucks at our heartstrings, ordinarily just rustling against each other like reeds, so that they now vibrate and ring out together, producing a pure and clearly audible chord; so in a sense it is we ourselves who answer our own questions. Awakened by a strange spiritual principle, we more clearly hear our inner voice, and our muddled musings become mesmerized in form and concept, congealing into clear pronouncements. This is just like in dreams, in which a strange voice edifies us concerning things outside of her ken, or about which we were at the very least in doubt; the fact notwithstanding that this voice that appears to introduce unknown truths, it does, after all, emanate from inside ourselves and express itself in intelligible words. It goes without saying that the Turk, by whom I naturally mean the hidden entity moving his lips, seldom needs to establish a psychological rapport with the questioner. A hundred questioners are superficially dispatched, one after another, as much as their individuality demands, and often enough, all that's called for is a keen insight spawned by the natural erudition or the quick-wittedness of the answering being, with no need to sound the depths of the question. But an exalted state of mind on the part of the questioner will presently affect the Turk in an altogether different way, and then he deploys the capacity that creates the psychic rapport, granting him the ability to respond from the questioner's innermost self. The Turk's hesitation to immediately answer such deeply probing questions is perhaps just the pause he permits himself to give him the time he needs to apply his enigmatic power. This is my heartfelt opinion, and as you can tell, the fabulous figure is not as contemptible to me as I gave you to believe before – perhaps I am taking this entire matter too seriously! But I do not wish to hide the fact that, if you go along with my take, I realize that I am not offering you any reassurance in your troubled state of mind!"

"You are mistaken, my dear friend," replied Ferdinand, "your thoughts on the matter fully concur with those that immediately came to mind and drove me into dark despair, which affords me wondrous reassurance;

cognizant as I am of the fact that I have to go about this by myself, it is a comfort to know that my cherished secret is safe, since my friend will faithfully keep it to himself like a sacred object entrusted to his care. But I must now mention a particular circumstance I had not thought of until now. As the Turk spoke the fateful words, it was as if I heard that ever-mournful melody sounding in my ears: '*Mio ben ricordati s'avvien ch'io mora*' in broken syllables — and then again it was as if a long-held note of that godly voice I heard that night wafted by."

"Then let me not conceal the fact," said Ludwig, "that just as you received the whispered answer, I happened to have my hand on the parapet surrounding the figure. I felt a vibration in my hand and it was as if a musical note — I can't well call it singing — glided along, resounding in the room. I did not pay it particular attention, since, as you well know, my entire imagination is forever infused with music, and I have consequently been deluded in the most wondrous ways; but I was more than a bit taken aback deep in my heart upon learning of the mysterious connection between that mournful note and the fateful occurrence in D—— that sparked your question to the Turk."

Ferdinand merely held it to be proof of his psychic rapport with his beloved that this invisible being behind the Turk should have likewise heard the music, and when the two friends proceeded in their discussion to delve deeply into the psychic connections between kindred spiritual principles, when the discussion gave rise to ever more lively and wondrous examples, it seemed to him as if the heavy burden of despair that had weighed down on his breast ever since receiving the Turk's answer was lifted from him; he felt himself emboldened to reflect on that fateful prediction. "How can I lose her," he said to himself, "she who forever holds sway in my heart of hearts, and manifests such an intense existence that could only be dissolved by my own demise?"

Hopeful at the prospect of shedding light on some of the conjectures that bore for both friends the weight of inner truth, they paid a visit to Professor X——. They found him to be a gentleman advanced in age, but with an alert appearance, girded in old Frankish attire, with small, gray eyes, and an unpleasant piercing gaze, his mouth twisted into a sarcastic smile that put them off.

When they expressed the wish to see his automata, he replied, "So, are you also lovers of mechanical artworks, perhaps even dilettante builders? You will find here in my collection devices that you won't find in all of Europe, indeed in the entire known world." The professor's voice had something extremely repugnant about it; it was a high-pitched, screeching, dissonant tenor that perfectly suited the market crier manner with which he touted his artworks. Making quite a racket, he fetched the keys and opened the tastefully, downright sumptuously decorated hall in which the works were kept. On a platform in the middle of the room stood a grand piano; directly beside it to the right there was a life-sized male figure with a flute in hand; to the left sat a female figure before a pianolike instrument, behind it two boys with big drums and a triangle. Far to the rear the two friends noticed the orchestrion, with which they were familiar, and the surrounding walls were all hung with chiming clocks. The professor ambled past the orchestrion and the clocks, and surreptitiously touched the automata; then he sat himself down at the piano and began playing pianissimo a marchlike andante; at the reprise, the flute player raised the flute to his lips and played the musical theme, and the boy quietly struck the drum in perfect rhythm, just as another brought a hardly audible chime from the triangle. Soon thereafter, the woman at the piano broke into hearty chords and, while pressing down on the pedals, managed to emit a harmonica-like sound. But then the music grew brisker and livelier, resounding in the entire hall; the clocks chimed in with the greatest rhythmic precision, the boy struck all the more loudly on his drum, the triangle rang out shrilly, and finally the orchestrion trumpeted and pounded in *fortissimo*, so loud that everything trembled and quaked, until with one last stroke the professor wrapped up his performance with a final chord. The friends applauded heartily, paying him the tribute that his self-satisfied smile seemed to demand. Approaching the automata, he prepared to offer up music-making of the same sort, but Ludwig and Ferdinand, as if they had previously agreed to do so, both offered the pretext of some pressing appointment that precluded their staying any longer, and promptly left the mechanic and his machines.

"Now wasn't all of that artful and beautiful?" asked Ferdinand.

But Ludwig let loose, as if in a fit of long-suppressed fury, "The devil take that damned professor— how badly we've been had! Where are the revelatory bits of information we were after? Whatever became of the instructive entertainment in which the professor was supposed to enlighten us, like the novices of Sais?

Ferdinand countered, "We did, after all, see some remarkable mechanical wonders, from a musical standpoint as well! The flute player is clearly the famous Vaucanson device, and judging from the finger movements, the same mechanism likewise appears to power the female figure, who manages to produce resonant, powerful tones: the coordination of the machines is remarkable."

"All that," replied Ludwig, "is precisely what drove me out of my mind! I am mightily worked up about and fed up with all that mechanical music – in which I include the professor's performance at the piano – so much so that I feel the strain in all my limbs, and won't get it out of my system for a good long time.

"For me, even the link between human beings and lifeless figures that mimic the human in appearance and movement, in actions and impulses, has something oppressive, uncanny, indeed something ghastly about it. I can well imagine that it must be possible by means of a built-in gearbox to have figures dance in an artful and nimble manner, and they must surely also be able to dance with people and engage in all manner of twists and turns, so that the living dancer grasps his lifeless, wooden partner, and swings her around, permitting the spectator to look for a minute without being revolted. But mechanical music is for me an entirely frightful and ghoulish thing, and in my view a good stocking-knitting machine infinitely surpasses the most perfect, splendid-looking music box.

"Is it only the breath blowing from the mouth that animates a wind instrument? Is it only the agile, supple fingers plucking notes from a string instrument that grip us with their mighty magic, stirring up in us such unknown, ineffable feelings linked to no earthly source, that arouse in us inklings of a distant spirit realm, awakening our higher being? Is it not, rather, the human spirit that just uses these physical devices to bring forth resounding notes from our deepest depths to the perceptible reality of life, so as to make them audible to the ears of others, and thereby elicit a wondrous hint of eternity from each note, like sparkling rays of light in the harmonic echo chamber of the spirit? To seek to manipulate valves, coil springs, levers, cylinders, and whatever else may comprise a mechanical device to make it sound musical constitutes, to my mind, a foolish and futile effort to make the medium itself spurt out that secret something that only the inner strength of the human spirit can bring to life and modulate by an absolute mastery of every movement. The greatest reproach one can make of a musician is that his playing is expressionless, thereby compromising the very essence of music, or rather eradicating the musical core of music; and even so, the most spiritless and insensitive instrumentalist can perform infinitely more subtly than the most sophisticated machine, it being unthinkable that the human essence should not find fleeting expression, even if but once in his playing, which, of course, in the case of the machine can never be possible.

"The effort of mechanics to imitate more and more closely the effect produced by human organs in eliciting musical notes, or by mechanical means to substitute for the same, constitutes for me a declared war against the human spirit, the power of which shines forth all the more brilliantly the more seemingly oppositional forces are wielded against it. It is for this very reason that the most accomplished mechanical music device is the most reprehensible to me, and a simple barrel organ that merely intends to produce mechanical effects by mechanical means is for me infinitely preferable to the Vaucansonian flute or harmonica player."

"I am absolutely in agreement," said Ferdinand. "For you have just expressed clearly in words what I have for the longest time felt in my heart of hearts, particularly so on our visit to the professor today. Without living and breathing so totally immersed in music as you, and consequently without being as sensitive as you to all musical abuses, the lifelessness and stiffness of mechanical music has repelled me for as long as I can remember, so much so that even as a child in my father's house a big chiming clock that sounded off every hour really grated on my nerves. What a shame that skillful mechanics apply their artistry and know-how to such wretched gadgets, rather than to the perfection of musical instruments."

"That's all too true," Ludwig replied. "Particularly in this regard, much could be done to perfect keyboard instruments; a skilled mechanic could do wonders, and it is really remarkable how far the piano, for instance, has advanced in its mechanical structure to favor tone and finger technique. But should it not be the task of top-notch musical mechanics to listen in on the most singular sounds of nature, to probe the musical notes that emanate from the most heterogenous bodies, and to attempt to capture this mysterious music in some sort of organon that complies with human will and sounds in response to his touch? All attempts to elicit notes out of metallic or glass cylinders, glass filaments, glass or marble strips, or to make strings vibrate and resound in ways other than the ordinary finger plucking or bow stroking, seem, therefore, to be most worthy of note. The only thing standing in the way of further progress in the endeavor to sound the depths of nature's profound acoustical secrets is that every flawed attempt pursued for the sole sake of ostentation or monetary gain is praised and shown off as the ultimate invention. It is for this reason that so many new instruments have come into being in such a short time, many with curious or showy names, and promptly disappeared and been completely forgotten."

"Your notion of a most highly developed musical mechanics is indeed very interesting," said Ferdinand, "although I cannot conceive the point or object of such an endeavor."

"We are speaking of nothing else here but the discovery of the most complete tone," replied Ludwig, "but I consider the musical note to be all the more complete the more closely it resembles the secret notes of nature which are not yet altogether severed from the earth from which they emerged."

"It may well be," said Ferdinand, "that I have not delved as deeply as you into these musical mysteries, but I admit that I do not completely catch your drift."

"Allow me at least to hint at my sense and concept of all this," Ludwig continued. "In the prehistoric beginnings of mankind, to borrow the notion of a brilliant writer on the subject (Schubert in his 'Thoughts on the Nocturnal Side of Natural History'), in man's primordial holy harmony with nature, infused with the godly instinct of prophesy and poesy, when the spirit of humanity did not embrace nature, but it was rather nature that embraced the human spirit, and the mother still nurtured from the depths of her being the wondrous person to whom she gave birth – at this time humanity was still enveloped, as if in a cloud of eternal rapture, with holy music, and wondrous notes heralded the arcane mysteries of its eternal ferment. I inferred an echo of the depth of our primordial attachment to music in the splendid legend of the music of the spheres, of which I first read as a boy in *The Dream of Scipio*, which filled me with fervent devotion, so that I often pricked up my ears on moonlit nights to try to detect a trace of such wondrous sounds in the whisper of the wind. But as I said before, such audible murmurings of nature have not as yet abated, for how else can we conceive of that air music or devil's bellowing from Ceylon, to which the aforementioned author Cicero alludes – a phenomenon that has such a profound effect on the human disposition that even the most serene spectator cannot fend off a deep sense of horror, and a shattering sympathy with those murmurings that so closely mimic human wailing. Years ago, I myself experienced a very similar natural phenomenon near the Curonian Lagoon in East Prussia. Far into the fall, I held up for a time on an estate in the area, and on quiet nights on which gentle winds blew all about, I heard long drawn-out tones that sometimes sounded like a deep, muffled pipe organ, sometimes like the muffled vibrating clang of a bell. I was often able to distinguish a deep F paired with augmented fifth C, and often I heard a resounding third E-flat, so that a piercing seventh chord chimed out with the sound of the deepest lament, filling my breast with the most profound melancholy, indeed riddling my heart with horror.

"There is something in the unnoticed genesis, crescendo, and dissipation of those natural notes that irresistibly grips our spirit, and the instrument set at its disposal will necessarily affect us to the same degree. It therefore seems to me that, taking its tone into account, the accordion most closely approximates that perfection, the measure of which is its effect on the spirit of the listener, and it is telling that precisely this instrument that so faithfully imitates those natural notes and has such a profound influence on the mood of the listener, should be not at all amenable to levity and insipid ostentation, but rather is grounded in the sacred simplicity of its idiosyncratic nature. Much in this regard will no doubt be accomplished by the recently invented so-called harmonichord, which by means of a secret mechanics set in motion by a touch of the keys and the swing of a barrel, in lieu of bells, makes strings vibrate and resonate. The player has almost greater control over the formation, crescendo, and gradual fading of musical notes than with the accordion, and it is only the tone of this instrument that sounds like it emanated from another world that has kept the harmonichord from becoming more popular."

"I have heard this instrument played," said Ferdinand, "and must confess that its tone moved me deeply, even though, in my view, it was not played to its best advantage. I feel I understand you now, even though I don't quite get the link between those natural notes, of which you speak, with the music produced by these instruments."

"Can it be," replied Ludwig, "that the music that resides in our innermost self is anything other than the music of nature, a secret sound hidden only from our higher consciousness, and which resounds only when compelled to do so, by passing through the body of the instrument mastered by the one who plays it? But in our dreams, in the strictly psychic workings of the spirit, the spell is lifted, and we hear those notes of nature wondrously produced and played in concert by familiar instruments, wafting down upon us, rising to a crescendo, and fading away."

"Your words bring to mind the aeolian harp," Ferdinand interrupted his friend, "what do you make of that ingenious invention?"

"Its attempts to coax out the notes of nature are indeed beautiful and most praiseworthy," Ludwig replied, "but to date it has evolved into little more than a piddling plaything, its potential thus reduced to naught. To my mind, much more impressive in concept than the aeolian harp, which as a mere musical deflector of wind currents has been reduced to a childish toy, is the weather harp, of which I once read. Rather thick wires spanned in the open air are made to vibrate by the passing breeze, and are said to resound in mighty tones. A broad field of inquiry in this domain remains open to the soulful, enlightened physicist and mechanic, and I believe that, given the momentum of advances in the natural sciences, further research will break in upon the sacred secrets of nature, and some things that are only now suspected will be revealed and made perceptible in the mysteries of life."

All of a sudden, a curious clang resounded in the air around them, which in its powerful crescendo greatly resembled the sound of the accordion. Gripped by terror, the two friends froze; the sound transformed itself into the mournful melody of a woman's voice.

Ferdinand reached for his friend's hand and pressed it hard against his breast; but Ludwig spoke softly and in a trembling voice, "*Mio ricordati s'avvien ch'io mora.*"

They happened to be standing outside the city, in front of the entrance to a garden surrounded by high hedges and tall trees. Right there before them, heretofore unnoticed, a sweet little girl who had been seated on the lawn playing, jumped up and said, "Oh how lovely, my sister is singing again, I must bring her another flower, since I already know that if I bring her brightly colored carnations, she'll sing even lovelier and longer." At this, she leapt forward with a great big bouquet of flowers in hand into the garden, the gate of which stood open, allowing the friends to peer in. But how stunned they were, seized with horror, upon spotting Professor

X—— standing there in the middle of the garden under a towering ash tree. Instead of the disconcerting ironic smile with which he received the two friends in his house, his face was now draped by a profoundly melancholic gravity, and his transfigured gaze seemed to peer upward into the hereafter hidden behind the clouds, the existence of which the wondrous sounds like a tremulous puff of wind passing through the air attested. He strode slowly and with a measured step up and down the central allée through the garden, everything in his path stirring with life; all around him a crystal tinkling rang out from the dark bushes and trees and streamed in wondrous concert like flames through the air, penetrating the soul of all who heard it and stirring the greatest rapture with inklings of the heavenly hereafter. The sun set, the professor disappeared among the hedges, and the plaintive notes faded in pianissimo.

The two friends finally returned in silence to the city, but as Ludwig was about to bid Ferdinand farewell, the latter pressed him in a tight embrace and whispered, "Stay true to me! Stay true to me! Oh, I can feel a strange force piercing my innermost self, stroking all my hidden heartstrings that now must ring out accordingly, even if I die in the process! Was the hateful irony with which the professor received us at his house not the expression of a deep-seated inimical tendency, and did he not simply seek to make short shrift of us by showing off his automata to preclude any closer contact with me in life?"

"You may very well be right," replied Ludwig. "I too have a hunch that in some way that presently remains a mystery to us, the professor has honed in upon your life, or rather, intruded in your mysterious psychic rapport with that unknown female presence. Perhaps against his will, intertwined with and fortified by that hostile force pitted against you, he himself is strengthening your rapport, bolstered in opposition; and it is conceivable that your approaching him may well be detestable to him for the very reason that your spiritual essence is opposed to his will, or rather, contrary to some conventional intention of his, reawakens all the memories of that psychic rapport, bringing it to life."

The friends resolved to try by all means to approach the professor again, and perhaps finally resolve the mystery that had such a profound impact on Ferdinand's life. The very next morning they planned a second visit, but an unexpected letter from Ferdinand's father compelled him to travel without delay to B——; hours later he was already rushing off by postal coach, though he wrote to assure his friend that nothing would keep him from seeing him again in J—— at the latest in two weeks' time.

Ludwig found it very strange that, shortly after Ferdinand's departure, he learned from the same somewhat elderly gentleman who had first told him of Professor X——'s influence on the Talking Turk that the professor's weakness for mechanical artworks was a secondary pastime, and that his primary research, to which he devoted himself body and soul, delved into all aspects of natural science. The man praised the professor's musical discoveries in particular, which, however, he had to date revealed to no one. His secret laboratory was a lovely garden at the city's edge, and oftentimes passersby had heard the most peculiar tones and melodies resounding from behind the hedge, as though the garden were inhabited by fairies and spirits.

Two weeks went by, but Ferdinand did not come back, and finally two months later Ludwig received a letter that read as follows:

"Read, and be amazed, but be apprised of what you perhaps already suspected after, as I hope you did, getting closer to the professor. The horses are just being changed here in the village of P——, as I stand and peer mindlessly into the distance.

"A coach driving by halts in front of a nearby open church; a simply dressed woman climbs out, followed by a handsome young man in a Russian military huntsman's uniform bedecked with medals; two men climb out of a second coach. The postman remarks: 'This is the foreign couple our pastor is due to wed today.' Without thinking, I enter the church at the precise moment when the pastor bestows his blessing at the end of the marriage ceremony. I look over— the bride is the singer in my dream. She catches sight of me and goes pale, she faints; the man standing behind her catches her in his arms, it is Professor X——. What transpired thereafter I don't know, not even how I got here— you'll find it out from Professor X——. A calm and serenity such as I have never felt before has taken hold of my soul. The Turk's calamitous fortune-telling was a damned lie engendered by a haphazard sound tapping with a shoddy device. Have I really lost her? Is she not eternally mine in the glowing core of my heart of hearts? You will not hear from me for quite a while, as I'm bound for K——, and perhaps also headed to the far north in P——."

Reading between the lines of his friend's words, Ludwig surmised all too clearly his state of mind, and the entire business became all the more puzzling when he learned that Professor X—— had never left town.

"What if," he thought, "it was merely a matter of the conflicts between inexplicable psychological relations, in which several people were perhaps concurrently involved, that spilled out into life and thereby effected otherwise unconnected external occurrences, such that one of those people misconstrued the import of that twisted internal state, firmly believing it to be a manifestation of something in himself? But perhaps in the future the unspoken premonition I have of good things to come will spill out and fulfill itself in life in such a way as to comfort my friend! The Turk's fateful prediction has been fulfilled, and perhaps this very fulfillment fended off the crushing blow that threatened my friend."

"So," said Ottmar, as Theodor suddenly fell silent, "is that all? How does it all turn out? What finally happened to Ferdinand, Professor X———, the lovely songstress, and the Russian officer?"*

"Did I not say from the start," Theodor replied, "that I only intended to relate an enigmatic fragment? It seems to me, moreover, that the strange story of the Talking Turk must necessarily remain fragmentary. What I mean is, the reader's or listener's imagination should only receive a few hefty jolts and then string out the rest for itself. But should you, dear

* Inspired by Boccaccio's *The Decameron*, Hoffmann situated the tale of "The Automaton" in an overall fictional narrative frame of a four-volume collection of novellas and fairy tales titled *Die Serapionsbrüder* (The Serapion Brethren), in which a group of friends, Ottmar, Theodor, Lothar, Cyprian, Vinzenz, and Sylvester, tell one another stories. The title derives from an actual celebratory gathering of Hoffmann's friends at his home held on the feast day of Saint Serapion. The celebrants and members of the short-lived literary brotherhood included Hoffmann's friend and first biographer, Julius Eduard Hitzig, and authors Friedrich de la Motte Fouqué, Adelbert von Chamisso, and Karl Wilhelm Salice-Contessa.

Ottmar, seek reassurance as to Ferdinand's fate, you need merely recall the conversation concerning the opera which I read aloud some time ago. It's the selfsame Ferdinand, perfectly fit in body and mind, setting out with a lust for life, whom we encounter here in an earlier period of his life, so all must have turned out for the best with his somnambulist love affair.

The Sandman

1816

Nathaniel to Lothar

You must surely all be worried sick not to have had word from me in such a long time. Mother, no doubt, is mad at me, and Clara may well believe that I am living it up here, having forgotten my beloved angel whose face is so deeply and indelibly graven in my heart and mind. But it isn't so; every day of the week and every hour of the day I think of you all and my lovely little Clärchen's figure floats past me in my dreams, smiling so sweetly at me with her bright eyes as she is wont to do whenever I walk in. Oh, how could I put pen to paper in this wretched state that till now distracted my every thought! Something awful came into my life – dark premonitions of a terrible impending fate cast their pall over me like the shadows of black storm clouds impermeable to any friendly rays of sunlight. Let me tell you then what happened to me. I have to tell you, that much I know, but just the thought of it prompts a mad burst of laughter. Oh, my dearest Lothar! How should I begin to make you fathom that what befell me just a few days ago could have such a devastating effect on my life! If only you were here, you could see for yourself – but by now you must surely take me for a deranged seer of spooks. In short, the terrible thing that happened to me, whose fatal impression I have tried in vain to forget, is this: a few days ago, on October 30, at twelve noon, a barometer salesman stepped into my room and offered me his wares. I bought nothing and threatened to throw him down the stairs, but he left promptly on his own.

You suspect, I imagine, that only the most extraordinary life-altering relations could have lent this occurrence such significance, indeed that the very character of that miserable peddler could have so cut me to the quick. And that is just what happened. I will pull myself together with all the strength of my willpower to quietly and patiently recount the circumstances of my early youth as plainly and clearly as possible so that you, with your alert mind, may take everything in and paint as clear as possible a picture of my condition. But even now as I begin, I can hear you laughing and Clara remarking: "What childish notions!" Laugh, if you like, have yourself a right hearty laugh at my expense! Be my guest! But God in heaven, my hair stands on end, and it seems to me as if I were begging you in my mad desperation to make me sound ridiculous, like Franz Moor did Daniel.* But it's time to begin!

Except for at lunchtime, we, my siblings and I, saw little of my father during the day. He must have been very busy. After supper, which was served at seven o'clock as is customary, all of us, my mother included,

---

* A reference to characters in *Die Räuber*, a play by Friedrich Schiller (1759–1805).

gathered in my father's study, and each took our place at a round table. Father smoked and drank a tall glass of beer. Often he told us many wondrous tales and would get so involved in the telling that his pipe went out, and it was my duty to fetch a burning wad of paper for him to relight it, a task that gave me the greatest pleasure. But many times, he would just give us picture books to look at and sit there in silence, propped up in his easy chair, blowing dense clouds of smoke, so that we were all enveloped in a fog. On such evenings Mother was very sad, and no sooner did the clock strike nine than she would declare: "Now children, to bed! To bed with you! The Sandman's coming, I can sense it!" And every time she said it, I really did hear the sound of slow heavy steps lumbering up the stairs; it must have been the Sandman. One time, the muffled thump and lumbering step sounded particularly grim to me, so I asked Mother as she led us away: "Mama, who is that evil Sandman who always chases us away from Papa? What does he look like?"

"There is no Sandman, my dear child," replied Mother; "when I say the Sandman is coming, all it means is that you kids are sleepy and can't keep your eyes open, as if somebody had scattered sand in them."

Mother's answer didn't satisfy me, indeed the notion that Mother only denied the existence of the Sandman so that we wouldn't be afraid took firm hold of my childish imagination – didn't I hear him with my own two ears coming up the steps? With a burning desire to know more about this Sandman and his connection to us children, I finally asked the old woman who took care of my youngest sister: "What kind of man is that, the Sandman?"

"Oh, Thanelchen," she replied, "don't you know yet? He's a bad man who comes to visit children when they won't go to sleep and flings a handful of sand in their eyes, so they scratch themselves bloody. Then he flings them in his bag and carries them off to the half-moon to feed his children. They sit up there in their nest and have crooked beaks like owls with which they pick out the eyes of naughty human brats."

So in my mind I painted a grim picture of that awful Sandman; as soon as I heard that lumbering step on the stairs I trembled with fear and horror. My mother could get nothing out of me but that one word stuttered amidst tears: "Sandman! Sandman!" Then I bounded up to my bedroom, and all night long I was tormented by the terrible presence of the Sandman. By the time I was old enough to know that all that business about the Sandman and his children's nest on the half-moon the nanny had told me couldn't possibly be true, the Sandman had become entrenched in my mind as a hair-raising spook, and I was gripped by dread and terror when I heard him not only come clambering up the steps, but also tearing open the door to my father's study and barging in.

Sometimes he stayed away a long time, but then he came more often, night after night. This went on for years, but I was never able to get used to that ghastly spook, nor did the grisly image of the Sandman ever fade from my mind. I got steadily more and more worked up about his dealings with my father; while some insurmountable reserve kept me from asking him about it, the desire grew stronger from year to year to find out the secret for myself – to see the fabled Sandman with my own two eyes. The Sandman lured me down the path of wonder, made me crave adventure with a longing that had taken seed in my childish mind. I liked nothing better than to hear or read fear-tingling tales of goblins, witches, sprites, and such;

but the Sandman remained at the top of my list of the grisly figures I scribbled with chalk and charcoal on tabletops, cupboards, and walls.

When I turned ten, my mother moved me from the nursery into a little room off the corridor not far from my father's study. We still had to make ourselves scarce at the strike of nine, when that unseen presence was heard in the house. From my little room I distinctly heard him enter my father's chamber, and soon thereafter it seemed to me as if the entire house filled with a strange-smelling vapor. As my curiosity grew, so did my courage – I was determined to find a way to make the Sandman's acquaintance. I would slip out into the corridor as soon as Mother had passed, but I was too late. By the time I reached the spot from which I might catch a glimpse of him, the Sandman had invariably already entered my father's study. Finally, driven by an overpowering urge, I decided to hide in my father's room and await the Sandman's appearance.

One evening, by my father's silence and my mother's sadness, I surmised that the Sandman was coming. Pretending to be very tired, I excused myself before nine o'clock and hid in a nook beside my father's door. The front door creaked, the slow, heavy thud of steps advanced through the vestibule toward the stairs. Mother hastened by me with my brothers and sisters. Quietly, I opened my father's door. He was seated in silence, as usual, with his back to the door, and did not notice me slip in behind the curtain drawn over a closet where he hung his clothes. Closer, ever closer came the thud of the steps, there was a curious cough and a scraping and a grumbling outside. My heart beat double-time in terror and expectation. Right there at the door came a powerful kick, a hefty blow on the latch, the door sprung open with a bang! Gathering all my pluck, I peeked out with great trepidation. The Sandman was standing there in the middle of the room in front of my father, the bright glow of the lamps lighting up his face. So the Sandman, the terrible Sandman, was the old barrister Coppelius who sometimes dined with us for lunch.

But the most hideous figure could not have instilled a deeper sense of horror in me than this Coppelius. Imagine a large, broad-shouldered man with a misshapen clumpish head, an ochre-colored face, gray, bushy eyebrows, beneath which a pair of piercing, greenish cat's eyes peered forth, and a big nose bent down over the upper lip. His crooked mouth often twisted into a crafty snicker, at which dark red spots appeared on his cheeks and a curious hissing tone issued from between his clenched teeth. Coppelius always dressed in an old-fashioned ash-gray coat, a waistcoat, and pants of the same color, with black socks and shoes affixed with tiny buckles. His minuscule toupee hardly covered his skull, his curls hung out over his big red ears, and a big half-hidden tuft of hair poked out from the scruff of his neck so as to reveal the silver clasp of his collar. His entire appearance was altogether repulsive and disgusting; but what disgusted us children the most were his big, knotty, hairy fists, so much so that we were repelled by anything he'd touched. He noticed this and consequently took great pleasure in finding this or that excuse to graze a piece of cake or some sweet fruit that our dear mother surreptitiously dropped on our plate so that, with tears in our eyes, repulsion kept us from enjoying a sweet tidbit that we would otherwise have savored. He did that same thing when, on holidays, our father poured us a little glass of sweet wine. He would then pass his fist quickly over it, even bring the glass to his blue lips and laugh a devilish laugh when we quietly sniffled in anger. He always called us the little beasts; we were not permitted to make a sound in his presence, and we cursed the hideous and hostile man who intentionally and maliciously spoiled our little pleasures. Our mother seemed to hate that disgusting man as much as we did, for as soon as he appeared her high spirits and easygoing cheerful manner faded into a sad and dour solemnity. Father behaved in his presence as if he were a higher being whose incivility one had to tolerate and whom one had to humor in every way possible. He only dared make timid suggestions in his presence, and made sure to serve him his favorite dishes and the finest wines.

So when I set eyes on this Coppelius I felt a grim shudder in my soul at the sudden realization that no one but he could be the Sandman, but now the Sandman was no longer the fairy-tale bogeyman who dragged children off to feed to his young in the owl's nest on the moon— no!— he was a hideous, ghastly fiend who brought misery, rack, and ruin— temporal and eternal— wherever he appeared.

Positively paralyzed with fear at the thought of being caught and severely punished, I just stood there with my head outstretched, listening through the curtain. My father received Coppelius respectfully. "Up now – to work!" the latter cried with a hoarse snarl, throwing off his coat. In grim-faced silence, father flung off his dressing gown and both men pulled on long black frocks. I didn't see where they came from. Father opened the folding door of a wall closet; but then I noticed that what I had long taken for a wall closet was not one at all, but rather a dark hidden space fitted with a small hearth. Coppelius stepped forward and a blue flame flickered up. All kinds of curious instruments were scattered about. Dear God! When my old father bent down toward the fire, he looked altogether different. A ghastly convulsive pain seemed to have twisted the gentle, honest features of his face into a devilish grimace. He looked just like Coppelius, who swung the red-hot tongs and fetched a bright flickering mass of ore out of the thick vapor, which he then assiduously hammered. It seemed to me as if human faces became visible all about, but without eyes – dreadful, deep, black hollows where the eyes ought to be.

"Eyes out, eyes out!" Coppelius cried with a muffled roaring voice. Gripped by wild terror, I let out a scream and burst out of my hiding place onto the floor. Coppelius grabbed hold of me and, baring his teeth, grumbled, "Little beast! Little beast!" Picking me up, he hurled me at the hearth so that the flames singed my hair. "Now we've got eyes— eyes— a lovely pair of children's eyes," Coppelius whispered. With his fists he grabbed glowing cinders from the flames which he was about to sprinkle in my eyes, when my father raised his hands, folded as in prayer.

"Master! Master! Let my Nathaniel keep his eyes! Let him keep them, I beg you!"

Coppelius let out a burst of shrill laughter. "Let the boy keep his eyes and whimper his lesson through life; but let us take a close look at the mechanism of the hands and feet." Whereupon he grasped me so hard that my joints snapped, twisted off my hands and feet, and reattached them here and there. He sputtered and lisped, "It's not right this way! 'Twas good the way it was!—The old man got it right!" Everything around me went dark, a sharp cramp flashed through my nerves and limbs— and then I felt nothing.

A warm and gentle breath wafted over my face, and I awakened as if from the sleep of death with my mother bent over me.

"Is the Sandman still here?" I stammered.

"No, my dear child, he's been gone a long long time, he won't hurt you!" my mother said, kissing and cuddling her recuperated little darling.

Why should I try your patience, my dearest Lothar! Why should I keep babbling in minute detail when there's still so much to be told? Suffice to say that I was caught eavesdropping and was mishandled by Coppelius. Fear and trembling had fetched me a high fever, with which I lay sick for several weeks. "Is the Sandman still here?" — That was the first clear word to issue from my lips and the sign of my recovery, my salvation. Let me just tell you the most terrible moment of my youth, then you'll be convinced that it's not the failing of my eyes that makes everything appear colorless, but rather that a dark destiny has really draped a veil of clouds over my life, which perhaps I may only rip through in death.

Coppelius stopped coming by; we were told that he'd left town.

It was about a year later, as we sat one evening at the round table, true to our old family custom. Father was very chipper and entertained us with delightful stories from the travels of his youth. Then, at the strike of nine, we heard the front door hinges creak and slow, leaden steps thumped through the hallways and up the stairs.

"It's Coppelius," said Mother, going pale in the face.

"Yes, it is Coppelius," Father confirmed with a weak and broken voice.

Tears streamed from Mother's eyes. "But Father, Father!" she cried, "must it be so?"

"This one last time," he replied, "it's the last time he comes here, I promise you. Just go, go with the children!— Go!— Go to bed! Good night!"

I felt like I'd been pressed into cold, heavy stone— my breath stood still! Mother grabbed hold of my arm when I remained standing there, motionless. "Come, Nathaniel, come along, please!" I let her lead me into my room. "Be quiet, be quiet, just go to bed!— sleep— sleep," Mother cried after me, but torn as I was by my inner fear and turmoil, I could not close an eye. The image of that hated, repulsive Coppelius stood there snickering at me with his sparkling eyes. In vain, I tried to erase the image from my mind. It must have been midnight already when a terrible boom went off, as if a cannon had been fired. The whole house rumbled, something rattled and roared past my door, and the front door slammed shut with a mighty clatter.

"That's Coppelius!" I cried out in terror, and leapt from my bed. Then came a piercing shriek and a wretched wail, and I rushed to my father's room. The door stood open, and a suffocating steam hit me in the face. The chambermaid cried out: "Oh, the master! The master!" In front of the steaming hearth, my father lay dead on the floor, his contorted face burnt black. My sisters howled and moaned around him, my mother lay unconscious at his side. "Coppelius, you cursed Satan, you killed my father!" I cried out, and immediately lost consciousness.

Two days later, when they laid my father in his coffin, his expression was once again mild and gentle as it had been in life. It was at least comforting to think that his pact with that devilish Coppelius could not have condemned him to eternal damnation.

The explosion had awakened the neighbors; the incident seemed suspicious to them, and they informed the authorities, who issued a warrant for Coppelius's arrest. But he had disappeared without a trace.

If I tell you now, my dearest friend, that the barometer salesman was none other than the accursed Coppelius, you will not, I trust, think ill of me for taking his inimical reappearance as a sign of bad things to come. He was dressed differently, but Coppelius's physique and facial features are too deeply engraved in my memory for me to mistake him for another. Moreover, Coppelius did not even change his name. He now pretends to be a Piedmontese mechanic and calls himself Giuseppe Coppola.

I have resolved to confront him and to avenge my father's death, come what will.

Don't tell your mother a thing about that terrible creature. Give a hug to my dear sweet Clara, I'll write her when I've calmed down a bit. Be well, etc. etc.

Clara to Nathaniel

It is true that you haven't written to me in quite a while, but I still believe that you think of me and hold me dear. I was surely very much on your mind, for though you intended to send your last letter to my brother Lothar, you unwittingly addressed it to me, not him. I tore open the envelope with joy and only realized the error upon reading the words: "Oh, my dearest Lothar." I know I ought not to have gone on reading after that, but rather to have handed the letter to my brother. But seeing as you sometimes reproached me in a childish teasing way that I had such a calm, ladylike, sensible disposition that, before fleeing a house about to collapse I would be inclined to quickly smooth out a wrinkle in the curtain, I dare hardly admit that the first lines of your letter upset me profoundly. I could hardly breathe— my eyes went blank. Oh, my dearest Nathaniel! What terrible thing could have burst into your life! Being separated from you, the possibility of never seeing you again, that thought pierced my breast like the sharp blade of a dagger. I read and read! Your description of that disgusting Coppelius is really horrible. Only now do I fathom that your dear old father died such a terrible and violent death. My brother Lothar, to whom I passed the letter, tried in vain to calm me down. The image of that despicable barometer peddler Giuseppe Coppola pursued me wherever I went, and I am almost ashamed to admit that he even managed to trouble my ordinarily unruffled and restful sleep with all sorts of nightmarish phantasms. But soon thereafter, in fact by the very next day, my mood calmed down. Don't be mad at me, my dearest one, if Lothar tells you that despite your strange premonition that Coppelius would harm you, I am once again my old cheerful, carefree self.

Let me confess here and now my firm conviction that all the awful and frightening things you speak of only happened in your imagination, and that the real outside world played little part in it. That old Coppelius may well have been repulsive enough, but the fact that he hated children made you and your siblings develop a real aversion to him.

Your childish imagination naturally associated your nanny's nursery account of the terrible Sandman with old Coppelius who remained a fantastic monster of the kind children fear so intensely, even though you didn't believe in the Sandman. The weird goings-on with your father at night were surely nothing other than alchemical experiments the two conducted together in secret, which would have vexed your mother since not only was a lot of money no doubt squandered in the process but, as is always the case with such laboratory assistants, your father became so consumed by the elusive craving for higher wisdom that he forgot about the family. Your father probably brought about his own death by a careless mistake, and Coppelius is not to blame. Can you believe that yesterday I asked the pharmacist next door if such a sudden deadly explosion ever occurred during chemical experiments? He said: "Yes, indeed," and described for me in his typical long-winded and minute manner how such a thing could happen, and in the process cited all kinds of curious-sounding substances I cannot now recall. Now you'll get angry with your Clara. You'll say: "Not a ray of the mysterious that embraces us with its invisible arms could break into that cold nature of yours. You only focus on the colorful surface of things and take a childish delight in the glittering golden fruit whose flesh contains a deadly poison hidden within."

Oh, my dearly beloved Nathaniel! Don't you think that even a cheerful, unaffected, carefree nature like mine could harbor an inkling of a dark force that insidiously strives to corrupt the sanctum of our inner self? But forgive me if, innocent girl that I am, I dare imply what I really think of that inner battle. I can't find the right words to say it and you're probably laughing at me, not because I mean to say something foolish, but because I am having such a hard time saying it.

If there is a dark force that can insidiously slip a perfidious filament into our innermost self to grab hold of us and drag us along on a dangerously destructive path that we would not otherwise have taken – if there is such a force, then it must reconfigure itself in our image, indeed it must become us; only in *this* way will we be inclined to believe in it and give it the space it needs to realize its shadowy end. If we have enough good sense, fortified by healthy living, to recognize strange and hostile influences as such, and to steadfastly hold to the path our nature and calling prescribe, then that sinister force will fail in the futile attempt to fashion itself in our image. It is also certain, Lothar adds, that we surrender ourselves to that dark physical force, it often makes us internalize strange figures that life flings into our path, so that we merely rouse the spirit which our vivid delusion makes us believe emanates from that figure. It is the phantom of our own self whose deep affinity and profound influence on our state of mind either damns us to hell or uplifts us into heaven.

You see, my beloved Nathaniel, that we, my brother Lothar and I, discussed at length the subject of dark forces and compulsions, a subject on which I have taken great pains to formulate an outline, and which now seems to me to be very profound indeed. I don't quite grasp Lothar's last point, though I have a sense of what he means and firmly believe it to be true. I beg you, erase the image of that ugly barrister Coppelius and the barometer peddler Giuseppe Coppola from your mind. Be assured that these strange figures have no power over you; only your belief in their malevolent power can, in fact, make them malevolent to you. If the deep upset of your soul did not cry out in every line of your letter, if your state of mind did not shake me up as profoundly as it does, in truth I could make light of your Mr. Sandman, Esq. and that barometer peddler Coppelius. Be cheerful— cheerful! I have decided to come to you and act as your guardian angel, and should that repulsive Coppelius dare reappear and trouble you again in your dreams, I will exorcize him with loud laughter. I am not in the least bit afraid of him and his loathsome fists, he will not spoil a tender tidbit with his barrister's touch or steal my eyes as the Sandman.

Forever, my dearly beloved Nathaniel, etc. etc. etc.

Nathaniel to Lothar

I am very sorry that – granted, on account of my own absentminded mistake – Clara recently tore open and read the letter I wrote to you. She wrote me a very profound philosophical response in which she took great pains to prove that Coppelius and Coppola only existed in my imagination and were phantoms of my own troubled self, phantoms that would be instantaneously reduced to dust if only I recognized them as such. It is indeed hard to believe that the spirit that emanates from such brightly smiling, sweet, innocent eyes could display such brilliant insight. She cites you. So you talked about me. You instruct her in logic so that she may learn to sort and filter out the wheat from the chaff. Better leave it alone! By the way, it's certain that the barometer peddler Giuseppe Coppola is not the old lawyer Coppelius. I've just begun attending the lectures of the recently arrived professor of physics, who, like the illustrious naturalist, is also named Spallanzani, and is of Italian descent. He has known Coppola for a good many years and, moreover, you can tell from the peddler's accent that he really is Piedmontese. Coppelius was a German, but no true-blue one, I think. I'm still not completely calmed down. Even if you and Clara take me for a dark dreamer, I cannot erase the terrible impression of Coppelius's accursed face. I'm glad, as Spallanzani claims, that Coppelius has flown the coop. This professor is a wondrous sort – a round little man with high cheekbones, a finely chiseled nose, pouting lips and small, piercing eyes. But you can get a clearer picture of him if you look at Chodowiecki's portrait of Cagliostro in any Berlin pocket calendar – that's just what Spallanzani looks like.

Recently, while climbing the steps to the lecture hall, I discovered that the glass door that is ordinarily covered with a curtain left a visible crack open at the side. A tall, very slender, well-proportioned, and splendidly dressed lady sat in the room at a little table on which she rested both her arms, her hands folded before her. She was seated just opposite the door, so that I got a good look at her angelically lovely face. She did not seem to notice me, and in fact her eyes were somewhat glassy— I'd almost be inclined to say they could not see. It seemed to me as if she were sleeping with open eyes. I felt the strangest rush of feeling, and therefore slipped quietly off to the auditorium next door. Later, I learned that the lovely figure I spotted was Spallanzani's daughter Olympia, whom for some strange reason he keeps locked up so that no one can come near her. I've begun to think there is something peculiar about her, that perhaps she's simple-minded. But why do I write you about all this? I could have told it to you more clearly and in greater detail in person. I might as well admit that I'll be visiting you in two weeks' time. I simply had to see my sweet angel-faced Clara again. By then the ill humor brought on (I must admit) by that annoyingly understanding letter of hers that sought to sound my depths will have blown over. Which is why I'm not writing to her today.

A thousand greetings, etc. etc. etc.

It would be impossible to imagine anything more incredible or more strange than what happened to my poor friend, the young student Nathaniel, which, dear reader, I have undertaken to tell you. Have you, gentle reader, ever experienced anything that so completely permeated your heart, your mind, and your thoughts that it supplanted all other notions? Something that simmered and seethed in you, that made your blood boil and flow like lava through your veins, and made your cheeks turn a fiery red. A thing that turned your gaze so eerie, as if it sought to grasp the presence of figures imperceptible to all other eyes in an empty room, as your words melted into dark sighs. Your nearest and dearest asked you, "What is it, friend? What on earth is the matter with you?" And you wanted to describe your state of mind in all the glowing colors and shadows and lights, and strained to find the words, and didn't know where to begin. But it seemed to you as if with your very first word you felt compelled to evoke all the wondrous, beautiful, horrible, laughable, frightening things that happened, so that your account would strike your listeners like an electric shock. But every word that came to mind, anything that language could conjure up, seemed colorless, frigid, and dead. You searched and searched, and stuttered and stammered, and the sensible questions of friends struck like icy gusts of wind that soon dissipated in the emotional cauldron within. But had you, like a bold painter, begun with a few audacious brushstrokes to set down the rough outline of your state, you would have easily been able to apply with great ease ever brighter dabs of color, so as to dazzle your friends with the living swirl of multifarious figures, and that they would see themselves, as you see yourself, in the middle of the picture that issued from your imagination.

No one, I must admit, gentle reader, ever actually asked after the story of young Nathaniel; but as you well know, I am one of those rum writers who, if burdened with impressions of the kind I've just described, feels as if anyone who happens to cross their path, indeed the whole world, is dying to know, "What's bothering you? Pray tell us if you please!"

So, I felt a pressing need to speak to you of Nathaniel's fateful path. The very wondrousness and strangeness of it consumed my consciousness, but for that very reason, and because I needed to make you, dear reader, likewise inclined and therefore able to bear the things I am about to tell, which is no small feat, I tormented myself as to how to begin my account in a significant, original, gripping fashion. "Once upon a time" – the nicest start to any tale – seemed too vapid! "In the small provincial town of S—— there lived…" – sounded a bit better, at least informative enough to pave the way for the climax. Or to begin right off *in media res*: "'The devil take you!' the young student Nathaniel cried out with a wild-eyed look of anger and dread at the sight of the barometer peddler Giuseppe Coppola"— this I had, in fact, already written down when I was suddenly struck by something droll in the wild-eyed look of the young student Nathaniel— but the story is not in the least bit comical. I could find no words to reflect even the faintest glimmer of the burning heart of the matter. So I decided to dispense with the beginning. Just take the three letters, gentle reader, that my friend Lothar was kind enough to pass on to me, as the outline of the picture, to which I will take pains to add more and more color in the telling. Maybe I will manage, like a good portrait painter, to conjure up a character such that you will find a convincing resemblance without knowing the original – indeed, that it will seem to you as if you had seen that person many times with your own two eyes. Maybe then, dear reader, you will believe that there is nothing more wondrous or more strange than life itself, and that all that the poet can do is convey a dark reflection of it in a lightly buffed mirror.

So as to clarify what the reader needs to know from the start, I must add to the aforementioned letters that shortly after the death of Nathaniel's father, Clara and Lothar, the children of a distant relative who likewise died and left them orphaned, were taken in by Nathaniel's mother. Clara and Nathaniel took a great liking to each other, to which no person on earth objected; they were therefore betrothed when Nathaniel left home to pursue his studies in G——, which is where we find him in his last letter, attending lectures by the famous professor of physics Spallanzani.

Now I could confidently press on with the tale; but at the moment I have such a vivid image of Clara's face before my eyes that I cannot look away, which is what always happened when she looked my way with her lovely smile. Clara could by no means have been considered beautiful; such was the opinion of all those who claimed to know a thing or two about beauty. And yet the architects of beauty praised the sleekness and symmetry of her stature, painters found her neck, shoulders, and bust almost too maidenly, but all were enamored of her Magdalen hair and raved about her luminous coloring. One of them, a real romantic, strangely enough compared Clara's eyes to a Ruisdael lake in which the azure-blue of a cloudless sky and the forest and flowering flora of the lush landscape of life were mirrored. Poets and thinkers were even more ebullient and said, "What lake – what mirror! Can one gaze at this girl without sensing heavenly music streaming from her eyes, music that reaches deep into our innermost selves, awakening and bestirring all our dormant passions? If we ourselves try to sing her praises and the song falls flat – a crude croon, a jumble of haphazard notes masquerading as a serenade – the fault is ours; Clara's lips say it all in their delicate smile.

That's the way it was. Clara had the healthy imagination of a cheerful, unaffected child, a deep, womanly, gentle disposition, and a downright sparkling sharp-sighted intelligence. The mystics and conjurers failed to impress her; for without saying much – idle chatter was anathema to her quiet nature – her bright gaze and that hint of irony in her smile said, "Dear friends, do you really expect me to take your ephemeral shadow figures for real live people with impulses and emotions?" For that reason, Clara was scorned by many as cold, emotionless, prosaic; but others with a sober grasp of all the twists and turns of life had a powerful affection for that tender, understanding, childlike girl, though none more so than Nathaniel, a young man seriously and passionately committed to the study of science and the arts. Clara was attached to her beloved with all her heart and soul, but when he went away to study, the first storm clouds troubled their life. With what rapture then, you can well imagine, did she fly into his arms when, as he let slip in his last letter to Lothar, he actually showed up in his hometown at his mother's doorstep. It was just as Nathaniel expected – as soon as he saw Clara again, he forgot all about the lawyer Coppelius and Clara's letter, and his upset disappeared.

Nevertheless, Nathaniel was right when he wrote to his friend Lothar that the appearance of that odious barometer peddler Coppola had had a damaging effect on his life. Everyone felt within days of his arrival that Nathaniel was a changed man. He fell into dark brooding spells and began to behave strangely, in ways that one would never have expected of him. Everything, his entire life, had become the stuff of dream and premonition; he kept saying that everyone who gave free rein to his fancies merely served as a plaything in the terrible game of dark forces, that all resistance was in vain, and all one could do was to meekly submit to the will of fate. He went so far as to maintain that it was foolish to believe that spontaneity could affect the arbitrary outcome of artistic and scientific investigations; he claimed that the passion needed to pursue such work does not come from our innermost selves, but rather from the external influence of a higher principle independent of our own free will.

Such mystical musings were altogether repugnant to the sensible Clara, yet it seemed futile to attempt to prove him wrong. It was only when Nathaniel insisted that Coppelius was the incarnation of the evil principal that had taken hold of him, pulling the strings from behind an invisible curtain, that Clara suddenly fathomed that this disgusting demon threatened to disrupt their happy love, grew very serious, and said: "Yes, Nathaniel, you're right, Coppelius is an evil and inimical principal, a devilish force that infiltrated your life, able to do dreadful things, but only if you refuse to banish him from your thoughts and feelings. As long as you believe in him, he does indeed exist and affect you; only your belief gives him the power over you."

Furious that Clara only accepted the existence of demons as a function of his state of mind, Nathaniel wanted to counter with a disquisition on the entire mystical teachings of devils and uncanny forces, but Clara, vexed in turn, cut him short by suddenly bringing up some altogether irrelevant matter, which made Nathaniel all the more angry. Those with cold, unreceptive hearts could not access such deep secrets, Nathaniel thought, without fully fathoming that he counted Clara among those with these lesser natures, which is why he did not stop trying to initiate her into those secret teachings. Early in the morning, when Clara helped prepare breakfast, he stood by her and read to her from all sorts of mystical texts, whereupon Clara protested. "But my dear Nathaniel, what if I were to blame *you* for the evil principal that's keeping my coffee from brewing? For if, as you wish, I were to drop everything and look you in the eyes as you read to me, then my coffee will boil over and burn and you won't get your breakfast!" Nathaniel slammed the book shut and ran in a rage to his room.

In the past he had had a charming talent for reading aloud the stories that he jotted down, to which Clara listened with the greatest pleasure; now his writings were dark, incomprehensible, shapeless, so that even though Clara said nothing, not wanting to hurt him, he sensed how unreceptive she was. Nothing was more deadly for Clara than this boring stuff; in every look and word she revealed her insurmountable intellectual ennui. Nathaniel's writings were indeed a crashing bore. His chagrin at Clara's cold, prosaic spirit grew; she simply could not shake off her displeasure at Nathaniel's dark, morbid, tiresome mysticism; and so the two drifted inwardly further and further apart without noticing it. Nathaniel himself had to admit that the figure of that repulsive Coppelius faded in his imagination, so that he had to take great pains to paint a vivid picture of him in his writings, in which he appeared as the bogeyman. Finally, he felt compelled to express that dark premonition that Coppelius would disrupt his happy love as the subject of a poem. In the poem he represented himself and Clara as bound by true love, but every now and then it was as if a dark fist reached into their life and ripped out any seed of joy that sprouted in the garden of their hearts. Finally, when they are already standing together at the marriage altar, that terrible Coppelius appears and touches Clara's sweet smiling eyes; they burst open against his breast, searing and burning like bloody sparks, where-upon Coppelius seizes Nathaniel and flings him into a flaming circle of fire that spins at the speed of lightning and hurls him about. Then comes a roar, as if the angry tempest whipped up the foaming waves of the sea so that they rear up in battle like white-hooded black giants. But through this wild roar he hears Clara's voice: "Can you not see me? Coppelius deceived you, those were not my eyes that burned in your breast, they were the glowing drops of your own heart's blood – I still have my eyes, just look at me!" And Nathaniel thinks: "It *is* Clara, and I am hers forever." Then it is as if the thought reaches into the circle of fire, stops suddenly, and the roar fades into a dull thud in the black abyss. Nathaniel peers into Clara's eyes; but it is the face of death that smiles back at him.

While engaged in the composition of this poem Nathaniel remained very quiet and collected, he polished and tinkered with every line, and since he chose to follow the rule of meter, he did not rest until everything fit together and sounded just right. When he was finally done with it and read the poem out loud to himself, he was totally appalled and, gripped by a wild sense of horror, cried out: "Whose terrible voice is this?" But soon the whole thing just seemed to him to be a very successful poetic text, and he was convinced that it would excite Clara's cold heart, although he failed to consider just where her excitement might lead and to what end he wished to frighten her with such gruesome images foreshadowing a terrible fate that would tear their love apart.

They sat together in his mother's little garden, Clara as cheerful as could be, because Nathaniel had not tormented her with his dreams and dark premonitions for the last three days, which he'd spent tinkering with the poem. Even Nathaniel spoke in a lively and spirited manner of funny things, like before, so that Clara said: "Now at last I have you all to myself again, you see how we drove out that repulsive Coppelius?" That reminded Nathaniel of the poem in his pocket which he'd intended to read aloud. He promptly pulled out the pages and started reading. Expecting the same tedious stuff as before, and prepared to endure it, Clara started quietly knitting. But as the storm cloud of his verse grew ever darker and darker around them, she let the knitted stocking sink into her lap and looked Nathaniel hard in the eye. Swept along by the fire of his poetry, his cheeks tinted bright red by the cauldron of stirred-up emotions, tears welled up in his eyes. Having finally reached the conclusion, he heaved a heavy sigh of exhaustion, gripped Clara's hand and sobbed, as though dissolving in inconsolable sadness: "Oh, Clara... Clara!"

She pressed him gently to her breast and said quietly, but very slowly and succinctly: "Nathaniel— my darling Nathaniel— throw that raving, senseless, insane fairy tale into the fire."

Nathaniel leapt up in a fury and, shoving Clara away from him, cried out, "You lifeless, cursed automaton!"

He ran off, leaving Clara completely mortified, weeping bitter tears. "He never loved me, he doesn't understand me!" she wailed at the top of her lungs. Lothar came striding into the arbor. Clara felt compelled to tell him what happened. Lothar loved his sister with all his heart; every word of her accusation struck him like a spark, so that the ill will he'd long felt for that muddle-headed Nathaniel now flared up into wild anger. He ran to find him, reproached him with harsh words for his inexplicable treatment of his beloved sister, and the irascible Nathaniel replied in kind. A wild and crazy fop faced off with a miserable, mundane man of the people. A duel was inevitable. They decided, according to the local academic custom, to meet behind the garden and draw sharp-bladed rapiers. Silently and stealthily they slipped by; Clara had heard and seen the heated argument, and spotted the dueling master bringing by the rapiers at dusk. She guessed what was about to happen. Lothar and Nathaniel had just reached the dueling ground and flung off their coats in brooding silence, a bloodthirsty fury pouring from their burning eyes, when Clara came bounding through the garden gate.

Sobbing, she cried, "Oh you barbaric beastly men! Cut me down right this moment before going at it with each other; for how am I supposed to go on living in this world if my beloved murders my brother, or my brother my beloved!"

Lothar let his sword sink and peered at the ground in silence, and all the heartrending love Nathaniel had felt in the sweet days of youth for his precious Clara once again flared up in him. The deadly weapon fell from his hand, he flung himself at Clara's feet. "Can you ever forgive me, my only, my beloved Clara! Can you forgive me, my dearest brother Lothar!"

Lothar was stirred by the profound pain of his friend; the three young people, now reconciled, embraced in a flood of tears and swore henceforth to faithfully hold by their love.

Nathaniel felt as though a heavy weight that had pressed him to the ground had been lifted from his shoulders, as though in resisting the dark force that had held him in its sway he had saved his entire being from the threat of annihilation. He spent three more blissful days with his nearest and dearest, and then rode back to G—— where he had to complete another year of study before returning for good to his native town.

Everything having to do with Coppelius was kept from his mother, since the three friends knew all too well that she could not think of him without trembling since, like Nathaniel, she too blamed him for the death of her husband.

Imagine how stunned Nathaniel was when, upon returning to his apartment, he found the entire building burned to the ground, so that only the charred walls still rose from the rubble heap. Braving the fire that had started in the laboratory of the apothecary on the first floor and then engulfed the house in flames from the bottom up, a few hale and hearty friends had nevertheless managed to dash up to Nathaniel's room and save his books, manuscripts, and instruments. They succeeded in carrying everything intact to another house where they rented a room for him, and where Nathaniel promptly moved in. He was not particularly surprised to discover that he lived directly opposite Professor Spallanzani, nor did it seem strange to him when he realized that from his window he could peer directly into the room in which Olympia often sat alone, positioned such that he could clearly recognize her figure, though her facial features remained blurred and vague. But after a while, it did strike him as strange that Olympia often sat for hours on end before a small table, perched in the same position she had been in when he once glimpsed her through the glass door, apparently engaged in no activity but clearly casting a fixed gaze in his direction. He likewise had to admit to himself that he had never set eyes on a lovelier female figure. But holding true to Clara in his heart, he remained largely oblivious to the allures of stiff and stone-cold Olympia, only every now and then casting furtive looks over his open compendium at the lovely statue – that was all.

He was just writing to Clara when he heard a light knock. Upon his invitation to enter, the door swung open a crack and Coppola's repulsive face peered in. Nathaniel felt a shudder of terror run through him. Mindful, however, of what Spallanzani had told him about his compatriot Coppola, and that he had given his sacred word to his beloved to lend no more credence to the Sandman Coppelius, he himself was ashamed of his childish fears; with a great effort he pulled himself together and spoke as calmly as possible, "I'm not going to buy a barometer, my dear friend, so you might as well be going!"

Coppola, however, stepped squarely into the room and spoke with a hoarse voice, his broad mouth twisted into an ugly laughter, his sparkling little eyes casting a piercing look beneath the wink of his long gray lashes. "Forget barometer, bah! I bring pair o' lovely peepers!"

Horrified, Nathaniel exclaimed, "Strange man, how can you have eyes for sale? Eyes? Eyes?"

But then and there Coppola shoved aside his barometers, reached into his deep coat pocket, and pulled out spectacles and eyeglasses which he laid out on the table. "Look— glass, glass, what you put on your nose, eyes a pretty, eyes a pretty!" At this, he pulled out more and more eyeglasses, so that the entire table was soon flickering and sparkling. A thousand eyes peeped and twitched and stared at Nathaniel, but he was unable to turn away from the table, and Coppola kept laying out more and more eyeglasses, and those glaring gazes landed ever wilder, helter-skelter, shooting their blood-red rays at Nathaniel's breast.

Overcome by frantic horror, Nathaniel cried, "Stop it! Stop it, you wretched creature!" He grabbed the man by the arm, even as Coppola, oblivious, reached yet again into his pocket to fetch more glasses to add to the heap that covered the table.

But Coppola shook himself free, and with hoarse, repulsive laughter, muttered, "Oh! This not for you! But look here, lovely glass!" And with that, he swept up all the eyeglasses, shoved them back into his coat pocket, and from another pocket pulled out a number of big and little telescopes and field glasses. As soon as the eyeglasses were out of sight, Nathaniel grew calm again and, mindful of Clara's words, had to admit to himself that the terrible spook was a figment of his own imagination, and that Coppola was an altogether honest craftsman and lens grinder, and could not possibly be Coppelius's cursed doppelgänger and shadow figure. He realized, moreover, that there was nothing strange about all the lenses that Coppola now laid out on the table, nothing ghastly like the eyeglasses. To make amends,

Nathaniel now decided to actually buy something from him. He reached for a small, very finely crafted pocket spyglass, and to test it, peered out the window. Never in his life had he come upon a spyglass that so cleanly and sharply brought distant objects before his eyes in such clear focus. He unintentionally peered into Spallanzani's room; Olympia sat there, as usual, at the little table, with her arms resting on it and her hands folded. Now for the first time Nathaniel espied Olympia's exquisitely lovely face. Only her eyes seemed strange – blank and dead. But as he brought her face in the spyglass into greater and greater focus, it seemed to him as if Olympia's eyes flashed open in moist moonbeams. It seemed as if she had only now acquired the power of sight; her glances grew livelier and livelier. Nathaniel lingered at the window, transfixed, unable to take his eyes off the lovely Olympia. He was awakened, as if out of a deep dream, by the sound of throat clearing and scraping. Coppola stood behind him.

"*Tre zecchini* – three ducats!" Nathaniel, who had completely forgotten the optician, quickly counted out the asking price. "Fine glass, fine glass – is it not!?" asked Coppola with his repulsive hoarse voice and his crafty smile.

"Yes, yes, indeed!" Nathaniel replied, greatly vexed. "Adieu, dear friend!" But Coppola cast several strange sidelong looks at Nathaniel and his room before taking his leave. The young man could still hear him laughing out loud on the stairway. "All right," Nathaniel muttered to himself, "he's laughing at me because I no doubt paid far too much for the little spyglass – far too much!" As he quietly whispered these words, a deep groan like that of a dying man resounded in the room. Nathaniel was so frightened he stopped breathing. But the sound had emanated from his own throat. "Clara's quite right," he said to himself, "to take me for a ridiculous, ghost-haunted idiot; it's perfectly insane, completely cockamamie of me to let the thought that I paid Coppola too much for the spyglass unnerve me to such a degree – and for no reason at all."

Then he sat himself down to finish writing the letter to Clara, but a glance out the window confirmed that Olympia was still seated as before, and then and there, driven by an irresistible urge, he jumped up, grabbed Coppola's spyglass, and remained glued to the window, riveted by Olympia's alluring visage, until his friend Siegmund called that it was time to come along to Professor Spallanzani's lecture. The next day the curtain was pulled shut in that fateful room across the way, and he could not catch sight of Olympia on that day or on the following two days, despite the fact that he seldom left his own window and constantly kept peering over with Coppola's spyglass. On the third day, even the blinds were pulled closed. Desperately pining and driven by a burning desire, he ran out to her front door. Impressions of Olympia's lovely figure hung in the air everywhere he looked; she stepped out from behind the bushes and the reflection of her big sparkling eyes beamed out at him from the clear brook. Clara's image had been totally erased from his heart – he thought of nothing but Olympia and wailed at the top of his lungs, "Oh you, my shining star of love, did you appear before me only to vanish again and leave me in the dark and desperate night?"

As he was about to return to his room, he became aware of noisy goings-on in Spallanzani's house. The doors were open, all kinds of devices were being carried in, the windows on the first floor were likewise open wide, busy housemaids swept and dusted the window boxes with large brooms while inside, carpenters and decorators banged and hammered. Stunned, Nathaniel remained standing there in the street; then Siegmund came over to him and said, laughing, "So what do you say about our old Spallanzani now?" Nathaniel assured him that he had nothing to say, since he knew absolutely nothing about the professor, but that he was rather surprised to discover such wild activity and housekeeping frenzy in that ordinarily dark and silent house. Siegmund informed him that Spallanzani was going to throw a big party the next day, including a concert and a ball, and that half the university was invited. The word was that Spallanzani was going to let his daughter Olympia, whom he'd fearfully kept sheltered from view, make her public debut.

Nathaniel received an invitation, and at the appointed hour, as carriages rolled up and lights shimmered in the elegantly decorated rooms, presented himself at the professor's house with a fast-beating heart. The party was large and glamorous. Olympia appeared, richly and tastefully attired. Everyone had to admire her finely chiseled face and graceful figure, although the strange stoop of her back and her bone-thin waist appeared to be the consequence of a too tightly tied girdle. There was a measured stiffness in her stance and step that some found displeasing, but that was ascribed to the stress of appearing in society. The concert began, Olympia played the grand piano with great skill and likewise brought off an *aria di bravura* with a clear, almost bell-like, pitch-perfect voice. Nathaniel was completely captivated; he stood in the last row and could not clearly make out Olympia's features in the candlelight. Without attracting notice, he therefore pulled out Coppola's spyglass and gazed through its lens at the lovely Olympia. Oh God! He now understood how ardently she gazed in his direction, how every note only seemed to sound clearly enveloped in a loving look that surged through his burning heart. The artful trills rang out in Nathaniel's ear like the heavenly hosannas of the spirit transfigured by love. When at last, following the cadenza, the long trill pierced the air all around him, he felt as though suddenly enveloped by her warm embrace. No longer able to control himself, he cried out in rapture and pain: "Olympia!" All heads turned to look at him, some laughing.

The cathedral organist twisted his face into an even dourer grimace than before and merely remarked: "Now, now!" The concert came to an end, and the ball began. Only to dance with her— with *her*! That was now the object of Nathaniel's deepest desire, all that he strove for; but how would he get up the gumption to ask her, the queen of the evening, for a dance? And yet – he himself had no idea how it happened – he found himself standing right there beside Olympia just as the music was starting up, and she had not yet been invited to dance. Hardly able to stammer a few words, he reached for her hand. It was ice cold, and he felt a terrible deathly frost surge through him. He looked into her eyes that greeted his gaze with love and longing, and at that very moment it was as if the pulse began to beat in her cold hand and the lifeblood began to glow warm within. As love's longing welled up, glowing hotter and hotter in Nathaniel's breast, he wrapped his arm around lovely Olympia and led her down the rows of dancers.

He had always thought himself to be a good dancer, able to hold to the beat, but from the altogether precise rhythmic steadiness of Olympia's step that often caused him to falter, he soon fathomed the failing of his sense of time. And yet he no longer wanted to dance with any other woman in the world, and felt like he would have killed on the spot anyone else who dared approach her to ask for a dance. But this happened only twice and, to his amazement, Olympia always remained seated until the next dance, when he did not hesitate to reach for her hand and pull her up again and again.

Had Nathaniel had eyes for anything but the lovely Olympia, countless tussles and tangles would have been unavoidable; for it was clear that the quiet, carefully muffled laughter that sounded here and there from the groups of young people was directed at the lovely Olympia, whom they followed with the strangest looks – it was hard to say why. Fired up by the dance and all the wine he'd drunk, Nathaniel shed his innate shyness. He sat beside Olympia, his hand in hers, and spoke with passion of his love for her in words that neither he nor she understood. But she perhaps grasped their meaning, for she peered without flinching right in his eyes and sighed again and again: "Oh, oh, oh!" Whereupon Nathaniel replied: "Oh you beautiful, heavenly woman! You ray of hope from the promised land of love! You deep spirit in which my entire being is mirrored," and more of the same. In response, Olympia kept sighing the same "Oh, oh!"

Professor Spallanzani walked several times past the blissful pair and smiled with a strange look of satisfaction. And though Nathaniel's spirit hovered elsewhere in another world, all of a sudden it seemed to him as if it grew curiously dark down here below in Professor Spallanzani's house. He looked around and noticed with a start that the last two lights in the empty hall were burning down to the wick and threatened at any moment to go out. Music and dance had stopped long ago. "Time to part, time to part," he cried in a wild and desperate voice, then kissed Olympia's hand, and leaned forward to kiss her on the mouth with his burning lips— but her lips were ice cold! And just as when he'd first touched Olympia's cold hand he had felt a shudder run through him, the legend of the dead bride suddenly flashed through his mind. But Olympia pressed him tightly to her, and in that kiss her lips seemed to come alive with warmth. Professor Spallanzani paced slowly through the empty hall, his steps muffled and, ringed by dancing shadows, his figure appeared terrifying and ghostlike.

"Do you love me— Do you love me, Olympia? Just that one word! Do you love me?" whispered Nathaniel.

But standing up, Olympia only sighed: "Oh, oh!"

"Oh yes, my precious, my beautiful star of love," said Nathaniel, "you rose in the firmament of my heart and will forevermore light up and trans- figure the darkness within!"

"Oh, oh!" Olympia responded, walking away. Nathaniel followed her until they stood before the professor.

"You chatted up my daughter in a right spritely manner," said the professor with a smile. "Well then, my dear Herr Nathaniel, if conversing with the simple-minded girl gives you pleasure, you're welcome to visit whenever you like."

Starry-eyed Nathaniel staggered off, with all of heaven's splendor bursting from his heart.

Spallanzani's party was the talk of the town in the days that followed. Despite the professor's great pains to make it a splendid occasion, the chat- terboxes found all sorts of unseemly and strange goings-on to dwell on.

They saved their sharpest barbs for the stiff and silent Olympia who, her lovely exterior notwithstanding, was saddled by the wagging tongues with a lot of completely nonsensical notions as to her sanity – and this was bandied about as the reason that Spallanzani kept her hidden for so long. Needless to say, Nathaniel was not pleased to learn of this, but he said nothing; what was the point, he reasoned, in proving to these dullards that it was their own nonsense that kept them from recognizing Olympia's profound and beautiful spirit!

"Do me a favor, brother," Siegmund said to him one day, "tell me how in Heaven a smart guy like you ever fell for the wax face of that wooden doll?"

Nathaniel was about to explode in anger, but then he pulled himself together and calmly responded, "Why don't *you* tell me, brother Siegmund, how a guy with an eye for beauty could be blind to Olympia's heavenly charms? But then again, it's just as well fate didn't make you a rival; for one of us would have had to fall in blood."

Realizing how things stood with his friend, Siegmund backed off, and after observing that in matters of beauty and love all is in the eye of the beholder, he added: "Still, it's funny that so many of us feel pretty much the same way about Olympia. She seemed to us – don't take it badly, brother! – strangely stiff and soulless. Her figure's regular, just like her face, it's true! She might well be considered beautiful, if her gaze were not so devoid of life, so totally lacking – you might say – the power of sight. Her step is strangely measured, every movement seems prescribed by clockwork gears and cogs. Her playing and singing has the unpleasantly precise soulless rhythm of a singing machine, which is true of her dance step too. This Olympia seemed completely weird to us, we didn't know how to make sense of her. It was as if she were only pretending to be a living being, and yet she unquestionably has her own way about her."

Nathaniel refused to give in to the bitter feelings that welled up in his heart at Siegmund's words; he checked his mood and simply replied, dead serious, "Olympia may indeed seem weird to you cold, prosaic types. The poetic temperament only reveals itself to like-minded souls! Her loving look fell on *me* alone, lighting up my senses and thoughts. Only in Olympia's love can I find myself again. You people think ill of her because she doesn't babble banalities like all the other shallow souls. It's true, she speaks little; but those few words are as vivid as hieroglyphs, revealing an inner world replete with love and a profound intellectual grasp of the eternal beyond. But you people just don't understand, all these words are lost on you."

"Beware, my brother," said Siegmund very softly, almost sadly, "it seems to me you're headed in a dangerous direction. You can count on me, if all else— no, I dare not say anymore!" Nathaniel suddenly realized that the cold, prosaic Siegmund was being very sincere with him, and so he took and shook the proffered hand with all his heart.

Nathaniel had completely forgotten that there was a Clara in this world whom he once loved; his mother, Lothar— everyone had slipped from his consciousness. He lived only for Olympia, beside whom he sat for hours every day, holding forth about his love, about life flushed with sympathy, about their psychic affinity – and Olympia listened to it all with deep devotion. From the depths of his desk drawers Nathaniel fetched everything he had ever written. Poems, fantasies, visions, novels, stories, to which all sorts of high-flying sonnets, stanzas, canzoni were added daily, and all of it he tirelessly read to Olympia for hours on end. But he had never had such a lovely listener. She did not embroider and knit, she did not peer out the window, she fed no birds, she played with no lapdogs, nor any cuddly cats, she practiced no paper cutting, nor did anything else with her hands, she held back no furtive yawns with a quiet forced cough – in short, for hours and hours she peered with a fixed and steady gaze into the eye of her beloved without fidgeting or budging, and her gaze grew ever livelier and more intense. Only when Nathaniel finally stood up and kissed her on the hand, and even on the mouth, did she respond: "Oh, oh!" Followed with, "Good night, my dear!"

"Oh, you beautiful, oh, you profound spirit," Nathaniel cried when he reached his room, "only you, you alone completely understand me." He experienced an inner bliss when he considered what a wondrous harmony manifested itself ever more each day between his and Olympia's spirits; it seemed to him as if Olympia had grasped his works, his poetic gift, from the depths of her soul, indeed that her voice came from the bottom of her innermost self. That must be true, he thought, for Olympia never uttered any more words than those already noted above. But in his most lucid moments, such as in the morning upon waking, when Nathaniel really thought about Olympia's total passivity and laconic manner, he shrugged it off. "What are words— words! Her heavenly gaze says more than any hollow language. Can any child of heaven fit herself into the narrow compass of a pathetic earthly need?"

Professor Spallanzani seemed to be absolutely delighted by the relationship between his daughter and Nathaniel, and he gave them all sorts of unequivocal signs of his approval. When Nathaniel finally dared to allude to a future bond with Olympia, a smile spread over the professor's face, and he replied that he would leave it to his daughter to decide of her own free will. Emboldened by these words, with burning desire in his heart, Nathaniel decided to implore Olympia the very next day to declare clearly in plain words what her dear loving look had long since told him, that she wished to be his forevermore. He searched for the ring that his mother gave him when he left home, to give to Olympia as a symbol of his commitment to their budding, blossoming life together. While looking for it, he happened on Clara's and Lothar's letters; indifferent, he flung them aside, found the ring, stuffed it in his pocket, and ran over to see Olympia.

Already from the front stoop, and from the vestibule, he heard a strange din that appeared to come from Spallanzani's study. A stamping of feet, a clatter, a shoving, a pounding on the door, interspersed with coarse words and hurled imprecations.

"Let go! Let me go! You wretch! You cursed creature! Did I put my life and limb on the line for that?"

"Ha ha ha ha! That was not our arrangement— it was me, me who made the eyes!"

"And I the mechanical clockwork!"

"Poor devil with your clockwork, you filthy cur of a simple-minded clockmaker!"

"Get out! Satan! Stop!"

"Organ-grinder!"

"Devilish beast! Stop— get out— let go!"

They were the voices of Spallanzani and that disgusting Coppelius that screeched and raged. Nathaniel burst in, gripped by an unspeakable terror. The professor held a female figure by the shoulders, the Italian Coppola held her by the feet, and they tugged and tore her here and there, furiously fighting for possession. Nathaniel recoiled in profound horror when he recognized the figure as Olympia. Flaring up in a wild fit of anger, he was about to tear his beloved out of their struggling grip— but at that very moment, Coppola yanked the figure free of the professor's hands with a mighty burst of strength and, pivoting, swung her in his direction, managing to land Nathaniel such a stunning blow that it made him tumble backward over the work table, toppling and knocking down the vials, retorts, bottles, and measuring glasses which all smashed in a thousand pieces on the floor. Then Coppola flung the figure over his shoulder and raced with a repulsive shrill laughter down the steps, so that the ugly dangling feet of the figure banged with a wooden thud and thump on the steps. Stunned, Nathaniel stood up. He had seen all too clearly that Olympia's deathly pallid wax face had no eyes, but black hollows in their stead; she was a lifeless doll.

Spallanzani thrashed around on the floor; glass shards had cut up his head, chest, and arms, and blood spurted as though from a fountain. But he pulled himself together. "After him, after him! What are you waiting for? Coppelius— Coppelius has robbed me of my finest automaton. Twenty years' work, life and limb invested— the clockwork, speech, step— all mine. The eyes— the eyes robbed from you. Cursed hellhound! After him! Fetch me back Olympia — there are her eyes!"

Nathaniel spotted a pair of bloody eyes peering at him from the floor.

Spallanzani grasped them with his uninjured hand and flung them at him so that they struck him on the breast. Then madness grabbed him with its burning claws and bored its way into his heart of hearts, tearing his thinking and feeling to shreds.

"Hopla, hoopla, hopla! Ring of fire, ring of fire! Spin around, ring of fire! Merrily, merrily! Wooden doll, hopla, lovely little wooden doll, turn, turn!"

And with that, Nathaniel flung himself at the professor and pressed his fingers to his throat. He would have strangled him if several people, roused by the racket, hadn't stormed in and torn the raging Nathaniel from the professor's neck, managing to revive the old man and thereby saved his life. As strong as he was, Siegmund was not able to restrain the madman, who kept on screaming in a terrifying voice, "Wooden doll, turn, turn!" and lashing about him with balled fists. Finally, it took the combined strength of many men to overpower him, fling him to the floor and tie him up. His words dissolved in a terrible beastly bellowing, and in this pitiful state, still raving in a ghastly frenzy, he was taken to the madhouse.

But before I continue, gracious reader, with my account of the fate of that poor unfortunate Nathaniel, those of you who took an interest in the masterful mechanic and maker of automata, Spallanzani, can rest assured that he completely recuperated from his wounds. He was forced to leave the university, as Nathaniel's story had caused a public uproar, and it was commonly held to be an altogether fraudulent swindle to try to pass off a wooden doll for a living person in proper society (for Olympia had effectively pulled the wool over their eyes). Jurists went so far as to call it a refined, and therefore all the harder to punish, swindle, which he succeeded in pulling off so skillfully that everyone (except for a few sharp-eyed students) was taken in – although they now put on a smart façade and pointed to all sorts of things that seemed suspicious to them at the time. But such smart alecks ultimately brought no hard-and-fast evidence to the case. For instance, could it possibly have aroused anyone's suspicion that, according to the testimony of one elegant invitee, Olympia more often sneezed than yawned? This, maintained said elegant invitee, was the automaton's hidden rewind mechanism that noticeably creaked in the process— and so on and so forth.

A professor of poetry and rhetoric took a pinch of snuff, snapped the tin shut, cleared his throat, and launched into his erudite discourse. "Most honored ladies and gentlemen, can't you see where the shoe pinches? The whole thing is an allegory – a long, drawn-out metaphor – do you catch my drift? *Sapienti sat!*"

But many honored gentlemen derived little consolation from this view; the story of the automaton had taken root, and a dreadful distrust of human figures seeped into their souls. In order to be completely convinced that they were not in love with a wooden doll, quite a few lovers demanded that their beloved sing something off key and dance out of step, that they embroider and knit while being read to, or play with the little pug; above all, they demanded that they not just listen, but also occasionally say something in such a way as to demonstrate that their words came from actual thought and feeling. As a result, the loving bond of many couples grew stronger than ever, while others quietly drifted apart. "One can hardly be certain about this," was the common excuse. Yawning was all the rage at social teas, but people refrained from sneezing, so as to dispel any suspicions. Spallanzani was obliged to skip town, as has already been said, to escape the criminal investigation into his fraudulent introduction of an automaton into human society. Coppola also vanished.

When Nathaniel awakened, as though from an oppressive and terrible dream, he batted his eyes open and felt himself infused with an indescribable sense of well-being and heavenly warmth. He lay in his bed in his room in his father's house, and Clara was bent over him while his mother and Lothar stood close by. "At last, at last, oh, my dearly beloved Nathaniel, you've pulled through at last, and now you're mine again!" Clara spoke the words with all her heart and took Nathaniel in her arms. Bright, burning tears of sadness and rapture poured from his eyes and he moaned deeply, "My Clara, my Clara!"

Siegmund, who had faithfully stood by his friend in dire moments, then entered the room. Nathaniel held out his hand. "You, my faithful brother in need, you never abandoned me."

Every last trace of madness was gone, and soon Nathaniel got better in the painstaking care of his mother, his beloved, and his friends. Fortune had, in the meantime, returned to the house; a miserly old uncle, from whom no one hoped to inherit a red cent, had died and left Nathaniel's mother a considerable fortune, as well as a small estate in a pleasant district not far from the city. There they intended to move together, Nathaniel with his Clara, whom he now planned to marry, and his mother and

Lothar. Nathaniel had become gentler and more childlike than ever, and only now really recognized the heavenly purity of Clara's radiant spirit. No one reminded him, not even breathing the slightest hint, of the recent past. It was only when Siegmund prepared to leave that Nathaniel remarked, "By God, my brother, I was headed down the path of no return, but in the nick of time an angel made me find the right way! It was my Clara, after all!" Siegmund cut him off, fearing that bitter memories might once again make him start raving.

The time came when the four happy people planned to move out to the small country estate. As they went walking through the streets of the city at midday, after buying some things here and there, the tall town-hall tower cast a long shadow over the marketplace.

"Hey," said Clara, "let's climb it one last time and gaze out at the distant mountains!" No sooner said than done. Nathaniel and Clara both climbed the steps, Mother went home with the maid, and Lothar, who was disinclined to mount the many steps, stayed down below. Now the two lovers stood arm in arm at the tower's highest lookout gallery and peered at the sweet-scented ring of woods, and the blue mountains loomed beyond like a giant city.

"Will you look at that strange little gray bush that seems to be slowly drawing near?" asked Clara. Nathaniel mechanically reached into his coat pocket, where he found Coppola's spyglass, and looked to the side. There was Clara standing in the eye of the lens. A spasmodic quiver started up in his veins and arteries. Turning deathly pale, he peered at Clara. Soon sparks of fire flashed from his rolling eyes; he let out a horrible holler like a hunted animal, jumped high in the air, and with a curious cackle, shrieked "Turn, little wooden doll, turn!" With a great burst of strength, he grabbed hold of Clara and tried to hurl her off the tower, but Clara clung for dear life to the metal railing.

Hearing the madman raving and Clara's terrified screams, Lothar clambered up the stairs, gripped by a terrible foreboding. But the door to the second flight of steps was locked. Clara's piteous screams sounded louder and louder. Consumed with anger and fear, Lothar hurled himself against the door, which finally gave way. Clara's cries grew fainter and fainter. "Help! Save me! Save me!" till her voice faded into silence.

"She's done for – murdered by that madman," Lothar screamed. The door to the lookout gallery was also locked, but desperation turned him into a lion and he broke down the door. God in heaven! Clara dangled in Nathaniel's mad grip over the edge of the cast-iron railing, only holding on by one hand. Quick as lightning, Lothar grabbed his sister, pulled her to safety, and at the very same moment heaved a balled fist into the madman's face, so that he tumbled backward and let go of his prey.

Lothar raced back down the steps, his unconscious sister in his arms. She was saved. Meanwhile, Nathaniel kept flailing about on the lookout gallery, jumping high in the air and shouting, "Ring of fire, turn! Ring of fire, turn!"

Stirred by the screams, a throng gathered below; in the midst of the crowd was the lawyer Coppelius, who had just come to town and gone straight to the marketplace. Some people wanted to climb the tower to capture the madman, but Coppelius laughed. "Ha ha, just be patient, he'll be down shortly on his own!" he said, looking on as the others raced up the steps.

Nathaniel suddenly stopped dead in his tracks, leaned down, spotted Coppelius below, and with a shrill shriek of "Ha! Eyes a pretty! Eyes a pretty!" leapt over the parapet. As Nathaniel landed, his skull smashed on the cobblestones. Coppelius disappeared into the crowd.

Clara was said to have been spotted years later in some distant town, seated hand in hand with a friendly man on a bench before the door of a lovely little country house, two bouncing boys playing at her feet. It might, therefore, be fair to suppose that Clara finally found the quiet domestic bliss that suited her cheerful spirit, which Nathaniel in his torn and troubled state could never have given her.

Intimations from the Realm of Musical Notes

1816

My father's little garden bordered on a forest full of sound and song. Year in, year out, a nightingale nested there in a lovely old tree, at the foot of which lay a large, oddly shaped stone dappled with all manner of wondrous moss and reddish veined rock. All that my father told of this rock had a fabulous ring. Many years ago, my father said, an unknown but stately gentleman came riding up to the squire's castle, a man of outlandish garb and arcane knowledge. Everyone found the stranger most peculiar; it was impossible to regard him for long without feeling a certain dread and, once having caught a glimpse of him, impossible to turn your bewitched eyes away again. In no time at all, the squire took a great liking to him – even though he confessed he always got a funny feeling in his presence – and broke out into cold chills when, over a heaping cup, the stranger got to speaking of the many distant, uncharted lands and the curious men and fauna he had become familiar with in his far-flung journeys. The gentleman then let his language dissolve into wondrous tones in which, without words, he made all manner of unknown mysterious things intelligible to his listener. But the squire could not break free of the stranger's spell, indeed could not listen to his stories often enough – stories which, in an inconceivable manner and clearly recognizable terms, evoked a dark, amorphous sense of foreboding.

Whenever the stranger sang all manner of wondrous sounding songs in some unknown language, accompanying himself on the lute, all who heard him were gripped as if by a supernatural force. "No mortal can play such music," they insisted, "he must be an angel able to transport the notes of the heavenly concert of cherubim and seraphim down to us here below on earth." The stranger ensnared the lovely young damsel of the castle with this indissoluble snare of sound. In the course of his instructing her in voice and lute, the two soon became intimate, and oftentimes the stranger made his way at midnight to the old tree, where the maiden was already waiting. Then, from a distance, one could hear her song and the entrancing plucked tones of his lute, but the melodies sounded so weird, so unearthly that no one dared draw near or betray the lovers' tryst.

One morning the stranger disappeared; although the maiden was sought out in every corner of the castle, she, too, could not be found. Riddled with fear, gripped by a sense of dread, her father swung himself onto a horse, and galloped toward the woods, crying out his child's name in inconsolable grief. When he came to the rock where the stranger had so often sat kissing the girl at midnight, the horse bristled its mane, whinnying and snorting; as if gripped by an infernal spirit, it refused to budge from the spot. Believing that the horse felt antsy about the curiously formed rock, the squire climbed down from the saddle to lead it past, but his blood curdled in a cramp of terror, and he stopped dead in his tracks at the sight of bright drops of blood welling up out of the stone. As if aided by a higher power, the hunters and peasants who had accompanied the squire managed with great effort to shove the stone to the side, and found the poor girl lying under it, her dead body riddled with stab wounds made by a dagger, the stranger's broken lute buried beside her. Ever since then, a nightingale nests on the tree where none had done so before, and sings at midnight in a mournful, soul-stirring manner; moss and weeds grew out of the blood, henceforth adorning the rock in a curious array of colors.

Since I was still a very young boy, I was not allowed to enter the forest without my father's permission; but the tree and especially the rock were an irresistible lure. Whenever the little rear gate in the garden wall was not locked, I slipped away to my beloved rock, my gaze transfixed by the won-drous mosses and herbs growing out of it, and the streaks of color in its surface. I often thought I could understand the figures and signs scratched into the stone, and it seemed to me as if I deciphered and grasped the arcane meaning of all manner of adventurous tales of the sort my mother had told me. Then gazing at the rock, I inevitably thought of the lovely song my father sang almost daily and which always so moved me that, forgetting my favorite games, I felt compelled to listen with tears in my eyes. And conversely, whenever I heard that song, my beloved mosses sprung to mind, so that both sometimes seemed entwined, and in my mind I was hardly able to tell the two apart.

It was at that time that my fondness for music grew stronger day by day, and my father, himself an able musician, took it upon himself to give me meticulous instruction, convinced that he was not only training me to be a first-rate instrumentalist, but also a composer. He may well have deduced my ambitions from the diligence – indeed the avid desire – with which I applied myself to improvising my own melodies and chords on the piano. My efforts evinced more expressive strength and coherence than one might have expected of a child. But I oftentimes burst into bitter tears, in a desperate fit of despair, resolved never to touch the piano again, since it always turned out sounding different from what I had intended when my fingers fumbled on the keys. Unknown songs that I had never heard streamed through my mind, and then it seemed to me as if, like arcane and fantastical musical notations, the moss on the stone conjured up these songs that sounded in my ears like the melodic whisper of spirits, and I became convinced that if one gazed upon them with true heartfelt love, the stone would burst out singing the songs of the murdered girl in the vibrant tones of her angelic voice.

And it did indeed come to pass that once, while peering at the rock, I managed to transport myself into a brooding, dreamlike state in which I was so moved by the sound of the girl's splendid singing sweeping through my ears that my breast ached with an extraordinary sweet pain. But as soon as I tried to sing and play back on the piano what I had heard, everything sank into a dark muddled mess. That made me altogether despondent, and when I was to play my practice pieces (which, compared to these mysterious songs, sounded repugnant and insufferable), I lost all patience. Consequently, I neglected all the necessary practice that might have helped me become a finished musician and, losing faith in my musical talent, my father finally gave up on my instruction.

When I later attended the high school in town, where music was also taught, my interest in it was reawakened in another way. The technical proficiency of many of my fellow students provoked my desire to emulate them. I made a great effort to match their prowess, but the more I mastered the mechanics of music, the less I succeeded in eliciting the tones of those exceptionally lovely melodies that once sounded in my mind. The music director of the high school – an old man who, it was said, was a master of counterpoint – taught me the basics of *basso continuo* and composition; he even attempted to introduce the principles of how to go about inventing a melody, and once having worked out a musical theme, I took great pains to make sure that all contrapuntal turns were in accord.

So I believed myself to be an accomplished musician, when, after a couple of years, I returned to the village where my father lived. In his house I found the little old piano at which I'd once sat for half the night, shedding tears of chagrin, trying in vain to bring forth the tones I heard in my inner ear. I also saw the wondrous stone again; but having grown smart and savvy, I laughed at the childish foolishness of my once having wanted to draw melodies from the moss. And yet, I could not disavow the fact that the shadowy spot beneath the great tree still elicited incredible musical intimations. Lying in the grass, my head leaning against the stone, the wind whistling through the branches still sounded like ghostly voices; but the melodies they sang that had long since taken root in my mind came alive again, resounding in my ear. How insipid, how tasteless my compositions pounded out by my faulty fingers on that old keyboard sounded; it was no music at all; my entire effort amounted to discordant trifling of absolutely no value. But I found solace in my dreams that tapped that splendid shimmering realm. I saw the stone, its red veins opened like dark carnations, their scent emanating in bright ringing rays. In the long rising notes of the nightingale, the rays condensed into the figure of a wonderful woman – a fleeting image of the girl from the castle – but then the image faded, dissolving back into heavenly music!

Our realm is not of this world, the musicians say, for where in nature can we find the prototypes of our art, as do the painters and the sculptors? Sound surrounds us, but musical notes, that is to say melodies conceived in the lofty tongue of the spirit world, live only in the hearts and minds of man. But is all of nature not infused with the spirit of notes in tandem with the spirit of music? Brought to life, the mechanically stroked sounding body bespeaks its being, or rather, its innermost essence bursts out into consciousness. It is as if the spirit of music stimulated by the sacred can only secretly express itself melodically and harmoniously by means of these audible echoes. The musician, that is to say he in whose innermost self music crystalizes into clear consciousness, is engulfed with melodies and harmonies every which way he turns. It is no empty image, no mere allegory when the maestro maintains that colors, scents, and beams of light appear to him as musical notes, and that he conceives a wonderful concert in their harmonic convolution. Just as, according to the dictum of a brilliant physicist, listening is a seeing from the inside, so for the musician seeing becomes a listening from the inside – that is to say, with what the eye captures, that most profound consciousness of the musical element, perceived by his spirit as vibrating in unison with it all; thus do the sudden incitements of the musician that spur on melodies spawned deep inside himself often give voice to the unconscious, or rather that which cannot be expressed in words, grasping the secret music of nature as the fundamental principle of life or the *primum mobile* of it all. The perceptible sounds of nature, the whispering of the wind, the welling up of mountain springs, and other murmurings first strike the musician's ear as individual notes, then as chords, then as melodies with harmonic accompaniment. Along with a recognition comes a mounting desire. And might the musician not ultimately comport himself in relation to the surrounding sounds of nature as does the hypnotist in relation to the somnambulist state, both applying their conscious will, to which nature always responds? The livelier, the more penetrating that recognition, the more the musician evolves in his ability to compose; the capacity to grasp and capture those natural stimuli in a grid of written musical notations with the aid of a particular cognitive ability is the hallmark of the art of composition. And so the musical score becomes the conjuring book through which one taps those most secret murmurings of nature found in life, so as to make them resound at will in a perceptible manner.

This ability to capture and transcribe the music resonating within is the fruit of a thorough artistic musical training resulting in a spontaneous, voluble mastery of musical notation, so that we produce a kind of hieroglyphic as an individualized language to express musical thoughts, evoking the most intimate link between note and word. But in music – this universal language of nature, in which there is no need for the link between the thought and its hieroglyph – wondrous secret sounds often swish past our ears and we attempt in vain to find the fitting notations for an auditory language resistant to transcription. Just as wonderful as the capture of music in musical notation is the dynamic emergence of music at the sight of these notes, and so musical amateurs able to read a score can gain an inkling of the dynamic element and conjure up the sound signified by a string of notes often spawned by a single moment of consciousness, irrespective of the fact that composition demands the highest degree of this cognitive capacity. It is only from that spontaneous, unconscious, inner impulse that sparks the consciousness of music that true music emerges; this we must admit, much as we are inclined to doubt random emanations of ecstasy in which the wondrous language of nature resonates. But how often do the words of the poet accord with the music resounding in the ear of the musician, and in general how often does the poet's language match up with the language of music? On occasion, the musician is clearly conscious of having conjured up the melody independent of the words, and it leaps forth in the delivery of the song as if awakened by a stroke of magic.

Should there not then exist a special physical rapport between poet and musician? Might it be that the poet's spirit, enthralled by the ecstasy of conception, inspired the musician, and the latter conceived the melody, so that the same string, as it were, resonated in tune in the echo chamber between his ears? As if completed masterworks of song, in which word and music that remain inseparably coalesced, could only come into being out of that lofty physical bond between poet and musician, so that the work was simultaneously versified and composed? As if oftentimes a third cognitive principle in nature were to loop a bond around both, and word and music were, like a message of love, to be conveyed from one to the other, just as butterflies transport the fertilizing dust from flower to flower? Music makes available the contact with yesterday. Often in the stillness of night, in a dark room, splendid songs flood the musician's ears. Is it not as if, at such moments, distant friendly spirits spoke with us, as if, indeed, even the voices of those long departed from this earth lived on in our heart of hearts, in the sounds of an ethereal singing? It is certain that the living remembrance of a friend with whom one had a musical bond can only be sustained in sound and song; resplendent melodies may pour forth from deep inside, but is that living remembrance of the departed friend not the embodiment of the friend himself?

It often seems to me as if I now have a better grasp of notions that only brushed past my soul when I was a boy. The legend of the wondrous stranger and the girl is a telling metaphor of earthly perdition through the malevolent influence of hostile force— the misuse of music— but then an uplifting to a heightened state— apotheosis through sound and song. My dream reveals itself as the interpretation of a wondrous presentiment at that sacred place. It is that which I hear; beauteous chords ring out, and their song radiates in wondrous melodies. My ever-constant force of will is rewarded, my willful musings are embodied by my music, and as long as I keep them in mind, music lives in my soul. But will I ever succeed in expressing the songs I hear, so that it may be audible to another listener? I don't believe I ever will, and when I contemplate transcribing all that I have heard and felt in musical notations, it is as if I were to betray a carefully guarded secret.

Should then the true essence of a musician only resonate most acutely in his music, and all that he gives the world remain nothing but a faint echo of the apparitions singing within?

The Fermata

1817

Hummel's lively, vital painting "Gathering in an Italian Locanda" became known after being exhibited at the Berlin Art Exhibit in the fall of 1814, where it caught many an eye and cheered many a spirit. A lush overgrown arbor— a table beset with wine and fruit— two Italian ladies seated on opposite sides, one is singing, the other playing a guitar, an abbot standing in the back between the two, serving as conductor. With raised baton he waits for the signora – her gaze raised heavenward – to complete her cadenza in an extended trill so that he can bring down the baton and the guitarist can strum a jaunty dominant cord. The abbot is full of admiration, infused with soulful delight, and yet all the while fraught with fearful premonitions. He will not miss the timely downbeat for the world. He hardly dares breathe. He looks like he would bind the wings and gag the mouth of every little bee, every little gnat, just to still the buzz. All the more noxious to him is the bustling innkeeper, now of all times bringing the ordered jug of wine at this most crucial moment. Behind them, a view of a leafy passageway, the greenery pierced with glimmering rays of sunlight, where a horseman has pulled up, and water is brought to his thirsty steed.

The two friends Eduard and Theodor stood before this painting. "The more I gaze at that, albeit no longer young, but truly virtuoso singer in her colorful clothes," said Eduard, "the more I delight in the perfect Roman profile and the lovely figure of the guitar player, the more that most admirable abbot amuses me, the more freely and powerfully the whole bursts into the buoyant confines of my real life— it is clearly a caricature in the purest sense, but full of zest and charm! Right here and now I'd like to climb into the arbor and pop open one of those wicker bottles beaming down at me from the table— it's as if I already had a sweet whiff of that fine wine— no, we cannot allow this artistic incitement to evaporate in the cold, prosaic air that surrounds us— let us honor that lovely work of art, that tribute to Italy's lust for life, and break open a bottle of Italian wine."

While Eduard spoke in broken sentences, Theodor stood by, listening in silence, deeply preoccupied. "Yes, let's do that!" he suddenly piped up, as if awakening from a dream; but he could hardly break free of the painting. He mechanically followed his friend, and when he soon found himself at the door, he cast a longing look back at the singers and the abbot. Eduard's proposition was easily realized. A wicker bottle very much like the one in the depicted arbor awaited them in the little blue cup room of the Sala Tarone directly across the street.

"It seems to me, my friend," Eduard remarked after they'd both emptied several glasses, and Theodor remained silent and very much still turned in upon himself, "it seems to me as if the painting affected you in a most peculiar manner, and not at all in the way it did me."

"I can assure you," Theodor replied, "that I, too, thoroughly delighted in all the lighthearted and charming allure of the painting, but the odd thing is that it faithfully portrays a scene I myself experienced in life, down to a precise portrayal of the depicted persons. You will admit, however, that even the most cheerful memories can trouble the mind if suddenly reawakened in such an unexpected, peculiar way, as if by a magic bolt of lightning. That is what just happened to me."

"From your own life?" Eduard interrupted in stunned amazement. "The painting, you say, depicts a scene from your own life? I immediately judged the depictions of the singers and the abbot to be faithful portraits of real persons, but do you really mean to say that you encountered them in real life? Pray tell, my friend, how this all fits together; it's just you and me here, nobody else is likely to show up at this hour."

"I'll gladly do as you wish," said Theodor, "but will, I regret, have to reach far back— all the way to my youth."

"I'm all ears, my friend," Eduard replied, "I know precious little about your younger years. If the telling takes more time than expected, we risk nothing more than having to break open another bottle – the prospect of which no one will take badly, neither us nor the innkeeper Signore Tarone."

"It took no one by surprise when I finally swept everything else aside and committed myself heart and soul to noble Musica," began Theodor, "since even as a boy I hardly cared a fig for anything else, and plunked away night and day on my uncle's clunky old piano. Music got short shrift in the small town where I grew up; there was nobody around to teach me except for an obstinate old organist, but he was a deadbeat arithmetician and tormented me with dark, awful sounding toccatas and fugues. But without letting myself be discouraged, I faithfully kept at it. The old fellow often banged something awful on the keyboard, but then all he had to do was play a fleet movement in his powerful manner for me to be reconciled with him and the art of music. Often then I found myself wafted into a wondrous state of mind, listening to some movement – especially one by old Sebastian Bach – almost resembling a ghostly tale, when I was gripped by shudders of delight of the sort we gladly embrace in the fantastic frenzy of youth. But a veritable Eden revealed itself to me when, in the dead of winter, the town piper gave a concert accompanied by a band of mediocre dilettantes, and because I could keep time, I was permitted to play the timpani in some symphony. Only later did I come to realize how ridiculous and madcap these concerts often were.

"Generally, my teacher played two piano concertos by Wolff or Emanuel Bach, a journeyman piper tormented himself attempting to play Stamitz, and the excise tax collector blew so mightily on his flute that he blew out both lanterns on the stage, which had to keep being lighted. Singing was out of the question, lest they risk the reproaches of my uncle, a great friend and aficionado of the musical arts. He still recalled with delight the old days when choirmasters from the four churches in town got together for a performance of "Lottchen am Hofe" in the concert hall. He extolled the tolerance with which the four singers came together to perform the piece, since in addition to the Catholic and the Evangelical, the Reformed congregation was divided into a German and a French contingent. The bespectacled French choirmaster refused to let go of

Lottchen and, as my uncle assured me, sang his part in a lovely falsetto of a pitch never heretofore emitted by a human throat.

"Meanwhile, back home (that is to say, in our town), a fifty-five-year-old demoiselle by the name of Meibel was eating away at her meager pension granted her as retired court singer, and my uncle rightfully thought that she still really ought to be able to emit a retiring little trill in concert for her money. She played hard to get and let them keep asking, but finally gave in, and so we finally got some *arias di bravura* in concert. She was a most peculiar person, this Demoiselle Meibel. I still have a vivid memory of her haggard little figure. With the score in hand, she had a very solemn and serious way of striding forward in a brilliantly colored dress and greeting the audience with a slight bow of the torso. She wore a rather outlandish headdress, to the front of which was fastened a bouquet of Italian porcelain flowers which had a strange way of shivering and nodding as she sang. When she finished singing and the audience responded with a good deal of applause, she handed the score with a stern expression to my teacher, who had the privilege of bringing forward a pug-shaped porcelain jar which she reached into with much ado to extract a pinch of tobacco. She had a ghastly, squawking voice, made all manner of droll twists and turns, and emitted curious coloraturas, and you can well imagine what impression all this posturing, along with her preposterous appearance, must have made on me. My uncle burst out in exalted hurrahs of praise hard for me to fathom, and I tended rather to favor my organist, a despiser of song who, in his venomous, hypochondriac manner, mercilessly parodied the droll old demoiselle.

"The more vigorously I shared my teacher's scorn for singing, the more he fired up my musical genius. He took great pains to teach me the principles of counterpoint, and soon I was composing the most contrived fugues and toccatas. I was playing one of these very contrived compositions of mine for my uncle on my birthday (I had just turned nineteen), when the waiter from our poshest restaurant strode in, announcing the visit of two foreign ladies who had just arrived in town. Even before my uncle managed to cast off his flowery dressing gown and get dressed, the announced guests strode in. You know how every manifestation of the foreign electrifies a sensibility raised in the confinement of small-town life – this appearance, in particular, that barged in unannounced in my life was ideally suited to strike me like a bolt of lightning. Just imagine two slender, tall Italian ladies colorfully attired in the latest fashion, swiftly, and yet gracefully, headed straight for my uncle with a virtuoso bravado, and addressing him with powerful and yet sonorous voice.— But what sort of strange language are they speaking?— only from time to time does it almost sound like German!— my uncle doesn't understand a word— confounded, he steps back— falling absolutely silent, he points to the sofa. They sit down— talking between themselves, their words sound like music. They finally manage to make it clear to my uncle that they are singers passing through town, they would like to give a concert here, and have come to him, since he appears to be in charge of organizing such musical events.

"Listening to them speak with each other, I deciphered their Christian names, and though I was totally bewildered by their duality before, it now seemed to me that I could more clearly register what each was saying. Lauretta, apparently the older one, her sparkling eyes beaming, addressed my poor confounded uncle with overwhelming vitality and lively gesticulations. Not overly tall, she was voluptuously built, and my gaze grew befuddled with heretofore unknown sensations. Taller, slimmer, with an elongated serious face, Teresina spoke little, but was more comprehensible. Every now and then she flashed the strangest smile – it was almost as if she reveled in the spectacle of my good uncle, who withdrew into his silk dressing gown as into a shell, and tried in vain to hide a traitorous yellow string with which to tie the garment shut, that instead kept slipping and unraveling from his breast where he clutched it.

"At last the two sisters got up. My uncle promised to arrange for the concert three days hence, whereupon he was respectfully invited, along with me, whom he introduced as a young virtuoso, for chocolate.

"Ceremoniously and with heavy steps we climbed the stairs to our rendezvous, both in an odd mood, as if headed for an adventure which we were not up to. After my uncle, having duly prepared for the occasion, discoursed many a fine phrase about art which neither he nor the rest of us understood, and I twice sank my tongue into the burning hot chocolate, but pulled a Scaevola,* smiling with stoic equanimity at the excruciating pain, Lauretta said she'd like to sing us something. Teresina took hold of a guitar, tuned it, and strummed a couple of chords. Never having heard that instrument played, I was greatly stirred by the muffled, mysterious sounding clang of the vibrating strings. Softly, Lauretta sang a note, which she held for a long *fortissimo* and then quickly broke out in a lively, ruffled figure which she held for one and a half octaves. I can still recall the opening line: '*Sento l'amica speme.*' Never having heard the like, I felt a fluttering in

* Gaius Mucius Scaevola, a legendary Roman youth captured by the Etruscans, who thrust his hand into a fire and held it there, without showing any sign of pain, to prove his bravery.

my breast. But the more Lauretta let loose, the song spilling ever more audaciously and freely from her lips, the increasingly fiery, scintillating notes enveloping my ears, my own inner music, so long numb and dormant, was ignited and flared up in mighty brilliant bursts of flame. Oh! It was the first time in my life I heard real music. Then the two sisters sang those solemn sonorous duets by the Abbot Steffani. Teresina's resonant, heavenly clear alto voice thrilled my soul. I could not hide how moved I was; tears streamed from my eyes. My uncle cleared his throat, casting disobliging glances at me, but it was no use – I was really beside myself with emotion. The two singers seemed to be pleased, and asked about my musical studies; ashamed of my musical dabbling, with the audacity prompted by my enthusiasm, I responded in all honesty that it was only today that I heard real music.

"*'Il bon fanciullo!'** Lauretta whispered sweetly and softly.

"When I got home, I was overcome by a fit of anger, grabbing all the toccatas and fugues I could lay my hands on, including the forty-five variations on a canonical theme the organist had composed and transcribed for me, threw everything into the fire, and laughed sardonically as the double counterpoint smoked and crackled in the flames. Then I sat down to my instrument and first tried to imitate the sounds of the guitar, and then the melodies sung by the sisters.

"'Will the little lad please stop squawking so egregiously and kindly lay his head on the pillow and go to sleep!' my uncle finally cried out at midnight, blew out both my candles, and returned to his bedroom from which he had emerged. I was obliged to obey. My dream revealed the secret of the

---

*The good child.

[238]

song – or so I believed – as I did a splendid rendition of '*sento l'amica speme*' in my sleep. The following morning, my uncle auditioned anyone in town who could stroke a fiddle or blow a pipe. He proudly sought to show off our local musical talent, but things didn't work out as he'd wished. Lauretta made a big to-do, but already in the recitativo the musicians made an awful clamor – none had the faintest notion of accompaniment. Lauretta screamed— ranted— wept in anger and impatience. The organist sat at the piano, and she assailed him with the bitterest reproaches. Struck dumb, he got up and walked out the door. The town piper, whom Lauretta called an '*Asino maledetto*'* clasped his fiddle under his arm and truculently plunked his hat on his head. He, too, made his way to the door. The other fiddlers and tooters packed up their bows, unscrewed their mouthpieces, and followed suit. Only the dilettantes looked around with weepy expressions, and the assize collector gesticulated and cried out, 'Oh God, how annoying!'

"All my timidity vanished in an instant. I threw myself in the path of the town piper, I begged, I implored, and in my fit of terror I promised him nine minuets with double trios for the town ball. I managed to mollify his injured pride. He returned to the conductor's stand, the other musicians stepped forward, and soon the orchestra was reassembled with only the organist missing. He was slowly ambling across the market square; no waving, no calling out to him drew him back. Teresina surveyed the scene with stubborn laughter; as irate as Lauretta had been before, she was now lighthearted. She overpraised my efforts, she asked if I could play the piano, and before I knew what I was doing I sat down before the score in the organist's place.

---

* Accursed ass in Italian.

I had never before accompanied a singer, or conducted an orchestra. Teresina sat down beside me at the piano and gave me each tempo, Lauretta cheered me on with a heartening bravo, the orchestra played along, everything sounded better and better. Everything became clear in the second rehearsal, and the effect of the two sisters' singing in concert was indescribable.

"Many festivities were planned for the prince's return to court, and the sisters were called upon to sing in the theater and concert hall; they decided to linger in our little town until such time as their presence elsewhere was absolutely necessary, and so they gave a few additional concerts. The public's admiration grew into a kind of madness. Only old Ms. Meibel took a pinch of tobacco from the pug-shaped porcelain jar and maintained that such shrieking was no proper singing. My organist never showed his face again, and I didn't miss him either. I was the most jubilant person on earth! All day long I sat beside the sisters, accompanied them, and wrote out the partitur each was to sing for their concert in the capital city. Lauretta was my ideal, her bad moods, her terrible irascible impetuosity – her virtuoso torment at the piano – all this I patiently endured! For it was she, she alone, who revealed to me what real music was. I started studying Italian and tried my hand at *canzonettas*. How ecstatic I was when Lauretta sang my compositions and even praised them! Oftentimes it seemed to me as if I had not even contemplated or conceived how it should sound, but it was only in Lauretta's rendition that the meaning emerged. I never warmed up to Teresina; she seldom sang, did not appear to pay me much mind, and it sometimes seemed to me as if she were laughing at me behind my back.

"It finally came time for their departure. Only then did I fathom what Lauretta had become for me and the impossibility of separating from her.

Often when she became *smorfiosa*,[*] she caressed me, even if in an altogether innocuous manner, but my blood began to boil, and it was only the curious coldness with which she confronted me that kept me from taking her in my arms, inflamed with the fury of love. I had a middling tenor voice which, while I had never trained it, I now quickly whipped into shape. I often sang with Lauretta those innumerable tender Italian *duettini*. As her departure drew near, we sang just such a duet – *'senza di te ben mio, vivere non poss'io.'*[**] Who on earth could endure such an emotional strain without springing to action? I threw myself at Lauretta's feet— I was at my wit's end! She raised me upright: 'But my dear friend! Dare we part?'— I pricked up my ears. She suggested I come to the capital with her and Teresina, seeing as I would one day have to leave that backwater if I wished to devote myself entirely to music.

"Just imagine someone who, having fallen into the blackest, most bottomless abyss, despairs of life, but at the very same instant he believes he has received the blow that tears him apart he finds himself seated in a bright and splendid rose arbor with hundreds of brilliant lights flickering about and a voice crying, 'Dearly beloved, you're still alive for now!'

"That's how I felt. To go along with them to the capital, that was my solemn resolve! I won't bore you with the details of how I began to insist to my uncle how I simply had to go to the capital city, which wasn't really all that far. He finally gave in, even promised to come along. What a glitch in my plans! I could not very well reveal my intention of traveling with the two Italian ladies. A bad cold that laid my uncle low finally saved the day. I

[*] Affected.

[**] I can't live without you, my dear.

[241]

rode off in the postal coach, but only to the next town, where I stopped to await the arrival of my goddess. A well-larded travel bag allowed me to make thorough preparations. Romantically inclined, I wanted to accompany the ladies on horseback like a protective paladin; I managed to procure a horse which, though not particularly stately, was, according to the man who sold it to me, a patient and dependable mount, and rode out at the agreed upon time to meet the singers. Soon the small, two-seated rig came slowly rambling along. One seat was occupied by the two sisters, and in the rear seat sat their chambermaid, the small, stout Gianna, a brown-haired Neapolitan. The carriage was otherwise heaped high with all manner of packing cases, boxes, and baskets from which traveling ladies can never be parted. Two little pugs perched on Gianna's lap and barked at me as I cheerfully greeted my eagerly awaited companions. Everything proceeded as planned; we had already arrived at the last station stop when my horse had the bright idea to want to return home. Guided by the presence of mind that in such instances severe measures would not be particularly effective, I tried, albeit to no avail, to employ gentler means, but my stubborn mount proved unmoved by my attempts at friendly persuasion. I wanted to go forward, he backward – all that I managed by painstaking means was that he rode around in circles instead. Teresa leaned out of the carriage and laughed heartily, while Lauretta, holding her face in her two hands, cried out at the top of her lungs, as if I were in mortal danger. Emboldened by desperation, I dug both spurs into the horse's ribs, but was in the selfsame instant hurled head over heels and landed on the ground. The horse stopped dead in his tracks and regarded me scornfully with his long, outstretched neck. Since I did not manage to rise, the coachman sped to my rescue,

Lauretta leapt out, weeping and shrieking, and Teresina kept on laughing. I had sprained my ankle and so was not able to remount the horse. How was I to proceed? The horse was tied to the carriage, and I was obliged to crawl in. Just imagine two relatively robust damsels, a fat chambermaid, two pugs, and a good dozen packing cases, boxes, and baskets, and me packed in on top of it all in a small two-seated rig— just imagine Lauretta's yammering at the uncomfortable seating arrangement— the howling of the pugs— the jabbering of the Neapolitan maid—Teresina's sulking— the unspeakable pain in my ankle, and you will fathom the pretty state I was in. Teresina, as she insisted, could stand it no more. We stopped, and with one leap she was out of the carriage. She untied my horse, sat herself squarely across the saddle and trotted and pranced on ahead of us. I must admit that she comported herself in splendid fashion. Her innate elegance and grace were even more in evidence on horseback. She had the guitar handed to her, and with the reins strung around her arm, sang proud Spanish *romanzas*, accompanying herself with sonorous strummed chords. Her light silk gown fluttered in the wind, the sunlight playing in shimmering reflections on the pleats, and the white feathers of her hat waved in time like nodding spirits cooing along. Her entire appearance was romantic to a tee, so much so that I could not take my eyes off Teresina, notwithstanding Lauretta, who saw her sister as a complete lunatic, and must surely have taken umbrage at her cockiness. But everything turned out well, the horse became compliant, or else the songstress was preferable to the paladin as a rider – to make a long story short, only once we'd reached the gates of the capital did Teresina crawl back into the buggy.

"If you had seen me then, reveling in all kinds of music – at the piano studiously practicing arias, duets and what have you – you would have been able to tell from my completely changed presence that I was infused with a wondrous spirit. Having shed all small-town timidity, I sat like a maestro before my score at the piano, directing the dramatic singing of my dear donna. My entire being – all my thinking – was done in sweet melodies. Unconcerned with contrapuntal musical confections, I wrote all manner of *canzonettas* and arias that Lauretta sang, albeit only in the privacy of her room. Why did she never want to sing any of my compositions in concert? – I just didn't get it. Teresina sometimes seemed to me to embody the very epitome of the rash romantic artist perched on her proud horse, stroking her lyre – I unintentionally wrote some serious highfalutin songs for her! – Still, it is true that Lauretta toyed with the notes like a capricious fairy queen. There was nothing she attempted that she didn't manage to pull off. Teresina couldn't produce a musical roulade – an appoggiatura maybe, a mordent at best, but her long drawn-out notes shimmered against a dark backdrop, and wondrous spirits came alive, peering with dark eyes deep into the heart's domain. I don't know how I could have been closed off to such a surge of musical feeling for so long.

"The time came for the sisters' benefit concert; Lauretta and I presented a long scene from an opera by Anfossi. She sang and I sat by, as usual, accompanying her on the piano. About to sing the last fermata, Lauretta summoned all her artistry. Nightingale twitters swelled and receded— notes held— then bright, ruffled roulades, followed by a burst of solfeggio! Truth to tell, this time it almost seemed to last too long. I felt a soft breath; Teresina stood behind me. At the same time Lauretta started toward a surging harmonic trill, which would then fall back into tempo.

Satan interceded, making me bang out the chord with both hands, and the orchestra followed at precisely the same moment that Lauretta produced her trill, the highpoint of her performance, intended to stun the audience. Piercing me with a livid look, she tore the score into pieces, flung them at my head so that the strips of paper fluttered around me, and ran in a frenzy through the orchestra into the adjoining room. As soon as the *tutti* came to a close, I ran after her. She wept, she raged. 'Out of my sight, you lout!' she shrieked at me. 'Vile devil, you brought my undoing— ruined my reputation, stained my honor— tarnished my trill— out of my sight, you cursed son of hell!' She leapt at me, but I escaped through the door. For the remainder of the concert, while someone else directed, Teresina and the kapellmeister managed to mollify the seething singer sufficiently so that she decided to appear again; but I was not permitted to return to the piano. In the last duet sung by the sisters, Lauretta really managed to bring off the surging harmonic trill, and was greeted with a thunderous ovation which put her in a wonderful mood. In the meantime, I could not get over the awful treatment I had suffered from Lauretta in the presence of so many strangers, and had firmly resolved to return to my native town the next morning.

"I had just packed my things when Teresina entered my room. Acknowledging my intent, she cried out in amazement, 'You want to leave us?' I explained that, after having suffered such humiliation from Lauretta, I could no longer remain in her presence. 'So it's the mad doings of a bedlamite, who already sincerely regrets her actions, that drives you away?' said Teresina. 'But where can you live out your art any better than in our company? With your sober response you alone can keep Lauretta from going off on another fit of hysteria. You're too acquiescent, too sweet, too gentle. You hold Lauretta's art in too high esteem. Her voice isn't half bad and she does have a great range, it's true, but all those over-exuberant flourishes, those immeasurably long held notes, those endless trills – what else are they but dazzling leaps to be admired like the daredevil high-wire sprints of a tightrope walker? Can such an audacious stunt stir our souls and move our hearts? I really can't abide the harmonic trill that you spoiled, it makes me feel uneasy and hurts my ears. And then that sudden rise of pitch, is that not a forced strain on the natural voice that only stirs us when it stays true to itself? I prefer the middle and the deep tones. A clearly sung note that touches us deeply, a true *portamento di voce* means more to me than anything else. No unnecessary embellishment, a firmly held note – a certain musical expression that encompasses soul and mood – that is real singing, and that's how I sing. If you don't care for Lauretta any longer, then think of Teresina, who holds you in her heart, since in your own unique fashion you will become my maestro and *compositore*. Please don't take it badly! All of your dainty canzonettas and arias can't hold a candle to the real thing!' Teresina sang with her sonorous rich voice a simple church canzone I had arranged some days ago. Never did I imagine that it could sound like that. The notes struck my ears with a wondrous force, tears of joy and delight welled up in my eyes, and I reached for Teresina's hand and pressed it a thousand times to my lips, swearing never to part from her.

"With a bitter, jealous rage, Lauretta observed my burgeoning relations with Teresina, all the while still needing me, for despite her artistry she was unable to rehearse anything new without assistance; she was bad at reading music and had trouble keeping time. Teresina read everything directly from the score, in addition to which her sense of timing was impeccable. Never did Lauretta's willfulness and her impetuosity manifest themselves more stridently than when practicing with a pianist. The accompaniment was always off— she treated it as a necessary evil— best not to hear the piano at all, keep it pianissimo— the pianist must always acquiesce— every cadence sounded different, just as she happened to construe it at that moment. But now I opposed her with firm determination, I countered her clumsiness, I proved to her that accompaniment without zest was unthinkable, that truly carrying a melody was markedly different from tactless fumbling. Teresina faithfully backed me up. I composed only church music and wrote all solos for a deep voice. Teresina likewise lorded it over me, but I put up with it, for she had a greater mastery, and (so I believed) a better grasp of German gravitas than Lauretta.

"We traveled through southern Germany. In a small town we met an Italian tenor who wanted to go from Milan to Berlin. My ladies were enchanted by their compatriot; he never spent a moment away from them, he took a particular liking to Teresina, and to my considerable chagrin I now played second fiddle to him. One time, just as I was about to enter their room with a musical score under my arm, I overheard a lively conversation between my ladies and the tenor. My name was mentioned – I hesitated and pricked up my ears. I was now so conversant in Italian that I didn't miss a word. Lauretta spoke of the tragic incident at the concert, when I cut off her trill through my untimely striking of the piano keys.

"'*Asino Tedesco*,'* cried the tenor; I felt like storming in and tossing the theatrical windbag out the window – but I held back.

* German ass.

[247]

"Lauretta continued that she had immediately wanted to get rid of me, but that, moved by my beseeching pleas, she decided out of pity to tolerate my presence and let me stick around, since I wanted to learn the art of bel canto from her. It was no small surprise to hear Teresina confirm this. 'He's a good child,' she added, 'now he's in love with me and writes everything for alto. He does have a middling talent, but he's got to work his way out of his typically German stiffness and stodginess. I hope to mold him into a *compositore* who can write a couple of competent pieces for me, since so little is written for alto voice, then I'll send him packing. He's a perfect bore with all his lovey-doveyness and pining, and he tries my patience with his tiresome and perfectly pitiful compositions.'

"'At least I'm rid of him now,' Lauretta interjected, 'you know how that pitiful fellow harassed me with his arias and duets, don't you Teresina?' Now Lauretta launched into a duet that I had composed and that she had praised to high heaven in the past. Teresina took up the second voice, and together they made mincemeat of my music. The tenor laughed so hard that the room resounded with his merriment – an icy chill ran down my spine – I made up my mind then and there. Silently I slipped away from the door and back into my room, whose window faced the side street.

"The post office was located across the street, and at that very moment the postal stagecoach to Bamberg pulled in, ready for boarding and to be loaded with mail. The passengers already stood lined up at the departure gate, but I still had an hour before the scheduled departure. I hastily packed my things, generously paid the entire bill for lodgings, and rushed off to the postal station. As I rode in the carriage across the wide street, I spotted my ladies with the tenor still standing at the window, leaning out at the blast of the post horn. I sat back in my seat and contemplated with pleasure the effect of the bitter note I left for them back at the inn."

With great gusto, Theodor slurped down the dregs of the glowing Aleatico Blanco that Eduard had served him, promptly popping open a new bottle, and skillfully draining off the droplet of oil at the neck. "I would never have suspected Teresina of such duplicity and perfidy. I can't get the pretty picture out of my mind of her seated on that horse that pranced about as she sang Spanish romanzas. That for me was the pinnacle of her artistry," Theodor reflected. "I can still remember the vivid impression that scene made on me. I forgot all my misery; Teresina truly seemed like a higher being. Such moments mark us and suddenly and forevermore epitomize some heretofore unformulated notion that time can never erase. When, on rare occasions, I managed to pull off a jaunty romanza, at the moment of composition that picture of Teresina in the saddle immediately emerged from memory and leapt to mind."

"Still," said Eduard, "let us not forget the artful Lauretta, and all your grievances aside, let us drink to the two sisters' health."

And so they did!

"Oh," said Theodor, "how the delightful fragrances of Italy waft forth from this wine— how a fresh burst of life sparks my nerves and infuses my veins!— Why in heaven's name did I have to have to go and leave that lovely land!"

"But wait," Eduard objected, "in all that you've told me so far, I see no connection with that heavenly painting, and so, I imagine, you still have more to tell me about the two sisters. It is clear to me that the ladies depicted in the painting can be none other than Lauretta and Teresina."

[249]

"They are indeed," replied Theodor, "and my wistful sighs reminiscent of that lovely land are a fitting prelude to what I still have to tell. Two years ago, before leaving Rome, I made a little sortie on horseback from the city. I passed a girl with a welcoming manner standing in front of a locanda out in the country, and I was struck by a whim of how pleasant it must be to let myself be served an ambrosial drop of wine by that sweet child. I halted at the door and peered through the leafy pergola pierced by bright rays of sunlight. Song and the sweet sound of plucked guitar strings echoed from the distance. I pricked up my ears, as the two female voices had a profound effect on me, generating a slew of dark memories I could not place. I dismounted from my horse, and listening intently to every note, slowly approached the pergola from which the music seemed to emanate. The first voice sang a solo canzonetta. The closer I came to the source of the music, the less I was gripped by that sense of the familiar that had first struck me. The songstress was in the process of singing a brilliant ruffling fermata. It eddied up and down— up and down— finally holding in a single extended tone— but then another female voice exploded in a vehement outburst— maledictions, execrations, invectives! A man protested. Another man laughed. The second female voice intervened. The dispute grew ever more heated, fueled with Italian *rabbia*.— Finally, I was standing right before the pergola— an abbot stormed out and almost knocked me over— he turned around to make sure I was all right, and I recognized the good Signor Ludovico, my musical gossip-monger from Rome. 'Well, for heaven's sake!' I cried out.

"'Ah, Signor Maestro! Signor Maestro!' he pleaded. 'Save me, please save me from these raging furies— from that crocodile— that tiger— that hyena— that devil of a girl! I admit it— I admit it— I beat time for Anfossi's canzonetta, and lowered my baton at the wrong moment in the fermata— I cut off her trill— but why did I look her in the eyes, that satanic goddess!— The devil take all fermatas— the whole lot of them!'

"Lurching along, I strode with the abbot into the pergola and recognized at first glance the sisters Lauretta and Teresina. Lauretta kept screaming and clamoring, Teresina kept admonishing her with heated words – with his bare arms crossed, the tavernkeeper looked on, laughing, while a girl set down new bottles on the table. As soon as the songstresses saw me, they fell upon me, exclaiming 'Ah, Signor Teodoro!' and showering me with caresses. The dispute was forgotten.

"'Look at him,' Lauretta said to the abbot, 'there's a real *compositore*, graceful like an Italian, strong like a German!'

"Tempestuously interrupting each other, they told of the good times we spent together, of my profound musical mastery, even as a young man— of our rehearsals— of the excellence of my compositions— never had they wanted to sing anything but what I wrote.

"Teresina finally let slip that she had been hired by an impresario as the lead tragic singer at the next carnival, but she now maintained that she would only sing provided that I was commissioned to write a tragic opera. The solemn, tragic was, after all, my special domain.

"Lauretta countered, on the other hand, that it would be a shame if I did not pursue my natural proclivity for the delicate, the graceful note, in short, for opera buffa. She had just been engaged as lead singer for an opera house, and it stood to reason that no one but I should compose the opera for her to sing. You can well imagine with what a bountiful burst of feelings I stood there between the two of them. By the way, as you can see, it's the very scene I overheard that Hummel depicts, and at precisely the same moment that the abbot misses the beat, upending Lauretta's fermata."

"But what of your hasty departure and the bitter note you left behind?" said Eduard. "Did the ladies not give it any more thought?"

"They spoke not a word of it, nor did I," replied Theodor. "My own rancor had long since faded and the memory of my adventure with the sisters amused me. The only thing I permitted myself was to tell the abbot how many years ago, while accompanying Lauretta in an aria by Anfossi, that same mishap with the fermata befell me as did him today. I squeezed the ups and downs of my entire time spent with those ladies into that tragicomic scene, and while taking a few pointed sideswipes at them, I gave them to understand the distance that subsequent years of life and artistic experience had given me. 'And it was a good thing that I put a stop to that fermata,' I concluded, 'the thing was likely to last a good long while longer, and I believe, had I let the songstress go on, I'd still be seated at that piano.'

"'But, Signor,' replied the abbot, 'what maestro can presume to hold the prima donna up to ordinary musical standards? Your misdeed in the concert hall, moreover, was much greater than mine here in the sundrenched pergola of a locanda – the fact is, I was only a virtual maestro, no one would set any store in it – and had I not been bewitched by the sweet fiery look of those heavenly eyes, I would not have made an ass of myself.' The abbot's last words proved salutary, for as he spoke, Lauretta, whose eyes had started sparkling again with fury, was mollified.

"We spent the rest of the evening together. Fourteen years – that's how much time had passed since I had parted from the sisters – change a lot.

Lauretta had aged considerably; even so, she was not without her charms. Much better preserved, Teresina had not lost her lovely figure, and her entire appearance was as before, thus she was fourteen years younger-looking than herself. On my request, Teresina sang some of the solemn songs that had moved me in the past, but it seemed to me as if they sounded different than they once had in memory. The same held true for Lauretta's singing, and though her voice had not noticeably lost any of its force or range, it sounded altogether different from the voice I preserved in memory. Already, this imposition of a comparison between my idealized memory and the not altogether gratifying reality upset me all the more so, since the sisters' comportment toward me, their feigned ecstasy, their indelicate admiration that did, after all, take on a patronizing tone, had already made me ill at ease. The droll abbot, who played up his role as the sisters' *amoroso*, and the good wine richly savored finally restored my humor, so that we all spent a very congenial time together. The sisters eagerly invited me to their room to discuss the essentials concerning the scores that I was to write for them. – I left Rome without seeing them again."

"And yet," said Eduard, "you are indebted to them for having awakened the music in your soul."

"Indeed," Theodor replied, "and for a slew of good melodies too, but for that very reason I should never have seen them again. Every composer preserves a vivid impression that time cannot crush. The spirit of music spoke forth in me, and that was the creative impetus that suddenly awakened kindred tendencies; it radiated from within and can nevermore be extinguished. No doubt all melodies that emanate from within us only seem to belong to the songstress who sings them, whose rendition ignited the first sparks. We hear it and just transcribe what they sing. But it is an inherited trait of us feeble mortals that, clinging to a clod of earth, we tend to want to drag down the otherworldly into the pitiful confinement of our earthly existence. And so we take the songstress as our beloved – sometimes even our wife! – The magic is extinguished, and the inner melody, inclined to communicate transcendent splendor, is reduced to a mundane lament over a broken soup bowl or an ink stain in new linen. Praise be to the composer who never again in his earthly life sets eyes on the one who by some arcane force managed to ignite the spark of his inner music. Although the youth may suffer the tempestuous throes of love's sweet torments and amorous despair when the lovely enchantress leaves him, her physical presence is transmuted into heavenly notes that live on in the eternal blossoming of youth and resplendent beauty, and from these notes are born the unmistakably original melodies. What else is the one who sparked those heavenly notes but an emanation of the highest ideal mirrored in and framed by an accidentally encountered figure."

"Curious, but plausible," said Eduard, as the friends emerged, arm in arm, from the Sala Tarone, and stepped out into the street.

Counselor Krespel

1819

The man of whom I'd like to speak is none other than Counselor Krespel of H——.

This Counselor Krespel was, in fact, one of the most peculiar people I've ever crossed paths with in life. When I moved to H——, where I intended to stay awhile, the whole city was talking about him, since one of his most harebrained devilries was just then in full flower. Krespel was renowned as a deft jurist and a capable diplomat. A ruling prince of little significance had turned to him to draft a document upholding his legal claim to a certain territory, the plan for which he proposed to submit to the emperor. The counselor carried out the prince's wish with the desired result and, since Krespel once complained that he had never found accommodations suitable to his needs, the prince assumed the total cost of a house that Krespel planned to have built entirely according to his own specifications to repay him for his help with the memorial. The prince even proposed to pay for the building site, as per Krespel's selection; but this Krespel did not accept, insisting rather that the house be built in his garden located in the loveliest district just outside the city gate. So he bought all the necessary building materials and had them transported to the site; he was then seen for days on end dressed in his curious gown (which, moreover, he himself had fashioned according to his own specifications), unloading lime, sifting sand, stacking the building stones in even heaps, etc. He had not spoken to a single master builder, nor had he thought of a ground plan.

One fine day he called on a worthy wall builder in H—— and bid him appear in the garden the following morning at daybreak along with all his apprentices and hired hands, a slew of odd-jobbers and the like to build his house. The architect naturally asked after the ground plan, and expressed considerable surprise when Krespel replied that none was needed, and everything would fall in line. When the master builder appeared the next morning with his people at said locale, he found a perfect square-shaped ditch, and Krespel said, "The foundation of my house is to be laid here, and then I ask that the four walls be raised until I say they're high enough."

"Without windows and doors, without transverse walls?" the architect interrupted, as if stunned by Krespel's madness.

"Just as I tell you, my good man," Krespel very calmly replied, "the rest will all work itself out."

Only the promise of generous payment finally prompted the architect to commence the ridiculous construction; but never has a building been built with more merriment, for the four walls rose with exceptional dispatch, the work accompanied by the constant laughter of the workers, who were treated to endless food and drink, until Krespel called out, "Stop!

Trowel and hammer fell still, the workers climbed down from the scaffolding, and as they circled around Krespel, every face seemed to ask, "So what now?"

"Take your place!" cried Krespel, who then ran to one end of the garden, turned around and slowly approached his perfect square; having arrived at the wall he reluctantly shook his head, ran to the other end of the garden, once again strode toward the square, and again did as before. He did the same thing several times, until finally striking with the tip of his nose hard against the walls, he cried out at the top of his voice, "Get to it, get to it, you workmen, break down a door, break down a door for me here!" He indicated precisely the length and width in feet and inches, and all was done as he ordered.

Then he went inside the house and smiled complacently as the architect remarked that the walls came to precisely the height of a stately two-story domicile. Krespel strode back and forth inside, followed by the masons with hammer and pickax, and when he cried out, "Here a window six feet high, four feet wide!"— "There a little turret three feet high, two feet wide!" the walls were promptly bashed in based on his specifications.

It was at this very time that I arrived in H——, and it was most amusing to watch as hundreds of people stood around the garden, and gave a loud cheer each time the stones flew out, and yet another window appeared where no one had expected it. Krespel had the house's remaining buildout and all accompanying tasks accomplished in exactly the same way, all hollowed out on the spot according to his precise orders. The absurdity of the entire undertaking, the growing conviction that everything would in the end work out much better than anyone expected, and in particular, Krespel's generosity – that, granted, cost him nothing – kept everyone in a good mood. Thus the difficulties necessarily precipitated by the unorthodox manner of building were redressed, and in no time at all a fully furnished house stood there – a house which, viewed from the outside, made the strangest impression since no one window resembled another and so on – but the interior of which evoked entirely its own sense of well-being. This was confirmed by everyone who entered, and I myself felt it when, after a closer acquaintance with him, Krespel invited me in. As a matter of fact, I had not until then exchanged so much as a word with the man; he was so preoccupied with the construction of his house that he did not even, as had heretofore been his wont, attend Tuesday lunches at the home of Professor M———, and informed the latter upon receipt of a personal invitation, that prior to the housewarming of his new home he would not set foot outside. All of his friends and acquaintances anticipated being invited to a big meal, but Krespel invited no one but the master builder, journeymen, hired hands, and handymen who had been involved in building his house. He treated them to the most lavish dishes; masons' helpers hungrily gobbled down partridge pâtés, apprentice joiners blissfully carved up roast pheasants, and hungry handymen managed to lay their hands on the most exquisite forkfuls of truffle fricassee.

That evening, the wives and daughters came for a great ball. Krespel took a turn waltzing with the wives, but then sat himself down with the musicians, grabbed a violin, and conducted the dance music until dawn.

The Tuesday following this festivity – in the wake of which Krespel was hailed as a friend of the people – to my considerable delight, I finally found him at Professor M——'s for lunch. You could not invent a more curious comportment. Stiff and clumsy in his movements, at any moment you would have thought that he'd collide with someone or something and do some damage. But that did not happen, a fact one might well have foreseen since the lady of the house did not display the least concern when he galivanted around the table set with the finest china, when he maneuvered his way toward the floor-to-ceiling-length mirror, nor even when he grabbed hold of a flowerpot of splendidly glazed porcelain and tossed it in the air, as if he wished to let the colors run. Krespel, in fact, examined everything on the professor's table with the most careful attention, even going so far as to climb onto a padded chair, take a painting down off the wall, and hang it up again.

All the while, he accompanied his actions with copious commentary vehemently expressed, sometimes (this was particularly conspicuous at table) jumping hastily from one subject to another, sometimes unable to let go of an idea, taking it up again and again, getting lost in all sorts of conceptual blind alleys, unable to find his way out until some other idea took hold. Sometimes his tone was gruff, howled at the top of his lungs, sometimes softly drawled, trilled; but the manner never matched the subject at hand.

If music was being discussed, a new composer lauded, Krespel chuckled and cantillated softly, "Would that the black-feathered Satan fling that accursed tone-bender ten thousand million fathoms into the abyss of hell!" Then he expostulated heftily and wildly about some diva: "She is an angel from heaven, emitting nothing but pure God-blessed tone and timbre— the bright ideal and starry constellation of all song!" And as he spoke, his eyes welled up with tears. All present had to be reminded that an hour ago they were talking about a famous female singer.

A roast hare was devoured, and I noticed that Krespel painstakingly gnawed off the flesh, left the bare bones lying on his plate, and made inquiries after the hare's foot which the professor's five-year-old daughter fetched for him with a friendly smile. Even during the meal, the children regarded the counselor with canny smiles, and now they got up from the table and approached him, albeit with bashful respect, maintaining a distance of three paces. What surprise lay ahead? I thought to myself. The dessert was served; then the counselor plucked a coffret out of his pocket that contained a little steel lathe. He promptly screwed this onto the table, and carved up the hare bones with unbelievable agility and speed into all sorts of tiny little canisters and boxes and balls which the children received with wild delight.

At the moment of rising from the table, the professor's niece asked, "How is our Antonia doing, dear Counselor?"

Krespel made a face, like someone who had just bitten into a bitter orange, but wished to appear as if he had just enjoyed something sweet. Soon this look twisted itself into a gray mask from which an altogether bitter, fierce, indeed it seemed to me, downright devilish derision spewed forth. "Our? Our dear Antonia?" he inquired in a slow, drawn-out, disagreeable singsong.

The professor soon interceded; in the punishing look he gave his niece, I understood that she had touched a chord that needs must disseminate a repugnant dissonance in Krespel's heart of hearts. "What's happening with the violins?" the professor asked in a right jovial manner, clasping the counselor by his hands.

At this, Krespel's facial expression lightened up and he replied with his loud voice: "Splendid, Professor, why just this morning I cracked open that capital instrument made by Amati, the one I told you about. What a stroke of good luck that it happened to fall into my hands. I hope that Antonia will give it a good workout with her bow."

"Antonia is a good child," said the professor.

"That's a fact, she is indeed," the counselor cried out, turning around quickly. In one fell swoop he had grabbed hat and stick, and leapt out the door. In the mirror I noticed that hot tears welled up in his eyes.

As soon as the counselor had departed, I dashed over to the professor to ask him to explain the business about the violins, and above all about Antonia.

"Well let me tell you," said the professor, "just as the counselor is in all other respects a one-of-a-kind, he pursues instrument building in the most peculiar manner."

"Instrument building?" I asked, altogether taken by surprise.

"Yes," the professor continued, "according to connoisseurs, Krespel fashions the most splendid violins being made nowadays; in the past, from time to time, if a fiddler struck his fancy, he let him or her play his instruments, but for quite some time now he has stopped doing so. Once Krespel finishes fashioning a violin he himself plays it for an hour or two, indeed with great vigor and captivating expression. Afterward, however, he hangs it among the others without ever touching it again or allowing anyone else to touch it. If there is any prized fiddle fashioned by an old master to be had by hook or by crook, the counselor buys it for whatever price asked. But just as he does with his own instruments, he only plays it a single time, before disassembling it to inspect and analyze the structural finesse. And if he fails to find what by his own criteria he happens to be looking for, disgruntled, he flings the mangled instrument into a great big closet already full of the scattered parts of other precious violins."

"But what about Antonia?" I hastened to inquire with keen interest.

"That, my friend," the professor continued, "that is a delicate matter that could arouse the counselor's greatest consternation, were I not convinced that, given his fundamentally good-natured character bordering on softness, it did not concern some secret consideration. When, many years ago, the counselor came to live in H——, he lived like an anchorite, with an old housekeeper in a house on X—— Street. Soon, on account of his curious ways, he aroused the curiosity of his neighbors, and as soon as he became aware of this he sought and found acquaintances. Just as in my house, people everywhere grew so accustomed to his presence that he became indispensable. His rough exterior notwithstanding, even the children took him to heart without burdening him with their attention, since despite all fondness, they maintained a certain respectful distance that shielded him from being overwhelmed. You have already seen how he has a way of winning over the children with all manner of amusements. We all held him for a confirmed bachelor, and he never gave us reason to doubt it. After having lived here among us for some time, he took a trip (no one knew where to), and returned several months later.

"The evening following his return, Krespel's windows were uncommonly lit up. This already made the neighbors take notice. But soon they bore witness to the altogether wondrously lovely voice of a woman accompanied by a pianoforte. Then the stroked tones of a violin resounded and wrestled in fiery combat with the voice. Everyone immediately recognized the counselor playing the violin – I myself joined the considerable crowd that had gathered before the counselor's house for the wondrous concert, and I must admit that the voices of the most famous female singers I'd ever heard sounded flat and inexpressive compared to the altogether singular singing style of that unknown diva that reached deep down into the heart of the listener. Never had I had the faintest inkling of these long-drawn-out notes, of this nightingale trill, of such billowing and breaking undulations, of this rising intonation to the forceful blast of a wind organ, of this subtly articulated tempering into the faintest breath. There was no one in the crowd who failed to be enveloped by that sweetest enchantment, and in the silence that followed her singing all you could hear were quiet sighs.

"It must have already been midnight when the counselor was heard speaking loudly, and based on what we could make out, another man's voice seemed to chime in with reproaches, and in between you could detect a girl's interrupted outbursts. The counselor yelled more and more vehemently, until finally he fell into that slow, drawn-out singsong tone that you know. His outburst was interrupted by a loud scream from the girl, followed by a deathly silence, until suddenly someone went stomping down the stairs and a young man staggered out sobbing, flung himself into a postal carriage waiting nearby, and whizzed away.

"The following day, the counselor appeared to be very merry, and no one had the courage to inquire after the incident of the night before. But when asked, the housekeeper replied that he had brought home a lovely young girl whom he called Antonia, and who sang just as sweetly as she looked. A young man also came along, who appeared to be on intimate terms with Antonia and must surely have been her fiancé. But the latter had been obliged to beat a hasty retreat, on the counselor's prompting. What relation Antonia bears to the counselor remains a mystery to this day, but one thing is certain – that he tyrannizes the poor girl in the most hateful manner. He watches over her, like Doctor Bartholo watches over his Mündel in *The Barber of Seville*; she's seldom even allowed to show her face at the window. When once, after her pleading entreaties, he finally gave in and took her out into society, he kept an eagle eye on her and could not stand that a single musical note be heard, far less that Antonia sing; moreover, she was no longer allowed to sing in his house. For the people of our city, Antonia's singing on that night consequently turned into something of a fantasy, a soul-stirring legend of a splendid miracle. Even those who did not hear her sing often remark if some female singer tries to make a go of it here: 'What kind of crude warbling is that? The only real singer worth her salt is Antonia.'"

You know all too well that I have a fondness for such fantastical affairs, and can well imagine how essential it was for me to make Antonia's acquaintance. I had often heard those public avowals concerning Antonia's singing in the past, but I never suspected that the beautiful one might be living right here and that she might be held by that madman Krespel, as if in the clutches of a tyrannical wizard. Naturally, the very next night I heard Antonia's magnificent voice, and since it was in a splendiferous adagio (which ridiculously enough, it seemed to me at the moment as if I myself had composed it), I solemnly resolved to save her, to break into Krespel's house, like a second

Astolfo into Alzino's* enchanted fortress, and free the queen of song from ignominious bondage.

Everything happened differently from how I had expected; for no sooner had I seen the counselor two or three times, and engaged in a heated discussion on the optimal structure of the violin, than he himself invited me to visit him at home. This I did, and he proudly showed me his precious collection of instruments. Some thirty violins hung in a cabinet, among which one stood out. Bearing all the marks of great age (engraved lion's head, etc.), it appeared to be hung higher than the others, and was bedecked with a corolla, as queen demanding the obeisance of all the others.

"This violin," observed Krespel, after I had asked him about it, "is a very remarkable, wondrous piece, the handiwork of an unknown master, probably from the time of Tartini. I am absolutely certain that there is something altogether extraordinary about this instrument's inner structure, and that if I disassemble it, a secret which I have long sought after would reveal itself. But – laugh at me if you wish – this dead thing, to which I alone can restore life and sonority, often speaks to me in a wondrous way, and the very first time I stroked its strings it seemed to me as if I were only the hypnotist able to elicit somnambulist notes, and that the instrument itself were expressing its own conception of music – please don't suppose that I am fool enough to give the least credence to such utter poppycock, but it is strange that I never considered myself worthy enough to disassemble that dumb dead thing. I'm glad now that I never did it, for since Antonia is here

---

* Characters in *Orlando Furioso*, a sixteenth-century Italian epic poem by Ludovico Ariosto (1474–1533).

I sometimes play her something on that violin – Antonia is glad, all too glad, to hear it."

The counselor spoke these words with evident emotion, which emboldened me to reply: "Oh, my most esteemed Counselor, would you not deign to play for her in my presence?"

In response to which, however, Krespel gave me a wry look and responded in that slow, drawn-out singsong tone of his, "No, no, my dear sophister!"

And that was the end of that. I was obliged to continue to admire all manner of somewhat childish rarities; until, finally, he reached into a light wooden box, pulled out a folded sheet of paper, and pressed it into my hands, speaking in a ceremonious manner, "You are a friend of art, please accept this little gift as a treasured souvenir that must remain ever precious to you!" With these words he very gently nudged me by both shoulders to the door, and embraced me at the threshold. Essentially, it was his way of symbolically kicking me out the door.

When I unfolded the paper, I found an approximately eighth of an inch of a fifth note string, accompanied by the words: "From the fifth note with which Stamitz, of blessed memory, tuned up his violin before playing his last concert."

The disdainful snub at my allusion to Antonia appeared to underline the fact that I would never set eyes on her; but that was not the case, for when I visited the counselor for a second time, I found Antonia in his room assisting him in the assembly of a violin. At first sight, Antonia's outward appearance made no lasting impression, but soon it was impossible to break free of the look of her blue eyes, her lovely rose lips, and her uncommonly delicate dulcet figure. Her face was very pale, but as soon as something witty or merry was uttered she flashed a sweet smile and a fiery flesh color spread across her cheeks, the rosy shimmer fading fast. I spoke in an altogether uninhibited manner with Antonia, and noticed Krespel giving me none of the Argus-eyed looks that the professor had imputed – he seemed rather to maintain a perfectly even-keeled expression, indeed to follow with interest my exchange with Antonia.

So it happened that I often dropped by the counselor's house, which resulted in a mutual acclimatization in our little circle of three that gladdened our hearts. The counselor continued to amuse me with his altogether singular comic mannerisms; and yet it was Antonia alone I cared about, attracted as I was by her irresistible allure, and I was consequently inclined to overlook some things that would otherwise have riled me. All too often, tasteless and tedious comments were mixed in with the hodgepodge of the counselor's other peculiar remarks, but what I found particularly odious was that whenever I turned the discussion to music, and song in particular, he would stop me with some altogether extraneous and most often mean-spirited remark in his noxious singsong voice, flashing his diabolical grin. From the great distress evident in Antonia's extremely sorrowful look I became aware that Krespel only did this to keep me from making any request that she sing. But I did not let up. With all the snags the counselor thrust in my way, my determination to surmount them grew, lest I lose my mind in my longings and intimations. I simply had to hear Antonia sing.

One evening, Krespel was in particularly high spirits; he had taken apart an old violin from Cremona and discovered that the tailpiece was set at a slightly greater slant than usual. "A significant discovery, particularly so for a performer!" I remarked and managed to spark some heated reflections from Krespel on how to play the violin. The notion that the old masters must surely have been inspired by the great and authentic virtuosos of song led directly to his observation that things are reversed nowadays, that singing is mangled by the singers' desire to follow the affected leaps and flourishes of instrumentalists.

"What can be more senseless," I cried out, jumping up from my chair, running to the pianoforte, and hastening to uncover the keyboard, "What can be more senseless than such convoluted embellishments which, instead of making music, produce a sound like that of dried peas poured on the ground!" I sang some of the modern frills you hear nowadays that whir like a mightily spinning top let loose, accompanying my singing with a couple of pounded chords on the pianoforte.

Krespel laughed profusely and cried out, "Haha! Methinks I hear our Teutonic Italians or our Italian Teutons attempting to interpret an aria by Pucitta or Portogallo, or some sort of maestro di capella, or rather *Schiavo d'un primo uomo*."

Now is the propitious moment, I thought. "Isn't it so?" I turned to Antonia. "Isn't it so, that Antonia knows nothing of such posturing?" I promptly let loose with a rendition of a lovely soulful ditty by old Leonardo Leo.

Antonia's cheeks flushed red, and a heavenly glow illumined her bliss-filled eyes— she leapt to the pianoforte— she parted her lips— but at the exact same moment Krespel shoved her away, grabbed me by the shoulders, and cried out in a strident tenor, "Sonny boy— Sonny boy— Sonny boy." And grasping my hand, with his head bowed politely, he promptly started singing very softly, "In effect, my most esteemed Master Scholiast, in effect, it would breech all good breeding, offend all good manners, were I to give loud and lively voice to my ardent desire that right here and now the Hellish Satan break your neck with a gentle twist of his fiery clawed fists, and in this way, as it were, expedite you to kingdom come; but my best wishes notwithstanding, you must admit, my dearest bosom buddy, that it is getting very dark out, and since no lantern is shining, even if I did not right this minute kick you down the stairs, you might well suffer injury to your dear bones. Do hurry home, and keep fond memories of your true friend, should you never more – you catch my drift? – never more cross his threshold!" Whereupon he took me in his arms, and spun around with me in his firm grip, slowly nudging me out the door, so that I might never again set eyes on Antonia. You will admit that, under the circumstances, it was not possible for me to give the counselor a proper thrashing, as he most definitely deserved.

The professor laughed heartily, and he assured me that I had forevermore burned my bridges with the counselor. Antonia was too precious, I dare say, too holy for me to play the part of pining lover at her window or scheming adventurer plotting to whisk her away. I left H——, shattered in body and soul. But as usually happens, the flamboyant colors of fantasy faded, and Antonia— yes, even Antonia's singing, which I had never heard, often resonated deep in my heart of hearts, soothing me with a soft rosy glow.

Two years later I was already employed in B——, when I set out on a trip in southern Germany. The towers of H—— reared up in the hazy red twilight. As I drew nearer and nearer I was gripped by an indescribable feeling of the most disconsolate angst; it burdened my breast like a heavy load, so much so that I couldn't breathe— I had to climb out of my carriage and stand in the open. But my trepidation grew into a physical pain. It soon seemed to me as if I heard the harmonies of a heavenly choir wafting through the air— the tones became more and more distinct, so that I was able to distinguish men's voices chanting a sacred chorale. "What is that?— What is that?" I cried out, as the sound pierced my breast like a burning dagger!

"Can't you see?" replied the coachman seated beside me. "Can't you see? They're burying someone over there in the churchyard!"

We were indeed driving past a churchyard, and I saw a crowd of people dressed in black standing around an open grave just then being covered with dirt. The tears coursed from my eyes; it was as if they were burying all the zest, all the joy of life. The carriage having advanced quickly, with a hill now cutting off my view, I could no longer peer into the churchyard. The choir went silent, and not far from the churchyard gate I noticed black-clad people returning from the burial. The professor with his niece on his arm, both in deep mourning, passed directly in front of the carriage without noticing me. His niece had a kerchief pressed against her eyes and was sobbing intensely. I suddenly felt unable to enter the city; I sent my servant on ahead with my things in the coach to my accustomed inn, leapt out, and ran into the surrounding fields that I knew all too well so as to rid myself of this mood that, being overheated and exhausted as I was, may well have simply been a physical consequence of the hardships of my long journey.

As I entered the allée leading to a pleasure garden, I witnessed the strangest spectacle. Counselor Krespel was being led forward by two mourners from whose grip he tried by all sorts of twists and turns to break free. He was, as usual, dressed in his peculiar, gray, homemade robe; but from his small triangular cap, which he wore in a martial fashion tilted toward one ear, there dangled an exceedingly long and narrow black crape ribbon that fluttered back and forth in the breeze. Around the middle he had bound a dagger scabbard, but instead of a dagger it contained a long violin bow. An icy chill ran down my spine; he's gone mad, I told myself, as I slowly followed behind. The men in mourning led the counselor to his door, where he embraced them with a loud burst of laughter. As soon as they departed, his glance fell upon me. I was standing directly beside him. He gave me a long blank look, then cried out in a muffled voice, "Welcome, Master Scholiast!—You understand, don't you!" He grabbed me by the arm and tugged me into his house— up the stairs, into the room in which the violins hung. All were enveloped in black crepe; the violins of the old masters were missing, and in their place hung a wreath of cypress.

I knew what had happened. "Antonia, oh Antonia!" I broke down, weeping and wailing inconsolably. The counselor stood there beside me with his arms crossed, as if struck dumb. I pointed to the cypress wreath. "When she died," the counselor said in a muffled and solemn tone of voice, "when she died, the tailpiece in that violin broke with a thunderous snap, and the wooden belly cracked down the middle. The faithful instrument could only live with her and through her; buried alongside her, it lies next to her in the coffin."

Shaken to the core, I sank into a chair, but the counselor started singing a merry song in a hoarse voice, and it felt downright eerie to see him leaping about on one foot, and with his hat on his head, dancing around the black crepe and the instruments hanging on the wall. I could not keep from emitting a piercing cry, when, with a twist, the counselor brought the crepe tumbling down upon me; it seemed to me at that instant as if, having enveloped me in crepe, he sought to tear me down into the terrible black abyss of madness. Suddenly, the counselor stood stock still and said in his singsong voice, "Sonny boy? Sonny boy? Why are you screaming? Have you seen the Angel of Death? That is always how the ceremony begins!" Then he strode to the middle of the room, tore the violin bow out of its sheath, held it in both hands over his head, and broke it so that it splintered into many pieces. Laughing out loud, Krespel cried, "Now the stick has broken over me, and you think I'm done for, don't you, sonny boy? Not at all! Not at all! Now I'm free— free— free! Hurrah, I'm finally free! Now I will build no more fiddles— no more fiddles— no more fiddles, I say!" The counselor sung these words in an unearthly, cheerful melody, as he once again hopped about on one foot. Terrified, I wanted to leap out the door, but the counselor held me tight, speaking to me in a cool and collected tone of voice: "Stay here, Master Scholiast! Please don't misconstrue these outbursts of pain tearing me apart with a martyr's torment as signs of madness, it's all on account of a dressing gown of my own confection I donned some time ago in which I wanted to look like fate itself or like God!"

The counselor kept babbling all manner of befuddled nonsense until finally he collapsed in a state of complete exhaustion. I called out for the old housekeeper, who came running, and was glad to find myself again outdoors. I didn't doubt for a moment that Krespel had gone mad, but the professor maintained the contrary. "There are people," he said, "from whom nature or some calamity tears away the veil behind which the rest of us engage in our mad doings unnoticed. They resemble thin-skinned insects that appear misshapen in the buoyant, visible squirming of their minuscule muscles, though they soon reassume their proper shape. Everything that in us remains merely imagined, in Krespel turns into action. The bitter irony that our well-behaved spirit ordinarily keeps under control in our conduct and actions, drives Krespel to mad gesticulations, twists, and turns. But that is his lightning rod. What emanates from the earth he gives back to the earth, retaining a flicker of the divine spark; and so, I believe, his mind is perfectly in order, notwithstanding the seeming madness of his antics. Antonia's sudden death may well weigh heavy on him, but I wager that the counselor will once again get his donkey trotting on course tomorrow." Things happened almost exactly as the professor predicted. The next day the counselor seemed back to his old ways, except that he declared that he would never again fashion violins, and never more play on one – a vow that I later learned he kept.

The professor's allusions confirmed my firm conviction that Antonia's intimate and painstakingly concealed tie to the counselor, as well as her sudden death, burdened him with a heavy sense of guilt for which he could not manage to atone. I resolved not to leave H—— without confronting him with the crime I suspected; I wanted to shake him to the core and thereby wrest a confession of his ghastly deed. The more I thought it over, the more I became convinced that Krespel was, without a doubt, a villainous scoundrel, and the fierier and more emphatic became my planned confrontation with him, evolving into a veritable rhetorical masterpiece. Thereby emboldened, and in a sweat, I ran to the counselor's house. I found him with a tranquil smile on his face, turning wooden toys on a lathe. "How in heaven's name," I let loose, "how in heaven's name can your soul concede a moment of peace, burdened as your conscience must be by that terrible deed, the viper's tooth sting of which surely torments you at all times?"

The counselor looked up surprised, laying aside his chisel. "But why, my most esteemed friend?" he asked. "Please do have a seat!"

But I kept at it, working myself up into a frenzy, accusing him to his face of having killed Antonia, and threatening him with the retribution of celestial justice. As a newly minted lawyer, I went so far as to assure him that I would do everything in my power to get to the bottom of his nefarious deed, and deliver him into the hands of legal authorities. I was indeed a bit taken aback, when at the end of my puffed-up pronouncement, without responding with a single word, the counselor regarded me with a quiet gaze, as if expecting me to continue. Which I did indeed attempt to do, but the words came out so loopy, so foolish sounding, that I immediately fell silent. Krespel basked in my discombobulation, a spiteful ironic smile spreading over his face. But then he became very serious and addressed me in a solemn tone: "Young man, you may take me for mad, altogether off my rocker; for this I forgive you since we are both locked up in the same madhouse. You reproach me for imagining myself to be God the Father, because you take yourself to be God the Son; but how can you presume to intrude in a life, to grasp its secret threads, when the warp and weft of it is and must remain beyond your ken? She is no more, end of story!" Krespel fell silent, got up, and strode back and forth several times in the room. I hazarded the request for clarification; he gave me a blank look, took me by the hand, and led me to the window, pushing both casements wide open.

With his arms cradling his head, he leaned out and, peering down into the garden, told me the story of his life. When he fell silent again, I left him, greatly moved and profoundly embarrassed.

Here, in brief, is the story of Antonia: Twenty years ago, having evolved into a full-fledged passion, the counselor's interest in seeking out and selling the finest violins of the old masters took him to Italy. At the time he had not yet begun to build instruments of his own, and so did not yet disassemble any old violins. In Venice he heard a performance by the renowned singer Angela ———i, who at the time starred in the lead role at the Teatro di S. Benedetto. Enticed not only by her outstanding artistic talent, he was also taken by Signora Angela's angelic beauty. The counselor sought to make her acquaintance and, despite his brusque manner, he succeeded brilliantly in winning her over with his jaunty and highly expressive way of playing the violin. Their most intimate relationship led in a matter of weeks to marriage, which was kept a secret from the world, not only because Angela was unwilling to leave the stage, but also because she refused to drop her famous stage name or even couple it with the cacophonous surname "Krespel."

Krespel described with a devilish irony Signora Angela's inimitable way of goading and tormenting him as soon as she became his wife. According to Krespel, all the willful and petulant ways of every prima donna congealed in Angela's petite figure. As soon as he sought to assert a spouse's prerogative, Angela sent a veritable army of *abbate*, *maestri*, and *academici*, ignorant of the nature of their relationship, to reprimand him as the most insufferable, discourteous lover, unwilling to bow to the signora's endearing caprices. After one such stormy scene, Krespel fled to Angela's country home where, fiddling away on his Cremonese violin, he forgot the day's woes. But not much time passed before the signora, who followed hot on his heels, stormed into the hall. In the mood to play the tender lover, she embraced the counselor, giving him sweet, pining looks, and lay her head on his shoulder. But lost in the world of his chords, the counselor fiddled on, so that the walls resounded, and it happened that with arm and bow he touched the signora somewhat ungraciously. She jumped back in a wild fury; "*bestia tedesca*"* she cried out, tore the violin out of the counselor's hands, and smashed it into a thousand pieces against the marble table. The counselor turned stiff as a statue before her; but then, as if awakened from a dream, he seized the signora with superhuman strength, flung her out the window of her own summer cottage and, without concerning himself with the consequences, fled to Venice – and from there back to Germany.

Only after a while did he realize what he had done; even though he knew that the window was hardly five feet above the ground, under which circumstances the imperative to toss her out made perfect sense to him, he nevertheless felt painfully perturbed, all the more so since the signora had given him to understand in no uncertain terms that she was expecting. He dared not make inquiries, and was quite surprised approximately eight months later to receive a tender note from his loving spouse, in which, not devoting so much as a syllable to the happenings at her country house, and following the news that she had just given birth to a darling little daughter, she added the heartfelt wish that the *marito amato e padre felicissimo*** please make his way back to Venice posthaste. Krespel did not do so; rather,

---

* German beast.

* Beloved husband and most happy father.

making inquiries of a trusted friend, he learned that the signora had landed light as a bird in the grass, and that the fall had had no physical, but only psychological consequences. Following Krespel's heroic deed, the signora had become a changed woman; she no longer made the slightest show of moody fits, mad whims, or any other vexing shenanigans. The maestro who composed music for the next carnival was the happiest man under the sun, since without the hundred thousand modifications he had in the past been obliged to suffer from the signora, she agreed to sing his arias as written. By the way, the friend added, it might be advisable to keep the manner of Angela's cure a tight secret, since otherwise divas would go flying out the window every day.

Greatly moved, the counselor ordered his horses to be hitched up, and climbed into the carriage. "Hold on!" he suddenly cried out. "Who knows," he muttered under his breath, "if the moment I make my appearance, the wicked imp does not once again take hold of Angela? Seeing as I already threw her out the window, what would I do if the same thing happened again? What options are left to me?" He climbed back out of the carriage and wrote a loving letter to his convalescing wife, in which he politely replied how kind it was of her to expressly laud the fact that, like him, their little daughter had a tiny mole behind the ear, and – he stayed in Germany.

The exchange of letters continued in a lively fashion. Assurance of love— invitations— laments at the continued absence of the beloved— frustrated longings— hopes, and all the rest flew back and forth, from Venice to H——, from H—— back to Venice. Finally, Angela came to Germany, and triumphed, as we know, as a prima donna on the stage of the

Great Theater in F———. Despite the fact that she was no longer young, she won everyone over with the irresistible charm of her wondrous singing. Her voice had not lost the least bit of its allure.

Antonia had in the meantime grown up, and the mother could not stop lauding the child in letters, how she was fast becoming a first-rate singer. This fact was confirmed by friends of Krespel who went to F——— to witness and admire the seldom seen phenomenon of two sublime divas performing together. None suspected the intimate connection the counselor had to the two. Krespel would have all too ardently liked to cast his loving eyes on the daughter who lived in his heart and who often appeared to him in dreams, but as soon as he thought of his wife he was overcome by a feeling of uneasiness, and so he stayed home among his dissected violins.

You must surely have heard of the promising young composer B——— in F———, who suddenly disappeared, nobody knows how. (Or did you perchance know him yourself?) He fell so head over heels in love with Antonia that, since the girl reciprocated his love, he appealed to the mother to sanction a union consecrated by art. Angela had no objections, and the counselor was likewise willing, all the more so since the young master's musical compositions found favor in his stern judgement. Krespel thought he had received word of the consummated marriage, but instead received a letter with a black seal signed by an unknown hand. Dr. R——— regrets to inform the counselor that Angela fell seriously ill as a consequence of a cold contracted in the theater, and died on the very day Antonia was to be wed. The ailing Angela had revealed to him, the doctor, that she was

Krespel's wife and that Antonia was his daughter; he had best therefore make haste to assume responsibility for the orphaned girl.

As much as the counselor was shaken by Angela's passing, it soon seemed to him as if a troublesome and sinister element had vanished from his life, and that only now could he breathe freely. The very same day he set out for F———. You won't believe how heartrending the counselor's description of first setting eyes on Antonia was. There was such a wonderfully evocative power in the bizarre twist of his facial expression, which I am hardly able to even begin to describe. Antonia had inherited all of Angela's amiability and beauty, but altogether lacked the ugly flip side of her mother's personality. There was not the slightest trace of a treacherous horse's forked hind hoof kick. The young bridegroom was on hand, as Antonia, who with her sweet soul immediately fathomed her peculiar father's profound appreciation of music, sang one of those motets composed by old Padre Martini that she knew the counselor had asked Angela to sing to him again and again at the height of their love. The counselor wept torrents of tears; never had he heard even Angela sing like that. The sound of Antonia's voice was altogether idiosyncratic and extraordinary, sometimes resembling an aeolian harp, sometimes more like the crescendo of a nightingale. The tones did not seem to spring from a human breast. Glowing with joy and love, Antonia sang and sang all of her most beautiful songs, and B——— provided the most delicate accompaniment in the intervals as only a lovestruck swain could do. At first Krespel listened, bathed in bliss, then he became thoughtful— silent— self-absorbed. At last he jumped up, pressed Antonia to his breast, and begged her in a quiet and muffled tone of voice, "No more singing, if you love me— it weighs heavy on my heart— the fear— the fear— no more singing!"

"No," the counselor later said to Dr. R——, "as she sang and the blush in her face contracted into two dark red spots on her pale cheeks, it was no longer a matter of foolish family resemblance, it was just what I feared."

To which the doctor, whose expression showed deep concern from the start of the conversation, replied, "It may well be that her condition is the consequence of a premature overexertion in singing, or perhaps nature is to blame. In any case, Antonia suffers from an organic pulmonary anomaly that gives her voice such wondrous force and, I am inclined to add, a sonority outside the sphere of ordinary human singing. But her early death is a likely related consequence; if she keeps singing, I give her at the most six months to live."

The counselor felt skewered by these words, as with a hundred swords. It seemed as if, for the first time, a beautiful tree bedecked with the most resplendent blossoms leaned into his life, and it was to be chopped down at the roots so as to never flower again. He made his decision. He told Antonia everything and gave her a choice – she could follow her fiancé, succumb to his allure and that of the world, but consequently court an early death, or she could give her father in his old age a sense of peace and happiness he had never before felt and, in this way, live for many more years. Antonia fell, sobbing, into her father's arms. Sensing that the coming moments would tear his heart to shreds, he did not wait for any further clarification. He spoke to the fiancé, but despite the fact that the latter assured him that not another note would ever spill from Antonia's lips, the counselor knew all too well that even B—— would not be able to withstand the temptation to at least hear Antonia sing his own arias. And even if instructed of Antonia's condition, the world, the musical public, would surely not let up on their demand to hear her sing, since when it comes to pleasure people are egotistic and cruel.

The counselor disappeared from F—— and arrived in H—— with Antonia. B—— fell into a fit of despair upon learning of their disappearance. He followed hot on their heels, caught up with the counselor, and arrived at the same time in H——.

"To see him just once and then die!" begged Antonia.

"Die?— Die?" cried the counselor in a wild rage, an ice-cold shudder passing through his heart. His daughter, the only being in the whole wide world who sparked in his innermost self a newfound joy, who by her very being reconciled him with life, forcibly tore herself free of his heart, and he, her fiancé, wanted the unthinkable to happen. B—— hastened to the piano, Antonia sang, Krespel played up a merry storm on his violin until the red spots appeared on Antonia's cheeks. Then he insisted they stop; but when B—— bid farewell, Antonia suddenly collapsed with a loud scream.

"I believed," (Krespel said to me), "I believed, just as I had foreseen it, that she really was dead, and having raised myself to the pinnacle of emotion I remained calm and sure of myself. I grabbed B—— by the shoulders, who in his torpor looked sheepish and ridiculous, and muttered (the counselor fell back into his singsong voice), 'Most esteemed piano master, since as you wanted and wished for, you really did kill your beloved wife, you might as well be off, unless you are good enough to linger until I run my shiny hunting knife through your heart, so that my daughter, who as you see, is rather pale, can get a little color from your worthy blood. Better run off now— but I could still fling a deft little blade at you from behind!' Muttering these words, I must have looked a little grim; for tearing himself free of my grip, he leapt forward with a scream, out the door, and down the stairs."

After B——— ran off, and the counselor sought to lift up Antonia, who lay unconscious on the ground, the girl raised her eyelids with a sudden deep sigh, however, soon she seemed to want to sink back into death. Krespel broke out in a loud, inconsolable wail. The physician whom the counselor's housekeeper fetched declared Antonia's state to be the consequence of a severe, but by no means fatal, fluke of nature, and indeed his daughter recovered much more quickly than the counselor had supposed. She favored her father with the most heartfelt childish love; she shared all his whimsies – his mad caprices and conceits. She helped him take old violins apart, and glue new ones together.

"I don't want to sing anymore, but to live only for you," she often said to her father with a soft smile, after someone invited her to sing and she declined. The counselor sought from then on, if possible, to spare her such moments, and consequently did not like to take her along on social visits and painstakingly avoided all music. For he knew all too well how painful it must be for Antonia to completely forsake the art that she had so thoroughly mastered. When the counselor had purchased and wanted to take apart the wondrous violin that he had subsequently buried beside her, she softly pleaded, "This one too?" He could not tell what obscure force compelled him to leave it intact, and to play on it. No sooner had he stroked the first notes than Antonia cried out in a loud and cheerful voice, "Oh, it's me – I'm singing again." There was indeed something altogether remarkable about the silver-soft tones of the instrument; they seemed to have been produced by the human breast. Krespel was profoundly moved, he played more superbly than ever, and when in bold partitas he fiddled with great gusto and a deep expressivity, and the music soared and sank, Antonia clapped her hands together and cried out in rapturous delight, "I did it! I really did it!" From then on, her life was infused with a great peacefulness and joy. Oftentimes she said to the counselor: "I'd like to sing something, father!" Then Krespel took the violin down from the wall where it hung and played Antonia's loveliest songs, and her heart was glad.

One night shortly before my arrival in town, the counselor thought he heard someone playing the piano in the room next door, and he soon clearly recognized B—— playing preludes in his particular way. He wanted to shoot up out of bed, but the sound hung like a heavy load over him; as if bound with iron bands, he was unable to budge. Then Antonia chimed in with soft, breath-like tones that soared and soared into a blaring *fortissimo*. The wondrous sounds came together in the deeply moving song that B—— had composed in the pious manner of the old masters. As Krespel recalled, he found himself in an inconceivable state, in which a deathly fear was bound up with a never before experienced rapture. Suddenly he was infused with a dazzling clarity, and at the same time he beheld B—— and Antonia locked in an embrace and peering at each other with silent rapture. The musical tones of the song and the accompanying piano lingered awhile without Antonia visibly moving her lips or B——'s fingers striking the keyboard. The counselor fell into a cloud of unconsciousness in which the image and the musical notes slowly dissolved. When he came to again, he was still gripped by the lingering wave of fear. He raced into Antonia's room. She lay still on the sofa with her eyes shut tight and a blessed smile playing on her lips, with her hand piously folded on her breast, as though asleep and dreaming of heavenly bliss and joyfulness. But she was dead.

Mademoiselle de Scudéry

1819

On the rue Saint-Honoré stood the little house of Mademoiselle de Scudéry, a favorite of Louis XIV and Madame de Maintenon known for her lovely verses.

Late, around midnight – it may have been in the fall of 1680 – there was such a loud knocking at the door that the entire hallway echoed with the sound. Baptiste, who in Mademoiselle's small household simultaneously held the positions of cook, butler, and doorman, had – with his mistress's permission – taken leave to journey to the country to attend his sister's wedding. So Martinière, Mademoiselle's lady-in-waiting, held down the fort on her own. Hearing the resounding knocks, she realized that, since Baptiste was away, the two were left to fend for themselves; it occurred to her that break-ins, burglaries, and murders were widespread in Paris at the time, and so she became convinced that a gang of hoodlums, knowing the house had been left defenseless, sought entry and, once let in, would act on their evil intentions. Consequently, she remained in her room, trembling and undecided, cursing Baptiste and his sister's wedding. Meanwhile, the knocks kept thundering through the hallway, and it seemed to her as if she heard a voice calling: *Open the door, for Christ's sake, do open the door!* Gripped by ever-mounting fear, Martinière finally grabbed the candlestick with the burning candle and ran out into the hall. There, she clearly heard the voice of the person knocking: "For Christ's sake, open the door!"

"Well," thought Martiniere, "that's definitely not the voice of a thief. Who knows, maybe it's a persecuted person seeking refuge in the home of my mistress, someone who is inclined to acts of kindness. But let us be careful!"

She opened the window and, trying to make her voice sound as manly as possible, called out to inquire as to who might be hammering at the door late at night, waking the entire household. In the shimmer of the moonlight breaking through the dark clouds overhead, she caught sight of a tall figure wrapped in a light gray coat, with a wide-brimmed hat pulled down low over the eyes. She then called out in a loud voice, so as to be clearly heard below, "Baptiste, Claude, Pierre, get up and have a look what ne'er-do-well is trying to break into the house."

A soft, almost plaintive voice replied from below, "Ach, Madame Martinière, I know it's you, dear lady, as much as you are taking pains to distort your voice. I also know that Baptiste has gone to the country, and that you are alone in the house with your mistress. Please just open the door, and don't be frightened. I must speak to the mademoiselle this very minute."

"What makes you think," replied Martinière, "that my mistress wishes to speak to you in the middle of the night? Don't you know that she is fast asleep, and that there is no way I am going to wake her from the sweet slumber that she, in her advanced years, badly needs!"

"I know," said the man standing below, "I know that your Mademoiselle has just set aside the manuscript of the novel *Clelia* on which she has been tirelessly working, and is at this very moment transcribing several verses which she plans to read tomorrow at the salon of the Marquise de Maintenon. I implore you, Madame Martinière, have mercy and open the door. You must know that it is a matter of saving an unhappy soul from perishing, that the honor, freedom, indeed the very life of a certain individual hangs on this moment in which I must absolutely speak with your mistress. Bear in mind that your employer would surely be eternally furious with you were she to learn that it was you who hard-heartedly rebuffed the poor unfortunate who implores her assistance."

"But why do you seek to elicit my mistress's compassion at this ungodly hour? Come back tomorrow at a proper time!" Martinière called down to the man below.

"Does destiny, when it is about to strike like a fatal bolt of lightning, give a damn about the hour? Open the door, have no fear of a poor suffering soul, helpless and abandoned by the world, hounded, beset by an inconceivable stroke of ill fortune, who begs to be rescued by your mistress from impending danger!" he responded.

Martinière heard how, following these words, the individual standing below moaned and groaned in abysmal pain; moreover, the gentle timbre of his voice, that of a very young man, touched her deeply. Feeling profoundly moved, she went to fetch the key without hesitating another instant.

No sooner had she opened the door than the man wrapped in the gray coat stormed in and, rushing past Martinière down the hallway, cried out in a wild voice: "Take me to Mademoiselle!"

Fearful, Martinière raised the candlestick and the shimmer fell on the deathly pale, terribly contorted face of a young man. Martinière almost fell to the floor in a burst of terror as the young man opened his coat and pulled the bare handle of a stiletto knife from a scabbard. He glared at her with sparkling eyes and cried out in an even more ferocious tone than before, "Take me to Mademoiselle, I told you!"

Martinière saw her mistress to be in the gravest danger, and all the love she felt for her cherished ladyship, whom she revered as a pious, faithful mother, flared up in her heart of hearts and engendered a courage of which she would not have thought herself capable. She hastened to fling shut the door to her bedchamber, which she had left open, stationed herself before it, and declared in no uncertain terms, "Your curious compartment inside this house hardly conforms with your pitiful words outside which, as I now see, ill-advisedly awakened my sympathy. You may not and shall not speak to my mistress at this ungodly hour. If you have no ill intent, you should not shun the light of day. Come back in the morning and present your case. Now, be gone!"

The young man heaved a heavy sigh, glared at Martinière with a terrible look, and brandished his stiletto. Martinière silently committed her soul to the Lord, but stood her ground, and looked the man in the eyes, pressing herself harder against the door to her bed chamber, through which the intruder would have to pass to get to her Ladyship.

"Let me go to your mistress, I tell you!" the man cried out again.

"Do what you will," Martinière replied, "I will not budge from this spot. Commit the evil deed you intended, you too will find your ignominious death on the Place de Grève, along with your accursed fellow cutthroats."

"Ha," cried the young man, "you are quite right, Martinière! I look like and am armed like a nefarious thief and murderer. But my comrades in arms have not been executed— no!— they've not been executed!" Casting poisonous looks at the woman, whom he had already frightened half to death, he raised his stiletto.

"Jesus!" she cried out, awaiting a fatal blow. But at that moment the clatter of arms and the clip-clop of horses' hooves became audible outside on the street. "Gentlemen of the constabulary! Gentlemen of the constabulary! Help! Help!" cried Martinière.

"Wretched woman, you seek my ruin – now I'm done for! All is lost, all is lost! Take this! Take it! Give it to Mademoiselle before morning – or tomorrow if you like!" Muttering these words quietly, the young man tore the candlestick out of the servant's grip, blew out the candle, and pressed a little coffret into her hands. "For the sake of your mortal soul, give that package to Mademoiselle," he cried, and ran out into the street.

Having fallen to the ground, Martinière got back up with difficulty, and felt her way in the darkened corridor back to her room where, thoroughly drained and unable to say a word, she sank into an armchair. Then she heard the jangle of the key she had left inserted in the front door lock. The house was locked, and uncertain, quiet steps approached her bed chamber. Glued to the spot, without strength enough to budge, she awaited the worst. Imagine her surprise when the door was flung open, and in the shimmer of a night-light she immediately recognized her honest colleague, Baptiste, looking pale as death and deeply disturbed.

"For the love of God, for the love of God, pray tell me, Madame Martinière, what in heaven has happened? Driven by terror— a premonition of terror!— I don't know what it was— something drew me away from the wedding last night! And here I am on our street. Madame Martinière is a light sleeper, I thought to myself, she'll surely hear me lightly tapping on the door and let me in. Then a formidable military patrol comes my way – cavalry, infantry armed to the teeth – confronts me and won't let me go. Fortunately, Lieutenant Desgrais of the Gendarmes, whom I know well, was among them; he spoke up as they shone the lantern under my nose. 'Well, for God's sake, Baptiste, what are you doing gadding about in the middle of the night? You've got to stay put and guard the house. Strange to find you here, we're out to catch us a big one tonight.' You can't possibly imagine, Madame Martinière, how these words moved me. But as I stood at the threshold, a cloaked man came bounding out with a shiny stiletto in hand, and gave me the run around. The house is open, the keys stuck in the lock— say, what the devil's going on here?"

Relieved of her mortal terror, Martinière told him all that had happened. Both she and Baptiste stepped inside the hallway and found the candlestick lying on the floor where the stranger had dropped it.

"There's no doubt in my mind," said Baptiste, "that our mistress was about to be robbed and murdered. The intruder knew, by your account, that you were here alone with Mademoiselle, indeed even that she was still awake bent over her writing; no doubt it was one of those crafty rogues who break in and stake out a place, to gauge all the circumstances that could aid in their dastardly assault. And the little coffret, Madame Martinière, I think we'd best fling it into the Seine where the current runs deep. Who can say for sure that some accursed fiend does not still have designs on our dear mistress's life, and that in opening the packet she would not drop dead like the old Marquis de Tournay did upon opening that letter he'd received from an unknown sender!"

Thinking it over for a long time, the two faithful servants decided to reveal everything that had happened to their mistress, and to hand her the mysterious little packet, which could after all be cautiously opened. Together they assessed every aspect of the appearance of the suspicious stranger, deciding that a secret might well be at play here that they could not resolve on their own, but had best leave the resolution to Her Ladyship.

Baptiste's concerns were well founded. At that very moment Paris was the stage for the most horrendous atrocities and, concurrently, the most devilish inventions of hell presented the simplest means to fulfill evil intent.

Like others of his calling, Glaser, a German apothecary and the best chemist of his day, engaged in alchemical experiments. He sought to discover the stone of wisdom. He was assisted in his work by an Italian named Exili. The latter employed his goldsmithing craft as a mere front. He only sought to master the skill of mixing, boiling, and subtilizing the poison elements – with which Glaser hoped to find salvation – and he finally succeeded in preparing a refined poison that killed either on the spot or slowly and left no traces in the body of the deceased, deluding the art and science of the doctors of the day who, failing to suspect poisoning, were obliged to ascribe the death to natural causes. As circumspectly as Exili went about his business, he was finally apprehended as a suspect in the sale of poison and brought to the Bastille. In the same cell, soon thereafter, they imprisoned Captain Godin de Sainte Croix. The latter had conducted for the longest time an illicit affair with the Marquise de Brinvillier, bringing scandal on the entire family. Since the marquis proved oblivious to the crime of his spouse, her father, Dreux d'Aubray, a police lieutenant in Paris, finally took it upon himself to separate the sinners with a warrant issued for the captain's arrest. Impetuous, without character, scorning piety, and inclined from youth to debauchery of all sorts, jealous, longing for revenge, Sainte Croix could not have found a more welcome boon than Exili's devilish secret which gave him the power to eliminate all his enemies. He became Exili's avid apprentice, and soon imitated his master so that, once released from the Bastille, he was able to go about his business on his own.

Madame de Brinvillier was a decadent woman; under the influence of Sainte Croix she became a monster. Seeking revenge, he induced her to poison her father under the guise of caring for him in his old age. Then, for the sake of the rich inheritance, to poison both her brothers, and finally her sister. The report of several such murders by poisoning set an example that led crimes of this sort to become an irresistible passion. For no reason other than taking pleasure in the act, like the chemist who takes pleasure in his experiments, poisoners often murdered individuals whose life or death made no difference to the perpetrator. The sudden demise of a number of destitute persons residing in the Hotel Dieu raised the suspicion that the loaves of bread, distributed by Madame Brinvillier on a weekly basis as a token of her piety and benevolence, contained poison. It is certain that the pigeon pies she set before her invited guests were injected with poison. The Chevalier du Guet and many other persons fell victim to these hellish repasts. Sainte Croix, his helper la Chaussée, and Madame Brinvillier managed for the longest time to hide their dastardly deeds; but the eternal scales of heavenly justice ultimately revealed the guile of the degenerate souls, making these evildoers pay the price here on earth. The poisons prepared by Sainte Croix were pounded into such a fine powder (Parisians dubbed it "inheritance powder") that, left lying about following its concoction, a single whiff sufficed to bring on instant death. Consequently, Sainte Croix wore a fine glass mask while whipping up the toxic substance. But one day, when he was about to pour the poison into a vial, the mask fell off, he inhaled the powder, and immediately dropped dead. Seeing as he had no heirs, the court ordered agents who hastened by to put a seal on his estate. There in a crate they discovered his entire hellish arsenal of poison, in addition to letters from Brinvillier that left no doubt as to her role as an accomplice. She fled, seeking refuge in a cloister in Liège. Desgrais, a gendarme, was sent to apprehend her. Disguised as a priest he appeared in the cloister where she hid out. He managed to arrange a love tryst with the wretched woman, luring her to meet him in a lonesome garden outside the city. But no sooner had she arrived than she was surrounded by Desgrais's deputies, the priestly lover suddenly revealed himself to be an officer of the gendarmes, and she was compelled to step into the paddy wagon that stood waiting outside the garden, surrounded by guards, and was driven straight back to Paris. La Chaussée had already been beheaded, and Brinvillier suffered the same fate; following the execution, her body was burned and her ashes tossed to the wind.

Parisians breathed a sigh of relief when that monster was disposed of, believing that that murderous weapon could no more be wielded against friend and foe. But word soon spread that the accursed Sainte Croix's diabolical art had been passed on to others. Like an invisible, insidious phantom, death insinuated itself in the most intimate relationships of the kind founded on family, love, and friendship, and swiftly and surely found its way to its unfortunate victims. He who stood today in the best of health teetered into sudden sickness and expired tomorrow, and the finest physician's art could not save him. Wealth – a lucrative position – a lovely, perhaps too youthful looking woman – all proved cause enough to fall victim. The most terrible distrust separated the holiest bonds. The husband trembled before his wife – the father before his son – the sister before her brother. Dishes at table remained untouched, wines poured among friends remained unsipped, and where merriment and jest had previously prevailed, feral looks were now exchanged in search of the hidden murderer. Fathers fearfully sought provisions to feed the family in the most far-flung districts, preparing their food in filthy sordid cookshops, fearing devilish treachery in their own homes. And sometimes even the greatest, most painstaking precaution was for naught.

In order to put a stop to this terror that was ever more getting out of hand, the king named a tribunal exclusively devoted to the investigation and punishment of these clandestine crimes. The so-called *chambre ardente* held its sessions not far from the Bastille and was presided over by Monsieur la Regnie. For the longest time la Regnie's best efforts, as zealous as they were, proved fruitless. The cunning Desgrais was handed the responsibilty of discovering this most secret corner of crime.

In the suburb of Saint Germain lived an old woman named la Voisin who dabbled in soothsaying and necromantic activities, and with the help of her accomplices, le Sage and le Vigoureux, succeeded in inducing fear and trembling in people not ordinarily given to weakness and gullibility. But she did more than this. Like Sainte Croix, she was one of Exili's disciples. Like her master, she prepared the finely ground, traceless poison, and in this manner helped unscrupulous sons come to early inheritances, and salacious women bed down a second, younger husband. Desgrais uncovered her secret, she confessed everything, and the *chambre ardente* condemned her to death by fire, which she suffered on the Place de Grève. A list was found in her possession of all the persons who had made use of her services, and so it came to pass that, not only did execution follow execution, but also heavy suspicion fell on even the most highly respected people. Consequently, Cardinal Bonzy was suspected of administering la Voisin's powder to all persons to whom, as Archbishop of Narbonne, he was responsible for paying pensions, all of whom he disposed of in short shrift. So too were the Duchess de Bouillon and the Countess de Soissons, whose names were found on the list, accused of dealings with the devilish woman, and even François Henri de Montmonrenci, Bourdebelle, Duke of Luxembourg, Peer and Royal Marshal, did not escape blame. He too was judged by the *chambre ardente*. He surrendered on his own accord to the prison in the Bastille, where Louvois and la Regnie had him locked in a six-foot deep hole. Months passed before it was decided that the duke's crime merited no punishment. Only on one occasion had he let Madame le Sage read his horoscope.

It is certain that blind zeal induced presiding judge la Regnie to commit excesses of force and acts of cruelty. The tribunal took on the character of the Inquisition; the slightest suspicion sufficed to hand out sentences of harsh imprisonment, and the establishment of innocence of those defendants facing execution was often left to happenstance. What is more, la Regnie had a ghastly reputation and underhanded ways, and soon invited the hatred of those whose avenger or protector he was supposed to be. Asked by him in interrogation if she had seen the devil, the Duchess de Bouillon replied: "I believe I am looking him in the eye at this very moment!"

While the blood of the guilty and suspected flowed in torrents on the Place de Grève, and furtive death by poisoning became ever rarer an occurrence, another form of evil mischief spread renewed concern. A band of thieves appeared to have resolved to take all jewels in their possession. No sooner purchased, and stowed away with the greatest care, than costly adornments disappeared in the most inconceivable fashion. Worse still, anyone who dared don jewels come evening was robbed on open streets or in dark alleyways, and sometimes even murdered. Those who escaped with their lives testified that a blow to the head hit them like a bolt of lightning, and once they had woken from their stupefied state, they found themselves divested of their valuables and lying in an altogether different place from where the blow had been delivered. The murdered victims, found almost every morning on the street or inside houses, all bore the same deadly wound. A dagger thrust through the heart, according to physicians' autopsies, had surely brought on such a swift and certain death that the victim must have sunk to the ground, unable to emit a sound. Who at the opulent court of Louis XIV did not engage in a secret amorous tryst at night, sometimes bearing a costly present? As if the scoundrels were in cahoots with the spirit world, they appeared to know exactly when such a meeting was to take place. Often the unfortunate victim did not even reach the house in which he envisioned indulging in love's bliss, oftentimes he dropped dead at the threshold, sometimes even at the door of his beloved who, horror stricken, would discover the bloody corpse.

Argenson, the Paris chief of police, rounded up all shady characters even the least bit suspect, and la Regnie sought to extract confessions, all to no avail. Guard details were strengthened and patrols multiplied, but no trace of the perpetrator could be found. Only the precaution of citizens arming themselves to the teeth and carrying a lantern helped somewhat, and still there were cases of a servant scared away with the toss of a stone, and the master robbed and murdered at the very same instant.

The strange thing was that despite all inquiries in all places where jewelry was bought and sold, not one of the stolen pieces ever turned up, so that there were no clues that might have been followed there either.

Desgrais seethed with rage that the scoundrels managed to elude even his cunning. Any neighborhood in which he happened to find himself was spared, while armed robbery and murder found its wealthy victims in districts where such crimes were least expected.

Desgrais resorted to the artful ruse of disseminating multiple Desgrais look-alikes so similar in gait, posture, speech, physique, and expression that even his bailiffs could not tell the real Desgrais from the fakes. In the meantime, he eavesdropped alone in the most remote corners of the city, risking life and limb, following at a distance this or that person who happened to be wearing precious jewelry. Whoever he tailed remained untouched; the perpetrators must have been onto even this measure. Desgrais got desperate.

One morning he appeared before tribunal president la Regnie, pale and shaken, deeply distraught. "What's the matter? What news do you bring? Did you dig up any clues?"

"Well, Your Honor," Desgrais faltered, at a lost for words, "well, honored Sir— last night— not far from the Louvre, the Marquis de la Fare was attacked in my presence."

"Oh, my God!" la Regnie shouted for joy. "We've got them!"

"Listen, just listen," Desgrais interrupted with a bitter smile. "First listen to the way things turned out. So I'm standing in front of the Louvre with this whole unsavory business weighing on my chest, brooding on the devils who've got me running circles around myself. Then this figure comes walking by with an uncertain step without seeing me. In the glimmer of moonlight, I recognize the Marquis de la Fare. I might well have expected him, I knew where he was slinking off to. He was hardly ten or twelve paces ahead, when another figure leapt up, as if out of the earth, knocked him down, and attacked him. Recklessly, taken by surprise at the moment that might have delivered the murderer into my hands, I cried out at the top of my lungs and with a mighty leap sprang out of my hiding place to accost him, whereupon I got all tangled up in my overcoat and fell flat on my face. I saw the culprit sprinting off, as if on the wings of the wind, so I pulled myself together and ran after him — making tracks, I blew on my horn — from the distance my bailiffs replied with their whistles — arms clanged, the clatter of horses' hooves thundered on all sides. 'This way! This way! It's Desgrais! Desgrais here!' I cried out, so that my voice rang out in the dark. I can still see the culprit clearly in the bright moonlight, turning here, there, trying to give me the slip. When we got to the rue Nicaise, his strength appeared to be giving out and I redoubled my efforts – he was fifteen paces ahead of me at the most.

"You'll outrun him, you've got him, the bailiffs are on the way!" la Regnie cried with fire in his eyes, grabbing Desgrais by the arm as if *he* himself were the fleeing murderer.

"Fifteen paces," Desgrais continued in a muffled voice, wheezing to catch his breath, "just fifteen paces ahead, the man jumped to the side, and passed through the wall, disappearing into the shadows."

"Disappeared? Through the wall? Are you mad!" cried la Regnie, retreating two steps and clapping his hands together.

"Call me what you will," Desgrais continued, stroking his brow like someone tormented by a bad conscience, "call me mad, Your Honor, call me a batty oaf who claims to see ghosts, but it's just like I said. I stood there stock still in front of the wall, as numerous breathless bailiffs came running up, the Marquis de la Fare – who had pulled himself together – with them, clutching a dagger in his hand. We lit torches, we tapped at the wall every which way; not a trace of a door, a window, an opening. It's a sturdy stone wall adjoining a house in which perfectly blameless people live. Today in daylight I reexamined everything. It's the devil himself making a fool of us!"

Desgrais's story was on everyone's lips in Paris. Everyone's head was filled with sorceries, necromantic antics, the devil's bonds of neighbors, le Vigoureux, the infamous priest le Sage; since the inclination to believe in the supernatural and the uncanny has always trumped all reason, people soon became convinced that, as Desgrais himself muttered in a huff, the Devil really was protecting the evil miscreants who had sold him their souls. One can well imagine that Desgrais's account was elaborated upon with florid details. The story was published together with a woodcut depicting a frightfully devilish figure, before whom Desgrais fell to his knees in terror, and sold on every street corner. It was enough to intimidate the public, and even to scare the living daylights out of the bailiffs who, come nightfall, fretful and trembling, wandered the streets draped with amulets and dripping with holy water.

Seeing all the efforts of the *chambre ardente* come to naught, Argenson went to the king to solicit the establishment of a new tribunal which would have even more power to track down and punish the perpetrators. Already convinced that he had accorded the *chambre ardente* too much autonomous license, and appalled by the horrid spectacle of countless executions ordered by the bloodthirsty la Regnie, His Majesty completely rejected the suggestion.

Another path was sought to win over the king.

In the rooms of Madame de Maintenon, where the king spent his afternoons and where he also had a habit of conferring with his ministers until late into the night, a poem was passed along to him in the name of all imperiled lovers, complaining that though gallantry demanded that they bring their beloved a precious gift, in so doing they put their life at risk. And though it was a matter of honor and passion to spill one's blood in chivalric jousts for the sake of one's beloved, falling prey to the sneak attack of a murderer against whom one could not arm oneself was an altogether different matter. The poem called for Louis, the glimmering Polaris of all love and gallantry, to cast his brilliant radiance upon the dark night and thereby illuminate the hidden black secret. The godly hero who fells all his foes will also wield his victorious shimmering sword and, as did Hercules with the Lernaean Hydra, and Theseus with the Minotaur, do battle with the beast that saps all the pleasure of love, and blackens all bliss into the grimmest grief and inconsolable sorrow.

Given how serious the situation was, this poem succeeded with witty, spirited turns of phrase to vividly depict how lovers were obliged to tremble with fear on their secret path to their beloved, how fear defused and nipped in the bud all the lusty anticipation of that adventure in gallantry. And since, moreover, the poem ended with a grandiloquent panegyric of praise to Louis XIV, the king read through it with evident delight. Having finished reading it, with his gaze still fixed on the paper, he promptly turned to Madame de Maintenon, read it again aloud, and asked with a wink and a smile what she thought of the imperiled lovers' plaint. She replied in her ever-serious manner, as always colored with a certain piety, that secret forbidden pathways to love trysts did not merit special protection, but that special measures had most assuredly to be taken to eradicate the terrible perpetrators. Dissatisfied with this wavering response, the king folded the paper. He was about to return to the undersecretary of state busy at work in the room next door when, with a sidelong glance, he noticed Mademoiselle de Scudéry, who happened to be present, seated on an easy chair not far from Madame de Maintenon. Striding toward her, the pleasant smile which had previously played on his lips and then been drained by annoyance once again took the upper hand. Standing directly in front of the writer and unfolding the poem, he spoke softly: "The marquise pretends not to give a hoot about the gallantries of our poor forlorn lovers, and prefers to sidestep forbidden pathways. But you, my dear Mademoiselle, what do you make of this poetic supplication?"

De Scudéry rose respectfully from her chair, and a fleeting blush swept like a last flash of twilight over the pale cheeks of the distinguished lady. Quietly bowing her head with her eyelids shut, she replied:

"Un amant qui craint les voleurs
*N'est point digne d'amour."**

Altogether astounded by the chivalrous spirit of these few words, the king flung the poem with its interminable tirades to the floor and, his eyes flashing, cried out, "By Saint Denis, you're right, Mademoiselle! I'll pass no measure that will sweep up the innocent along with the guilty just to coddle cowardice! Let Argenson and la Regnie do their job!"

The following morning, Martinière described in vivid detail all of the grue-some doings of the day, recounting for her mistress all that had transpired in the previous night and, trembling with fear, handed her the mysterious little coffret. Both she and Baptiste, who stood in the corner, all white in the face, anxiously and apprehensively crushing his nightcap, hardly able to speak, pleaded with their mistress, for the love of God and all his saints, to take the greatest precaution in opening the packet. Weighing and scrutiniz-ing the sealed secret in her hand, de Scudéry replied with a smile, "You're both seeing ghosts! The accursed assassins lurking out there, who, as you

---

* A lover who fears thieves / Is surely not worthy of love.

yourselves admit, are apprised of the ins and outs of every household, know all too well that I'm not rich, that this house holds no precious treasures worthy of murder, and that you and I make poor pickings. Why would they want to take my life? Who could desire the death of a person of seventy-three years of age, who never pursued anyone but the villains and miscreants in the novels of her own making, who spun mediocre verses that surely sparked no one's envy, who will leave no inheritance other than the negligible holdings of an old spinster who occasionally attended court, and a few dozen finely bound books, the rims of the pages embossed in gold! And you, my dear Martinière, though your description of the stranger sounds truly frightful, I cannot imagine that he harbored any evil intent. So then!—"

Martinière leapt back three paces and Baptiste sank half to his knees with a muffled *Ach!* as their mistress pressed on the protruding steely knob, and the lid of the coffret sprang open with a twang.

Imagine how stunned the mademoiselle was when a couple of lavish, diamond-studded armbands and similarly bedecked necklaces glimmered in the packet. She removed the jewelry, and as she admired the wondrous craftsmanship of the necklaces, Martinière ogled the opulent armbands, and kept exclaiming that even the vain Madame Montespan did not possess such brilliant bangles. "But what in heaven's name are we to make of this?" asked de Scudéry. At that very moment she caught sight of a little folded slip of paper at the bottom of the packet. She rightfully expected that it would contain a resolution to the mystery. But no sooner did she read what was written on it than the note fell from her trembling hands. She cast a telling look to the heavens and sank, as if half-unconscious, into her easy chair. Martinière and Baptiste leapt toward her in a fright. "Oh," she cried out, her voice choked with the tears that were streaming from her eyes. "Oh, the insult, oh, the profound humiliation! Must I endure this in my old age! Did I imprudently commit some outrage like a brash young thing? Oh, God, can words muttered half in jest be apt to elicit such a monstrous interpretation! Can a person like me, the epitome of virtue, irreproachably pious since childhood, be ensnared into making criminal common cause with the devil?"

The old woman held a handkerchief to her eyes, weeping and sobbing so intensely that Martinière and Baptiste were so perplexed and nonplussed they did not know how to help ease their mistress's terrible pain.

Martinière picked up the fateful note from the ground. On it was written:

> *Un amant qui craint les voleurs*
> *N'est point digne d'amour.*

Your sharp-witted spirit, most honored lady, helped prevent us from being tracked down, we who take advantage of the right of the stronger over the weak and cowardly to acquire treasures otherwise destined to be ignobly squandered. As a token of our appreciation, please accept this jewelry. It is among the most precious that we have managed to get hold of in a long time, even though, honored lady, you ought to be adorned in far more splendid embellishments than these. We beg you not to withdraw your friendship and your gracious best wishes.

The Invisible Ones

"How is it possible? cried Mademoiselle de Scudéry, once she had recovered somewhat from the initial shock. "How is it possible that anyone might have the shameless effrontery to take a wicked taunt to such a degree?" The sun shone brightly through the crimson silk curtains, so the jewels lying beside the open coffret on the table were lit up in a reddish glimmer. After peering at them awhile, the mademoiselle hid her face in horror, and ordered Martinière to immediately remove the terrible adornments dripping with the blood of the murdered victims. After sweeping the necklaces and armbands back into the little box, the servant thought it would be most expedient to surrender the jewels to the chief of police, and to reveal to him all that had happened, from the appearance of the troubled young man to his having left the packet.

Mademoiselle de Scudéry got up and paced quietly back and forth in the room, as if pondering what to do next. She then bid Baptiste go fetch a sedan chair, and ordered Martinière to help her get dressed, as she intended to hasten to the Marquise de Maintenon.

Taking the coffret of jewelry with her, she had herself carried to the home of the marquise at the precise time when, as she well knew, the latter would be alone.

The marquise was stunned at the sight of the mademoiselle, ordinarily the epitome of dignity – indeed, despite her advanced age, the picture of kindliness and grace – who entered with tottering steps, her face twisted and pale. "What in heaven's name happened to you?" she called out to the cowering old lady, who, completely beside herself and hardly able to stand upright, rushed to reach the easy chair that the marquise pushed toward her. Finally able to speak, the mdemoiselle related how profoundly mortified she was to find herself the butt of such a thoughtless jest as a result of her poetic reply to the petition of the imperiled lovers. Following a blow-by-blow account of all that had transpired, the marquise judged that Mademoiselle de Scudéry took the strange occurrence too much to heart, that the derision of profligates was never of a pious, gallant sort, and finally asked to see said jewelry.

De Scudéry passed her the open coffret, and no sooner had she laid eyes on the precious adornments, than the Marquise let out a cry of amazement. She took out the necklaces and armbands and strode with them to the window where, first letting the jewels shimmer in the bright rays of sunlight, she promptly held the delicate gold work up close to her eyes to behold with what wondrous art and craft every clasp of the entwined necklaces was fashioned.

All of a sudden, the marquise pivoted round to the mademoiselle and cried out, "You must know, my dear Mademoiselle, that this could not possibly be the handiwork of anyone but René Cardillac!"

René Cardillac was then the most adroit goldsmith in Paris, one of the most artful craftsmen and most extraordinary people of his time. Rather short of stature, albeit broad-shouldered and of a strong and muscular build, Cadillac, already well into his fifties, still had the vigor and dexterity of a youth. His thick head of curly reddish hair and squashed, glistening visage further added to the effect of his extraordinary vigor. Had Cardillac not been known all over Paris as the most upright, unselfish, open, straight-shooting man of honor, always ready to help his fellow man, the altogether quirky expression of his small, deep-set, sparkling green eyes might well have put him under suspicion of guile and ill will.

As already stated, Cardillac was not only the most skilled practitioner of his craft in Paris, but perhaps anywhere in his time. Endowed with a profound grasp of the nature of precious stones, he knew how to handle and set them such that jewelry initially considered unremarkable emerged from his workshop imbued with a remarkable splendor. He took on every commission with a burning desire and charged so meager a price that it seemed to bear no relation to the result. And he was then tireless in his execution. Day and night you could hear him hammering away in the workshop, and oftentimes when the task was almost completed, the shape suddenly displeased him or he began to doubt the finesse of a jewel setting or a tiny clasp – cause enough to fling the entire piece back into the crucible and to start again. So every confection became a consummate masterpiece that made the client pause in amazement. But then it was almost impossible to make him part with the finished product. With a thousand pretexts he held the customer off from week to week, from month to month. To no avail, clients offered to pay him double; he would not accept a Louis d'or more than the agreed-upon price. And when, finally, he was obliged to succumb to the urging of a persistent customer and hand over the jewelry, he could not refrain from giving vent to the most profound vexation, the rage that boiled within. Should he feel compelled to deliver a more significant work of great value, perhaps worth several thousand, given the costliness of the jewels and the extremely delicate gold crafting, he was often inclined to run around like a madman, cursing his work and everything around him.

But as soon as someone else would come running up behind him and cry out at the top of his lungs: "René Cardillac, wouldn't you like to fashion a necklace for my wife— armbands for my daughter, etc.," he would suddenly stand still, glare at the person with his beady eyes and, rubbing his hands together, ask, "What have you got?"

Whereupon the new customer would pull out a coffret and say: "Here are the jewels, not particularly special, ordinary stones, but in your hands – !"

Cardillac would not let him finish his sentence, but would tear the little box out of his hands, take out the jewels that really weren't worth much, hold them up to the light, and cry out with delight, "Well, well— common stuff?— not on your life!— lovely stones— lovely stones, let me take a crack at them! And if you don't mind parting with a handful of Louis d'or, I'll add a few more little stones that will sparkle in your eyes like the blessed sun itself."

To which the new customer always replies, "I'll leave everything to you, Master René, and pay what you wish!"

And without fail, whether the fellow is a wealthy burgher or a noble at court, Cardillac impetuously flings his arms around his neck, squeezes and kisses his new customer, says he's happy again and that the job will be done in a week's time. Then he hurries home, hastens into his workshop, and hammers away, and in a week's time he has whipped off a new masterpiece. But as soon as the person who commissioned it pays the modest requested price and expects to take the finished work, Cardillac becomes cantankerous, gruff, truculent.

"But Master Cardillac, please bear in mind, tomorrow is my wedding."

"I don't give a hoot about your wedding, ask again in two weeks!"

"The piece is completed, here's the money, I must have it."

"And *I* tell you that I still have to make some modifications and so can't give it to you today."

"And *I* tell you that if you don't hand over the piece, for which I am willing to pay double, you will soon see me back here with Argenson's armed guard."

"Then may Satan torment you with a hundred red-hot pincers and hang three hundredweights on this necklace so that it strangles your bride!" Whereupon Cardillac stuffs the jewelry into the bridegroom's breast pocket, grabs him by the arm, flings him out the door, so that he tumbles down the entire flights of stairs, and standing at the window, he laughs like the devil upon seeing the poor young man wiping his bloody nose with a handkerchief, limping away.

Nor could anyone explain how, as often came to pass, after Cardillac enthusiastically undertook a commission, he suddenly implored the client with all manner of temper tantrums, with the most moving protestations, sobbing and weeping, to retract the commission. Some people highly esteemed by the king, some by the common folk, offered considerable sums of money in vain just to acquire the smallest piece of Cardillac's handiwork. The artisan flung himself before the king and begged His Majesty for the favor not to have to work for him. In much the same manner he declined Madame de Maintenon's every commission, indeed he once responded with an expression of utter disgust and dismay at her request to fashion a small ring emblazoned with the emblems of the arts to give to Racine.

"I bet," responded Madame de Maintenon, "I bet that even if I were to send a messenger to Cardillac to at least find out for whom he fashioned this jewelry, he would hesitate dropping by, as he might perhaps fear a new commission, and does not want to work for me. Even though, as I hear, he has for some time now let up on his pigheaded obstinacy and works harder than ever, handing over his finished work on the spot, albeit with great displeasure and a twisted expression."

De Scudéry, who desperately wished that the jewelry be returned to its rightful owner posthaste, if still possible, replied that it might be a good idea to inform Master Crank right off that no new commission was asked of him, but rather his assessment of some jewelry. The marquise concurred. Cardillac was sent for and, as if he were already on his way, a little while later he entered the room.

As soon as he set eyes on de Scudéry, he seemed taken aback, like someone who, suddenly confronted with the unexpected, promptly forgets the demands of social niceties. He bowed down low and reverentially before the venerable old lady first, and only then turned to face the marquise. Pointing to the adornments laid out on the table with the dark green throw cloth, the latter asked point-blank if they were his handiwork. Cardillac cast a fleeting glance at it then, looking the marquise right in the eye, hustled the precious pieces back into the little coffret lying beside them and gave it a hefty shove away from him. With a flushed face and an ugly smile playing on his lips, he replied, "Yes, indeed, Madame la Marquise, one would have to be ill acquainted with the work of René Cardillac to believe for an instant that some other goldsmith might have fashioned this jewelry. Of course, it's of my fabrication."

"Be so good as to inform us then," the marquise continued, "for whom you fashioned it."

"For myself," Cardillac replied, and when both Maintenon and de Scudéry eyed him with amazement, the one full of mistrust, the other with eager anticipation as to how this whole matter would turn out, he added, "you might find it strange, Madame la Marquise, but it's true. Just for the sake of enjoying the splendid challenge, I gathered together my most precious stones and took great pleasure in working more diligently and more meticulously than ever before. Not long ago these pieces vanished inexplicably from my workshop."

"Thank God," cried de Scudéry, her eyes sparkling with joy. As swiftly and nimbly as a young girl, she leapt up from her easy chair, strode toward Cardillac, and lay both hands on his shoulders. "Here it is," she declared. "Take back, Master René, the precious property that nefarious thieves stole from you!" She then proceeded to recount in detail how she came to gain possession of the jewels.

Cardillac listened in silence with a downcast gaze. He only interrupted every now and then with a half-muttered: "Hm!— Is that so!— Ei!— Haha!" now flinging his hands back, now quietly stroking his chin and cheeks. And when de Scudéry came to the end of her story, it was as if Cardillac struggled with a string of the strangest thoughts that had struck him while listening, as if a conclusion refused to follow and fall in line. He stroked his brow, he sighed, he rubbed his hand over his eyes, as if indeed to quell tears. Finally, he seized the coffret proffered by de Scudéry, slowly sank to one knee, and said, "Fate has destined you to receive this jewelry, most noble, worthy Mademoiselle! Only now do I recall that I thought of you while fashioning it, indeed that I made it for you. I beg you not to refuse to accept and wear this jewelry as the best that I have made in a long time!"

"Now, now," replied de Scudéry in jest, "what can you be thinking, Master René? Does it behoove a lady of my advanced age to galivant about decked out in such precious stones? And whatever prompted you to make me such a lavish gift? Come now, Master René, were I as lovely as the Marquise de Fontange and wealthy to boot, I wouldn't let this jewelry out of my hands, but what should these flaccid arms do with such vain adornment, what should this sagging neck do with that glimmering necklace?"

Cardillac had in the meantime risen to his feet, and spoke with a troubled look, as if beside himself with emotion, continuing to hold the coffret out to Mademoiselle de Scudéry. "Be so charitable, Mademoiselle, and take this jewelry. You cannot imagine how much I admire your sublime virtue, in what great esteem I hold you for your merits! Please accept my modest gift as a token of my innermost feelings."

And since de Scudéry continued to hesitate, Madame de Maintenon took the coffret out of Cardillac's hands, and said, "Well for heaven's sake, Mademoiselle, you are forever talking of your advanced age. But what do we, you and I, have to do with age and its burden? And don't carry on like a shameless young thing who would gladly help herself to the sweet fruit if only she could have it without stretching out a little finger! Do not spurn the worthy master by refusing to accept what a thousand others will never possess for all the money, begging, and pleading in the world!"

Madame de Maintenon had in the meantime pressed the coffret into Mademoiselle de Scudéry's hands, whereupon Cardillac fell to his knees before her, kissed the hem of her skirt— her hands— sighed— groaned— sobbed— jumped up— ran around like a lunatic, overturning chairs, tables, making porcelain and glasses rattle and, in a mad dash, raced out the door.

Altogether at her wit's end, de Scudéry cried out, "For the love of God, what's got into that man!"

To which the marquise, herself in an ebullient mood bordering on uncustomary waggery, laughed out loud and said, "There we have it, Mademoiselle. Master René is head over heels in love, and has set out, according to common practice and the established custom of true gallantry, to besiege the bastion of your heart with lavish gifts." Madame de Maintenon kept up the pleasantry, exhorting de Scudéry not to be too beastly with her desperate would-be paramour. The mademoiselle, giving vent to an innate caprice, let herself be carried away by a thousand whimsical fancies. She maintained that, matters being as they were, finally succumbing to such entreaties, she had no choice but to present to the world the unheard-of example of a seventy-three-year-old goldsmith's bride of impeccable noble blood. Maintenon offered to braid the bridal crown and instruct her in the duties of a good homemaker, of which, surely, such a maidenly neophyte as she could not know much.

And when, finally, Mademoiselle de Scudéry picked up the coffret of jewelry and rose from her chair to be on her way, all the jest notwithstanding, she once again became very serious. "But Madame la Marquise!" she said, "I will never be able to don this jewelry. However it came into being and whatever just transpired, it passed through the hands of that infernal knave, committed with a devilish daring, indeed by a pact with the devil himself, to robbery and murder. I am filled with horror at the thought of the blood that stains these glittering bijoux. And I must admit that I even found something strangely skittish and weird in the way Cardillac carried on. I cannot dispel a dark inkling that there is some terrible and gruesome secret hidden behind all this, but when I try to paint a clear mental picture of the entire business, I cannot even begin to guess what that secret might be, and what in heaven's name the honest, upright Master René, a model citizen, might possibly have to do with some evil, accursed business. But this much is certain: I will never be able to bring myself to don this jewelry."

The marquise maintained that her friend was taking her scruples too far; but when de Scudéry asked her on her honor, were their places reversed, what she would do, she affirmed in all seriousness that she would rather toss the jewels in the Seine than ever wear them.

De Scudéry rendered Master René's curious comportment in charming verses that she recited the following evening at Madame de Maintenon's apartments before the king. It may well be that, having stilled all sinister apprehension, and at the cost of ridiculing Master René, she managed to paint a priceless picture in brilliant colors of the comic encounter, including a parody of herself, the seventy-three-year-old goldsmith's bride of noble birth. Suffice to say, the king laughed himself silly and swore that Boileau-Despréaux had met his match, and that de Scudéry's poem was the most hilarious ever written.

Many months later, as chance would have it, de Scudéry happened to ride over the Pont Neuf in the glass-topped coach of the Duchesse de Montansier. The invention of the glass-topped coach was still so recent that curious onlookers crowded round when such a vehicle appeared on the street. So it came to pass that the gaping rabble ringed Montansier's coach on the Pont Neuf, almost blocking the horses' path. Suddenly, de Scudéry heard a cursing and swearing, as a man shoved his way through the unruly crowd with fisticuffs and jabs in the ribs. And as he drew near, she was struck by the piercing look of a deathly pale, grief-stricken youth. The young man kept his gaze glued to her, fighting his way forward with elbows and fists until he came to the carriage door, which he hastened to tear open; he tossed a note onto de Scudéry's lap and, giving and receiving shoves and punches, disappeared in the crowd. With a cry of horror, Martinière, who was seated beside de Scudéry, sank back in a faint on the cushioned bench. To no avail, de Scudéry tugged at the bell and cried to the coachman; as if possessed by an evil spirit, he whipped the horses until, foaming at the muzzle, spewing their spittle, they reared up and finally thundered across the bridge in a fierce gallop. De Scudéry emptied the bottle of her smelling salts on the face of the unconscious woman, who at last opened her eyes and, writhing and shaking, hanging on to her mistress for dear life, her face riddled with terror and horror, piteously groaned, "Holy Mother of God! What did that awful man want? Ach! It was him, it was him, the same one who brought you the coffret on that dreadful night!"

De Scudéry reassured the poor woman, reminding her that nothing terrible had befallen them, after all, and that they would have to see what was written on that slip of paper. She unfolded it and found the following words:

> An evil circumstance that you had in your power to prevent, is about to push me over the abyss! I beg you, like a son his mother with whom he has an eternal bond, in the burning fervor of a child's love, to find an excuse to take the necklace and armbands you received from me back to Master René Cardillac to have some aspect altered. Your well-being, your very life depends on it. If you fail to do so before tomorrow morning, I will force my way into your apartment and kill myself in your presence!

"Then there's no doubt," de Scudéry remarked, once she had read the note, "even if the mysterious young man really does belong to the band of despicable thieves and murderers, that he harbors no evil intent toward me. Had he succeeded in speaking to me that night, who knows what light might have been shed on some strange incident, some dark link to the sordid scheme, for which I now rack my brain in vain, chasing after the most tenuous intimation. But let things turn out as they will. I shall do what this note bids me, if only to rid myself of the deplorable jewelry, which seem to me to be hellish talismans of evil. True to longstanding custom, Cardillac will likely not want to let them out of his hands again."

The very next day, de Scudéry resolved to return the jewelry to the goldsmith's atelier. But it was as if all the leading lights of Paris conspired on that very morning to besiege her with verses, plays, and anecdotes. No sooner had la Chapelle completed the scene of a tragedy with which he was slyly convinced he would best Racine than the latter himself made an appearance and with a king's pathetic soliloquy wiped out his rival, until Boileau shot his flares into the dark and tragic heavens just so as not to be hemmed in forever against the colonnade of the Louvre by the architectonic chattering of Doctor Perrault.

It was high noon by then, when de Scudéry was expected at the home of the Duchesse de Montansier, and so the visit to Master René Cardillac had to be postponed until the following morning.

Burdened with a strange disquietude, de Scudéry could not rid herself of the image of the young man. Something about him moved her deeply, stirring a faint dark memory, as if she had seen that face, those features, somewhere before. Fearful dreams disturbed the slightest slumber, she felt troubled, indeed guilt-ridden, by the thought that her rash failure to meet his desperate plea with a helping hand had shunted him into the abyss, as if it had been up to her to deflect some ruinous occurrence, and thereby avert an awful crime! Come morning, she bid Martinière to hurriedly help her get dressed, and had herself driven with the coffret in hand to the goldsmith's digs.

Streaming toward the rue Nicaise, where Cardillac lived, a crowd gathered before his door yelling, raging, clamoring to get in, the gendarmes stationed around the house straining to hold them back. In the wild, chaotic din, angry voices cried out, "Tear him limb from limb, crush the cursed murderer!"

At long last, Desgrais appeared on the scene with an armed detail, ploughing a path through the thick of the throng. The front door flew open, and a man shackled with chains was brought out and led off, his appearance met with the most dreadful volley of oaths from the raging rabble. No sooner had Mademoiselle de Scudéry, half out of her mind with a terrible premonition, realized what was happening, than a shrill wailing welled up in her throat. "Forward! Let's go!" she frantically cried out to the coachman, who managed to make the crowd scatter with an adroit, swift turn of the wheel, and pulled up at Cardillac's door. There de Scudéry saw Desgrais, and at his feet a young girl of astounding beauty, her hair in disarray, half-undressed, with a wild terror and a look of inconsolable despair, clasping his knees and calling out to him in the grip of the most dire and hellish grief, "But he's innocent! He's innocent!" Desgrais's best efforts and those of his deputies notwithstanding, no one could manage to release her grip and raise her from the ground. Then, finally, a hefty, hulking brute clumsily grabbed her by the arms and dragged her away from Desgrais, then carelessly fumbled and let go of the girl, who, tumbling down the stone steps, hit her head, and silently collapsed on the street.

De Scudéry could not contain herself any longer. "In Christ's name, what happened, what's going on here?" she shouted, flinging open the carriage door, and stepping out.

Deferentially, the crowd made way for the honorable lady, who saw a couple of compassionate women pick up the girl and sit her on the steps, dabbing her forehead with water. She approached Desgrais and emphatically repeated her question.

"The most awful thing happened," said Desgrais. "René Cardillac was found dead this morning with a dagger wound. His assistant Olivier Brusson is the murderer. He has just been carted off to prison."

"And the girl?" cried de Scudéry.

"Madelon, Cardillac's daughter," Desgrais replied. "The nefarious fellow was her lover. Now she's crying and carrying on, shouting again and again that Olivier is innocent, absolutely innocent. If she was an eyewitness to the murder, we'll end up having to drag her off to the Conciergerie for questioning." Having said these words, Desgrais cast a look so spiteful and malicious at the girl, that de Scudéry trembled. While remaining motionless, the girl breathed quietly, incapable of uttering a word, her eyes shut tight. Nobody knew what to do, whether to take her into the house or stand by until she came to. Deeply moved, with tears in her eyes, de Scudéry gazed at the innocent angel, revolted by Desgrais and his henchmen. Then came a stamping of feet on the stairs, as they brought down Cardillac's corpse.

Deciding on the spot, de Scudéry cried out, "I'll take the girl home with me. You can take care of the rest, Desgrais!"

Muffled mutters of approval ran through the crowd. The women picked up the girl; everyone pressed forward to help, a hundred hands tried to lend support, and as the girl was swung through the air into the coach, blessings poured from everyone's lips on the noble woman who wrested the innocent child from the clutches of the bloodthirsty court.

Thanks to his best efforts, Seron, the most famous physician in Paris, finally managed to bring Madelon back to consciousness after she had been lying completely unresponsive for hours. De Scudéry followed up on the doctor's care by igniting a few faint rays of hope in the girl's soul, until a mighty storm of tears pouring from her eyes allowed her to give vent to her feelings. In brief moments of lucidity, in between bursts of sobbing induced by the overpowering force of the most piercing pain that caught words in her throat, she somehow managed to relate all that had happened.

Around midnight Madelon had been awakened by a quiet knocking at the door of her room, and heard Olivier's voice bidding her to rise immediately, as her father lay dying. Aghast, she jumped up out of bed and opened the door. His expression contorted by extreme distress, dripping with sweat, and a lantern in hand, the pallid-faced Olivier advanced with shaky steps toward the workshop, and she followed. There she found her father stretched out on the floor, with a blank expression in his eyes, his body gripped by a death rattle, about to give up the ghost. Wailing, she flung herself upon him, only then noticing his blood-soaked shirt. Olivier gently pulled her away and proceeded to try to wash out a gash in the left breast side with balsam of Peru and thereafter dressed the wound. In the meantime, her father returned to consciousness; he stopped emitting the death rattle, and peered first at her, then at Olivier with a soulful look, gripped her hand, placed it in Olivier's hand, and gave them both a hefty squeeze. Both Olivier and she fell to their knees before her father, whereupon Cardillac raised himself upright with a sharp grunt, but promptly collapsed again and, with a heavy sigh, expired. The two wept and wailed. Olivier recounted how, at Cardillac's behest, he had accompanied his master on an errand the night before on which the goldsmith was attacked in his presence, and how, not believing the wound to be fatal, with the greatest effort he hauled the heavy man home. At the crack of dawn, alerted by the thumping, wailing, and loud weeping, the concierge and his wife came upstairs and found them still kneeling, inconsolable, beside her father's corpse. Then came a loud noise; the gendarmes stormed in and dragged Olivier off to prison as his master's murderer. Madelon added the most moving description of the virtue, piety, and devotion of her beloved Olivier. How he held his master in the highest esteem, as though he were his own father, how her father returned his love and esteem to the same degree, how despite his modest origins her father approved of him as his future son-in-law, as his manual dexterity matched his devotion and his noble nature. All this Madelon related with great emotion, as if from the bottom of her heart, and concluded by insisting that if Olivier had stuck a dagger into her father's breast in her presence, she would sooner have believed it to be a ruse of Satan than to credit him capable of such a terrible, monstrous crime.

Profoundly moved by Madelon's unspeakable suffering, and inclined to believe Olivier innocent of the crime, de Scudéry made inquiries and found all that the girl had said about the relationship between master and journeyman to be validated by the testimony of others. The concierge and the neighbors were unanimous in their praise of Olivier for his exemplary level-headed, pious, faithful, and diligent behavior; no one had a bad word to say about him, and yet in speaking of the dreadful act, everyone shrugged their shoulders and said it was incomprehensible.

In court, as de Scudéry later learned, Olivier adamantly denied the crime with which he was charged with a clear conscience, and maintained that his master had been attacked and knocked down on the street in his presence, but that he was still alive when he carried him back home where, alas, he soon died. This too concurred with Madelon's account.

Again and again de Scudéry sought, from various sources, to have the most minute circumstances of that terrible incident confirmed. She made inquiries as to whether there had ever been a dispute between master and journeyman, whether Olivier showed any signs of that irascibility that all too often grips the most even-tempered person, leading him to commit capricious acts that would appear to have been contrary to his nature. But the more impassioned Madelon was in her portrayal of the quiet domestic bliss in which the three lived, bound by the most heartfelt affection, the more the slightest shadow of a doubt as to Olivier's culpability in the murder disappeared from the mademoiselle's mind. Carefully reviewing every last detail, proceeding under the assumption that, notwithstanding all that spoke for Olivier's innocence, he was, in fact, Cardillac's murderer, de Scudéry could find no conceivable motive for his having committed that terrible act that, in any case, deprived him of all claim to happiness.

He is poor, but nimble-fingered. He succeeds in gaining the confidence of the master, he loves his daughter, the master approves of his love, his happiness and prosperity are assured for the rest of his life. But may he have been driven by God knows what motive, overpowered by ire, to assault his benefactor, his father, with murderous intent, what devilish hypocrisy could possibly have compelled him to act as he did following the murder? Absolutely convinced of Olivier's innocence, de Scudéry decided to save the blameless youth, come what may.

Before soliciting the intercession of the king himself, she decided that it would be most expedient to turn to the court president, la Regnie, to bring to his attention all of the circumstances that spoke for Olivier's innocence, and thereby perhaps to awaken in his soul a favorable opinion of the accused that might be communicated to sway the judges in their ultimate ruling.

La Regnie received de Scudéry with all the deference due the venerable lady held in such high esteem by the king himself. He listened in silence to all that she put forth regarding the terrible act, Oliver's relations to the deceased, and his impeccable character. However, the only indication that her words did not fall on totally deaf ears was a subtle, almost sardonic smile with which he heard her protestations and tearful admonitions that every judge dare not be the enemy of the accused, but rather also take everything into account that spoke in his favor.

When de Scudéry, completely drained, finally fell silent and wiped the tears from her eyes, La Regnie responded, "It is altogether worthy of your virtuous heart, my dear Mademoiselle, that you, moved by the tears of a young girl in love, should believe all that she alleges, that you are not inclined to grasp even the possibility of such a terrible deed, but things stand differently with a judge accustomed to tearing off the mask from such an insidious dissimulation. It is indeed not my responsibility to unravel the course of a criminal trial for anyone who asks. Mademoiselle, I do my duty, and pay no mind to the judgment of the world. Let the miscreants tremble before the *chambre ardente*, that knows no other punishment than blood and fire. But in your eyes, honored Mademoiselle, I do not wish to be taken for a severe and cruel monster, therefore permit me in a few words to paint a clear picture of the bloody culpability of that young scoundrel who, heaven help us, fell prey to the grip of vengeance. Your astute mind will then spurn the good-heartedness that does you honor, but by no means befits my office. Now then! In the morning René Cardillac is found murdered by a dagger wound. No one is with him but his journeyman Olivier Brusson and his daughter. In Olivier's bedchamber the authorities discovered a dagger fresh dabbed with blood that precisely fits the wound. 'Cardillac,' claims Olivier, 'was cut down last night before my very eyes.' 'Did someone want to rob him?' 'That I don't know!' 'You accompanied him, and did not manage to resist the murderer? To hold fast to him? To cry for help?' 'The master strode fifteen, perhaps twenty paces in front of me, I followed him.' 'Why in all the world did you hold so far back?' 'That's the way the master wanted it.' 'What in heaven's name drove Master Cardillac out into the street so late at night?' 'I have no idea.' 'But ordinarily he never left the house after 9 PM?' In response to which Olivier falls silent, deeply distraught, starts sobbing, sheds tears, swearing by all he holds holy that on that night Cardillac did indeed go out and found his death. But please mind, Mademoiselle. It has been proven with almost absolute certainty that Cardillac did not leave the house that night, consequently Olivier's contention that he went out with him is a bold-faced lie. The street door is affixed with a heavy lock, which in unlocking and locking makes a piercing racket, after which the door rattles something awful and howls on its hinges, so that, as repeated attempts have confirmed, the infernal racket resonates even on the topmost floor of the house. Now then, old Master Claude Patru lives on the ground floor with his old lady-in-waiting, a person of almost eighty years of age, but still fit as a fiddle. On that evening, both of these people heard as, true to his common custom, Cardillac came down the stairs at nine o'clock sharp, locked and barricaded the door with copious clanks, rattles and squeaks, then climbed the steps again, recited his evening prayers out loud, and then, as one might surmise from the sound of a door slammed shut, retreated to his bedroom. Master Claude suffers from insomnia, as is often the case with older folk. On that night, too, he could not shut an eye. It must have been nine-thirty when the housekeeper turned on the light in the kitchen where she'd been pacing back and forth, and sat down at the table beside Master Claude to flip through an old chronicle while the old gentleman, quietly ruminating, alternately sat himself down in an easy chair and got up again and, so as to foster fatigue and bring on sleep, paced quietly back and forth in the room. All was peaceful and quiet until midnight. Then they heard above them heavy steps and a hard fall, as if a hefty weight fell to the floor, and immediately thereafter a muffled moaning. Both he and she felt a sudden burst of fear and trepidation. A cold inkling of the terrible act, the one that had just been committed, passed through them. Come morning, the crime committed in the darkness finally came to light."

"But for the love of God and all that's holy," de Scudéry interrupted, "given all the circumstances I just enumerated in detail, can you conceive of a single motive for this hellish deed?"

"Hm," replied La Regnie, "Cardillac was hardly poor, having in his possession some splendid precious stones."

"But was the daughter not due to inherit it all?" objected de Scudéry. "You forget that her betrothed, Olivier, was about to become Cardillac's son-in-law."

"He was perhaps obliged to share the spoils or even do the killing on behalf of others," replied la Regnie.

"Share? Kill on behalf of others?" de Scudéry asked in stunned amazement.

"You must know," the presiding judge continued, "surely you must know, my dear Mademoiselle, that Olivier would have been condemned and executed long ago on the Place de Grèves if his murderous deed did not have direct bearing on the veiled secret threat still terrorizing all of Paris. Olivier clearly belongs to that heinous band that still manage to pull off their audacious devilries and go unpunished, shamelessly flouting the most stringent surveillance and investigations of law enforcement. He will – nay, *must* – be the key to unraveling the mystery. Cardillac's wound is a dead ringer for all the others inflicted on the street and in the homes of the murdered and looted victims. The most determining factor is that, since Olivier's arrest, all murders and lootings ceased. Paris streets are once again as safe by night as by day – proof enough that Olivier may well have been the leader of that murderous band. He has as yet refused to confess, but there are ways to make him speak against his will."

"And Madelon," cried de Scudéry, "what about that faithful, innocent dove!"

"Well, well," said la Regnie with a spiteful smile, "who can give assurances that she's not in on the plot! What did she care about her father, she only shed tears for the murderous lout."

"What are you saying!" cried de Scudéry. "It's not possible. Not for her father! That girl!"

"Is that so!" la Regnie continued. "Just think of Brinvillier! You will have to forgive me if perchance I soon find it necessary to snatch up your protégé and lock her up in the Conciergerie."

De Scudéry shuddered at such an abominable suggestion. It seemed to her as if no loyalty, no virtue could endure in the presence of this terrible man, as if in his heart of hearts he could conceive of nothing but murder and bloody guilt. She got up.

"Be human!" Those were the only words she managed to painstakingly bring from her lips in her breathless state. About to descend the stairs, to which la Regnie had ceremoniously conducted her, a curious thought came to her mind – she could not say what got into her – and with a rapid pivot she asked, "Might I be permitted to visit the unfortunate Olivier Brusson?"

La Regnie regarded her with a dubious expression, his face thereafter twisting into that distinctive and repulsive smile of his. "No doubt," he said, "no doubt, my good Mademoiselle, trusting your own intuition rather than the facts at hand, you wish to verify for yourself Olivier's guilt or innocence. If your modesty does not make you blanch at a sinister sojourn, if you are not loathe to face the very picture of depravity in all its nefarious shades, then the door of his cell in the Conciergerie will stand open to you for two hours. You will be introduced to the wretched Olivier, whose fate appears to concern you."

The fact is, de Scudéry was not convinced of the guilt of the young man. Everything appeared to speak against him – indeed, in the face of such convincing facts, no judge in the world would have reacted differently from la Regnie. But the picture of domestic bliss, as Madelon had painted for de Scudéry in the most expressive terms, outshone any suspicion of evil intent, and so she preferred to hypothesize some inexplicable secret than believe a foregone conclusion which she rejected in body and soul.

She intended to have Olivier again recount everything that happened on that fateful night, and as much as possible to elucidate a secret that perhaps remained closed to the judges, since it seemed to them to be useless to pay it any more mind.

Upon arriving at the Conciergerie, de Scudéry was led into a big, bright chamber. Not long after that, she heard a rattling of chains. Olivier Brusson was brought in. But as soon as he appeared in the doorway, de Scudéry fainted. By the time she regained consciousness, Olivier had vanished. She begged to be taken back to her carriage, to be gone, gone from the chambers of wicked depravity. Dear God! She had immediately recognized Olivier Brusson as the young man who flung the note into her carriage on the Pont Neuf, the same person who had brought her the coffret of jewels. Any doubt was now dispelled, and la Regnie's terrible suspicion was confirmed. Olivier Brusson belonged to the terrible band of cutthroats, he definitely murdered his master. And Madelon? Never having been so bitterly deceived by her intuition, chilled to the bone by a diabolical force in which she did not believe, de Scudéry wavered in her faith in all she held to be true. She conceded to the terrible suspicion that Madelon may have been in on the plot, and that she might have played a role in the grisly deed. Once an illusion has been dispelled, it is human nature to take pains to depict one's disillusion in the most glaring colors; thus, in assessing Madelon's comportment down to the most minute detail, de Scudéry found much to support a suspicion of guilt. Even some things that had heretofore appeared to attest to her innocence and purity, now seemed an unmistakable sign of criminal malice and cold-blooded dissemblance. That heartrending wailing, those bloody tears might well have been prompted by a mortal terror, not of seeing her beloved condemned to death, but rather of herself being brought to the executioner.

[328]

Having resolved to rid herself of the snake feeding on her good nature, de Scudéry stepped out of her carriage. As she entered her apartment, Madelon flung herself at her feet. With a heavenly gaze no less faithful than that of an angel of God, her hands folded in front of her heaving breast, the girl wept and begged for help and comfort. Taking pains to pull herself together, de Scudéry strove to speak with a tone of voice imbued with as much seriousness and composure as she could muster. "Go!— Go, my girl, and console yourself for the murderer who will meet his just punishment for the scandalous crimes he committed! May the Holy Virgin keep you from bearing the weight of the murderous guilt on your own shoulders!"

"Then all is lost!" Having uttered these words, with a piercing cry Madelon collapsed. De Scudéry let Martinière tend to the girl, and departed to another room.

All torn up inside, having had enough of it all, de Scudéry no longer wanted to live in a world full of hellish deceit. She bemoaned the bitter trick of fate that had accorded her so many years to foster her faith in virtue and constancy, only in old age to dispel the lovely illusion that had illuminated her life.

As Martinière led Madelon away, de Scudéry heard the girl quietly moaning and wailing, "Dear God!— Her too!—The monsters have pulled the wool over *her* eyes too!— All's lost!— My poor, unfortunate Olivier!" The words touched her deeply, yet again awakening in her heart of hearts the suspicion of a dark mystery, and the belief in Olivier's innocence.

Beset by contradictory emotions, absolutely distraught, de Scudéry cried out, "What demon from hell got me embroiled in this wretched business that will be the death of me!"

At that very moment, Baptiste strode into the room, looking pale, aghast with the news that Desgrais was waiting outside. Ever since the horrid trial of la Voisin, Desgrais's appearance in a house was the certain harbinger of an imminent accusation, hence Baptiste's shocked expression which prompted her to ask him with a smile, "What is it, Baptiste? The name de Scudéry appeared on la Voisin's list – isn't that it!"

"But for heaven's sake," replied Baptiste, trembling all over, "how can you even say such a thing? Desgrais, the terrible Desgrais, is acting so secretive, so imperious, he can't wait to see you!"

"Well then," said de Scudéry, "well then, Baptiste, make haste to bring that person so odious to you in at once. I at the very least have nothing to fear from him."

"The presiding judge," declared Desgrais upon entering the room, "His Honor, Monsieur la Regnie, has sent me with a request, my dear Mademoiselle, your acquiescence to which he would not presume were he not cognizant of your virtue, your courage, and if the last hope of bringing to light the perfidious guilt of the accused did not rest in your hands, not to mention if you yourself were not already embroiled in the matter of the grim trial before the *chambre ardente* that is keeping us all breathless with anticipation. Ever since seeing you, Olivier Brusson has gone half mad. As much as he previously appeared to be on the verge of confessing, he now swears again in the name of Christ and all saints that he is completely inno-cent of the murder of Cardillac, even though he would gladly suffer the death that he says he earned. Please note, my dear Mademoiselle, that the last ancillary remark clearly indicates an admission of culpability in other crimes that burden his conscience. And yet we have failed to elicit another word from his lips, even the threat of torture falls flat. He begs, he implores us to set up a meeting with you. Only to *you*, to *you* alone will he tell all. Do please deign, my dear Mademoiselle, to hear Brusson's confession."

"How," cried de Scudéry, beside herself with anger, "can I serve as an instrument of this bloodthirsty court; do you expect me to betray the trust of that poor unfortunate person so as to deliver him to your judgment? No, Desgrais! Even if Brusson were the nefarious murderer you make him out to be, I could never conceive of so roguishly going behind his back. I would never reveal a single one of his secrets – secrets which, were he to reveal them to me, would remain locked in my breast like the stuff of a sacred confession."

"Perhaps," replied Desgrais with a hint of a smile, "perhaps, my dear Mademoiselle, your attitude may change once you have heard Brusson out. Did you not beg the presiding judge himself to be human? What could be more human than heeding Brusson's misguided request, and thereby making a last attempt to avoid resorting to the torture that Brusson has so long merited? Rest assured, most esteemed lady, you will not be required to set foot again in those dark chambers that fill you with dread and disgust. In the still of the night, without any big to-do, Olivier Brusson will be brought like a free man to your house. While he will be under guard, no one will be listening in, so that he may freely confess all. I can vouch with my life that you will have nothing to fear from that dreaded individual. He speaks of you with fervid devotion. He swears that only the dark calamity that kept him from seeing you sooner precipitated him into the abyss. And then it will be up to you to reveal as much as you see fit of that which Brusson confesses. Might you be persuaded to concede?"

De Scudéry looked down, thinking long and hard. It seemed to her as if she was called upon to heed a higher power who demanded of her the resolution to some deep dark mystery, as if she could no longer elude the wondrous slings of fortune into which she had involuntarily slipped. Making her mind up suddenly, she spoke with dignity. "God will grant me composure and fortitude; bring Brusson here, I will speak with him."

Just like the night when Brusson brought by the coffret, someone knocked at the front door at midnight. Having been informed of the upcoming visit, Baptiste opened the door. A cold shudder ran down de Scudéry's spine when she heard the soft steps and muffled mutterings of the guards who brought Brusson echoing in the corridor of her house.

Finally, the door to her room opened quietly. Desgrais entered, followed by Olivier Brusson, unshackled and dressed in decent clothes. "Here, honored Mademoiselle, is Brusson," said Desgrais, who bowed deferentially and left the room.

Brusson dropped to his knees before de Scudéry and raised his folded hands in supplication as tears streamed from his eyes.

Turning pale, de Scudéry gazed down at him, unable to utter a word. Though disfigured by grief and terrible pain, the pure expression of a trustworthy spirit shone through the twisted countenance of his youthful face. The longer de Scudéry let her eyes rest on Brusson's face, the more it brought to mind the memory of a beloved person she could not quite place. All dread drained away and, forgetting that Cardillac's alleged murderer stood there before her, she spoke with her characteristic quiet kindness. "So, Brusson, what do you have to say to me?"

Still kneeling before her, emitting a sigh of deep and poignant sadness, the young man replied, "Oh, my worthy, most esteemed Mademoiselle, has every trace of your memory of me faded?"

Eying him more closely, de Scudéry replied that she did indeed perceive in his features a certain resemblance with a once beloved person, and that it was only this resemblance that permitted her to surmount the profound abhorrence she felt before a murderer, and to quietly hear him out.

Pained by these words, Brusson quickly rose to his feet and took a step back, with his gaze fixed on the ground. Then he spoke to her in a whisper. "Have you completely forgotten Anne Guiot? Her son Olivier? The boy you so often rocked on your knees stands here before you."

"Oh, my God!" cried de Scudéry, covering her face with both hands and sinking into the pillows. Mademoiselle indeed had cause enough to be horror-stricken. Anne Guiot, the daughter of an impoverished bourgeois, had from early childhood lived with de Scudéry, who cared for her as a mother for a beloved child, raising her with the greatest trust and care. And when Anne came of age, a handsome, upright young man named Claude Brusson asked for her hand in marriage. Since he was a highly skilled watchmaker likely to do well in Paris, and Anne dearly loved him, Mademoiselle de Scudéry had no qualms about ascenting to her ward being wed to him. The young couple set up a household and lived together in quiet happy harmony, the knot of love being tied even more tightly between them when the young woman gave birth to a beautiful boy, the spitting image of his lovely mother.

De Scudéry idolized little Olivier, whom she wrested from his mother for hours, often days at a time to pamper and coddle. Consequently, the boy became so accustomed to her that he was just as glad to spend time with her as with his mother. After being in business for three years, Brusson's commissions diminished day by day due to the jealousy of his competitors until finally he could hardly keep his family fed. In addition to this, he was consumed by longing for his native Geneva, and so it came to pass that the family moved there, regardless of the resistance of de Scudéry who offered all possible support. Anne wrote a few more times to her benefactress, then stopped writing, and the mademoiselle felt compelled to believe that the happy life in Brusson's hometown superseded the memory of former days.

Twenty-three years had passed since Bruson left Paris with his wife and child to live in Geneva.

"Oh, horror!" cried de Scudéry, once she had somewhat recuperated from the shock, "Oh, horror! So you are Olivier? The son of my dear Anne! And now…!"

"Yes, indeed," Olivier retorted, quiet and composed, "yes, indeed, my esteemed Mademoiselle, you could never have imagined that the boy you coddled like a most loving mother, whom you rocked on your knees, in whose mouth you stuffed treat after treat, whom you called by the sweetest nicknames, might have grown into a youth who would one day stand before you, accused of the most terrible crime! I am not blameless, the court can rightfully link me to certain crimes; but though I hope to die honorably, be it by the hand of the executioner, I am innocent of murder, I am blameless in the death of the poor unfortunate Cardillac!" With these words, Olivier started trembling and teetering. De Scudéry pointed in silence to a small chair beside him, upon which he let himself sink.

"I have had time enough," he went on, "to prepare myself for this tête-à-tête with you, which I perceive as merciful heaven's last favor, and have braced myself sufficiently to attain enough peace of mind to tell you the story of my terrible, incredible misfortune. Please be merciful enough to hear me out, as much as the resolution of a mystery that you would never have suspected will surprise you and fill you with horror. If only my poor father had never left Paris! As far back as my memories of Geneva reach, I am drenched with the tears of my inconsolable parents, myself brought to tears by their incomprehensible laments. Later I fully fathomed the complete extent of the dire need, the utter misery in which my parents lived. My father found all his hopes shattered. Brought down by great grief, crushed by disappointment, he died at the very moment when he finally managed to apprentice me to a goldsmith. My mother spoke so much about you, she wanted to tell all to you, but then she was overcome by the despondence born of misery. That and a touch of false pride that often gnaws at the fatally wounded spirit kept her from carrying through on her resolve to reach out to you. A few months after my father's death my mother followed him to the grave."

"Poor Anne! My poor Anne!" de Scudéry cried out, overwhelmed by grief.

"Thanks and praised be to the eternal heavenly power that she has gone to the great beyond, and so will not see her beloved son pass under the hand of the executioner, branded with shame!" Olivier wailed at the top of his lungs, flashing a wild and terrible look. His cry aroused unrest outside the door, agitated steps went back and forth. "Ho ho," Olivier muttered with a bitter smile, "Desgrais alerted his henchmen, as if I could escape from *here*. I was badly treated by my master, even though I did my best work, and even surpassed his skills. It so happened that a stranger once came to our workshop to purchase some pieces of jewelry. When he set eyes on a necklace that I made, he patted me on the shoulder and gave me a friendly look, gazing at the piece. 'Well, well, my young friend, you did a superb job,' he said. 'Truth to tell, I don't know anyone who could surpass your skill but René Cardillac, unquestionably the greatest goldsmith in the world. You really ought to seek him out; he'd gladly take you on in his workshop, I'm sure, since you have what it takes to assist him in his artful craft, and he's the only master goldsmith from whom you could still learn a thing or two.' The stranger's words touched me deeply. I could no longer sit still in Geneva, but had a burning desire to leave town. I finally managed to sever my apprenticeship to my master and came to Paris, where René Cardillac initially received me coldly and curtly. I did not let up, insisting he give me work, as trifling as it might be. He instructed me to fashion a little ring for him. When I brought him the completed work, he peered at me with his sparkling eyes as if he wanted to look deep into my soul. Then he said, 'You are an able, honest journeyman, you can move in with me and help me in my workshop. I will pay you well, you'll be happy here.' Cardillac kept his word. I had already spent many weeks there without having seen Madelon, who, if I'm not mistaken, was staying at the time with one of Cardillac's cousins in the country. At last she arrived. Oh, God in Heaven, how can I describe the effect on me once I set eyes on that angelic person! Has ever a man been as smitten as I was! And now— oh, my Madelon!"

His misery made him fall silent. He held both his hands in front of his face and burst out sobbing uncontrollably. Finally managing with great effort to overpower the wild pain that gripped him, he continued speaking.

"Madelon gave me a friendly look. She came more and more frequently to the workshop. I was overjoyed to realize that she loved me. As closely as her father kept watch, a few furtive squeezes that Cardillac did not seem to notice confirmed our bond. I resolved to first earn his favor and achieve full mastery of the craft before seeking Madelon's hand in marriage. One morning, as I prepared to start work, Cardillac strode before me, his face consumed with a dark look of fury and contempt. 'You are no longer needed in my workshop,' he began, 'be gone from my house within the hour and never let me set eyes on you again. I need not tell you why you have outlived your welcome. For you, poor devil, the sweet fruit you're yearning for hangs too high out of reach!' I wanted to speak in my defense, but he grabbed me with a strong fist and flung me out the door with such a great force that I fell down and badly bruised my head and arm.

"Incensed, torn up by pain and fury, I left the house and finally found a kindhearted acquaintance at the outer edge of the Faubourg Saint Martin who let me stay in his garret room. Ever restless, I found no peace of mind. Come nightfall, I prowled around Cardillac's house, imagining that Madelon might hear my sobbing, my desperate laments, and that she might manage to whisper to me from her window without being overheard. All manner of reckless plans crossed my mind, plans in the fulfillmet of which I hoped to ask her to cooperate. A high wall with hollowed-out pedestals, and old, half-disintegrated sculpted statuettes abuts Cardillac's house on the rue Nicaise. One night I was standing close to one of these sculptures, peering up at the windows which open onto the courtyard closed in by the wall. Suddenly I noticed a light go on in Cardillac's workshop. It was midnight, and Cardillac was never normally awake at that ungodly hour; he always made it a habit of going to bed at nine o'clock sharp. My heart started beating with uneasy apprehension as I imagined an incident that might block my access. But then the light went out again almost immediately thereafter. I pressed up against the statue, into the space behind it, but bounced back, feeling something press up behind me, as if the statue had come alive. In the faint shimmer of moonlight, I noticed the statue slowly turning, and a dark figure slipping out from behind it, descending the street with silent steps. I leapt back against the statue, which now stood, as before, hard against the wall. Instinctively, as if driven by some inner force, I slunk after the dark figure. Directly in front of a statue of the Madonna, the figure turned around, revealing its face in the shimmer of a burning streetlight set atop the statue. It was Cardillac! I was overcome with an unfathomable burst of fear and an uncanny sense of dread. As if in the grip of a magic spell, I felt compelled to follow close on the heels of that ghostly sleepwalker. Although it was not the time of the full moon, I took the master to be in the grip of sleepwalking. Finally, Cardillac disappeared sideways into darkness. With the sound of a short, all too familiar, throat-clearing cough, I realized, meanwhile, that he had stepped into the gateway to a house. 'What does it mean, what is he up to?' I asked myself, pressing myself hard against the wall of the house. Not long after that, a man came singing and trilling a tune, with a luminous tuft of feathers and his feet bedecked in jingling spurs. Like a tiger pouncing on its prey, Cardillac slipped from his hiding place and lunged at him, bringing him down with a gasp. With a cry of horror, I leapt forward. Cardillac was on top of the man he knocked to the ground. 'Master Cardillac, what are you doing!' I cried out loud.

"'Damn you!' Cardillac screamed, running past me at lightning speed and disappearing.

"Altogether beside myself, hardly able to budge, I approached the man flung down. I knelt down beside him; perhaps, I thought, he could still be saved. But there was not a trace of life left in him. In my deathly fear, I failed to see that the gendarmes had closed in around me. 'Another one of those devils laid low— hey hey, young man, what are you doing here, are you a member of the band? Off with you!' they cried out as one and took me into custody. I was barely able to stammer that I could not possibly have committed such a grisly deed, and that they had best leave me in peace.

"Then somebody flashed the light of a torch in my face and cried out, laughing, 'Why, it's Olivier Brusson, the goldsmith journeyman who works for the good Master René Cardillac! Yes, indeed, *he's* one of those street thugs who murder people on the street! Looks just the sort! He's just the kind of cutthroat to cower over his corpse and let himself be caught. What'd you do, boy? Fess up!'

"'Right in front of me,' I replied, 'somebody jumped that guy, knocked him down, and ran off as I cried out. I wanted to see if the guy knocked down was still alive.'

"'Not so, my boy,' one of the cops picking up the corpse cried out, 'that one's done for, pierced through the heart with a dagger thrust, as usual.'

"'Hell's bells!' said another, 'again we got here too late, like yesterday!' At this, they cleared off with the corpse.

"I can't even describe the state I was in; it was as if a bad dream were taunting me, as if I would wake at any minute and be stunned by the mad delusion— Cardillac— the father of my beloved Madelon, a nefarious murderer!— Legs gone limp, I collapsed on the stone steps of a house. The morning sun shone ever more brightly overhead; an officer's hat, richly bedecked with feathers, lay there before me on the pavement. Then the hard reality dawned on me: Cardillac's bloody deed was perpetrated on the very spot where I sat. Horrified, I ran away.

"Completely bewildered, practically insensate, I was seated there in my garret room when the door flew open, and in stormed René Cardillac. 'For Christ's sake, what do you want?' I cried out to him.

"Oblivious to my state of mind, he approached me and smiled with quiet calm and an affability that further enhanced my sense of horror. He dragged over an old, shaky footstool and sat himself down beside me where I lay, struck dumb, in a bed of straw.

"'Now then, Olivier,' he began, 'how are you doing, my poor boy? It really was villainously shabby of me to hasten to kick you out of my house. I miss you every which way I turn. I just now happen to have a commission which I cannot possibly complete without your assistance. What do you say you come back to work with me in my atelier? Cat got your tongue? Yes, I know I offended you. I won't deny that I was mad at you for fooling around with my Madelon. But upon reflection and closer consideration, I have come to the conclusion that, given your skill, your diligence, your devotion, I could not wish for a better son-in-law than you. Come along with me then, and let's see how you can go about making Madelon your wife.'

"Cardillac's words cut me to the quick; shuddering at his malice, I found myself at a loss for words. 'You hesitate,' he continued with a sharp tone of voice, his sparkling eyes piercing my heart, 'you hesitate – perhaps you have other things to do today and can't make it to my place. Maybe you intend to visit Desgrais, or to introduce yourself to d'Argenson or la Regnie. Beware, my boy, that the claws you hope to draw out to destroy others don't grab you and tear you to shreds.'

"At this, I gave vent to all the deep indignation stewing in me. 'Let them,' I cried out, 'let them with terrible deeds on their mind bandy about the names you just cited – I have no business with them.'

"'As a matter of fact,' Cardillac continued, 'as a matter of fact, Olivier, it will bring you honor if you work with me! I am the most famous master goldsmith of my time, so highly esteemed for my loyalty and integrity that any malicious slander would fall back on the head of the slanderer. And as far as Madelon is concerned, I must confess that you owe my indulgence to her persistence. She loves you with an intensity of which I would not have thought the delicate child capable. As soon as you were gone, she fell to the floor before me, hugged my knees, and swore with a thousand tears that she could not live without you. I thought, she's just imagining, as is often the case with such young things in love, that she's smitten when the first milksop makes eyes at her. But in truth, my Madelon grew sickly and weak, and when I tried to talk her out of such nonsense, she called out your name a hundred times. What else could I finally do if I didn't want to see her driven to distraction! Yesterday evening I told her I had given in and would go fetch you today. Overnight she blossomed like a rose and awaits you now beside herself with a lover's longing.'

"May God in Heaven forgive me, but I myself don't know how I suddenly came to be standing the next day in Cardillac's house, with Madelon shouting out for joy, 'Olivier, my Olivier, my beloved, my husband!' She wrapped her arms around me, pressed me tightly to her breast, so that, enraptured with delight, I swore by the Virgin and all that is holy, never, never to leave her again."

Shaken by the memory of this decisive moment, Olivier fell silent. "How ghastly!" de Scudéry cried out, horrified at the crime of a man whom she had taken to be the very epitome of virtue and rectitude, "René Cardillac is a member of the murderous band that has for such a long time turned our city into a den of thieves?"

"Did you say 'a band,' Mademoiselle?" Olivier interrupted. "Such a band never existed. It was Cardillac and Cardillac *alone* who, with reprehensible resourcefulness, sought out and found his murder victims throughout the city. The fact that he was the sole perpetrator, accounts for both the secret of his precise planning of these crimes and the unresolved difficulty to date in tracking him down. But do let me go on, the continuation of my story will help elucidate the secrets of the most despicable and at the same time unhappiest of people. Anyone can well imagine the impossible situation in which I now found myself in the household of the master goldsmith. The step was taken, there was no going back. At times it seemed to me as if I myself had become Cardillac's murderous henchman – only in Madelon's loving arms did I forget the agony of guilt that tormented me, only by her side did I manage to blot out any external sign of the nameless grief I felt. When busy with the old man in his workshop, I could not look him in the eye, nor was I able to exchange words, given the horror that made me tremble through and through in the presence of this unspeakable monster who in the daylight hours fulfilled all the virtues of the faithful, tender-hearted father, the upright burgher, and come nightfall concealed his awful acts. Madelon, the pious, angelic child, doted on him with a daughter's love. My heart was pierced with pain at the thought that, if ever that concealed miscreant got his due, having pulled the wool over his daughter's eyes with the hellish guile of Satan, she would fall prey to the direst despair. That in and of itself kept my lips sealed, and for that very reason I would have gladly accepted a criminal's death. Even though I was privy to considerable insights, having overheard the talk of the constabulary, Cardillac's misdeeds, motives, and manner of execution remained a mystery to me. But I did not have long to wait for their elucidation.

"One day, Cardillac, who ordinarily aroused my revulsion, was working away in high spirits, joking and laughing, lost in his thoughts. Suddenly, he thrust aside the piece of jewelry on which he had been working so that precious stones and pearls rolled around, impetuously rose to his feet, and said, 'Olivier, things can't remain this way between us – our present rapport with each other is intolerable to me! What Desgrais and his henchmen in all their painstaking investigations failed to discover, chance thrust into your hands. You caught me in the act of my nightly endeavors, to which my unlucky star drives me, there's no denying it. It was also your misfortune that made you follow me in the shadow of night, your muffled footsteps enabling you to go unnoticed, like a tiny forest creature, so that I who can ordinarily pierce the darkness with the attentiveness of a tiger, pacing the streets, attuned to the buzz of a fly and the slightest other sound, failed to notice your presence. Your unlucky star, my fine fellow, led you to me. Hoodwinking you, under the present circumstances, is no longer an option. Therefore, you shall know everything.'

"*Never again will I be your fine friend, you two-faced scoundrel!*— This I wanted to cry out, but the utter horror with which Cardillac's words filled my heart gagged my mouth. Instead of words, all I managed to emit was an incomprehensible gurgle.

"Cardillac sat himself back down in his work chair. He wiped the sweat from his brow. Profoundly taken aback by the memory of what I'd witnessed, he seemed hard-pressed to get ahold of himself. At last he began: 'Wise men like to speak of the extraordinary impressions pregnant women are apt to have, of the wondrous influence such lively, unconscious impressions can have on the child they carry within. I was told a fantastic story about my mother. When she was one month pregnant with me, she and some other women witnessed a sparkling court festivity held at the Trianon. Her glance fell on a gentleman in Spanish costume with a glittering diamond necklace around his neck, which she could not take her eyes off. Her entire being was filled with the desire to possess that string of sparkling stones which seemed to give its wearer an otherworldly aura. Many years ago, before my mother married, the same gentleman stalked her virtue, but found himself rebuffed with repugnance. My mother recognized him again, but now it seemed to her as if the shimmer of those glittering stones transformed him into a higher being, the very epitome of splendor. The gentleman noticed my mother's yearning, fiery looks. He thought he might now have more success with her than before. He managed to draw near, and even to separate her from her friends and lure her to a lonely spot. There he clasped her in his arms with lusty intent – my mother reached for the lovely necklace, but at that same moment he sank down and dragged my mother with him to the ground. I do not know whether he suffered a sudden stroke, or whether it was for some other reason, but suffice it to say he dropped dead. My mother's best efforts were in vain; she could not manage to release herself from the arms of the corpse locked in rigor mortis. With his cavernous, unseeing gaze locked upon her, the dead man dragged her to the ground. Her shrieking call for help finally reached the ears of distant passersby, who rushed over and tore her free of the arms of her frightful would-be lover. The terrible shock sent my mother to a sickbed. It was thought that she would lose me, the child growing in her, but she recovered and the delivery proved more successful than anyone could have hoped.

"'But the lingering shock of that terrible experience made its mark on me. My unlucky star hovered above me and showered me with sparks that ignited the strangest inherited trait. Already in earliest childhood I was bedazzled above all else by glittering diamonds and golden jewelry. It was taken to be a perfectly common childish inclination, but it proved to be something else, for even as a boy I stole gold and jewels wherever I could lay my hands on them. Like a practiced connoisseur, I soon developed an instinct for distinguishing between fake costume and real jewelry. Only the real deal caught my eye – the fake stuff, like gold-plating, left me cold. The father's crass inclinations bequeathed avidity to the son. Just to be able to handle gold and precious stones, I gravitated to the goldsmith's trade. I took pains to master the craft and soon became the foremost practitioner.

"'Then began a period in my life when my impulse, so long kept in check, erupted and grew into an indomitable drive to grab anything I laid my eyes on. As soon as I completed and delivered a commissioned piece of jewelry I fell into a state of inner turmoil, into a desolation that robbed me of sleep, vigor, and the will to live. Like a ghost, the person for whom I labored haunted me day and night, decked out with my jewelry, and a voice whispered in my ear: *It belongs to you, after all— it belongs to you, after all— take it back— what good do diamonds do the dead?* Until, finally, I resorted to the art of thievery.

"'Having access to the homes of the rich and powerful, I quickly seized every opportunity. No lock withstood my ability to crack it, and so, soon enough, the jewelry I'd fashioned was back in my hands. But that was not enough to quell my disquiet. That uncanny voice vented, scoffed at me, and cried out in my ear: *Ho ho, a dead man dons your jewels!* I myself can't say how it happened that I developed an unfathomable loathing for those for whom I crafted jewelry. Yes indeed, a lust to kill them stirred in my heart of hearts, an urge that made me shudder. Around that time, I bought this house. I came to an agreement with the owner – here in this room we sat celebrating the signing of the contract over a bottle of wine. Night fell, and he was about to leave when the erstwhile owner said to me, "Listen, Master René, before you go, I must reveal to you a secret about this house." He unlocked that hidden recess in the wall, shoved aside the rear partition, bent over, and opened a trapdoor. We descended a steep, narrow stairway, came to a small portal which he unlocked, and stepped out into the rear courtyard. Then the old gentleman who sold me the house approached the outer wall, pushed on a slightly protruding iron handle, and a piece of the wall pivoted such that a man could easily slip through the opening and reach the street. You must once see the escape hatch for yourself, Olivier, probably designed by sly monks from the cloister formerly located here to secretly slip in and out without being noticed. It's made of a piece of wood cemented over and painted on the outside that lets out onto a hollow recess containing the statue of a saint, likewise carved of wood, but made to look like stone. The entire structure, including the statue, is designed to turn on invisible hinges. Dark thoughts came to mind as I considered this contrivance; it seemed to me as if deeds still undreamed of were foreordained and preconceived. I knew that I had just recently delivered to a gentleman at court a piece of lavish jewelry destined to adorn a dancer at the opera. The threat of a tortuous death did not dissuade me— the thought of a ghastly deed held to me like a shadow— Satan kept whispering in my ear!— I moved into the house.

"'Bathed in a cold sweat of fear I staggered, sleepless, around in my room! In my mind's eye, I saw the man sneaking along to a rendezvous with the dancer carrying my jewelry. In a fit of rage, I jumped up, flung on my coat, descended the secret stairway, and slipped through the trapdoor in the wall out into the rue Nicaise. He came walking along, I assaulted him, he cried out— but grabbing hold of him from the rear, I thrust a dagger in his heart— the jewelry was mine! Having done so, I felt a calmness, a profound sense of satisfaction seeped into my soul the like of which I had never felt before. The ghostly urge evaporated, Satan's whispering voice went silent. I knew then what my unlucky star demanded of me. Henceforth, I had to yield to that urge or else perish in my restraint.

"'Now you know it all, Olivier, the secret that feeds and foments my craft and cunning! Do not think that just because I am driven to do things beyond my control that all feelings of sympathy and compassion common to most have failed me. You know what a tough time I have parting from and delivering a piece of jewelry on which I've worked, how I absolutely refuse to work for some people whose death I do not desire, and how, even while perfectly well cognizant that on the morrow I will have blood on my hands, today I really would much rather call it quits with a fisticuff, knocking out the owner of my little bijou and reclaiming what's mine.'

"Having revealed all of the above, Cardillac proceeded to lead me to a secret vault and granted me a privileged peek at his jewel cabinet. The King himself has none finer. On a label attached to each piece of jewelry he had clearly noted for whom it was made, and the date on which, through theft or murder, it was acquired.

"'On your wedding day,' said Cardillac in a pained and solemn tone of voice, 'on your wedding day, Olivier, you will swear a sacred oath, with your hand on the holy cross, that upon my death, all these riches are to be destroyed in a manner I will make known to you. I do not wish for a single soul, least of all Madelon and you, to come into possession of this blood-tainted hoard.'

"Trapped in this labyrinth of crime, torn by love and horror, rapture and revulsion, I was like the damned to whom a fair angel beckons heavenward with a smile while Satan holds him fast in the grip of his burning claws, and the loving smile of that pious angel in whose gaze all heavenly bliss is mirrored becomes the most tormenting of his tortures. I contemplated leaving – even suicide – but for Madelon! Blame me, blame me, my most esteemed Mademoiselle, that I was too weak to fight off a passion that kept me tightly ensnared in crime, but am I not bound to atone for it with a disgraceful death?

"One day, Cardillac came home unusually cheerful. He hugged Madelon, gave me the friendliest look, drank a vintage wine at dinner – as he only did on high holidays and celebratory occasions – sang and made merry. Madelon left the table and I rose, intending to go to the workshop.

'Stay seated, my boy,' Cardillac cried out, 'no more work today. Let us drink another glass to the good health of the worthiest, most sublime lady in Paris.' After we had clinked and he had emptied a glassful, he said, 'Tell me, Olivier! How do you like this verse?

Un amant qui craint les voleurs
n'est point digne d'amour!'

"Then he recounted what happened with the king and yourself at the apartments of Madame de Maintenon, and added that he had long held you in higher esteem than any other living soul, and that endowed with such great virtue, in the face of which his evil urge shrinks back, that even adorned with his finest piece of jewelry you would never stir his animus or spark a murderous intent in him. 'Listen, Olivier, what I have decided to do. Some time ago I was commissioned to fashion a necklace and armbands, and even furnish the precious stones, for Henrietta of England. The work went well, as never before, but it tore at my heart when I pondered parting with those bijoux that had become my most precious treasure. You know of the princess's unfortunate assassination. I kept the jewelry and now wish to send it in the name of the hunted band of thieves, as a sign of my high esteem and my gratitude, to Mademoiselle de Scudéry. In addition to bestowing this telling token of my admiration on de Scudéry, this gift will also bring ridicule on Desgrais and his associates, as they deserve. You must bring her the bijoux!'

"As soon as Cardillac mentioned your name, Mademoiselle, it was as if a dark shroud had been pulled back and the bright and beautiful picture of my happy early childhood appeared in brilliant colors in my mind's eye. My soul was soothed with a wondrous balm, a ray of hope before which the dark demons disappeared.

"Cardillac must have interpreted the impression his words made on me in his own fashion. 'My plan appears to please you,' he said. 'I must confess that an imperious inner voice commanded me to do so, a voice altogether different from the clamor, like the craving of a ravenous beast of prey for sacrificial lambs. Sometimes I am overcome with a queasy feeling inside – a profound agitation, the dread of something awful – the chill of which wafts from some distant elsewhere and grabs me by the throat. It then feels as if those deeds committed by that unlucky star with me as its tool might well one day be associated with my immortal soul that plays no part in such doings. In such a state of mind, I decided to fashion a lovely diamond tiara for the Virgin in the Church of Saint-Eustache. But every time I tried to get to work on it, I was overwhelmed by a wave of that fear and trembling, and so had to give up on it. It now seems to me, in dispatching to de Scudéry the most exquisite handiwork I ever fashioned, as if I were humbly offering a sacrifice to virtue and piety incarnate and beseeching her intercession on my behalf.'

"Knowing every last detail of your customary habits, my dear Mademoiselle, Cardillac told me precisely how and when to deliver the jewelry he had packed up in a little coffret. I was enraptured in body and soul, for it seemed to me that heaven itself had, through the mouth of that wicked Cardillac, revealed to me the path of escape from the hell that I, an outcast and sinner, had long pined after. That's what I thought. Altogether against

Cardillac's will, I wanted to get through to you. As Anne Brusson's son, as your former ward, I thought I would fling myself at your feet and tell you everything. I felt quite confident that, bearing in mind and moved by the indescribable misery that poor, innocent Madelon would have suffered from the discovery of the truth about her father, taking the secret into consideration, your lofty, keen-witted spirit would surely have come up with a plan to proceed without revealing the truth about the accursed evil of Cardillac. Don't ask me how I imagined you would proceed, I have no idea— but that you would find a way to save Madelon and me, of that I was as firmly convinced as is my faith in the comforting succor of the Holy Virgin. You know, Mademoiselle, that my plan that night was thwarted. However, I did not lose hope of succeeding another time. But then it came to pass that Cardillac suddenly fell out of his jubilant state. He slunk about in a foul humor, stared into space, muttered incomprehensible words, punched with his fists, as if fighting off hostile forces – his spirit seemed tormented by evil intent. He kept on this way for the entire morning. Finally, he sat himself down at his work table, jumped right up again in a fit of anger, peered out the window, and muttered in a serious and sinister tone of voice, 'I wish after all that Henrietta of England had worn my jewelry!' The words filled me with horror. I now knew that his sick spirit was once again gripped by the terrible specter of death, that Satan's voice once again rang out in his ears. I realized that your life was threatened by that accursed murderous devil. If only Cardillac had his jewels back in his hands, you would be saved. The danger grew with every passing moment. Then I spotted you on the Pont Neuf, pressed my way through the crowd to your coach, and flung you that scribbled note begging you to bring the jewelry back to Cardillac at once. You did not come. My sense of dread grew into despair when, the next day, Cardillac spoke of nothing else but the priceless bijoux that flashed before his eyes all night. I was quite certain it had to do with the jewelry he had bid me give you, that he was hatching a murderous plot that he planned to carry out that very night.

"I had to save you, even if it cost Cardillac's life. After evening prayers, as soon as Cardillac locked himself in his room, as was his wont, I climbed through a window out into the courtyard, slipped through the opening in the wall, and stood watch nearby, hidden by the cloak of night. It wasn't long before Cardillac came out and slipped off stealthily down the street. I followed hot on his heels. My heart beat quickly as he approached the rue Saint-Honoré. Cardillac had disappeared. I decided to plant myself in front of your door. Then a policeman came singing and whistling by, without noticing me, just as another had that other time when chance made me a witness of Cardillac's murderous deed. But at the self-same moment a dark figure leapt out and fell upon him. It was Cardillac. Intent on stopping this murder, with a loud cry, in two or three steps I reached the spot. Not the constable, but Cardillac sunk to the ground with a death rattle. The constable dropped his dagger, drew his sword out of his sheath, ready to fight me off, suspecting that I was the murderer's henchman, but bolted when he realized that, paying him no mind, all I careed about was the corpse. As it turns out, Cardillac was still alive. After picking up the dagger that the policeman let drop, I loaded him onto my shoulders and, with great effort, carried him home, and through the secret gap and passageway up to his workshop.

"You know the rest. As you see, my esteemed Mademoiselle, my only misdeed was not turning Madelon's father over to the authorities, and so putting an end to his crimes. I am innocent of any spilled blood. No torture will force me to confess the secret of Cardillac's crimes. I do not wish that, despite the fact that the good Lord kept her father's criminal guilt hidden from the eyes of his virtuous daughter, the entire terrible truth of the past now be suddenly revealed to Madelon, tearing her apart, nor that the world's vengeance exhume the corpse from down under, and that the executioner now brand the stain of disgrace on his decayed bones. No, let my beloved bemoan my lost soul as her innocent fallen lover. Time will mollify her pain, but the pain of knowing the hellish deeds of her beloved father would be more than she could bear."

Olivier fell silent, but then suddenly burst into tears and flung himself at de Scudéry's feet and begged, "You are convinced of my innocence, I know you are! Have mercy on me, please tell me how Madelon is doing?"

De Scudéry called to Martinière, and moments later Madelon came running in and wrapped her arms around Olivier's neck.

"All's well now that you're here. I knew that this most noble lady would save you!" Madelon kept crying out the same words again and again, and Olivier forgot his fate, all the menace that still weighed upon him, and at that moment he felt free and blissfully happy. Both lamented in the most moving fashion how much they'd suffered for each other, and embraced each other one more time, and wept tears of joy to have found each other again.

Had de Scudéry not already been convinced of Olivier's innocence, the sight of the two oblivious to the world around them, their distress, and their unspeakable sufferings, in a state of utter bliss in the most intimate bond of love dispelled any lingering doubt. "No," she cried out, "only a pure heart is capable of such soulful oblivion!"

The bright rays of daybreak shone through the windows. Desgrais knocked quietly on the door and reminded them that it was time to take Olivier Brusson away, since it would be impossible to do so later without causing a stir. The lovers had to separate.

The dark premonitions that swept over de Scudéry from the moment Brusson first entered her house were confirmed in the most awful way. Innocent though he was, she saw the son of her beloved Anne so ensnared in this unsavory business that it hardly seemed conceivable to save him from an ignominious death. She admired the youth's heroism, preferring to die burdened with guilt rather than to reveal a secret that would surely prove a death blow to his beloved Madelon. Wracking her brain, considering the entire realm of possibility, she could not come up with a plan to save the poor young man from the claws of that terrible court. Even so, she resolved in her heart of hearts to spare no sacrifice to avert the appalling injustice that was about to be committed. She agonized over all sorts of schemes and plans bordering on the rash and risky, only to promptly scrap them. Losing every last glimmer of hope, she fell into deepest despair. But Madelon's unconditional, pious, childish trust, the idealized way in which she spoke of her beloved who would surely soon be ruled innocent of any guilt, and embrace her as his lawfully wedded wife, uplifted de Scudéry to the same degree as she was deeply moved by it.

Finally, so as to do something, de Scudéry drafted a long letter to La Regnie, in which she wrote that Olivier Brusson had demonstrated to her in the most believable fashion his complete innocence in the death of

Cardillac, and that only the heroic resolve to take a secret with him to the grave, the revelation of which would cast a blight on innocence and virtue, kept him from making a confession before the court that would absolve him of any suspicion, not only that he killed Cardillac, but also that he had any ties whatsoever to the accursed band of murderous thugs. De Scudéry took the greatest pains and tapped all the eloquence she could mobilize in an attempt to melt la Regnie's hard heart. Several hours later la Regnie replied that it gladdened his heart that Olivier Brusson completely vindicated himself before his highborn, noble benefactress. But as to Olivier's heroic resolve to wish to take a secret with bearing upon the murder with him to the grave, he very much regretted that the *chambre ardente* could not honor such heroic courage, and would be obliged to employ the necessary means to break his will. In a matter of three days he hoped to be privy to the strange secret, the revelation of which would, in all likelihood, shed light upon the circumstances of the murder.

De Scudéry knew only too well what that terrible la Regnie meant by the necessary means to break Brusson's heroic resolve. Now it was certain that the poor unfortunate boy would undergo torture. In the throes of mortal terror, de Scudéry finally fathomed that she would need the advice of a lawyer to ask for a stay in the interrogation. Pierre Arnaud d'Andilly was at the time the most famous barrister in Paris. His comprehensive legal knowledge and his profound powers of reasoning were matched with utter integrity and absolute moral virtue. De Scudéry went to see him, and told him everything possible without divulging Brusson's secret. Convinced as she had been that d'Andilly would take on and apply his best efforts to the defense of the innocent young man, she was soon sorely disappointed.

D'Andilly listened in silence to all she had to say, and then replied with a smile in the words of Boileau: "*Le vrai peut quelque fois n'être pas vraisemblable.*"* He averred to de Scudéry that the striking causes for suspicion against Brusson substantiated la Regnie's resolve to proceed with interrogation, and that said resolve should by no means be considered cruel or hasty, but rather altogether in accordance with the law, insisting indeed that he could not do otherwise without failing to attend to proper judicial procedure. He, d'Andilly, could not venture to attempt by the most adroit argumentation in Brusson's defense to save him from torture. Only Brusson himself could do so, either by a candid confession or at the very least through the most precise account of the circumstances surrounding the death of Cardillac, which testimony might then give rise to a new assessment of the case.

"Then I will fall to my knees before the king and beg for mercy," cried de Scudéry in a half-suffocated voice, beside herself in a burst of tears.

"For heaven's sake, don't do that, esteemed Mademoiselle," d'Andilly cried back. "Save that as a last resort, for should it fail to sway His Majesty, your cause would forever be lost. The king would never pardon a criminal of this sort – he would arouse the bitter admonishment of his threatened subjects. It might still be possible by a discovery of Brusson's secret or by some other means to dispel the suspicion against him. That would be the time to beg for the king's pardon, not asking him to counter what has been proven or not proven in court, but rather appealing to his heartfelt conviction."

De Scudéry was necessarily compelled to bow to the counsel of the wise and experienced d'Andilly. Sunk in deep distress, wracking her brain,

---

* "At times, truth may not seem probable." Nicolas Boileau-Despréaux (1636–1711).

trying to figure out what, in the name of the Holy Virgin and all the saints in heaven, to do to save the poor unfortunate Brusson, she sat up till late at night in her room, when Martinière entered, announcing the arrival of the Count de Miossens, colonel of the King's Guard, who urgently requested leave to speak with her.

"Begging your pardon," said Miossens, taking a soldierly bow, "begging your pardon, esteemed Mademoiselle, if I take the liberty of barging in on you at such a late hour. We soldiers live by other rules, I hope you will forgive me – Olivier Brusson leads me to you."

With keen anticipation of what she might learn, de Scudéry cried out: "Olivier Brusson? That most unfortunate of men? What do you have to do with him?"

"That's what I thought to myself," Miossens continued with a smile, "that the mention of your protégé's name would suffice to capture your attention. The whole world is convinced of Brusson's guilt. I know that you hold another opinion resting solely on the assertion of the accused, as I've heard. My position is different. No one can be more convinced than me of Brusson's innocence in the death of Cardillac."

"Speak, oh speak!" de Scudéry cried out, her eyes sparkling with rapture.

"It was I," insisted Miossens, "I myself, who knocked down the gold-smith on the rue Saint-Honoré not far from your house."

"For the love of all saints, you— you!" cried de Scudéry.

"Yes, indeed," Miossens continued, "and I swear to you, Mademoiselle, that I am proud of my deed. I must tell you that Cardillac was the most reprehensible, duplicitous scoundrel, that it was he who underhandedly murdered and robbed, and for such a long time eluded all traps set for him. I myself can't say how and why I first harbored suspicions of that old lout, when with evident agitation he delivered the jewelry I had commissioned, when he took pains to inquire for whom the piece was made, and when, in a stealthy fashion, he managed to ascertain from my valet when I was in the habit of visiting a certain lady. I had long been struck by the fact that the unfortunate victims of that most rapacious crime all bore the same deadly wound. There was no doubt in my mind that the murderer was practiced in deadly assault and confident that the blow would immediately kill his victim. If he missed his mark it would mean a fight to the finish. This led me to take a precaution so simple that I cannot fathom why others did not resort to it long ago, and so saved themselves from the clutches of deadly menace. I wore a light suit of body armor under my waistcoat. Cardillac attacked me from the rear. He held me with immense force, but the confident dagger thrust struck against iron. At the same time, I broke free of his grip and thrust the dagger I held ready into his breast."

"And yet you kept silent?" demanded de Scudéry. "You did not testify before the court as to what transpired?"

"Please permit me," Miossens continued, "permit me, esteemed Mademoiselle, to point out that such a testimony would ensnare me in a messy legal business, if not lead to my complete undoing. Would la Regnie, in his tireless effort to sniff out criminals every which way he turned, have ever believed me had I accused the upright Master Cardillac, that epitome of piety and virtue, of attempted murder? Would not the sacred sword of justice have promptly turned its pointed edge against me?"

"That's impossible," cried de Scudéry, "given your noble birth, your social status."

"Is that so?" Miossens retorted. "Just think of the Marshall of Luxembourg, who was imprisoned in the Bastille on suspicion of murder by poisoning simply because of a predeliction for having his horoscope told by le Sage. No, in the name of Saint Denis, I wouldn't concede a hair's breadth or the tip of my ear to that rabid la Regnie, dying to stick his knife into all our throats."

"But by remaining silent, you ensure that the innocent Brusson is bound for the gallows!" de Scudéry cut him off.

"Innocent," replied Miossens, "innocent, my good Mademoiselle, is that how you characterize the accomplice of that accursed Cardillac, who stood by him in his dastardly deeds, a man who earned death by execution a hundred times over? No, by God, *that* blaggard deserves to die, and the fact, most esteemed Mademoiselle, that I revealed to you the true circumstances of the case, was done on the supposition that you might somehow be able to make use of my secret on behalf of your protégé without delivering me into the bloodthirsty hands of the *chambre ardente*."

Enraptured in her heart of hearts to see her firm belief in Brusson's innocence confirmed so conclusively, she did not hesitate to tell all to the count, well aware as he already was of Cardillac's crimes, and to urge him to go with her to d'Andilly. All was to be revealed to the lawyer under a pledge of confidentiality, and his counsel sought as to how to proceed.

Once de Scudéry had told all to the barrister in precise detail, d'Andilly again inquired after the most minute details of the case. In particular, he asked Count Miossens if he, too, was firmly convinced that he had been attacked by Cardillac, and if he would be able to identify Olivier Brusson as the individual who carried off the corpse.

"In addition to the fact that I clearly recognized the goldsmith in the bright moonlight," Miossens replied, "I also saw in la Regnie's possession the dagger with which Cardillac was laid low. It is my dagger, clearly distinguishable by the fine handiwork of the hilt. Having stood on that night one step away and clearly able to make out all the facial features of the youth, whose hat had fallen, I would surely be able to recognize and identify him again."

D'Andilly looked down for several minutes in silence, then he spoke: "There is absolutely no way by ordinary means to save Brusson from the clutches of justice. For Madelon's sake, he does not wish to identify Cardillac as a murderer. Even if he did so, and managed, by revealing the existence of the secret exit door, to account for the stolen loot, he would still be condemned to die as an accomplice. The same would hold true were Count Miossens to testify in court concerning the true circumstances of the incident with the goldsmith. A postponement in the proceedings is all that we can seek. Count Miossens must beget himself to the Conciergerie, request a meeting with the prisoner Olivier Brusson, and recognize him as the individual who carried off Cardillac's corpse. He must hasten to call on la Regnie and say, 'In the Rue Saint-Honoré I saw a person laid low, I stood directly beside the body as another leapt forth, bent down to the body and, sensing a flicker of life left, hoisted him onto his shoulders and carried him off. I recognized Olivier Brusson as the man who carried him off.' This testimony will require the court to once again interrogate Brusson, in the presence of Count Miossens. Now then, the torture will be averted and the investigation continue. It will then be the right time to turn to the king himself. I will leave it to your ingenuity, my dear Mademoiselle, how best to approach His Majesty. In my opinion, it would be advisable to reveal the entire secret to the king. Count Miossens's testimony will support Brusson's confessions. A covert search of Cardillac's house may perhaps prove fruitful. Brusson cannot be saved through law alone, but based on His Majesty's inkling of extenuating circumstances, mercy may mitigate the sentence where the judge would be compelled to order punishment."

Count Miossens listened carefully to d'Andilly's advice, and matters proceeded as the barrister predicted.

Now the time came to approach the king, and this was the touchiest matter, since His Majesty so abhorred Brusson, whom he held to be the sole loathsome murderer who had so long kept Paris in a state of fear and trembling, that even the most offhand mention of the trial would bring on a fit of blind anger. True to her precept never to speak to the king of unpleasant things, Madame de Maintenon rejected any intervention regarding this matter, and so Brusson's fate fell entirely into the hands of de Scudéry. After mulling things over for quite a while, she came to a resolve and promptly carried it out. She donned a black robe of heavy silk, adorned herself with Cardillac's precious jewels, hung a long, black veil over her face, and appeared in this manner at the apartments of Maintenon at the hour when the king was customarily present.

The noble figure of the venerable mademoiselle decked out in this ceremonious attire had a majestic air that must surely have aroused great respect, even among the loafing riffraff that customarily milled about in the antechambers. All dutifully stepped aside, and when she entered the reception room even the astonished king arose and strode toward her. The priceless diamonds in the necklace and bracelet immediately caught his eye and he cried out, "Heavens, those are Cardillac's jewels!" And turning then to Maintenon, he added with a comely smile, "See, Madame la Marquise, how our lovely bride mourns her bridegroom."

"Oh, Honored Sire," de Scudéry replied, as if perpetuating the ruse, "how would it befit a bride in mourning to deck herself out in such finery? No, I have completely cut myself off from that goldsmith, and would no longer have given him a thought, were I not haunted by the heinous image of how, having been murdered, his body was carried off."

"How's that?" inquired the king. "How in heaven's name! You saw the poor devil being dragged off?"

De Scudéry related in a few words, not yet mentioning Brusson's involvement, how by chance she happened to be passing in front of Cardillac's house as the murder was discovered. She evoked Madelon's distraught state, the profound impression that the poor child had made on her, the manner in which, amid the whoops of the mob, she saved the girl from Desgrais's clutches. With ever growing and more fervent interest, the king listened to her account of the scenes involving la Regnie, Desgrais, and finally alluding to Olivier Brusson himself. Deeply moved by the force of the most poignant description of life in de Scudéry's impassioned telling, the king did not immediately realize that she touched upon the hateful trial of Brusson, the man he found so loathsome, and could not manage to get a word in edgewise, only succeeding every now and then to give vent to his mounting emotions with a burst of air. Incensed at the outrage of it all, before he fully fathomed and managed to make sense of all that he had just heard, de Scudéry had already flung herself at his feet and begged for mercy for Olivier Brusson.

"What are you doing," the king exclaimed, grabbing her by both hands and drawing her into a chair. "What are you doing, my dear Mademoiselle? You surprise me in the strangest way! That is such a terrible story! What guarantees the truth of Brusson's bizarre account?"

De Scudéry replied, "Miossens's testimony, the search of Cardillac's house, and my inner conviction— dear God! Madelon's virtuous heart, the same virtue I recognized in that poor unfortunate Brusson!"

About to reply, the king turned upon hearing a sound at the door. Louvois, who had just been working in the room next door, looked in with a troubled mien. The king got up and followed Louvois out the door. Both de Scudéry and Maintenon considered this interruption dangerous, for once having been taken by surprise, the king would likely take care not to fall into the same trap twice. But several minutes later the king returned, strode swiftly back and forth a few times in the room, then positioned himself face to face with de Scudéry with his hands crossed behind his back, and whispered half in silence without looking at her, "I would like to meet your Madelon!"

"Oh, my most gracious Majesty," de Scudéry replied, "what great, great fortune you bestow on that poor, unfortunate child! A mere wink from you is all it takes to have the girl prostrate before you."

And then she scurried toward the door as fast as she could in her black dress, called out, "The king wants Madelon Cardillac to appear before him!" and promptly returned, weeping and sobbing with rapture and deep emotion. Having anticipated such royal kindness, she had brought Madelon along. The girl remained with Madame la Marquise's lady-in-waiting, with a brief petition in hand drafted by d'Andilly. Moments later she lay speechless at the king's feet. Fear— bewilderment— deep veneration— love and pain— a muddle of all these emotions made the seething blood flow ever more quickly through all her veins.

Her cheeks glowed bright purple— her eyes glittered with luminous pearls of tears that filtered through her silken lashes and fell from time to time upon her lovely lily-white breast. The king appeared to be bedazzled by the wondrous beauty of the angelic child. He gently lifted the girl from the ground, then made a gesture as if wanting to kiss her hand that he held in his. He let her hand fall again and peered at the lovely child with a tear-soaked gaze, which attested to he himself being choked with profound emotion.

Quietly Maintenon whispered to de Scudéry, "Is she not the spitting image of La Vallière, that dear little thing? The king is reveling in the sweetest stream of memories. Your game is won."

As quietly as Maintenon whispered, the king appeared to have heard her words. His face flushed red and his gaze withered Madame. He read the petition that Madelon had handed him, and spoke then in a mild and kindly voice, "I am well inclined to believe that you, my dear child, are convinced of the innocence of your beloved; but let us hear what the *chambre ardente* has to say!"

With a swift and gentle motion of the hand the king dismissed the girl, who was about to drown in a flood of tears.

De Scudéry realized to her horror, that the memory of La Vallière, as favorable to her cause as it had first appeared, had the contrary effect on the king's mood as soon as Maintenon mentioned her name. Might it be that the king was somehow so vexed by the memory that he was on the point of sacrificing beauty, or perhaps His Majesty felt like the dreamer who, stirred by a fleeting magical image he thought to embrace, mourned its fast fading. Perhaps he no longer saw before him his erstwhile mistress La Vallière, but rather thought of Soeur Louise de la Miséricorde (La Vallière's cloister name in the convent of the Carmelite nuns she joined), whose memory pained him with her piety and penance. What else was there left for de Scudéry to do now but quietly wait for the king's decision?

Count Miossens's testimony before the *chambre ardente* had in the meantime become known and, as is often the case, public opinion being easily driven from one extreme to another, the very same man who had first been maligned as the most reprehensible murderer and whom the crowd threatened to tear to pieces even before being brought to the execution site, was now bemoaned as the innocent sacrificial lamb of a barbaric justice system. Only now did the neighbors recall his virtuous way of life, his great love for Madelon, his devotion, and the total commitment of body and soul he brought to the old goldsmith. Great throngs often gathered in a threatening manner before la Regnie's palace, crying out: "Let Olivier Brusson go, he is innocent!" and even throwing stones at the windows, so that la Regnie was obliged to seek the protection of the gendarmes before the infuriated mob.

Many days went by without de Scudéry having the least knowledge of how Olivier Brusson's trial was proceeding. Inconsolable, she repaired to the apartments of Madame de Maintenon, who assured her that the king was silent about the matter, and that it did not seem advisable to remind him of it. But when Maintenon inquired with a strange smile how dear little La Vallière was doing, de Scudéry became convinced that deep inside the heart of the proud woman seethed a chagrin concerning a certain matter that could well entice the irascible king into a psychic territory to which she herself was barred. De Scudéry now fathomed that nothing more was to be hoped for from Maintenon.

Finally, with d'Andilly's help, de Scudéry managed to establish that the king had had a long secret talk with Count Miossens. Further, that Bontemps, the king's trusted valet de chambre and chargé d'affaires, had been to the Conciergerie and had spoken with Brusson, and finally that this Bontemps had gone to Cardillac's house with a company of men and spent a considerable amount of time there. Claude Patru, the occupant of the ground-floor apartment, confirmed that all night long he heard a rumbling overhead, and it is certain that Olivier was present, for he clearly recognized his voice. This much was certain, that the king himself sought to investigate the true connection between the facts of the case; what seemed incomprehensible, however, was His Majesty's lengthy hesitation to come to a decision. La Regnie must surely have done his utmost to keep his teeth firmly planted in any victims who sought to be released from his clutches. This spoiled any hope of germinating the truth.

Almost a month had gone by, when Madame de Maintenon sent word to de Scudéry that the king wished to see her that evening at Maintenon's apartments.

De Scudéry's heart beat double-time, cognizant that Brusson's fate was about to be decided. She told poor Madelon, who fervently prayed to the Virgin and all the saints in heaven to instill in the king's heart the conviction of Brusson's innocence.

And yet it seemed at first as if the king had forgotten the entire matter; as usual, engaged in charming chitchat with Maintenon and de Scudéry, he did not devote so much as a syllable to poor Brusson. At long last, Bontemps appeared, approached the king, and whispered a few words so quietly that both women were unable to catch the drift. De Scudéry was on tenterhooks. Finally, the king got up, walked toward her, and spoke with a radiant expression. "I wish you luck, my dear Mademoiselle – your protégé, Olivier Brusson, is free!"

Tears welling up in her eyes, unable to utter a word, de Scudéry wanted to fling herself at the king's feet. But he held her back from so doing, saying, "Now, now, my dear Mademoiselle, you ought to be a parliamentary lawyer and fight out my lawsuits, for by Saint Denis, your powers of persuasion are second to none. But be that as it may," he added in a more serious tone of voice, "whosoever rises to the defense of the cause of virtue itself is not immune to the insidious accusations of the *chambre ardente* and all the courts of law in the world!"

De Scudéry finally found the words to express her gratitude in the most glowing terms. The king interrupted her, announcing that she awaited expressions of far more fiery thanks in her own house than he might expect of her, for it was likely that at this very moment the fortunate Olivier Brusson was embracing his Madelon. "Bontemps," the king concluded, "will pay out to you a thousand Louis d'or in my name as a dowry for dear little Madelon. May she marry her Brusson, who hardly deserves such good fortune, but then let both of them leave Paris. That is my wish."

Martinière came running toward her mistress, followed by Baptiste, both greeting her with faces glimmering with joy, both cheering, and crying out, "He is here!— He is free!— Oh, the dear young folks!"

The jubilant couple fell to de Scudéry's feet. "Oh, I always knew that you, you alone would save my bridegroom," cried Madelon.

"Dear God, I never lost faith in you, my mother," Olivier cried, and both kissed the hands of the worthy lady and shed a thousand hot tears. They embraced again and affirmed that the otherworldly bliss of this moment offset all the nameless sufferings of the past days, and they swore never to be separated from each other until death do them part.

A few days later they were united by the blessings of a priest. Even if it had not been the will of the king, Brusson would not have been able to remain in Paris, where everything reminded him of that terrible time of the misdeeds of Cardillac, and where a chance mishap revealing the dark secret to more people could have adverse consequences and forever disrupt his peaceful life. Immediately after the wedding, with the blessings of Mademoiselle de Scudéry, he moved with his young bride to Geneva. Richly endowed by Madelon's dowry, and given his exceptional skill in his craft, and his virtuous demeanor, the two enjoyed a happy, carefree life together. The selfsame aspirations were fulfilled that had failed his father and led him to an early grave.

A year after Brusson's departure from Paris, a public proclamation signed by Harloy de Chauvalon, Archbishop of Paris, and by the barrister Pierre

Arnaud d'Andilly, let it be known that a penitent sinner as a sacrament of penance bequeathed to the church a lavish stolen fortune of diamonds and jewelry. Everyone who had until the end of 1680 been divested of jewelry on the public street by an attacker with murderous intent was invited to get in touch with d'Andilly, and, should the description of the stolen jewel perfectly match that of any of the pieces found in said treasure hoard, and should there be no other doubt as to the legitimacy of said person's rightful claim, would retrieve the jewelry. Many of those among Cardillac's prey who had not been murdered but merely knocked unconscious by a fisticuff found their way to the barrister's offices, and to their considerable surprise, got their stolen jewelry back. The rest of the treasure was left to the Church of Saint-Eustache in Paris.

My Cousin's Corner Window

1821

My poor cousin suffered the same fate as the famous Paul Scarron. Like him, my cousin completely lost the use of his legs as a consequence of an intractable illness, and only with the greatest effort, with the help of sturdy crutches and the aid of the nervous arms of a sullen invalid who betimes served him as orderly, was he able to shuffle from his bed to an easy chair packed with cushions, and from the armchair back to bed. But there was another similarity between my cousin and the famous Frenchman, whose particular brand of elusive humor landed far afield of typical French wit and, notwithstanding his meager output, accorded him a permanent place in the French literary canon. Like Scarron, my cousin plies his pen; and like Scarron, he is endowed with a particularly lively spirit and in his own way works wondrously humorous whimsies on the page. To the credit of this German writer, however, let it be noted that he never deems it necessary to spice up his little piquant bowls of words with asafetida, to tickle the gums of German readers allergic to such flavor enhancers. He makes do with the noble spice of wit, which, while stimulating, also fortifies the effect. People like to read what he writes; it is said to be satisfying and pleasurable to read, though I can't make head nor tail of it. I tend to tire of my cousin's entertainments, and find it far more congenial to listen to him than to read him. But it is precisely this indomitable proclivity to writing that brought dark calamity upon my cousin's life; the most pernicious illness, with which he is beset, could not manage to obstruct the swiftly coursing cogs of his imagination forever whirring inside his head, churning out story after story. Consequently, he has kept at it, pumping out all manner of charming narratives despite the considerable pain it costs him. But the nasty demon of his malady has of late blocked the usual route which his thoughts must traverse so that he might transfer them to paper. As soon as my cousin seeks to commit something to the page, not only do his fingers cease to serve him, but also the thought itself dissolves and fades from consciousness. This made my cousin lapse into the darkest depression.

"Cousin!" he addressed me one day in a tone of voice that scared me. "Cousin, I'm done for! I feel like a batty old painter who sits for days on end before a blank, framed, stretched, gessoed canvas, telling everyone who drops by about his lush and lovely painting. I'm giving up on my futile attempts to create, and thereby commune with the world by granting external shape to the images in my mind! My spirit is retreating into its hermitage!"

Ever since then, my cousin has refused to be seen by me or by anyone else. His grumpy old invalid caretaker barred us from entering, growling and snapping like a mad dog inclined to bite.

It should be noted here that my cousin lived several flights up, in a rather small and low-ceilinged garret room – the customary quarters of writers and poets. What is the effect of the low ceiling? It presses on the imagination, making it spew forth and fabricate a high, vaulted ceiling, reaching up all the way to the glimmering blue sky. Thus the poet's narrow quarters, just like the minuscule, walled-in, ten-foot-square garden upon which he looks out, may not be spacious in width and length, but retains an uplifting altitude. My cousin's lodgings are located in the nicest quarter of the capital city, looking out on the great marketplace* which is surrounded by glorious edifices, and in the middle of which stands the colossal and beautifully conceived theater. My cousin resides in a corner house; peering out the window of a little chamber, his gaze takes in the entire panorama of that grandiose market square.

It just so happened to be market day when, elbowing through the crowd, I made my way up the street, already spotting from afar my cousin's corner window. I was more than a bit surprised to make out in the window frame the familiar red cap my cousin wore on good days. Furthermore, upon coming closer, I saw that he had donned his stately Warsaw dressing gown and was smoking his Turkish Sunday pipe. I saluted him, waving my handkerchief. I managed to attract his attention, and he responded with a genial nod which made me hopeful as to his state. I bounded up the steps. The invalid opened the door; a burst of sunlight had smoothed out his face, ordinarily riven with runes and wrinkles, into a more or less tolerably welcoming mug. He informed me that the master was seated in his easy

* Hoffmann's last lodgings, at Taubenstraße 31, corner Charlottenstraße 38/39, overlooked the Gendarmenmarkt in Berlin.

chair and receptive to visitors. The room had been tidied up, and on the bed curtain a sheet of paper was fastened with the words in large bold script:

"*Et si male nunc, non olim sic erit.*"*

Everything seemed to suggest a renewed burst of hope, a newly roused life force. "Hey," my cousin called to me as I entered his chamber, "so you've finally come, cousin; do you know that I had a real hankering to see you? Who the devil cares what you may think of my immortal works, I'm still fond of you because you're a cheerful guest and *amusable*, if not exactly amusing." Taking in the prickly compliment from my ever-candid cousin, I felt my face go red.

"You appear to believe," my cousin continued, without paying my expression of consternation any notice, "you no doubt believe me to be in complete recovery, or at least not unduly suffering from my condition. That is certainly not the case. My legs remain faithless vassals, disloyal in their service to their lord, and wanting nothing more to do with the rest of my miserable carcass. Which is to say, I am unable to budge, and have to cart myself graciously back and forth in this wheel-chair, aided by my old invalid caretaker while he hums the most melodious military marches from the war years. But this window is my consolation; through it the life of the street rises toward me, and I feel myself uplifted by its ceaseless ferment. Come, cousin, do have a look out my window!"

I sat myself down opposite my cousin on a tabouret small enough to fit in the narrow space before the window. The view was indeed striking and surprising. The entire marketplace looked like a single, dense, tightly packed

---

* If things are bad now, they may take a better turn in the future. (From an ode by Horace).

crowd, so that one was inclined to believe that an apple tossed in its midst would never touch the ground. Tiny patches of all sorts of different colors glimmered in the sunlight, which gave me the impression of a bed of tulips waving in the wind, and I had to admit to myself that the spectacle was quite agreeable, but tiresome in the long run; small groups of agitated persons could stir up a dizzying squall that resembled the not unpleasant delirium of an oncoming dream. In all this I assessed the pleasure that that corner window might afford my cousin, and openly admitted as much.

In response to which, however, my cousin clapped his hands over his head, sparking the following conversation between us:

My Cousin: Cousin, dear cousin, I can now confirm that you have not the slightest spark of writing talent. You lack the first prerequisite ever to follow the footsteps of your worthy, lame cousin; namely, an eye able to look clearly. That marketplace offers you nothing but the spectacle of a bewildering, checkerboard square of people engaged in meaningless agitation. Hah hah, my friend, in my eyes it all evolves into a slew of civic scenarios of daily life, and my spirit, like that of a hearty Callot or a modern Chodowiecki, whips off sketch after sketch with jaunty enough contours to attract attention. Let's see, cousin, if I can teach you how to grasp at least the bare rudiments of art. Look straight down at the street below— here, take my looking glass— do you notice the curiously attired person with the big basket of groceries on her arm, presently engaged in heated discussion with a brush maker, who together appear to be quickly concocting arrangements other than those involved in bodily nourishment?

Me: Yes, I see her. She has a gaudy, lemon-yellow kerchief wrapped in the French manner, turban-like around her head, and her face as well as her entire being clearly identifies her as French. Probably a woman left behind from the last war, in debt up to her ears, engaged in feathering her own nest.

My Cousin: Not a bad guess. I wager the husband is counting on some branch of French ingenuity for a favorable outcome, so that his wife manages to fill her shopping basket to the brim with a slew of purchases. Now she's plunging back into the throng. Dear cousin, why don't you try to follow her various peregrinations without losing sight of her; the yellow kerchief should do as a guidepost.

Me: Oh, how that burning, yellow dot cuts through the crowd! Now she's already near the church— now she's bargaining over something at some stand— now she's off again— Oh, dear, I've lost sight of her— no, over there she pops up again— there, at the poultry stands— she's grasping a plucked goose— assessing it with knowing fingers—

My Cousin: Well-done, cousin, fixing one's gaze begets a clear looking. But instead of my tiresomely trying to tutor you in the art of looking, an art that cannot really be learned, let me rather make you aware of all manner of enchanting doings going on before our very eyes. Do you see that wench over there in the corner, paying no mind to the throng, elbowing her way through?

Me: What a splendid appearance— with her silk hat, oblivious in its capricious shapelessness to fashion's dictates, with brilliantly colored feathers waving in the wind— with a short silk mantle, its color to its original absence of hue— and on top of it a perfectly decent shawl— the floral trim of her yellow calico dress reaching down to her ankles— blue-gray stockings— laced boots— behind her a stately maid with shopping basket, a knitted bag weighed down with a sack of flour— God save us from the angry glances that silken personage is casting around her! With what determined fury she is breaking her way through the thick of the throng— the way she's touching everything, vegetables, fruit, meat, etc.; the way she's eyeing, fingering, haggling over everything, and not buying a single thing.

My Cousin: She makes an appearance on every market day; I call her "the rabid housewife." I imagine she must be the daughter of a wealthy burgher, perhaps of a prosperous soap maker, whose hand in marriage some low-ranking ministerial privy secretary took considerable pains to wangle. Heaven may not have endowed her with beauty and grace, but her neighbors considered her a most efficient domestic planner, and she is indeed very efficient, and busies herself every day from morning to night in such a dreadfully efficient manner that her poor husband doesn't know what hit him and would rather take refuge where pepper grows. With drums beating and trumpets sounding, all records of purchase, order slips, retail trade, and of all other household needs are kept up to date, and so the privy secretary's household resembles an encasement in which a wind-up clock regularly sounds off with a mad symphony composed by the devil himself; more or less every fourth market day she is accompanied by another maid.—

*Sapienti sat!** – as you may remark – but no, no, this troop of characters taking shape here would be worthy of Hogarth's immortalizing pencil. But have a look at the third doorway of the theater!

Me: A couple of old biddies seated on low stools – their entire wares set out in a bunch of medium-size baskets before them – the one containing

---

* Latin saying: Enough said!

colorful kerchiefs, so-called fandangles, intended to hoodwink fools, the other filled with a supply of blue and gray stockings, knitting wool and the like. They're seated in a huddle – they whisper into each other's ears – one is savoring a cup of coffee; the other, seemingly completely enraptured by the subject of their conversation, forgets the spot of schnapps she intended to pour down the hatch. A perfect pair of physiognomies! What demonic laughter – what jocular gesticulations they make with their brittle, bony arms!

My Cousin: These two old biddies remain seated side by side, and despite the different nature of their wares, presenting no commercial competition, keep glaring at each other with hostile looks, and dare I trust my practiced prowess in physiognomics, keep swapping colorful snide remarks. Oh, look, look, my dear cousin, they are forever melding in body and soul. The rag woman dishes out a cup of coffee to the stocking stocker. How are we to interpret this act? I know! Just a few minutes ago a young girl, no more than sixteen years old, pretty as a picture, whose external appearance and manner bespoke meager means, was attracted by the fandangles to one of the baskets. She was drawn to a white scarf with a colorful border, which she may well have needed. She bargained over the price, the old woman plied all the wiles of the mercantile arts, spreading out the scarf and making its brightly colored border shimmer in the sunlight. They came to an agreement. But when the poor girl unwound her meager monetary reserve from the tip of her handkerchief, the ready cash did not meet the mark. With burning red cheeks and tears in her eyes, the girl backed off as quickly as she could, while the old biddy, scornfully cackling, folded up the kerchief and tossed it back into the basket. Colorful swear words must have been exchanged. But then it seems that the other old devil knew the girl and the sad story of her impoverished family, dishing out a scandalous chronicle of improvidence and perhaps even criminal acts to cheer up the bluffed basket proprietress. The cup of coffee surely capped off a crude, sly dog string of slanders.

Me: Not a word of all that you've deduced, my dear cousin, may be true, but as I behold the two old biddies, your explanation seems so plausible that I am inclined to believe it, like it or not.

My Cousin: Before turning our backs on the theatrical spectacle, let us have a look at the plump, jolly woman with round healthy cheeks, hands folded beneath her white apron with stoic composure, seated on a straw stool, with a stock of brightly polished spoons, knives and forks, glazed earthenware, porcelain plates and tureens of outdated style, teacups, coffee-pots, assorted socks, and what have you, spread out on white sheets, so that her goods, more than likely acquired at stock auction, comprise a veritable *Orbis Pictus*.* Without altering her facial expression, she calmly takes in the offers of the bargainers, whether likely to amount to a sale or not, and pokes one hand out from under her apron only to take in payment from a customer whom she permits to carry off the procured object. This is a calm, canny tradeswoman likely to amount to something. Just four weeks ago her entire stock consisted of roughly a half-dozen fine woolen socks and the same number of drinking glasses. Her holdings grow with every market day, and the fact that she brings no better stool, and continues to keep her hands hidden under her apron, attests to a stoic spirit, and that she is not likely to let herself be misguided by good fortune to pride or haughty

---

* A children's schoolbook widely used in Europe from the seventeenth to the nineteenth century.

presumption. How then does this scurrilous idea suddenly leap to mind! At this very moment I conjure up in my imagination a malicious little devil, like the one planted under the chair of the pious lady in that Hogarth print, here having crept under the tradeswoman's seat, jealous of her good fortune, slyly sawing off the legs of her stool. Blam! She falls among her glass and porcelain, and the entire business is in shambles. Which would lead to her veritable bankruptcy.

Me: In truth, dear cousin, you have taught me how to better screw up my eyes. As I let my eyes wander over the colorful mêlée of the madding crowd, my gaze falls every now and then on young girls accompanied by cleanly attired cooking women, lugging glimmering shopping baskets, roaming around the market, haggling over domestic necessities on display. The girls' tastefully modest attire and their entire manner leave no doubt that they come at the very least from prosperous bourgeois backgrounds. How is it that such girls as these come to market?

My Cousin: That's easy enough to explain. For some years now it has become customary for even the daughters of high-ranking government officials to be sent to the marketplace to learn the ropes of that aspect of household management relating to the purchase of foodstuffs.

Me: Indeed, a laudable practice, which in addition to its hands-on utility must necessarily lead to a sense of domestic responsibility.

My Cousin: Do you really think so, cousin? I rather think the contrary. What else can buying something for yourself teach a person but an admiration for objects offered for purchase and a familiarity with the current market price? A future housewife has other ways of learning how to recognize the freshness from the appearance of a vegetable or a nice cut of meat, etc., and the meager benefit of the so-called penny saved remains a moot point, far outweighed by the downside, seeing as the accompanying cook has already come to an unspoken understanding with the salesperson. Never, for the sake of innumerable pennies saved, would I expose a daughter of mine to the risk of consorting with the riffraff, overhearing a dirty joke, or having to swallow loose talk from the mouth of some churlish wench or wastrel. And then there is the matter of a certain questionable speculation as to the prospect of easy conquest by some love-starved young lad in blue uniform riding by on horseback— but look, look, cousin! What do you think of that girl by the fountain just now advancing toward us, accompanied by that elderly cook? Take my looking glass, take my looking glass, cousin!

Me: Yes, indeed, what a prize, she's the very picture of comeliness and amiability— but look how bashfully she walks with downcast eyes— every one of her steps is timid— wavering— demurely she clings to her chaperone, who guides her through the thick of things with accelerated offensive maneuvers— I've got my eye on them— now the cook is stationed in front of baskets of vegetables— she's haggling— she yanks the little one toward her, who averts her gaze and swiftly, swiftly, plucks the money from her purse and hands it to the cook, relieved to get away— I can't lose sight of her, thanks be to that red shawl— they seem to be searching in vain for something— at last, at long last, they linger in front of a woman peddling fresh vegetables from splendid little baskets— the winsome little one's attention is riveted to a basket full of lovely white cauliflower— the girl herself picks out a fresh head and drops it in the cook's basket— but, wait, that shameless hussy— just like that, the cook takes the head out of the basket, lays it back in the vendor's basket, and selects another, while I can see from the hefty shaking of her bonneted head that she chides the poor girl, who for the first time in her life sought to act independently.

My Cousin: What do you imagine are the feelings of that girl being introduced to the precepts of a domesticity wholly abhorrent to her delicate sensibility? I know that lovely little one; she's the daughter of a privy finance counselor, a natural, totally unaffected soul, endowed with a true feminine feeling and with that savvy and sense of tact young women of that sort always possess. Hold on, cousin! That's what I call a fortuitous conjuncture. Over there, around the corner, comes the very antithesis of this one. What do you say to that other girl, cousin?

Me: Oh, what a sleek, slim figure!— young— fleet-footed— facing the world with a brash, uninhibited look— a sunny expression— merry music in her movements— how cool and carefree she courses into the crowd— the servant following her with a shopping basket doesn't look a day older than her, and there is an unmistakable cordiality between them— Mademoiselle is decked out in splendid duds, her shawl is modern— her hat matches the rest of her attire— every stitch of her clothing handsome and decent— oh, dear! What do I see? Mademoiselle is wearing white silk shoes. Cast-off ball pumps at the marketplace! The longer I look at that girl the more I'm struck by a certain singularity I can't put into words. It's true, she makes all her purchases with a painstaking sedulousness, always picky, bargains and bargains, speaks, gesticulates, all with a lively mien and manner almost bordering on tension; but it seems to me she's after more than mere household necessities.

My Cousin: Bravo, bravo, cousin! You're gaining keener insight, I must say. Look closely, my most esteemed fellow, her modest attire notwith-standing – the fleet-footedness in and of itself should be a clue – the white silken pumps at market must surely reveal that our mademoiselle belongs to the ballet or perhaps the theater. What else she's after ought soon to become apparent— hah, I guessed it! Look there, dear cousin, a bit to the right, just up the street, and tell me who you catch sight of on the sidewalk, in front of the hotel, practically all by his lonesome?

Me: I see a tall, slender youth in a yellow, short fleece coat with black collar and steel buttons. He's wearing a little red, silver-threaded cap, beneath which lovely black curls peek out almost too flamboyantly. The expression of his pale, manly, finely shaped face sets off his short black mustache on the upper lip. He's holding a briefcase under his arm – no doubt a student about to attend a collegium – but his feet are firmly planted on the ground, his gaze turned toward the market, seemingly oblivious to the collegium and all else.

My Cousin: You've hit the nail on the head, cousin. His entire attention is turned to our actress. The time has come; he approaches the big fruit stand in which the freshest fruit is appealingly piled atop the heap, and appears to ask for a particular fruit not easily reachable. It is altogether impossible that a good midday meal should not include fruit for dessert; consequently, our little actress is constrained to wrap up her business at the fruit stand. A round, red, luscious-looking apple slips seductively out from between dainty fingers— the yellow-clad gent picks it up— the little the-ater enchantress responds with a charming curtsy— the conversation has been kicked off— the acquaintance, no doubt already made before, wraps up with reciprocal advice and affirmative nods concerning the admitted difficulty in selecting oranges, as prelude to the impending rendezvous, surely not the first, of varying scenarios and at different locales.

Me: Let the son of the Muses flirt and opine about selected oranges as much as he likes; I couldn't care less, all the less so since my best beloved, the privy secretary's daughter, has just turned up again at the corner, near the main entrance to the theater, where the florists display their colorful wares.

My Cousin: I'm not inclined to cast my glance at the flowers, dear cousin; I have my reasons. The saleswoman, who as a rule has the loveliest floral array of carnations, roses, and other rarer blooms, is a very attractive, pleasant-tempered girl, ever striving after greater refinement of the spirit; whenever she's not busy selling flowers she is assiduously reading books bearing the emblem of Kralowski's great literary army, which spread culture into the farthest corners of the capital. A flower girl engaged in reading is an irresistible sight for a writer of belletristic inclination. Once, long ago, when my path led me past the florists – the flowers are on display for purchase every day – I caught sight of the flower girl engrossed in her reading and stopped in surprise. She sat there as if in an arbor of blossoming geraniums, with an open book on her lap, her head resting on her hand. The hero of whatever story she was reading must have just faced impending danger, for the girl's cheeks glowed read, her lips quivered, she seemed completely oblivious to her surroundings. Cousin, let me frankly confess a writer's weakness. I was completely captivated – I scurried back and forth, wondering what the girl might be reading. This thought preoccupied my entire being. The essence of a writer's vanity awoke and tickled my suspicion: might it be one of my own works that just now transported that girl into the fantastic world of my imaginings? Finally, I plucked up my courage, approached her, and asked after the price of a batch of carnations arrayed in a far corner of her stand. While the girl went to fetch the carnations, I muttered, 'What might you be reading, my lovely child?' and picked up said book. Oh! Heaven above, it really was a work of mine, none other than ———. The girl fetched her flowers and immediately quoted a modest price. Never mind the flowers, never mind the carnations; that girl was for me at that moment the most precious reading public of the entire elegant coterie of readers in the capital. Beside myself, all fired up with an author's most profound feelings, I asked with feigned indifference if she liked the book. 'Oh, my dear Sir,' replied the girl, 'that's an odd book. In the beginning it sends you for a loop; but then it's like you're sucked in.' To my considerable surprise, the girl gave a clear account of the story, so that I realized she must have read it several times. She repeated that it was a really odd book, sometimes she laughed out loud in the telling, sometimes she was on the edge of tears; she advised me, in case I hadn't yet read it, to pick it up that afternoon from Mr. Kralowski's lending library, seeing as she changed books every afternoon.

Now for the big stunner. With downcast eyes, with a voice as sweet as the honey from Hybla, and the smile of a blissful author, I let slip: 'Here, my dear angel, here before you in the flesh stands the author of the book that gave you such pleasure.'

Speechless, she gazed at me with big eyes and an open mouth. I took this as an expression of the greatest astonishment, nothing less than a stunned rapture that the sublime genius whose dynamic imagination produced such a work should suddenly appear among her geraniums. Perhaps,

I thought, as the girl's expression remained unchanged, she did not believe that the sudden appearance before her of the illustrious author of ——— was not at all a matter of fortuitous happenstance. I sought to the best of my ability to convince her that said author and I were one and the same. But it was as if she were turned to stone, not a word slipped from her lips but: "Hm— so— is that a fact— you don't say—."

But how should I make clear to you the profound humiliation that overcame me at that moment? It so happened that the girl never imagined that the books she read had previously been composed by someone. She had not the slightest notion of a writer or a poet, and I truly believe, after a bit of cross examination, once her pious childlike faith became apparent, that she believed God made books grow like mushrooms.

Sheepishly I inquired again as to the price of the carnations. In the meantime, an altogether different dark idea of the provenance of books must have taken root in her imagination; for as I counted out the coins, she inquired in perfect naivete if I produced all the books in Mr. Kralowski's stand. Quick as lightning I made tracks with my carnations.

Me: Cousin, dear cousin, that's what I'd call recompense for a writer's vanity; but while you were telling me your tragic tale, I did not take my eye off my little darling. At least at the florist's stand that overbearing kitchen demon gave the girl free rein. The surly kitchen governess had set down the heavy market basket on the ground and lost herself in indescribably delirious chitchat with three fellow cooks, first crossing her plump arms, now with hands on her hips, arms akimbo when prompted by the rhetorical expression of her dialogue. Contrary to biblical prescription, her choice of words was, shall we say, more peppery than yes, yes and no, no. Just look what a splendid bouquet of flowers the lovely angel selected and had delivered to her home by a hale and hearty lad. What's this now? No, I don't approve of her stopping in passing to sample cherries from a little basket; how will the fine bit of cambric cloth she has probably got on survive the stain of the fruit?

My Cousin: Her youthful craving of the moment couldn't give a hoot about cherry stains, for which there are potassium oxalate and other tried-and-true household cleansing remedies. Blame it on her childish naivete that the young thing in her retrieved autonomy lets herself be enticed by the seedy lures of the marketplace. For quite some time now I've had my eye on that man over there standing near the wagon, beside the second water pump, for whom a peasant woman is just now dishing out a cheap plum jam out of a large vat – I must admit that he remains a mystery to me. First off, dear cousin, you must admire the agility of the woman, who, armed with a long wooden spoon, attends to the business, serving quarter, half, and whole pounds of the stuff, and then turns to the voracious little nibblers, holding out their folds of paper, and even their fur caps, with lightning speed dishing out a desired dab, which that ilk promptly proceed to lap up as a tasty morning tidbit – caviar of the simple folk! Her skillful serving of the plum jam with the sweep of a wooden spoon brings to mind a thing I heard when I was a kid, how at a well-appointed peasant wedding the food was so splendidly served that a threshing flail was employed to dish out a delicate rice pudding with a thick crust of cinnamon, sugar, and cloves. Each of the esteemed guests had only to lazily open his mouth wide to receive his due portion, and everything transpired in like manner as in some fabled land of milk and honey. But say, cousin, have you focused on the man in question?

Me: I have indeed! What do you make of that curious character? At least six feet tall, wind-weathered, back straight as a poker! The tip of a wig peaks out from behind a small, squashed, tricorn hat, its swishing tail hugging his back. His snug-fitting, gray coat – cut according to long-outdated fashion – is buttoned up from top to bottom, without a single pleat, and as he strode toward the wagon, I noticed that he had on black pantaloons, black stockings, and big tin buckles on his shoes. What might he have squirreled away in that rectangular box resembling a peddler's kit he keeps clasped tightly under his left arm?

My Cousin: Just keep your eye on him, you'll find out presently.

Me: He's lifting the cover— the sun is shining in— radiant reflections— the box is lined with tin— doffing his little hat, he is bowing almost reverentially to the plum-jam lady. What an original, expressive face— tightly clasped lips— a hooked nose— big, black eyes— thick, bushy eyebrows— a high forehead— black hair— his heart-shaped toupee painstakingly combed, with little ringlets of hair dangling over the ears. He hands the box to the peasant woman, who promptly proceeds to fill it with plum jam, and hands it back with a courteous curtsy. Following a second bow, the man takes his leave— he winds his way to the herring barrel— pulls a bottom drawer out of the box— drops in a couple of salted fish acquired for a pittance— a third drawer, as I now notice, is reserved for coriander and other root-based herbs. Now he's crisscrossing the market this way and that in long, deliberate strides, until he is captivated by an array of dappled poultry spread out on a table. Like everywhere else, here too he bows down low before beginning to bargain— he talks up a blue streak with the woman tending the stand, who listens with a particularly friendly mien— he carefully sets his box down on the ground and snatches up two ducks which he proceeds to calmly stuff into a big sack— heavens! He stuffs a goose in too. The turkey he just contemplates with a loving look— he can't refrain from at least fondling it with index and middle finger— he's lifting his box up lickety-split, bows down most obligingly to the poultry dealer, and breaking free of the seductive lure of coveted wares, he makes tracks directly for the butcher's stall— is the man a cook purchasing provisions for a feast, I wonder?— He buys a leg of veal which he still manages to stuff into his massive sack. Having now completed his purchases, he strolls up Charlottenstraße with such a decorous and suave manner that it seems to me he must hail from some foreign land.

My Cousin: I've racked my brains enough about this exotic character – tell me, cousin, what do you think of my hypothesis? This man is a master draughtsman who has taught his trade at various middling schools and is perhaps still so engaged. He has managed to amass a pretty penny through all manner of activities; he is stingy, distrustful, insufferably cynical, a confirmed bachelor— beholden to only one god— his belly. His sole pleasure is eating well, needless to say alone in his room— he has no servants, attends to everything himself— on market days, as you have seen, he fetches his provisions for half a week, and prepares his meals for himself in a little kitchen alcove adjoining his squalid room, which, seeing as the cook always pleases his master's palate, he then proceeds to dispatch with a greedy, indeed animal-like, appetite. As you yourself noticed, dear cousin, he skillfully and purposefully converted a paint box into a market basket.

Me: Enough of that repulsive fellow!

My Cousin: Why repulsive? A worldly-wise observer of my acquaintance claims it takes all kinds of curious codgers, and he knows what he's talking about, since variety is the spice of life. But if you dislike that man so much, dear cousin, I can offer another hypothesis about what he is, does, and dithers. Four Frenchmen, all Parisians no less, a French language instructor, a master fencer, a dance instructor, and a pastry chef, all came in their youth to Berlin at the same time, toward the end of the previous century, and all managed, as they could hardly fail to do, to make a good living. Ever since the moment of their first meeting in the coach that brought them together, they established close friendships with one another, remained united in heart and soul, and passed every evening together after a good day's work, true to their French heritage, in lively conversation over a frugal supper. The dance instructor's legs had grown stiff, the fencing master's thrust unnerved with age, the French language instructor challenged by professional rivals conversant in the latest Parisian turns of the tongue, and the tasty creations of the pastry chef surpassed by more inventive, younger palate ticklers trained by the most intractable Parisian gastronomes.

But each member of the faithful foursome had already feathered his nest. They all moved into a spacious, altogether agreeable apartment – albeit situated in an outlying district – gave up their businesses, and true to old French custom, lived content and carefree, since they had all managed to weather and surmount the hardships and burdens of that difficult time. Each had cultivated a useful skill of great benefit to society. The dance instructor and the master fencer visited their old students, high-ranking veteran military officers, court chamberlains, lord high chamberlains, and such; since they had the most genteel clientele, they continued to gather the latest gossip to entertain the friends who didn't go out. The French language instructor rummaged through the antique dealerships to keep digging up French publications the language of which the Académie Française had approved. The pastry chef kept the kitchen well stocked; he not only did all the shopping, but also saw to the meals, in the preparation of which an old French manservant assisted. Aside from the latter, and following the death of a toothless old Frenchwoman who had worked her way down from governess to scullery maid, a chubby lad whom the four friends had taken in from among the French orphans saw to their domestic needs. See that fellow clad in a sky-blue frock shuffling along over there with a basket of dinner rolls on one arm and a basket of heaped-up salad fixings in the other? So, in the blink of an eye, I have transformed the repulsive, cynical German draughtsman into a genial French pastry chef, and I believe that not only his attire but also his entire manner fits the bill.

Me: This inventive contrivance is a credit to your writerly talent, dear cousin. But for some minutes now I've had my eye on those tall white feathers poking out of the thick of the crowd. Finally, the figure decked out with them emerges, standing over there beside the water pump— a tall, slender wench not at all bad-looking— her pink silken overcoat looks brand new— her hat is of the latest fashion, with a white lace veil attached to the front— she wears white kid gloves. What compels this elegant lady, probably invited to lunch, to press her way through the crowded market? Whatever her ultimate destination, does she too belong to the class of lady shoppers? She stops and motions to a shabby, dirty old woman, a lively picture of misery, yeast in the dough of humanity, laboriously limping after her with a half-broken basket on her arm. Upon reaching the corner of the theater building, the elegant lady stops to give a pittance to the blind veteran leaning against the wall. With some difficulty, she pulls the glove off her right hand— heaven help us! A blood-red and rather manly fist emerges. But without any hesitation she presses a coin into the blind man's hand, runs out into the middle of Charlottenstraße without paying her shabby companion any more mind, and hastens on to the grand avenue Unter den Linden.

My Cousin: To rest up, the old woman set the basket on the ground, and in a single glimpse you can survey all the purchases of the elegant lady.

Me: Verily, a marvel to gaze upon. A head of cabbage— many potatoes— some apples— a small loaf of bread— a couple of herrings wrapped in paper— a sheep milk cheese not of a particularly appetizing hue— a mutton liver— a small shrub of roses— a pair of slippers— a bootjack— and what have you—

My Cousin: Be still, be still, dear cousin, enough rosy superfluities! Look closely at that blind man to whom misery's child gave alms. Could there be a more stirring picture of undeserved human misery and pious, God-fearing resignation? With his back to the wall of the theater, both dried-out, bony hands resting on a cane held out before him so that the careless crowd does not trample on his feet, his corpse-pale face raised heavenward, his military cap pressed down over his eyes, he stands there motionless at the same spot from early morning until the market closes—

Me: He begs, even though blind veterans are well cared for.

My Cousin: You are quite mistaken, dear cousin. This poor man serves as the hired help of a woman who hawks vegetables and who belongs to the lower echelon of such salespersons, since the upper echelon peddle their greens from baskets packed on carts. This blind man comes every morning loaded down like a packhorse with heaping baskets of vegetables, so that the heavy load almost bends him to the ground, and he can only advance with a wobbly step, holding himself upright with the aid of a cane. A big-boned, robust woman whom he serves, or who perhaps only uses him to transport the produce to market, hardly makes much of an effort to help when he almost succumbs to the burden, gruffly grabbing him by the arm and dragging him to the spot where he now stands. Here she takes the baskets from his back and carries them off, leaving him standing there, and without paying the slightest attention to him until it's time for the market to shut down, when she once again loads the empty or only partially empty baskets onto his back.

Me: How curious, even if an individual's eyes are not shut or some other visible impairment is not apparent at first glance, that one can nevertheless always immediately recognize blindness from the upward-turned tilt of the head unique to the blind; it seems to suggest an eternal striving to behold something in the eternal night that envelops the blind.

My Cousin: There is for me no more stirring sight than that of such a blind man with head uplifted who appears to be peering into the distance. The reddish tint of sunset has forever faded to dark for that man, but his inner eye still strives after a glimpse of the eternal light shining toward him, offering solace, hope and salvation in the hereafter – but I am becoming too solemn. Every market day that blind veteran provides me with a wealth of observations. You will note, dear cousin, how this poor man elicits the beneficence of Berliners. Droves of people regularly pass him, and not one fails to give him a handout. But the diverse mode and manner with which such pittances are passed along – that's what interests me the most. Observe for a while, dear cousin, and tell me what you see.

Me: Just now, three, four, five heavyset, sturdy housemaids are walking by; their shopping baskets, some of them packed to the brim with heavy goods, almost straining their fleshy arms right down to the blue nerve-endings; they have all reason to hurry, to divest themselves of their load, and yet each one lingers a moment, reaches hastily into the basket, and presses a coin into the blind man's hand without even looking at him. This payment appears to be an essential and indispensable part of market day activities. You're right about that. Here comes a woman whose outfit, whose entire bearing clearly bespeaks a life of comfort and prosperity— she stops in front of the invalid, pulls out a purse in which she searches and searches, but no coin seems small enough to fulfill the act of charity she feels impelled to perform— she calls to her cook— it seems that she, too, has run out— she must first make change by trading with the vegetable dealers— finally the threepence piece destined for charitable contribution has been procured— she taps on the blind man's hand so that he may notice that he is about to receive something— he opens the palm of his hand— the benevolent lady presses the coin into his hand and closes the fingers of his fist around it so that the lavish gift not be lost. But why does the dainty little mademoiselle pitter-patter back and forth, coming closer and closer to the blind man? Hah, scurrying by, she plunked a coin into the blind man's hand, so quickly, in fact, that surely no one but me captured the act in the sight of my looking glass – that was definitely more than a threepence piece. The proper, portly gentleman in the brown coat who comes ambling over is surely a member of the upper crust. He, too, stops before the blind man and engages in a lengthy conversation, blocking the way of others, thereby hindering them from handing him their pittance – at last, at long last he pulls a hefty green purse out of his pocket, takes pains to slowly snap it open, and rattles up such a storm in the change, I believe I can hear it tinkling up here at my window. *Parturiunt montes!** But I really want to believe that, torn by the misery of the blind man, that noble philanthropist intends to shell out a pretty penny. Given these observations, it seems to me that the blind man must bring in a considerable sum on market day, and what surprises me is that he accepts it all without the least display of gratitude; only a silent movement of the lips, which I seem to detect, indicates that he utters something that might be a thank-you – but even this lip movement I only notice from time to time.

My Cousin: Complete and total resignation, that's the apt expression. What good is money to him? He can't use it; only in the hand of another, whom he must heedlessly trust, does it attain its value – I may be altogether mistaken, but it seems to me that the woman whose baskets of produce he carries is a nasty profiteer who takes complete advantage of poor folks like him, in addition to which she most likely confiscates all the money he takes

---

* A Latin quotation from Horace: *Parturiunt montes, nascetur ridiculus mus.* Literally: The mountains are in labor and a piddling mouse will be born. By implication: To make a mountain out of a molehill.

in. Every time she brings back the empty baskets, she harangues the blind man, in direct relation to the good or bad business she did that day. Already the blind man's deathly pale face, haggard figure, and tattered clothing allow us to suspect that his situation in life is lamentable, and it would be the task of an active philanthropist to investigate this insidious relationship.

Me: Surveying the entire market, I notice that sheets are spanned like tents over the carts of flour, according it all a picturesque appearance, granting the eye a point of reference from which to consider the colorful crowd.

My Cousin: The white flour carts and the flour dusted miller's lads and lasses with their rosy red cheeks, each one a *bella molinara*,* clues me in to something altogether different. I am saddened not to see a family of coal mongers who ordinarily peddle their wares directly opposite my window, there in front of the theater, and have been reassigned a spot on the other side of the market. The head of the charcoal dealer's family is a big, robust man with an expressive face— marked features— vehement, almost violent in his movements— suffice to say the very epitome of a charcoal dealer as commonly depicted in novels. On a solitary stroll in the woods I once actually ran into this man, an encounter that might well under other circumstances have given me the chills, but his amicable disposition came as a godsend at that moment. In stark contrast to him, the second member of the family is an altogether droll, strangely twisted fellow, hardly four feet tall. You know, dear cousin, that there are people of peculiar build; at first sight you take them for hunchbacked, and yet on closer consideration you cannot rightly tell where exactly their hump is located.

---

* An allusion to *Die Schöne Müllerin* (The Lovely Miller Maiden), a song cycle by Franz Schubert (1797–1828), based on poems by Wilhelm Müller (1794–1827).

Me: Apropos of which, I remember the naïve turn of phrase of a quick-witted military man who had business dealings with just such a misshapen fellow, and for whom the unfathomable nature of the latter's bodily build prodded his wit. "A hump," he said, "that fellow has a hump; but who the devil knows where that hump of his is planted!"

My Cousin: Nature initially conceived the idea of building the little charcoal burner into a giant figure, some seven feet tall – for so do his colossal hands and feet suggest, almost the biggest that I have ever seen. This modest little fellow, draped in a big-collared coat with a curious fur cap plunked on his head, is in a constant state of restless agitation; with an unsettling agility he leaps and scurries back and forth, now here, now there, and takes pains to play the role of the most beloved, charming character, the *primo amoroso* of the marketplace. He does not let a single woman pass, unless she belongs to the upper class, without puttering after her, uttering endearments with his own inimitable posturing, gestures, and grimaces befitting only of a charcoal burner. Sometimes he carries his gallantry so far in the course of a conversation as to suavely sling an arm around a girl's hip, and taking his cap in his hands, praise her beauty, and proffer his chivalrous services. Strangely enough, not only do the girls allow him to take such liberties, but they give the little creature a friendly nod and appear to condone his gallant advances. This little fellow is surely endowed with a rich dose of natural wit, the essential talent for drollery, and the ability to express it. He is the Pagliaccio, *le tausendsasa*,* the life and soul of every event, known in the entire region surrounding the woods in which he lives; without his presence, no child's baptism, nuptial feast, no last dance to

---

* Jack-of-all-trades.

wrap up a wedding, no proper banquet can take place; his pleasantries are prized and laughed at all year round.

Since the charcoal burner's children and any and all maidservants are left at home, the visible rest of the family comprises two women of robust build and dark, sullen expression, for which the coal dust caught in the folds of the face may well be blamed. The touching attachment of a great big spitz, with whom the family shares every bite that they themselves gobble down during market, offers ample proof of the upright nature and good-hearted patriarchalism of the charcoal burners' household. The little man, moreover, is endowed with great strength, of which the family makes ample use to lug the sold sacks of charcoal to clients' homes. I often saw him loaded down by the women with a good ten baskets full, which they heaped one on top of the other on his back, and he hopped off with it as though it weighed nothing at all. Seen from the rear, this fellow looked about as droll and quixotic as you can imagine. Naturally one could not see the worthy figure of the little fellow himself, but only the most massive sack of coal with a little pair of feet attached to the bottom. He looked like a fabulous creature, a fairy-tale-like kangaroo leaping about the market.

Me: Look, look, cousin! Somebody's making an awful racket over there in front of the church. Two vegetable peddlers are probably engaged in a tiresome squabble over mine and thine, and with fists balled up at their sides, are exchanging the most colorful language. The crowd converges— a dense circle surrounds the disputants— their voices grow louder and shriller by the moment— ever more ferociously do they go at it, hands waving with menace in the air— they move ever closer to bodily contact— the altercation is on the verge of breaking out into fisticuffs— the police break it up— how? Suddenly I notice a group of glittering helmets butting in between the disputants— a moment later, the female friends of the two sides manage to mollify the hotheads— the fight is over— without the help of the police— the two women return quietly to their respective vegetable baskets— the crowd, which only a couple of times, probably in response to particularly agitated moments in the dispute, expressed their approbation with loud cheers, is dissipating.

My Cousin: You will notice, dear cousin, that in the entire time we've been looking out the window this was the only squabble that broke out on the marketplace, and that, ultimately, it was hushed by the crowd. Even more serious, more threatening disputes are generally broken up in this way by the crowd, which presses in between the disputants and pulls them apart. Last market day, there was a big raggedy fellow with a churlish, wild-eyed expression stationed between the meat and fruit stands who suddenly got into a squabble with the butcher boy just then passing by. With the awful club that he held strung over his shoulder like a rifle, he promptly lunged at the boy, which would have instantly laid him low, had the latter not adroitly sidestepped the blow and leapt into the butcher stand. Here, however, he armed himself with a big butcher's cleaver, intending to chop at his assailant. All circumstances seemed to indicate that this altercation would be resolved with a murderous blow, and become a case for the criminal court. But the female fruit vendors, the whole lot powerful ladies of portly build, felt impelled to embrace the butcher boy so tenderly and firmly that he could not manage to break free of their grip; he stood there with weapon raised above his head, as it is said in that emotional dramatic description of the angry Pyrrhus: "So, as a painted tyrant, Pyrrhus stood, /

And like a neutral to his will and matter, / Did nothing." In the meantime, other women, brush makers, bootjack vendors, etc. surrounded the attacker, granting the police time to take the fellow, likely a recently released convict, into a custody.

Me: So there is, in fact, a sense among the people for the order to be preserved, which can only be very fruitful for everyone.

My Cousin: In general, dear cousin, my observations of goings on in the marketplace have confirmed my belief that the people of Berlin have undergone a remarkable transformation since that catastrophic period when an impudent, overconfident enemy overran the country and tried in vain to break their spirit, which leapt back up with renewed force like a squashed spiral coil. In short: the people have improved in their ethical comportment; and if on a warm summer afternoon you watch the crowd break up camp and hightail it to Moabit,* even among the common chambermaids and day laborers you will notice an altogether remarkable effort toward courteous behavior. Much the same as the individual, the masses have undergone profound change, and given their *nihil admirari*.** They have, so it seems, become more supple in manner. In the past, Berlin's hoi polloi were gruff and brutal; as a stranger, for instance, you could hardly ask after a street or a particular address, or anything else, for that matter, without receiving a rude or sarcastic response, or being made a fool of with false information. Gone is the Berlin street urchin likely to take advantage of the least excuse, a somewhat garish getup or someone having suffered a laughable accident, and respond with the most reprehensible prank. For those

* A formerly working-class neighborhood in the heart of Berlin.

** Latin expression, roughly translatable as: to be surprised by nothing.

young hoodlums peddling cigars at the gates of the city who hoodwink gullible out-of-towners, those rogues who spend their lives in Spandau or Straußberg, or, as just recently happened to one of their ilk, who end up on the gallows, are by no means comparable to the Berlin street urchin of old. The latter was not some vagabond, but rather an ordinary apprentice craftsman and – it almost seems ridiculous to say it – in all his godlessness and depravity, still held by a certain *point d'honneur* and was not lacking in a droll sense of humor.

Me: Oh, my dear cousin, let me tell you how just recently I was the shameful butt of just such an insidious lark. I was walking in front of the Brandenburg Gate and was followed by Charlottenburg carters who invited me to rest my weary legs and climb aboard. One of them, a lad of sixteen or seventeen at the most, carried his effrontery so far as to grab me by the arm with his filthy fist. 'Take your hands off me!' I snapped. 'So, my good Sir,' the youth replied perfectly calmly, gaping at me with a hollow look in his eyes, 'why should I not lay my hands on you; are you perhaps not an honorable gentleman?'

My Cousin: Haha! This lark really is one of those sprung from the stinking depths of depravity. The sassy repartees of Berlin's female fruit vendors were renowned, and one even did them the honor of characterizing such jibes as Shakespearian, despite the fact that, when you get right down to it, their energy and originality consisted above all of the shameless cheek with which they famously dished out the vilest filth. In the past, the marketplace was the hotbed of bickering, brawls, bamboozlement, and petty theft, and no honest woman would dare do her own shopping there lest she expose herself to such unsavory goings-on. For not only did the hucksters turn their skullduggery on themselves and everyone else, but there were also unsavory types, like the ragtag contingent in military regiments culled from every corner of the world, who went there with the express purpose of stirring up trouble so as to go fishing in muddy waters. Notice, dear cousin, in contrast, how nowadays the marketplace presents the pretty picture of well-being and perfect harmony. I know that enthusiastic purists inveigle against this apparent picture of public propriety, suggesting that with this imposed politeness of manners the folksiness will also be polished off and forfeited. I, for my part, am of the firmest conviction that a people who treat the locals and strangers alike, not with gruffness or sarcastic contempt, but rather in a civil manner, will by no means thereby forfeit their character. Such purists would surely take issue with one striking example in support of the truth of my contention.

The crowd had thinned out more and more; the market was growing emptier by the moment. The female vegetable vendors packed some of their empty baskets on a wagon that rolled up— they lugged others off themselves— the wagons full of flour drove off— the female florists hauled off their leftover stock of flowers on big pushcarts— the police proved most efficient at keeping everything running smoothly, in particular the wagon order. This steady flow of carts would have kept running on its own if every now and then a schismatic peasant boy had not taken it upon himself to chart his own new Bering Strait diagonally across the square, and dash audaciously through the fruit stands toward the entrance to the German church. This elicited much shouting and much troublesome maneuvering on the part of the adroit charioteers.

"This market," said my cousin, "is even now a faithful likeness of the eternally meandering course of life. Brisk activity, the necessity of the moment drove the crowd together; in a matter of minutes the whole place is deserted, the voices that had until now become entangled in a chaotic din fell silent, and the desolate square all too vividly illustrates the grim saying: 'What was, was!'"

A clock sounded, the surly invalid strode into the cubicle and remarked with a twisted look: "It would behoove you, Sir, to finally leave the window and come eat, as the served dishes will otherwise grow cold."

"So, you've still got an appetite after all, dear cousin?" I asked.

"Oh, yes," he replied with a pained chuckle, "as you will soon be able to attest for yourself."

The invalid servant rolled him into the room. The proffered dishes comprised a middling soup bowl filled with a beef broth, a single soft-boiled egg propped up in a heap of salt, and half of a dinner roll.

"A single bite more," my cousin quietly and wistfully remarked, as he pressed my hand, "even the most minuscule additional piece of the tenderest meat engenders the most excruciating pain, dispels my last ounce of courage to face life, and extinguishes the last little spark of humor that flashes every now and then."

Motioning in the direction of the sheet of paper attached to his bed screen, I flung myself on my cousin's chest and pressed him hard against me.

"Yes, cousin," he cried out with a voice that cut me to the quick and filled me with heartrending sorrow. "Yes, indeed: *Et si male nunc, non olim sic erit!*"

My poor cousin!

[403]

Facing the Music: The Melodious Imaginings of E. T. A. Hoffmann

An Afterword

On weekdays I'm a jurist, and a bit of a musician, my Sundays are devoted to drawing, and come evening I'm a quick-witted author until late at night.

E. T. A. Hoffmann

Not far from his perch at the corner window overlooking Gendarmenmarkt, the central marketplace in Berlin where Hoffmann last surveyed life, paralyzed and in the painful end stage of syphilis, his tombstone in Cemetery III of the congregations of the adjacent Jerusalem Church and New Church bears an epitaph that reads like an abridged resumé: "E. T. W. Hoffmann, Counselor of the Court of Appeal, outstanding in accomplishment, as author, composer and painter." The man better known to posterity as E.T.A. Hoffmann plied diverse talents and packed parallel careers into a mad-dash life that lasted a mere forty-six years.

Born on January 24, 1776, in Königsberg, East Prussia, Ernst Theodor Wilhelm Hoffmann later opted to change his second middle name to Amadeus in homage to Mozart. Alongside the wildly imaginative tales for which he is justifiably famous, Hoffmann also composed eight operas and light operas, twenty-three musical themes for plays, ballets, and melodramas, multiple masses, a miserere, a symphony, thirty vocal works, and sixteen piano sonatas and chamber music pieces, most of which have either been lost or forgotten. He also wrote landmark music criticism notable for, among other insights, a keen appreciation of the felicitous marriage of words and notes in operas and other vocal compositions.

Speaking through his fictional alter ego, Kapellmeister Johannes Kreisler, in tongue-in-cheek writings published in various literary journals of the day, Hoffmann burst into print, fording the divide between tune and text.

But while his own richly evocative fictions inspired the memorable melodic creations of others, notably Jacques Offenbach's opera *The Tales of Hoffmann*, Pyotr Ilyich Tchaikovsky's ballet *The Nutcracker*, and Robert Schumann's *Kreisleriana* (Opus 16), Hoffmann himself never achieved the success he sought on the concert stage. Yet like few other authors before or since, music informed every fiber of his being, seeping into the very marrow of his writing, not only inspiring narratives directly relating to musical themes, but also infusing his phrasing with a rich mellifluence that leaves the reader with the sense of stories sung.

Consider the following passage from "Ritter Gluck," Hoffmann's first published narrative, drafted in 1809 and issued in the *Allgemeine musikalische Zeitung*, in Leipzig, a respected musical newspaper at a time when music really mattered in cultivated German society; Hoffmann subsequently included it in his first collection, *Fantasiestücke in Callots Manier* (*Fantasy Pieces Conceived in the Manner of Caillot*), published in 1814. An account of the narrator's meeting with a mysterious stranger who may either be the eponymous composer Christoph Willibald Gluck or else a brilliant lunatic, the tale is an attempt to compose with words a virtual tone poem evoking the psychic state of musical inspiration:

> Hah, how in heaven's name is it possible to even intimate the thousand some odd paths to musical composition! It is a broad thoroughfare, which all romp along, whooping and crying: 'We are the anointed ones! We've made our mark!' Passing through the ivory gate, you reach the realm of dreams; there are precious few who see the gate even once, and far fewer who ever pass through it! [...] Madcap figures pass back and forth, but they have character – some more so than others. They keep a low profile on the high road; you can only catch sight of them on the far side of the ivory gate. [...] Many are entrapped by their reverie in the realm of dream, they dissolve in their dreams [...]; but only a handful, awakened from their dream, [...] arrive at the truth— the supreme moment has come: contact with the eternal, an unspeakable experience! The sun looks on, it is the tonic triad, from which chords, starlike, shoot down and spin around you with flaming filaments. Enmeshed with fire, you lie there, until Psyche swings herself up to the sun.

Music constituted for Hoffmann a kind of sacred spell and as such may have proved too holy, too precious, too ineffable to toy and tinker with. But words bore no such aura and were consequently free to fiddle with, unencumbered with self-imposed restrictions.

"Ritter Gluck" can also be read as a kind of confessional. In the persona of the narrator, Hoffmann acknowledges his own failed attempts at musical composition. His interlocutor is clearly an embodiment of the author's own musical musings and longings. The fact that Hoffmann was best able to evoke such sonorous euphoria in words, rather than notes, must have proved both immensely gratifying and infinitely frustrating to him.

In any case, music continued throughout the author's life to embody for him both an artistic and a spiritual ideal after which he strove. This intangible ideal not only inspired fiction directly relating to music, but also sparked in the echo chamber of his imagination such fulminous outbursts as "The Sandman" and "The Golden Pot," the two enigmatic tales for which he is best known. In these and other phantasmagorical narratives, Hoffmann allowed himself to take prodigious artistic liberties, wildly leaping back and forth across the border between the physical and the metaphysical, the perceived and the imagined, the accessible and the unattainable, hazarding with language the daring leaps of his musical idols, Mozart and Beethoven. The astute reader can sense the notes pulsing inside his words and recognize his narratives as the quasi-musical compositions that they are.

⌣⟶

The opposition between the accessible and the ideal also plays itself out in his plots. In both "The Sandman" and "The Golden Pot," Hoffmann's male protagonists waver between their attraction to actual flesh-and-blood women and the seemingly irresistible lure of ideal objects of desire – an

automaton in the former narrative and a sultry green snake in the latter –
invariably opting for the ideal over the actual and consequently descending
into madness. One cannot help but wonder if his characters' unflinching
preference for the impossible was a consequence of the "grass is always
greener" syndrome, or rather, contingent on some unresolved childhood
trauma in the author's own life.

Fascinated by the man and his imaginings as a potential minefield for
psychoanalysis, Sigmund Freud repeatedly sought to posthumously stretch
him out on the virtual analytic couch and dig into his dreams. In Freud's
late work, *Der Mann Moses und die monotheistische Religion* (*Moses and Mono-
theism*), completed in 1939, he included the following aside:

> E.T.A. Hoffmann liked to trace back the source of the wealth of
> characters that fed his fictions to the play of images and
> impressions he gleaned as a suckling babe at his mother's breast on
> a weeklong journey by postal coach.

Much as the author might have fostered this far-fetched fiction about himself, it is impossible to confirm, indeed unlikely, that such a rife imagination
could have been stoked by even the most precocious infant's photographic
memory.

What is certain is that Hoffmann mythologized his childhood and his
mother. He was the product of an unhappy union; his parents separated in
1778, when he was only two years old, at which point he lost contact with
his father and moved back with his emotionally cold mother to her mater-
nal home. The reconstituted household was headed by a strict, unforgiving

grandmother, two batty maiden aunts, and a repressed, albeit musically inclined, bachelor uncle, whose sole saving grace from the boy's perspective was that he encouraged him to take up music. A virtual automaton, his mother often spent the whole day motionless, staring into the void, and died in despair a year later. His uncle had studied law, but abandoned the profession after losing his first court case, withdrawing into premature and permanent retirement. Except for a kindly childlike aunt, the adults remained essentially aloof to the child in their midst. Hoffmann came of age in this emotionally arid environ, taking refuge in his reveries, embroidering his longings with imagined memories of intimacy with an idealized and loving mother.

Freud had already delved into Hoffmann's rife imagination in a famous early essay, "Das Unheimliche" ("The Uncanny"), written in 1919, in which he hailed the author as "the unsurpassed master of the uncanny in literature." In the essay, Freud focuses his attention on "The Sandman," a tale of a student's descent into madness, dated on the original manuscript, "One o'clock in the morning, November 16, 1815," and first published in his short story collection *Die Nachtstücke* (The Night Pieces), in 1817.

Traumatized in childhood by an ominous sometime associate of his father who half-jokingly threatened to tear out the inquisitive boy's eyes, Hoffmann's protagonist, Nathaniel, later conflates a traveling oculist with his childhood bugbear; through the lens of a spyglass he buys from the latter he glimpses and immediately falls head over heels for Olympia, the dazzling daughter of his professor, and promptly drops his old flame Clara. Olympia, alas, turns out to be an automaton. Upon witnessing the comely robot have her eyes torn out and thereafter be literally torn apart in the course of a quarrel between the professor and the oculist, Nathaniel suffers a nervous breakdown. He returns to his native town, where Clara, with whom he has since reconciled, cares for him in his convalescence. All appears to be going well between them, until Nathaniel goes off the deep end again, believing he has spotted his old demon in the crowd, and in a psychotic fit, attempts to toss Clara from a tower window, from which he ultimately leaps to his death.

Freud traces a fondness for mechanical automata back to a common childhood fixation, reminding with considerable insight "that at a very early age of make believe, the child does not distinguish sharply between the living and the lifeless and is particularly fond of treating its doll as a living being."

Freud furthermore conflates the eyes with the genitals, and concludes that "the uncanny element in 'The Sandman' can be traced back to fear of the child's castration complex" – a somewhat far-fetched contention perhaps more linked to Freud's own fixations than those of Hoffmann.

Whatever childhood trauma it does or does not tap, the terrifying tale and its author had a profound literary influence, particularly abroad, nourishing the eerie narratives of Edgar Allen Poe, Nathaniel Hawthorne, Nikolai Gogol, and Oscar Wilde, among countless other authors of note. "The Sandman" also inspired a novel by German novelist and screenwriter Thea von Harbou, which in turn inspired her husband, film director Fritz Lang, to collaborate with her on the silent film classic *Metropolis*. French Surrealist André Breton viewed E.T.A. Hoffmann as a pivotal forerunner and pathfinder and included "The Sandman" in his *Anthology of Black Humor*, published in 1940. The tale later primed the American science fiction writer Philip K. Dick to pen his tour-de-force novel, *Do Androids*

Dream of Electric Sheep?, upon which Ridley Scott based his 1982 cult classic film, *Blade Runner.*

However we choose to interpret such enigmatic tales as "The Sandman" and "The Automaton," also included in this collection, Hoffman's interest in and concern about the early-nineteenth-century mechanized figurines featured at fairs in his day – particularly those that also play music and still decorate Christmas show windows to this day –"constitutes one of the earliest condemnations of the burgeoning industrial omnipresence of machines," as one biographer, Peter Braun, points out. "He saw in them, not only a threat to human beings, but also, and in particular, a menace to music," excising the vital human element of variability and reducing it to a stiff, mechanical motor of music.

"The Golden Pot," first published in 1814 in the third volume of his *Fantasiestücke in Callots Manier,* likewise traces a student's descent into folly. The love object here is an imaginary green talking snake named Serpentina, first glimpsed by the delirious protagonist, Anselmus, wriggling around the trunk and branches of an elderberry tree. The shape of the snake evokes phallic phantasies, but we had best leave it to future Freudians and biographers to delve into Hoffmann's complex libido.

Hoffmann's fascination with madness was informed by his acquaintance with the physician Adalbert Friedrich Marcus, who in 1789 founded the Bamberger Allgemeine Krankenhaus, where he treated emotionally disturbed patients with hypnotic methods based on Franz Anton Mesmer's theory of animal magnetism.

What matters to posterity is not so much the root of his intuition, as how Hoffmann the writer transformed such infantile traumatic flashes into unforgettable fiction. A thin, little man with deep-set eyes, sharp features, and porcupine-like, spiked hair, with a fiery temperament and wit enough for multiple personalities, Hoffmann apparently penned the tales bubbling up from his unconscious at lightning speed. According to his diary, he wrote "The Sandman" over a period of eight days, while simultaneously attending to the responsibilities of his day job as a jurist.

This is how his friend Julius Eduard Hitzig described him in the first biography devoted to the author:

> Hoffmann was very short in stature, had a yellowish skin color,
> very dark, almost black hair that sprouted from low down on his
> forehead, gray eyes that did not express much when he was still
> and peering forward, but which sparkled and took on an
> uncommonly crafty look when he winked, as he often liked to do.
> His nose was fine and bent, his mouth tightly closed. [...] He
> particularly prized his muttonchop whiskers, and combed them
> carefully close to the corners of his mouth. [...] In his entire
> outward appearance, one was particularly struck by an
> extraordinary sprightliness.

Hoffmann peppered his texts with revelatory clues concerning his character, as, for instance, in the comic description of his fictional alter ego, Kapellmeister Johannes Kreisler:

His friends maintained that nature tried a new recipe when cooking up his character traits, and the experiment had failed. Too little of the phlegmatic had been added to his over-excitable disposition; his imaginative faculty all too often got fired up to a dangerous degree and upset the balance of his equilibrium, a character trait absolutely essential to the artist, enabling him to get along with the world, and to compose works of the sort that the world really needs to a higher degree than they even know.

There is another hardly veiled self-portrait in "The Golden Pot":

… such an individual need be of a childlike poetic disposition. This disposition is often found in youths who are scorned by the crowd on account of the great simplicity of their manner and because they are totally lacking in worldly sophistication.

In yet another passage, from "Counselor Krespel," Hoffmann's tale of a maniacally overprotective father who forbids his daughter to sing, first published in 1818 in his friend the Baron de la Motte Fouqué's popular literary journal *Frauentaschenbuch*, the author once again appears to be describing a character with definite parallels to himself:

"There are people," he said, "from whom nature or some calamity tears away the veil behind which the rest of us engage in our mad doings unnoticed. They resemble thin-skinned insects that appear misshapen in the buoyant, visible squirming of their minuscule muscles, though they soon reassume their proper shape. Everything that in us remains merely imagined, in Krespel turns into action. The bitter irony that our well-behaved spirit ordinarily keeps under control in our conduct and actions, drives Krespel to mad gesticulations, twists, and turns. But that is his lightning rod. What emanates from the earth he gives back to the earth, retaining a flicker of the divine spark; and so, I believe, his mind is perfectly in order, notwithstanding the seeming madness of his antics.

Krespel, it turns out, has a perfectly rational reason for preventing his daughter from singing. The story was inspired by the actual case of the sickly seventeen-year-old singer Minna Brandes, whom Hoffmann had heard sing in Königsberg; having been forbidden to sing on doctor's orders as a strain on her fragile health, she declined to follow the medical advice and died of consumption six years later.

Like Krespel, Hoffmann had a rational, pragmatic side counterbalancing the erratic bent of his wild emotional swings and imaginative frenzies. He summed up his attitude and aesthetic in a line from *The Serapion Brethren*,[*] the epistolary narrative frame of a collection of his tales:

> I believe that the bottom of the heavenly ladder, upon which we
> seek to clamber to reach the higher regions of consciousness, must

[*] The Serapion Brethren was also the name of a Berlin literary and social circle to which he belonged.

be grounded in real life, so that our readers can clamber up after us. If the reader who climbs higher and higher finds himself in a fantastic magical realm, he will be more likely to believe that this realm still belongs as an integral part of his life, and is, in fact, the most wondrous and splendid part of that life.

Another notable German-speaking author likewise trained in the law, Franz Kafka, who also juggled the responsibilities of a mundane day job with nightly reverie, and is in many ways a kindred spirit with Hoffmann, took up a similar ladder metaphor, albeit with a Kafkaesque twist, in a diary notation:

> … all things that occur to me to describe don't strike me from the root, but rather from somewhere in the middle. Just try to grab it, try to embrace a blade of grass that grows out from the middle of the stalk. A select few can do it, so for instance, Japanese jugglers balanced on a ladder not resting on firm ground, but rather on the uplifted soles of a half-reclining partner, a ladder not propped up against any wall either, but rather just rising in the air.

It might not be all that far-fetched to perceive a link of influence between Hoffmann's automaton, the cause of the protagonist's violent demise in "The Sandman," and the insidious device in Kafka's dark fantasy "In the Penal Colony" that inscribes the body of the condemned with his crime and immediately thereafter implodes.

Like Kafka, Hoffmann, too, kept a firm foothold in the sober reality of the law. Having studied law, he pursued a professional career as a mid-level bureaucrat in the judicial administration of the Prussian state. Prussia at the time extended well beyond the borders of the present-day German state of Brandenburg, encompassing large swathes of present-day Poland, including Posen (Poznań) and the cosmopolitan metropolis of Warsaw. Hoffmann started out as a probationary court judge in Posen and rose to the rank of judge in Berlin's prestigious court of appeal. By most accounts, he faithfully and diligently carried out his legal responsibilities, oftentimes going out of his way to promote justice and freedom of expression in an absolutist state.

In Posen, he met and married Maria Thekla Michaline Rohrer-Trzcińska and lived happily, if not ever after, then at least for a while. But time and again, the disparate strands of his character unraveled and his pen got him into trouble. An accomplished draughtsman, among his many creative talents, Hoffmann was fond of drawing caricatures of individuals of his acquaintance. In 1802 his caricatures of major-generals and other high-ranking officers in the Prussian military and local landed gentry found their way onto satirical masks at a carnival celebration. Discovered as the artistic trickster behind the lark, Hoffmann, who had been anticipating promotion to state councillor and transfer to the capital city of Berlin, was indeed promoted, but as a sanction for his insubordinate antics was shunted off to the onomatopoeic sounding backwater hamlet of Płock.

Two years later, Hoffmann managed to get himself transferred to Warsaw, where he reveled in the cosmopolitan atmosphere and the plenitude of cultural activities. His family life was also enriched by the birth of a daughter whom he named Cäcilia, after St. Cecilia, the patron saint of musicians. In Warsaw he met and befriended a fellow jurist, Julius Eduard Hitzig, who would become a lifelong ally and his first biographer. Born Isaac Elias Itzig, Hitzig added an H to camouflage his identity as the cultivated scion of a well-to-do Jewish family, and he later converted to Christianity. Neighbors as well as professional colleagues, the two men flung open their windows on warm summer nights, and Hitzig was fond of leaning out to listen to the music Hoffmann played. Well-read and well-connected in literary circles, Hitzig introduced his friend to the Romantic literature of the day, and later to many of the leading German Romantics writers.

His friendship with Hitzig notwithstanding, Hoffmann's attitude to Jews has been studied by scholars, some going so far as to suspect a Jewish caricature in his portrayal of the villainous character who threatened to pluck out the child's eyes in "The Sandman." Certain insidious antisemitic clichés crept into such tales as "The Selection of a Bride." It should be noted, however, that in harboring such prejudices, Hoffmann was no different from most of his contemporaries.

Among his administrative duties in Warsaw, the man who had changed his own middle name from Theodor to Amadeus was tasked with the assignment of surnames to Warsaw's Jewish community, who as per Jewish tradition, had heretofore gone by patronymics. According to Norman Davies, in his *Heart of Europe: The Past in Poland's Present* (Oxford University Press, 2001), Hoffmann undertook the task with a capricious whimsy: "Before dinner, or on an empty stomach, he issues serious or melancholy surnames, after dinner more amusing ones." On one occasion, apparently following a prolonged bout of drinking with a military man of his acquaintance, Hoffmann hastily dubbed unsuspecting individuals of Jewish provenance with military names, such as Festung (Fortress), Pistolet (Pistol), Szyspulver (gunpowder), Trommel (drum), etc.

Like so many other creative artists, Hoffmann was surely a bundle of contradictions. His prickly personality did not always sit well with those who knew him. Contemporary assessments by his fellow German Romantics vary. Unfailingly defending him, Hitzig remained a devoted friend, lauding Hoffmann in the biography he wrote after his death. Wilhelm Grimm, on the other hand, considered Hoffmann brilliant, "but unsavory." Jean Paul held him to be an out-and-out madman. A friend and frequent dinner partner in Berlin, author Adelbert von Chamisso dubbed him "the king of tomfoolery." Poet Clemens Brentano called him "an eccentric, but honest chum." Writer and journalist August Varnhagen von Ense held him to be "an honest friend, without guile and malice, whose sense of humor nevertheless proved brash and disquieting, and could be equally insightful and fatuous."

Hoffmann offers a veiled fictionalized self-appraisal in his novel *The Devil's Elixir*, written in 1814:

I am what I appear to be, and don't appear to be what I am, an inexplicable riddle to myself, I am a divided self.

Whether out of restless temperament or necessity, he changed locales with some frequency, from Posen to Płock, to Warsaw, to Berlin, to Bamberg, where he landed a position as theater director, from which he was fired soon thereafter, compelling him for a time to eke out his existence as a piano teacher.

In one profoundly embarrassing and socially devastating instance, Hoffmann's infatuation with an underage piano student in Bamberg, Julia Mark, led to a scene, compelling him to skip town. Next stops Leipzig and Dresden. Marriage did not keep his excesses in check. Always a heavy drinker and carouser, back in Posen he is rumored to have been the author of an anonymous sado-masochistic novel, *Sister Monica*, issued by a book dealer-publisher of his acquaintance. In one of his many extra-marital involvements he contracted the syphilis that would first cripple him, then do him in.

And when it was not his own shenanigans that got him into trouble, history played a hand. Prussia's provisional military alliance with Russia against France led Napoleon to occupy Warsaw. Refusing to swear allegiance to the Gallic emperor and the newly installed French puppet administration, Hoffmann was again obliged to decamp.

⌣

Hoffmann's allegiance to his native Prussia did not, however, keep him from speaking and reading French, and admiring French culture and literature. French influence found its way into his work, notably in one of his most accomplished and successful works, "Mademoiselle de Scudéry," inspired by Voltaire's *Le Siècle de Louis XIV*, and other books which he borrowed from a Berlin lending library in 1818. In Voltaire's text, Hoffmann found the historic inspiration for one of his only female protagonists, Madeleine de Scudéry (1607–1701), aka Mademoiselle de Scudéry, a poet and writer of popular novels, a favorite of Louis XIV and his mistress and later wife, Madame de Maintenon. Hoffmann wove an intricate murder mystery from historic threads, which was published in the fall of 1819 in the popular almanac *Taschenbuch für das Jahr 1820*. The narrative, in which Hoffmann combined his legal expertise with his imaginative prowess, proved an immediate sensation, stirring interest in all of Hoffmann's writing. The publisher was so pleased that, to foster future contributions, he gifted the author fifty bottles of wine.

According to literary scholar Richard Alewyn, "Mademoiselle de Scudéry" is the earliest prototype of the detective genre, a clear influence on Edgar Allan Poe's "The Murders in the Rue Morgue." Against the backdrop of a series of unsolved murders plaguing Paris, the plot revolves around the inexplicable actions of a young journeyman goldsmith in love with his master's daughter, wrongfully accused of murdering the master, and yet refusing to defend himself. After the young man has already been found guilty and condemned to death, Mlle. de Scudéry manages, against all odds, to ascertain and prove his innocence and gain clemency from the king. Unlike the uncanny tales for which Hoffmann is most famous, this story is an astounding intertwining of irrational actions and clearheaded, rational thinking. De Scudéry may well be the first, and surely one of the most astute female sleuths, a model for Agatha Christie's Miss Marple, among others. And in his characterization of the master goldsmith, a certain René Cardillac, at once an artist and a madman, Hoffmann gives us one of the great criminal masterminds in world literature whose heirs must surely include Robert Louis Stevenson's Dr. Jekyll, Sir Arthur Conan Doyle's Professor Moriarty, and Ian Fleming's Goldfinger.

Whereas historical sources provided the seed, and rational thought is adroitly employed to tie loose knots, the twists of the imagination are always Hoffmann's primary compass. A character named Theodor (coincidentally also the author's original second middle name) in the story "Die Serapionsbrüder" espouses Hoffmann's literary aesthetic:

> Nothing is more distasteful to me in a story, in a novel on the floor of which the fantastic world has wiggled its way, than that it be swept so clean with an historic broom so that not a kernel, not a grain of dust remains, when you return home, so resigned that you feel no more longing to look behind the curtains. In contrast to which, many a fragment of a spirited story sinks deep into my soul and affords me a lasting pleasure, since fantasy stirs its own vibrations.

The defeat of Napoleon permitted a penniless Hoffmann to return to the Prussian civil service. He moved back to Berlin in 1814 to accept an initially unpaid position, and then a permanent appointment as judge in the court of appeal. Yet again he got himself into trouble by parodying a sometime superior and mocking the court system in his satirical novel *Master Flea*. But Hoffmann agreed to make cuts and weathered the crisis.

It was here in Berlin, from 1814 until his death in 1822, juggling administrative responsibilities with creative drive, that he finally achieved success and celebrity. In Berlin, he reconnected with Hitzig, who had also been transferred there. Hitzig introduced Hoffmann to the Romantic writers Adelbert von Chamisso, Ludwig Tieck, and Friedrich de la Motte Fouqué, the latter also a publisher.

Throughout his life, despite all the ups and downs, personal scandals and professional pitfalls, Hoffmann kept creating.

His greatest musical triumph, the opera *Undine* – for which he composed the music based on a libretto by Friedrich de la Motte Fouqué, and the noted architect, city planner, and painter Karl Friedrich Schinkel designed the set – premiered at the Königliches Schauspielhaus in Berlin in 1817, and proved a critical and popular hit talked about all over town. In retrospect, viewed by some musicologists as the first Romantic opera, the combined effect of the music, text, set, and costumes, was among the influences on Richard Wagner's notion of the *Gesamtkunstwerk*. Alas, after fourteen sold-out performances, a fire burned the theater to the ground, also destroying the set and costumes. Hoffmann himself witnessed the fire from his window across the way, at his last place of residence, Taubenstraße 31. The flames threatened to leap across the way and consume his building. He later described the scene in a letter to a friend:

> I was seated at my desk, when my wife came rushing in from the
> room next door, her face pale as a sheet, and said: 'My God, the
> theater is burning!' – Neither she nor I for a moment lost our
> heads. When firemen, including some whom I counted among my
> friends, knocked on the door, we had already, with the aid of our
> cook, transported curtains, bed and other furniture to safety in a

room to the rear, thus diminishing the risk of their catching fire. […] In the front rooms, all the windowpanes shattered and the oil paint on the window frames and doors melted and dripped down in the heat.

It was here at this same window overlooking the marketplace, between the months of February and April 1822, in between acute spasms of pain, and almost completely paralyzed in the late stage of syphilis, that Hoffmann dictated his last completed narrative, "My Cousin's Corner Window." It appeared shortly thereafter in several installments in the journal *Der Zus-chauer*, weeks before the author's death.

The aforementioned text is included in this collection, not because it is among the author's best or most representative pieces of writing – far from it; Walter Benjamin derided its descriptions as "backward-looking Biedermeier," in contrast to Baudelaire's and Poe's progressive modes of presentation – but precisely because it is his last published account, and because it reveals the wheels of his keen faculty for observation still turning, albeit without plot, with no other narrative end than to take in the world around him until his last conscious blink.

Translating that last completed story into English felt to me at times like eavesdropping on the privacy of a fading mind. But Hoffmann put the words out there, so he must have welcomed the prospect of eyes from the future peering in. Celebrating seeing and telling till the end, this text reads like his last will and testament, bequeathing his disintegrating consciousness and its last fruits to posterity. Perched at his corner window overlooking the marketplace, scanning the open book of the crowd, harvesting impressions, Hoffmann kept compulsively secreting a narrative thread, spinning fiction out of life, forever enticing posterity in the web of his imaginings. According to Hitzig, he was still spinning a yarn, dictating another unfinished tale, "The Enemy" with his dying breath – before finally facing the music.

Peter Wortsman

New York, August 2020

Acknowledgments

My translation of "The Sandman" originally appeared in *Tales of the German Imagination, from the Brothers Grimm to Ingeborg Bachmann*, an anthology selected and translated by Peter Wortsman, Penguin Classics, UK, 2012; was reissued as a stand-alone volume by Penguin Little Black Classics, Penguin Classics, UK, 2016; and as a bilingual Chinese-English edition, Penguin Little Black Classics, 2019.

archipelago books

is a not-for-profit literary press devoted to
promoting cross-cultural exchange through innovative
classic and contemporary international literature
www.archipelagobooks.org